PRAISE FOR ALEXAN

Huntress M

A Thriller Award Nominee for Bes
A Suspense Magazine Pick for Best Thriller
An Amazon Top Ten Bestseller

"This interstate manhunt has plenty of thrills...keeps the drama taut and the pages flying."

—*Kirkus Reviews*

"The intensity of her main characters is equally matched by the strength of the multilayered plot...The next installment cannot release soon enough for me."

—*Suspense Magazine*

"Who you know: Agatha Christie, Gillian Flynn, Mary Higgins Clark. Who you should read: Alexandra Sokoloff."

—*Huffington Post Books*

The Price

"Some of the most original and freshly unnerving work in the genre."

—*The New York Times Book Review*

"A heartbreakingly eerie page turner."

—*Library Journal*

"*The Price* is a gripping read full of questions about good, evil, and human nature...the devastating conclusion leaves the reader with an uncomfortable question to consider:

'If everyone has a price, what's yours?'"

—*Rue Morgue magazine*

The Unseen

"A creepy haunted house, reports of a 40-year-old poltergeist investigation, and a young researcher trying to rebuild her life take the "publish or perish" initiative for college professors to a terrifying new level in this spine-tingling story that has every indication of becoming a horror classic. Based on the famous Rhine ESP experiments at the Duke University parapsychology department that collapsed in the 1960s, this is a chillingly dark look into the unknown."

—*Romantic Times Book Reviews*

"Sokoloff keeps her story enticingly ambiguous, never clarifying until the climax whether the unfolding weirdness might be the result of the investigators' psychic sensitivities or the mischievous handiwork of a human villain."

—*Publisher's Weekly*

"Alexandra Sokoloff takes the horror genre to new heights."

—*Charlotte Examiner*

"Alexandra Sokoloff's talent brings readers into the dark and encompassing world of the unknown so completely, that readers will find it difficult to go to bed until the last page has been turned. Her novels bring human frailty and the desperate desire to survive together in poignant stories of personal struggle and human triumph. But the truly fascinating element of Sokoloff's writing is her deep dig into the human psyche and the horrors that lie just beneath the surface of our carefully constructed facades."

—*Fiction Examiner*

Book of Shadows

"Compelling, frightening, and exceptionally well-written, *Book of Shadows* is destined to become another hit for acclaimed horror and suspense novelist Sokoloff. The incredibly tense plot and mysterious characters will keep readers up late at night, jumping at every sound, and turning the pages until they've devoured the book."

—*Romantic Times Book Reviews*

"Sokoloff successfully melds a classic murder-mystery whodunit with supernatural occult overtones."

—*Library Journal*

The Harrowing

Bram Stoker and Anthony Award Nominee for Best First Novel

"Absolutely gripping…it is easy to imagine this as a film. Once started, you won't want to stop reading."

—*The London Times*

"Sokoloff's debut novel is an eerie ghost story that captivates readers from page one. The author creates an element of suspense that builds until the chillingly believable conclusion."

—*Romantic Times Book Reviews*

"*Poltergeist* meets *The Breakfast Club* as five college students tangle with an ancient evil presence. Plenty of sexual tension, quick pace and engaging plot."

—*Kirkus Reviews*

shadow moon

Also by Alexandra Sokoloff

The Huntress/FBI Thrillers

Huntress Moon: Book I
Blood Moon: Book II
Cold Moon: Book III
Bitter Moon: Book IV
Hunger Moon: Book V

The *Haunted* Thrillers

The Harrowing
The Price
The Unseen
Book of Shadows
The Space Between

Paranormal

The Shifters (from The Keepers Trilogy)
Keeper of the Shadows (from The Keepers: L.A.)
D-Girl on Doomsday (from *Apocalypse: Year Zero*)

Nonfiction

Stealing Hollywood: Screenwriting Tricks for Authors
Writing Love: Screenwriting Tricks for Authors II
"A Woman Wouldn't Do That" (in *Hollywood vs. the Author)*

Short Fiction

The Edge of Seventeen (in *Rage Against the Night*)
In Atlantis (in *Love is Murder*)
The New Girl (from Nasty Woman Press)

Learn more about the author at: **AlexandraSokoloff.com**

shadow moon

Book VI of the Huntress/FBI Thriller Series

alexandra sokoloff

ISBN-13 9781950696000

Cover design by Cissy Hartley
Cover photo by Professional Fine Art

For Siegrid, who knows all the roads

Author's Note

The Huntress series takes place over six months of the present, and multiple timelines in the past. *Shadow Moon* is a culmination of those characters and storylines, and it is very strongly recommended, by me and every reader who has ever found the books, that you experience the series in order:

Huntress Moon
Blood Moon
Cold Moon
Bitter Moon
Hunger Moon
Shadow Moon

Welcome to the hunt.

Alexandra Sokoloff

Chapter 1

Salton Sea: three weeks ago
Singh

Desert wind blows through the mosaic of cracks and holes in the walls of the abandoned motel.

FBI Special Agent Antara Singh lies on the concrete floor, breathing shallowly beneath the cloth blindfolding her eyes. She can smell the blood of the man Cara Lindstrom has just murdered. A heavy, coppery stench, fouled with the body fluids of Detective Gilbert Ortiz.

She feels fingers on her ankles, cold, expert hands tightening circles of rope, pulling them taut to bind her legs.

She hears Lindstrom step back...and feels an explosion of sensation: a boot connecting with her rib cage, her kidneys, as Lindstrom systematically kicks her. Damaging blows, but she experiences them more as motion and impact than pain. The narcotics Lindstrom has given her are already taking effect.

There are soft, booted footsteps on the concrete floor, retreating.

Singh suspends her breath to listen.

Lindstrom's presence is gone. Singh is alone in the shell of the derelict hotel lobby.

She knows what she has been left with.

The body of an overweight young man slumped in a chair behind a table laden with video equipment, blood pooling at his feet from his slashed throat.

And a platform in the center of harsh klieg lights. Its surface red, drenched in blood. Ortiz's naked body spread-eagled on the top of the platform, gutted, bloodied beyond recognition.

In her drugged state, Singh's mind drifts above her own body and she sees herself as part of the gruesome tableau as well. Blindfolded, bound, bruised.

A cover story for her own part in the carnage.

Her consciousness falls back into her body as someone bursts through the front door of the lobby. Two sets of footsteps. Heavy. Male. There is a paralyzing instant of terror that it is the men, the online trolls who attacked her in the parking garage, or the ones who had paid Ortiz in the hope of assaulting Cara…

Then there is a familiar voice calling her name, a rush of motion as someone hurls himself to the ground beside her… the touch of familiar, beloved hands as Damien gathers her into his arms.

Her partner. Her rescuer. The man she has just deceived in a way she would never in her life have expected or wanted.

Damien pulls off her blindfold. He kneels above her, his regal face harrowed with worry. Her ASAC, Matthew Roarke, hovers behind him.

Men she would trust with her life. Men she must now lie to…

The full effect of her ordeal and the narcotics hits her and she passes gladly into the dark relief of unconsciousness.

Chapter 2

San Francisco – present
Singh and Roarke

The San Francisco Bay is a gleaming mirror of the city today.

Singh stands in Roarke's office, looking past his desk, out the window at the glimmering bay beyond. Perhaps it will be the last time she sees this view, from this building.

She has rehearsed her speech in the shower, during her morning and evening meditations, while walking on the white sand beach during the week she has just passed in the Maldives with Damien, "recovering" from her ordeal in the desert. She has spent days preparing her words, her mind, her heart, for what she knows she must do.

She meets Roarke's eyes and lifts her arm, extends her letter of resignation…

Her ASAC will not let her speak. He stares into her face, does not acknowledge the envelope in her fingers.

"I called you in because I'm sending you to Portland. Special Agent Snyder is putting his case files in order in preparation for his retirement and he needs a researcher to help. I'm assigning you."

She opens her mouth to protest and he cuts her off again. "This is not a request. I am ordering you on assignment."

She inclines her head in acknowledgement and steps to the door, then turns back and speaks quietly, a reminder of their last conversation.

"Do you think that things are better?"

He stares at her, through her, and says flatly, "I'll need you to turn your sidearm over to me."

A seemingly unrelated request, which has everything to do with everything. He no longer trusts her with her weapon.

Her face flushes, a high burn in her cheeks. But she nods, and removes herself to her cubicle to fetch her sidearm.

She surrenders it to Roarke in a wordless exchange. After, she walks down the corridor—not back to the bullpen, but to the elevators, down to the lobby of blue-veined marble, out the front doors.

It is only when she steps into the chill of the outside that she realizes how badly she is shaking.

Roarke stood at the window watching Singh cross the Civic Center Plaza, as if viewing her from behind the reinforced glass of a prison wall.

He found himself wishing he had been the one to leave.

His life seemed unbearably constrained. He longed for the sound and touch of the wind, the vast stretch of desert vistas. The wilderness.

He knew banishing Singh was hypocrisy of the highest order. Her words had taken him back to that last conversation in the desert. It was where he lived now, in his mind, that windy night when he'd stood in the palm grove, calling out for Cara.

Had he heard her say, *"Come"*?

Or was that his own, desperate imagining?

The truth was, he had been half a breath away from following her out into the desert, never to return.

We are all mad, here.

Chapter 3

San Francisco - present
Singh

Singh walks blankly across the Civic Center Plaza, with its pollarded mulberry trees and statues and bundled-up homeless, toward one of the grand marble buildings surrounding the square. She mounts the stairs of the Asian Art Museum, moves between the slender columns of the building.

The expansive lobby and open galleries are instantly calming.

She finds her way to an inner gallery, to a stone bench among the familiar gods and goddesses: Tara, Shiva, Vishnu, Lakshmi, Saraswati, and sits in the midst of the statues to examine her sentence.

Banishment to Portland to assist Agent Snyder in what is essentially administrative paperwork. What used to be called secretarial work.

Exile—under the supervision of a psychological profiler. Who presumably will be able to monitor her for signs of violence, even psychosis.

An elegant solution, she must admit, to a problem that must have caused Roarke no end of sleepless nights since the bloody standoff in the Salton Sea desert, under the Hunger Moon.

She had expected almost anything else. Firing. Arrest.

Last month she had been teetering on the brink of insanity. And had certainly crossed the line into criminality.

She had not killed the Palm Desert sheriff's detective, Ortiz. That bloody task had been Cara Lindstrom's. But Singh had been an accomplice, in thought and deed.

And she had been planning for a far more direct and consequential action, before Roarke had intervened at the last moment. It had been a fever dream of an idea. Singh is not herself sure if she would have been able to go through with it.

She does not know if she is grateful or resentful that Roarke stopped her.

The man she intended to kill, the man Roarke prevented her from killing, has left the administration and is trying to foment other right-wing takeovers in other countries presently vulnerable to his toxic agenda of racism and dominionism.

Perhaps that is one definition of "better."

There is still a madman in office, doing damage every hour of every day that he is allowed to remain.

But she has not been fired. Her ASAC is not arresting her, nor institutionalizing her, though these things may come.

The thought is only a dull ache.

She looks around at her goddesses, and bitterness wells up inside her.

Where is your power? Why have you abandoned us?

Privileged men have asserted their privilege, have beaten back the progress of decades.

But as soon as she thinks it, she recalls Roarke, and Damien.

Not all men, she reminds herself, without irony.

As if in response to the thought, she hears quick, agile footsteps on the polished gallery floor and looks up to see Special Agent Lam, criminalist on the office's Evidence Response Team.

He drops onto the bench beside her, so wiry and ebullient he seems to bounce. "I only have a minute. Talk fast."

She explains the verdict, and Lam nods sagely. "So, kind of like house arrest."

She smiles without humor. "Under the supervision of one of the world's leading criminal profilers."

"Yeah, Roarke must really think you're off the deep end." Lam says, reading her thoughts. He is being matter-of-fact because it takes the sting out of the truth. "Still, working with Snyder!" He strokes his cheekbones with his fingertips. "See the green? Pure envy, girl."

The legendary Chuck Snyder had been the Supervisory Special Agent of BAU 3 in its heyday: the Bureau's Behavioral Analysis Unit, which provides investigative support in solving serial and mass murders and other violent crimes to local law enforcement throughout the country. In semi-retirement Snyder travels the world instructing law enforcement agencies in the psychology of the most violent offenders. Roarke's own powerhouse resume includes his early days as an agent working with Snyder.

"When do you leave?" Lam queries her.

"Tomorrow."

He does a cartoon double-take. "Whoa. What are you going to tell Epps?"

She gives him a despairing look. He claps a hand to his forehead. "Honey. Better you than me. Gotta go. Give me a hug and keep me posted."

After a quick embrace, he sprints off. Without his presence, the gallery falls into resonant silence.

Distance. Evaluation. Supervision.

She looks up at the towering figures of the divinities.

Perhaps Roarke is exactly right.

Damien, of course, is in a rage. A rage she recognizes as concealing hurt, bewilderment, fear. He prowls the wide-open space of her loft condominium, darkly seething, dangerously close to eruption. "The hell does Roarke think he's doing?"

Damien still has no idea how close Singh had come to something irrevocable. She suspects he is choosing not to know. They have never talked about the discrepancies in her story of that bloody night.

Nor had she told him her intention to resign that morning. Now, of course, she has been spared that conversation.

She begins, "It is a great privilege. Working with Agent Snyder—"

It is proof of his distress that he does not let her finish her sentence. "I don't care who it's for. It's grunt work. Makes *no* sense to put you on it. Let a rookie handle it."

She speaks carefully, "I do not believe it will be for long. Portland is an hour and a half flight from here, no more. I can be back each weekend. And it is an opportunity to work with one of the great minds of the field. I could not ask for a more opportune assignment. It is as if it has been designed precisely for my needs."

She means more by this than she is telling.

But her genuine interest in the post does not come out of thin air. Damien knows that since the team first encountered Cara Lindstrom, Singh has become enthralled by the science of profiling. And she has already worked briefly with Agent Snyder. During the hunt for Lindstrom, the two agents began work on an extensive list of unsolved U.S. murders which Cara might have been responsible for.

When Snyder had told Singh she had an aptitude for the work, she had felt the psychic tug of *dharma:* her true path. Profiling seems to her a way to quantify the darkness she has always been terrified of and fascinated with, in equal measure.

All these things are true. She can say then without compunction. She says them to Damien now, stepping close to him and putting her hands against his chest. "I feel it is a destiny of sorts."

She feels his strong and elegant body melding with hers, hears the wild racing of his heart. And she knows she has won, for now. Damien is too honorable to stand in the way of something she truly wants. She is using his own nature against him.

She has not told him everything. She does not, for example, tell him that she has surrendered her sidearm. She knows full well he would never let her go if he knew just that one fact. And that is far from all that she has held back.

But she cannot tell him of her dark descent, or that she needs to be away partly to be away from him.

Because since that night in the desert, alone with Cara Lindstrom, she no longer knows what she is capable of.

Chapter 4

Portland, Oregon – present
Snyder

Snyder wakes with the adrenaline surge of danger, the absolute knowing that he is not alone.

His heart is already thumping hard enough to quiver the mattress, but he forces himself to lie still in his bed, to absorb and catalogue the sense of presence.

The sounds in the living room are faint, but discernible.

An intruder in his house.

Moving as silently as all his training affords him, he reaches out toward his bed stand. Eases the drawer open. Feels for the service weapon he hasn't had to use in fifteen years and has never wanted to.

Its heft is familiar: implacable and lethal.

He slides out from under the covers, stands in the dark of his bedroom in bare feet and pajamas, and listens with all of his senses.

Soft slides on the polished hardwood floors.... the whisper of paper...

The sound of searching? Or of approach?

He moves across the room, one ninja step at a time, *heel ball toe*, wincing at the crackle of joints sounding off like cannon fire in the dark. The popping sounds recede, but the arthritis in his feet burns, a silent scream. He is too aware of the degeneration of strength. He is seventy-two.

But he can still shoot.

He stops at the closed bedroom door to regulate his breath.

Then he clasps his left hand around the cold, round doorknob. Slowly, slowly, he twists it and eases the door open…

He inches out the doorway, his eyes adjusting to the dark.

It hits him like a wave, taking his breath away.

He can feel it, *smell* it. It is madness out there in the outer room. And in all his years hunting the worst of the worst, he has never been so afraid.

He forces himself forward, down the hallway, stopping at the arch of the living room entry with heart racing…

Then he hits the lights from the hall and presses his back against the wall, listening.

Silence. Stillness.

Weapon leading, he steps into the archway….

And confronts chaos.

The room is deranged. The house has been ransacked. Someone has torn through his case files, the boxes of his life's work. Each box is a tomb, with unspeakable evil written on the pages of the files. The lids are off now, the files scattered. He can hear the cries and screams of countless victims unleashed from within.

A sound comes from behind him, a quick shuffling and a thud. He spins, poised to fire…

… as a stack of files topples over, sliding in slow motion off the table, pouring papers onto the floor.

His breath rasps as he gasps in to calm his racing heart.

And as he stands shaking, the out of control feeling recedes, like a wave curling back from the shore.

He steels himself, grips his weapon, and searches the house, room by room, checking windows and doors.

There is no one but him. Whatever was there has left. For now.

He returns to the living room and confronts the evidence, leans against the door frame, sagging.

"Matthew," he says softly to the empty room. "He's back."

Chapter 5

Portland, Oregon – present
Singh and Snyder

She walks through the Portland airport, under skylights in soaring white ceilings. A wide, round indoor courtyard is lined with artisanal shops selling gooseberry pie, local wines and olive oils. A tall, slim, long-haired young man plays ethereal music on some New Age string instrument as tall as he is.

She reflects that Roarke could have sent her to any number of miserable, isolated, cultureless posts across the United States. She is grateful that her exile is to such an oasis.

She picks up the keys to an SUV at the rental counter, as her assignment will involve transport of file boxes. Agent Snyder lives in the Laurelhurst district, a ten-minute drive from downtown. She resolves to go there immediately, without stopping to check in to her hotel.

The descent into Portland had provided stunning scenery: views of snowy Mount Hood and the conical dormant volcanos known as the Three Sisters, a city enclosed by the twin ribbons of the Willamette and Columbia Rivers, and hundreds and hundreds of miles of deeply forested mountains and lakes.

The drive from the airport into Portland proper boasts more glimpses of deep forest. With such a landscape spread out before her, it is clear to Singh why so many serial killers over the years had been able to operate for such long stretches of time in this area, and so prolifically, without detection. There could be bodies every few feet and no one would ever find them.

The topic is in her thoughts because she knows that Roarke's very first case as an FBI agent with Agent Snyder was investigative support on such a case in this area, resulting in the capture of a nefarious killer of teenage runaways involved in survival prostitution. Robert Jonah Barker, aka the Street Hunter, had savaged five known victims in Seattle and two in Portland, dumping an untold number of other bodies in wilderness areas before Roarke and Snyder brought him down.

Her bloody thoughts are interrupted by the GPS announcement of her arrival at Agent Snyder's house. It is tucked into a cul-de-sac in a forested neighborhood of old historic homes. Massive trees drift with mist under ominously darkening Portland skies.

Singh walks up the path to a beamed house with tall glass windows, half hidden in a clutch of pine trees. The front door is red, the top arched and rounded, like something from *Lord of the Rings.* Lam would approve, of the Tolkien and of the color. Singh knows that in Asian cultures a red door is auspicious, a color employed for the entrance of shrines and the homes of high-ranking officials. Both of which arguably apply to Agent Snyder. She feels a flutter of nervous anticipation as she steps up to the porch.

He opens the door before she can knock, and his face lights as he sees her. "Agent Singh, we meet at last."

Some of her consults with him on the Lindstrom case have been by videoconference, so she is familiar with his face. There is an ascetic nobility there, reminiscent of a battlefield surgeon or a priest. But she is unprepared for the pleasant, slightly erotic rush of testosterone she feels in his actual presence. At seventy-two, Snyder is still a virile and arresting man, lean and craggy, his eyes intent, encompassing.

He steps gallantly aside for her as she passes into the house. In the dark-paneled hall, he takes her coat, smoothly helping her off with it as if this is a Golden Age Hollywood movie instead of a meeting of trained federal agents.

He hesitates before the arch of the inner door, and a look of what seems to be unease flickers on his face. "I have to warn you, it's not pretty in there."

She is puzzled. But all becomes clear when she steps into the living room.

The room is tastefully furnished, masculine, elegant. Underneath. But the lovely bones of the house are buried in a chaos of filing boxes and scattered files.

"My housekeeper gave up on me some time ago," Snyder admits, as Singh looks around in dismay.

The trail of files continues into the study, a spacious room with wall-to-wall bookshelves. There is a large sitting area, a huge desk, tall windows that look out at the green forest beyond a redwood deck.

And boxes. At least a hundred more.

The number would not trouble her, on its own. But the boxes have been—ransacked, it looks like. Folders scattered randomly. Papers pulled out of files. There are thick unopened manila envelopes, and pages of printouts stacked in piles on every available surface. Singh feels an inexplicable disquiet about the disorder.

"It's overwhelming, I'm aware," Snyder says, and she hears the undercurrent of anxiety in his voice.

"Not at all," she assures him, although she suppresses a shiver. *The horrors that must reside in these boxes.* She can only begin to imagine.

She forces herself to focus, to evaluate the task at hand.

She has always had a passion for order, and even now she is calculating the solution. She will rent an indoor storage space, climate controlled, suitable for paper documents and audio and video files, and begin with the unmolested boxes. Label them and remove them to the storage space, beginning a clear arrangement by date. One must be able to walk into the storage space and instantly find a file by year, month and day, without even a chart as a guide. Then she and Agent Snyder can work in the house, sorting the loose papers and files.

It should not take more than a week or two. Damien will be happy to hear it.

She turns to Snyder and explains her plan. "We will begin tomorrow."

His face clouds. "I'm afraid it's not that simple. These case files need to be catalogued."

She feels a prickling at the back of her neck. A foreshadowing. "I am not sure what you mean. Catalogued in what way?"

"We need to input all the cases into ViCAP."

Singh looks around at the room, the chaos of boxes. "These cases were never entered into ViCAP?"

He is speaking of the FBI's Violent Criminal Apprehension Program, which maintains a database of details of violent crimes from across the country that law enforcement officials can use to search for similar, possibly related crimes.

As Agent Snyder answers her, she can feel the agitation in his voice. "Before I let the files go, I wanted to be sure. I started checking my own list of cases to make certain that the data had been entered by the local police agencies. Out of a hundred cases I queried, only five had been logged into the database by the police or Sheriff's department responsible for the cases."

Singh can only stare at him, numb. She has used ViCAP many times during her tenure as an agent. So she is familiar with the overwhelming problem of it.

The ViCAP database is theoretically the premiere technological tool to take down serial predators: rapists, domestic abusers, pedophiles, mass murderers, serial killers. In actual practice, the highly touted system is barely functional, because of law enforcement agencies' consistent failure to input case data into the database. In short, the chances of getting a hit on a case, a match, are nearly non-existent.

Agent Snyder speaks quickly now. "For several months I've been requesting the full files from every case I ever provided investigative support on. If we input just the cases here in this room, we can raise the number of cases currently in the system by almost a full percent, nationwide."

He turns in a slow circle. "One thousand cases. Each of them impacting dozens, if not hundreds, of victims, family members, friends, and future victims. Any number of open cases that could be closed if some of these perpetrators were in the database."

There is such a stark plea in his eyes that her heart twists in her chest. The simplicity of his plan underscores the grotesque neglect of the system. If more persons in law enforcement had just a tiny fraction of Snyder's diligence, the database could have been grown by God alone knew how much over the years. Saving countless lives.

At the same time, Singh is in near shock at the magnitude of the job ahead of them. She looks around at the room and struggles to get her mind around the scope of the task. It requires putting every single case from Snyder's files into a lengthy ViCAP form. One hundred and one categories of questions, requiring sometimes pages of detail. Charts to fill in. Crime scene photos to scan and upload.

Hundreds of file boxes, each with dozens of case files....

"But we must hire others," she protests faintly. She will use her own money if she must.

"No. No one else," he says, so harshly she takes an involuntary step backward. "I need to review," he says, with a strange urgency. "*We* need to review. I need you to check my inputs. I need to run some recollections by you. We need to do it right. And I can't trust..."

He stops, and Singh has the distinct feeling that he is withholding something crucial. Something even massive.

He finishes, quietly. "I can't trust anyone but you."

Chapter 6

Portland - present
Singh

Singh's downtown hotel is geared to corporate travelers. Her suite is spacious and functional: a living area with executive desk, a kitchenette, a separate bedroom, a deck with a chair and table looking out on the misty river and the many bridges that span it.

She stands blankly at the sliding glass doors. Outside the rain has begun, a dense curtain of gray.

Before leaving Agent Snyder's house, she had spent several hours establishing some order by boxing the loose files by year and clearly labeling the boxes.

Enough time spent to get a sense of the depths of depravity contained within.

It is a heavy feeling on its own, but there is something else, as well. An overwhelming sense of unease that Agent Snyder is keeping something from her.

She reaches for her phone and attempts to call Damien, hoping to talk it through, to find comfort from his strong, steady voice. But he is not answering.

She leaves a message and remains standing for a moment in the middle of the room, still unsettled. Then she moves into the bedroom to unpack. Almost immediately she abandons the task.

Instead she removes a few items from her suitcase. Candles scented with frankincense and vanilla, verbena and basil. Several books of matches. And a journal. Something she has turned to increasingly often in these chaotic times, a means of grasping for sanity.

Something else she has kept from Damien.

She moves out again to the living area with the journal and a candle, curls on the sofa.

She opens the book and begins.

Chapter 7

Cajon Pass, California - June 2005
Cara

She pushes the gas pedal against the floor of the old Honda as it winds its way upward on Interstate 15 through the Cajon Pass.

It is so expansive, the vistas, the layers of hills building upward along the fault line that cracked the valley in two and created the pass between the San Bernardino and San Gabriel ranges. Train tracks snake through the jagged mountains past stunning pale Tule rock formations. The immensity of the landscape is pure exhilaration.

She hasn't seen much of California in the daylight, except on official transport. Her joyriding has been at night, so she has viewed the world largely by the light of the moon. Now the sun on the rocks is almost blinding.

As exciting as the daylight driving is the fact of her own car. She bought it outright, a five-year old Honda, because they are reliable and so common as to be anonymous. Used, so she could pay cash, with a registration sticker good for another six months, so she will not need to file paperwork. She will not have to return it at the end of the night, to the street of the rightful owner. She can buy her own food and camping supplies and stock it as her own home.

Her goal is to be across the state border before dark. The money is hers. She hasn't stolen it. But having lived thirteen years in the social services and criminal justice systems, she knows innocence has nothing to do with anything in life. When a great deal of money is involved, people will want to find her. And this is a great deal of money.

Innocence is also not the right word. She is a murderess. But no one knows that, except possibly that angry, pockmarked sheriff's detective, Ortiz, whom she hasn't seen in four years, now. She has killed a number of other men since the first. And no one else has come looking for her yet.

She has told no one she is going: not her aunt, not the group home, not the high school. She would have been kicked out of the group home anyway; at eighteen the foster care system abdicates all responsibility for its charges. And she doubts anyone in the system will do much to try to find her. She knows all too well. Kids go missing all the time. Girls, boys, all ages. Snapped up by the men in vans, running from abuse, just running.

The school will not look for her either. She has been less than four months at this one and has kept the lowest profile she could manage.

She is eighteen years old.

She has been incarcerated, medicated, and regulated from the time she was five.

And now she is free.

* * * *

Singh looks up from the journal. City lights illuminate the fog in eerie light outside the balcony doors.

Of course, what she has just written is all speculation.

What Singh knows is that at the age of eighteen, Cara Lindstrom came into an insurance settlement for the massacre of her family, a million-dollar life insurance policy that would have accrued substantially more in the thirteen years since the murders of the Lindstroms.

And the very day after that inheritance was triggered, Cara disappeared simultaneously with the money, which vanished from the account where it had been held for her in trust.

She took nothing with her—not that she had more than the most basic possessions in the group home in Oceanside where she was living. She had not quite finished her senior year in high school and as far as Singh knows, she never did. Since then there had been no public record of her whatsoever, until that fateful day that Roarke saw her standing on the sidewalk behind FBI Special Agent Greer, just before Greer was crushed by a commercial truck.

But Singh has spent many hours, days, weeks, tracking Cara's whereabouts as part of the FBI team's investigation into Greer's death, which opened up the whole mystery of Cara Lindstrom and a decades-long trail of murders.

She has been piecing together Cara's entire life. At first simply listing facts. Making a timeline of critical dates: the massacre of her family by the serial killer known as the Reaper, her half-year with an aunt and the aunt's young family before she was given up to the Social Services system, her two years of incarceration in Youth Authority after having seriously injured a much older boy whom Singh suspects tried to assault her in the group home where they were living.

And then her first murder, at fourteen. An adult counselor from that group home who may well have been in on that botched assault.

Singh has a file, pages and pages of hundreds of names. Male murder victims who are plausibly Cara's work. She has compiled lists of suspicious deaths along with actual murders. A bigoted talk show host drowned in his bath, his bloodstream overloaded with prescription opiates. A film director known for his graphic, gleeful rape scenes, who ran his car off a steep curve of Mulholland Drive late one night. Victims whom Singh cannot bring herself to mourn.

And there is a file within that file of the most plausible among them: those who died by fatal wounds to their throats.

It is a story that Singh fully suspects spans the entire United States, over a period of sixteen years. All evidence she has gathered as part of the San Francisco team's pursuit of Lindstrom.

Lindstrom is no longer in the Bureau's jurisdiction. The FBI's case on Lindstrom was officially closed after her arrest and incarceration by the San Francisco police department. Once Lindstrom jumped bail she became entirely the problem of the parole board.

In truth, Singh has no idea where Cara might be, or if she even survived the encounter in the Salton Sea. Since that night, Singh has found no sign of the Huntress. And she sometimes feels bereft, haunted by the loss of Cara's strange and pervasive presence in her life.

So the journaling has been her way of coping. The timeline has become something more intimate, a kind of active imagination. Journaling what might have been Cara's thoughts.

To put herself into the mind and body of another person, a being as complex as Lindstrom, is a relief from her own tormented present. It is a puzzle to be solved, a mystery, a meditation, all rolled into one.

She knows she should sleep. Instead, she writes long into the night. It is her peace in unthinkable times. Her wish to believe that monsters are being battled and slain. That some form of justice is being done.

A stand against the atrocities in Agent Snyder's boxes.

Chapter 8

Portland – present
Singh and Snyder

The fog is thick around her as Singh stands on the doorstep of Agent Snyder's house and rings the bell. She can hear it echoing faintly inside the house.

Unease stirs in her chest.

She presses the doorbell again, and waits. When no response comes, she punches in the code that Agent Snyder has given her for the security system.

She opens the front door, closes it behind her, stands in the dim hall and calls out, "Agent Snyder?"

No response comes back. The house is still. And for no immediately apparent reason her heart begins to race.

She quiets her steps, moves slowly into the living room… and stops in her tracks.

The boxes of files that she so carefully arranged are in disarray again.

She stands in the room and feels the same sense of...

Chaos? Derangement? Madness?

There is movement behind her and she twists around... to see Agent Snyder in the doorway.

He is dressed as he was yesterday, trousers and a sweater, but there is a faraway look on his face that makes him appear to have just awakened. His smile of greeting dies on his face as he stares behind her at the files. He seems as startled by the disorder as she is.

She forces her voice steady. "Have you been looking for something, Agent Snyder?"

He turns to look at her. She feels a chill at the blankness of his eyes. Then his face clears and he is himself again. "Forgive me. I was reminiscing last night. I was up too late and... left things in disarray."

She feels heat in her face. She is certain that he is lying.

Why?

He turns his face away from her to avoid her gaze, stoops to picks up a case file. "I didn't realize I'd gone so overboard." He casually places the file on an end table and turns to her, with his body blocking her view of the file.

"Let's not worry about the boxes," he says. "We should start our input."

For the moment, she chooses to say nothing. But as she follows him toward the study, she glances back at the file he has left behind. Facing down, so she cannot read the label.

Agent Snyder, you are hiding something from me. What is happening, here?

In the study, they begin the grim task of inputting the data into the ViCAP form.

Singh's nerves are already jangled from the morning's strange beginning. The work does not help. It is both tedious and horrifying.

The length of the questionnaire is one of the sticking points for the law enforcement agents and detectives who balk at completing the form.

For Singh, the difficulty of the task is the oppressive weight of the atrocities she is cataloguing. Almost entirely serial rape and serial homicide—which is almost always what serial rape, unchecked, will evolve to. The questions are a catalogue of every horror human beings have been known to inflict on other human beings. Questions about the offender's fetishes. Questions about the specific assaults and their duration and the order in which they occurred. Questions about binding, about torture, about insertion of objects into bodily orifices. Questions about body disposal and about whether the offender returned to re-assault the corpse. To properly complete the forms, she must enter excruciating details of dehumanization and dismemberment.

And so very many of the perpetrators are still out there, uncaught. Because stopping these atrocities has not been made a priority—

Her heart begins to race. She pushes back from her keyboard, dizzy…

She is back in the underground parking lot of her loft building. The darkness is resonant with the faint whiff of oil and gas fumes—and the sense of presence. A rasp of breath. A low whistle.

Adrenaline shoots through her like a lightning bolt. And all at once the voices surround her in the dark. Multiple men, whistling, chirping like birds. She sees their shadows on the concrete walls… hears the catcalls.

"Muslim cunt." "Black bitch."

"Here, pussy pussy pussy… I've got something' for you."

"Get ready –"

"Gonna get fucked till your ass bleeds."

"Gonna wish you never left Dumbfuckistan…."

Her heart is hammering, so thunderous it echoes off the concrete walls and floor. Then an explosion as a weapon is fired. A bullet cracks against a nearby vehicle, shattering glass—

She is jolted by the touch of a hand on her shoulder.

She starts back in her chair… and stares up into Agent Snyder's face, creased with concern.

"Agent Singh, that's enough. We're done for today."

"I am perfectly all right—" she begins to protest. But her breath is rapid and shallow and she fools Agent Snyder not for a moment.

"You are not. And I'd be disappointed if you were."

Through the racing of her own heart she realizes she has been deep in a PTSD flashback. She is grateful and amazed that Snyder understands.

He speaks lightly, allowing the charade that nothing of consequence has happened. "Let's have tea and enjoy the sun. We get it seldom enough in Portland."

And again with that old-school gallantry, he extends a hand to help her up.

She excuses herself to the bathroom to splash cool water on her face and compose herself. When she exits the toilet, she can hear Agent Snyder moving in the kitchen, making the tea.

She stands for a moment in the hallway. Then quickly, silently, she slips back into the living room.

She crosses on cat feet to the end table where Snyder placed the file he'd picked up from the floor.

She glances back over her shoulder… then turns the folder over to read the label.

The date is 2009. And the case is the Street Hunter killings.

Before Agent Snyder can discover her, she moves quickly out through French doors into the garden.

It is Asian in design, with a fountain, ornamental shrubbery, Buddhist statuary. An oasis of tranquility. Singh turns her face to the sun and breathes in to slow her pulse.

"That's better," Agent Snyder says, as he steps outside, carrying two huge steaming mugs.

"Yes," she agrees, and takes the tea he offers her. "Thank you."

He stands, contemplating his fountain. "These are terrible times for women, I know." She glances at him, startled. He gestures back toward the house. "I hope you can remember that what we are cataloguing is not normal, average male behavior."

"No," Singh murmurs. "It is not normal."

"My best estimate is fifteen to twenty percent of the male prison population is psychopaths. But that fifteen to twenty percent is responsible for at least half of violent crime in this country. In a rational world it wouldn't be that hard to prevent this specific population from doing so much damage."

Instead we reward the perpetrators, she thinks. *We elect them to high office.* But she sips her tea and remains silent.

He looks at her briefly, and answers as if he has heard her. "Canada mandates national training in their ViCLAS database entry. If the Bureau collected data on perpetrators at the same population ratio as Canada does, ViCAP would contain more than 4.4 million cases. Instead, we have fewer than 90,000. It's the first thing I told Matthew when we began to work together."

It is an unexpected opening to question him about the file he has concealed from her. Impulsively she takes it.

"That was here, in Portland was it not? On the Street Hunter case?" she asks. Casually, she hopes.

"Oh, no. Years before."

This is unexpected. The story in every article she has ever read on the subject is that the Street Hunter was Roarke's first case as an agent.

"Before he was an agent, then?" she asks.

The older agent's mouth quirks in a smile. "Matthew was born an FBI agent. It was the Bureau that had to catch up to him. I first met him at Quantico. He came for an internship the summer after he graduated from university. 2005."

Singh believes strongly in synchronicity. That there is an order in the universe that reveals itself in glimmers of what some dismiss as coincidence. It does not escape her that 2005 is the year she had been immersing herself in last night. The year Cara disappeared from the system.

She does the math quickly. In 2005 Cara had been eighteen. Roarke would have been twenty-two.

Agent Snyder is speaking.

"In 2002 there was a wave of high-profile child abductions. I consulted on two of them. Danielle Van Dam, age seven, kidnapped from her bedroom in San Diego and murdered by her neighbor. Four-year old Samantha Runnion, abducted from her front yard in Stanten, California. Raped, strangled, her body left in Cleveland National Forest."

Singh flinches inside.

Agent Snyder is deep in his memory, now. "President Bush likened the phenomenon to terrorism. That year the Amber Alert was born. For the next several years, there was an intense media focus on stranger abductions. And in 2005, Matthew was working for the San Luis Obispo police department, his senior year in college."

Chapter 9

San Luis Obispo, California - June, 2005
Matt

In the black of sky, a million stars tremble around the full moon. And he stands trembling below, in the dark outside the house in the large wooded yard.

The front door stands open, a rectangle of black. He can hear her calling from inside. Crying. A small, terrified female voice.

A strong wind blows over the surrounding land, swirling dust demons across the fields. A feeling of doom closes in, threatening to suffocate him.

Run. Get away, before it gets you...

The girl cries again, an agonized voice from the darkness within.

Help her. Have to help her.

He forces himself through the open doorway, into the entry hall. Cold moonlight streams through tall arched windows...

Terror turns every cell in his body to ice. On the floor around him is a pool of dark. He is up to his ankles in it, and it is not cold, like water, but warm...

And those crumpled shapes, on the floor around him, not sleeping, no. The eyes are open, staring… an entire family, slaughtered—

Matt Roarke wrenched his way out of sleep.

He lay with his heart pounding against his rib cage, in his own bed, in his own apartment. His alarm would've gone off in five minutes anyway, but he was relieved to have woken himself. He'd been having the same dream on and off since he was nine years old, and he didn't need to see how it ended.

He threw off his sheets and stood, to get ready for his job at the San Luis Obispo Police Department.

By the time he'd showered, the dream was forgotten.

San Luis Obispo's quaint downtown was a warren of Mission architecture and historical buildings. The funky shops, New Age boutiques and walkable streets belied the roughness of the city underneath, statistically one of the more violent in California.

Matt pushed through the doors of the police department so energetically he got a "Slow down, kid," from the desk sergeant, Rodriguez.

It was true, he was restless this morning. There was an anticipation… a buzzing in his temples that usually… usually… meant something big was going to happen.

Something good? Something bad?

He never knew which, when this feeling came. But something.

He headed into the bullpen, where six detectives hunched over desks, eating, typing. Except for Bello, who sprawled in his chair like some big nesting spider. "Hey, *College*," Bello called out to him. "How was your weekend? You finally pop that cherry?"

Matt could feel his face and jaw muscles tense, but he was pretty sure he kept it from showing. He'd had plenty of practice not reacting. There were sixty sworn officers in the department and he figured he'd taken shit from every one of them.

Most of them were good guys, and cops seemed to thrive on insult humor. Matt had played sports in high school, he knew the drill. He endured the ribbing, mostly took it for what it was. Blowing off steam. Passing the time. But there were a few men in the department that made him uneasy. Bello and a couple of his friends.

Bello didn't actually think Matt was a virgin. He was just trying to goad Matt into talking about Caitlin, his girlfriend. And not about her personality or her major or her thoughts. Bello wanted details. What they did. In bed.

Not in a million years, he thought at Bello.

Compared to Bello and the rest of them, Caitlin was a kid. It sickened Matt that a police detective, someone who was supposed to be protecting and defending, could act so much like—well, the bad guys.

Bello's needling about Caitlin was by far the worst of it, but he was constantly baiting Matt in other ways. It seemed to him sometimes that Bello and his friends wanted what Matt had. He couldn't understand it. They were the adults. They were the ones with all the freedom to make their own choices. Matt was impatient to be where *they* already were: out of college, into the world.

He moved through the bullpen into the corner he'd claimed as his own, to set up the day's work. It was admin, secretarial stuff, really. Typing in reports for the detectives. Getting old reports into the new computer system. But he liked it because it gave him an overview of crimes, a steady tutorial on how to—and how *not* to—file reports.

He'd first volunteered for police duty in high school, with the Explorer program in Palo Alto. His academic parents supported his choice, they just didn't like it much. And Matt loved and respected his parents, but on this point, he didn't give a damn what they thought. He'd decided on law enforcement a long, long time ago.

In college he kept up the volunteer work with the San Luis Obispo Sheriff's Auxilliary Volunteer Patrol, to get training and experience in observation and radio skills. Then Search and Rescue in the summer for CPR and emergency medical training. A psychiatric internship at Atascadero State Hospital, as part of his Criminal Psychology field major.

All that volunteering had paid off exactly how he'd intended: it got him a real job with the SLO police department this year. And the waiting, the marking time, was almost over. Almost. He'd graduate from Cal Poly this month. And he'd applied for an internship he would give just about anything to get: a summer working at Quantico for the FBI.

Being an FBI agent was a non-negotiable goal of his life, had been since he was nine years old. But today the thought of the internship brought a ripple of worry. It was only a few weeks to graduation and he hadn't heard from the program yet. He'd been so focused on getting the internship that he'd made no other plans for the summer, including with the girlfriend that Bello was so keen to get details about.

Unease swept over him. His stomach had been in knots since he'd woken up—

And it hit him.

The dream.

He'd had the dream again.

An isolated desert ranch house at night. A warm, dry, dusty wind whispering through a grove of eucalyptus trees. The split rail gate creaking open and shut, as if it was breathing.

Walking up the stone pavers to the house, toward a gaping hole of a door...

And the massacre inside. An entire family, slaughtered.

All but one...

It was a real thing that happened years ago, when Matt was nine years old. Three ordinary families, really not any different from Matt's, slaughtered at night in their own homes. The whole state, parts of the whole country, had been gripped with the terror of it. The killer never caught... but there had been not a trace of him in the last thirteen years. There was no danger now.

Matt knew that.

But it had been a defining moment in his life. The lightning bolt that had set him on the law enforcement path. He had dreamed about it for years, had dreamed *her,* too—the girl who had survived the third and final massacre. Cara Lindstrom, five years old, a tiny blond waif. Her family slain around her, her own throat cut by the monster the media called The Reaper. She'd faced the most horrifying evil... and had lived through the encounter.

She'd started something in him. A vow, a path, a mission. He would save people. One day he would be old enough to make a difference.

The dream still came to him periodically.

Like an omen.

He'd dreamed it last night. He'd dreamed of *her.* Calling him.

He swallowed through a dry mouth. His stomach was roiling again, so bad he thought he was going to be sick...

And then all hell broke loose in the station.

"Code Adam!" "All officers and detectives in the bullpen *now.*" "Drop what you're doing and listen up!"

As the frenzied shouts continued and officers swarmed into the bullpen, Matt pieced it together.

It was law enforcement's worst nightmare. Not just a missing child—a verified stranger abduction.

Matt could barely rein in his agitation as Sergeant Rodriguez briefed the room.

"Eight-year old girl walking home from school to her grandmother's house. Perp described by witnesses as a white male, late twenties to early thirties. Grabbed her off the sidewalk—threw a sleeping bag over her and lifted her into the trunk of a dirty blue Subaru parked at the curb."

Every alarm bell that could go off was going off. AMBER alert. Tracy Collier's name and description on electronic billboards on freeways all over the state. Bulletins out to local TV and radio stations. A press conference scheduled outside the police department in an hour.

Matt could feel fury blazing through his veins, a shocking sensation. He didn't just want to see this guy caught. He wanted to kill him.

He had to work to pull himself together when he heard his name.

"Roarke. You're on the hotline."

Matt felt it like a slap in the face. *Phones?* He wanted to be out there. Hunting.

Rodriguez must have caught the look on his face. "Listen, Junior. These cases get solved on tips. We need a break. You grab that phone and you make it happen."

Matt managed a "Yes, *sir*!"

He gritted his teeth. And reported to the conference room and grabbed the phone.

For five hours he did nothing but field calls. The tip line was a dizzying view into human nature. People who wanted to help. People who wanted attention. People who were off-the-charts crazy.

And a few pond scum who just wanted to fuck with the cops. Luckily those were too dumb even to pull off a prank phone call. Matt wrote down their information dutifully and found new ways of coolly communicating *"Go straight to hell where you belong"* without actually saying the words.

But pay off it did.

It wasn't Matt who caught the tip. It came in on another line—a witness had spotted a white male in his thirties who fit the description of Tracy's abductor, driving a dirty blue Subaru into Bishop Peak Natural Reserve.

It was electrifying… and terrifying. Taking the girl up into that remote area meant only the worst intentions.

Alerts went out to four agencies: San Luis Obispo Police Department, SLO County Sheriff's Department, the Sacramento Bureau field office and Fish and Wildlife. All leapt into action, sending personnel to converge on the three hundred fifty-four acre reserve with all-terrain vehicles, mountain bikes, horses, search dogs.

As the SLO police scrambled in the bullpen, Matt was up on his feet, pushing his way forward through the swarming chaos of officers and detectives.

"Sergeant Rodriguez, sir—"

Rodriguez wheeled on Roarke, barked, "Roarke, I told you. Stay on that phone."

An order was an order. There was a reason for the chain of command. And in the chain of command, Matt was less than a snail.

But.

The other thing was, he *knew* that park.

Hiking was his sanctuary. Those weekend excursions, nine or ten hours on a mountain, covering the distances, working his body into an adrenaline high. Hiking slowed his natural impatience, cooled his quick temper. He'd hiked every trail up to Bishop Peak. He'd camped there. He'd fixed the map of the reserve in his head, one Sunday at a time.

All those hikes must count for something. It must mean he should be out there, in the park, searching, instead of inside, tied to a phone.

So he steeled himself, and he told Rodriguez what he had to say. "Sir, I have my Emergency Medical Response card. I volunteered for the Sheriff's Search and Rescue team two years ago. I'm CPR certified. And I know Bishop Peak."

The sergeant looked about to explode. But this was what Matt admired about Rodriguez. He listened. He *heard.* And he did now.

Wasting no words, Matt outlined his experience in the park.

Rodriguez's voice was gruff and grudging, but he gave Matt a nod. "Tell Camden to take over your phone. Go."

Matt grabbed his backpack from the locker room and hustled out to the parking lot.

He had a bigger, emergency pack in the trunk of his car. Hiking boots, water, trail foods, compass, nylon rope, flint, first aid kit, a headlamp for night hiking. Keeping a pack ready was something he'd done ever since he'd started driving partly because this was California and his parents were freaks about earthquake preparedness. But part of it was that whole law enforcement mindset. Always being prepared for the call.

Like now.

He made only one quick stop at a gas station convenience store for bottles of cold water and trail bars, but his assigned search party was already gathered when he caught up with them at the Bishop

Peak trailhead, assembled under a shelter of gnarled oak trees. Even in late afternoon, the sun was blazing. Matt could feel the heat radiating from the sandy path, up through the soles of his boots, as he looked over the assembled ten men and two women: deputies from the SLO Sheriff's department, several park rangers, and a few community volunteers. Matt's civilian clothes and youth stuck out.

The search party leader spread out a map of the area, separated into grids, broken into areas related to terrain. He divided the team into two, one to cover the Bishop Peak trail and one to search the Felsman Loop, then assigned the volunteers to specific areas of the grid and passed around Xeroxed copies of the maps.

A sheriff's deputy handed out photos and gave the volunteers a detailed report of the clothing Tracy had been wearing: a T-shirt with a sunflower design and jeans, red Keds, a Bratz backpack.

The photo showed a cute kid: mocha skin, braces, pigtails. Someone who should be jumping rope or playing tetherball in a schoolyard. Anything but this.

Matt's face tightened as he stared down at the sketch of the man who'd taken her. No one looked benevolent in a composite. But the hairs on the back of Matt's neck bristled at the sight of him: hollow cheeked, stringy hair, unfocused eyes.

Their group coordinator took note of all of their cell phone numbers, those who had them. "We search the trails and any shelters first. Any runners here?"

Matt raised his hand, along with a few others.

"I want you folks to run your assigned trail to get out ahead of the slower searchers. When you get to the end of your marked section, start back parallel to the trail and search the less likely hideouts, further from the trail. No one is to go past the 'End of Trail' sign—even though you won't be at the top of the peak. He's not going to be taking her to the top. He'll want something off-trail and secluded."

The coordinator cautioned them to look out for light reflections, and listen for any anomalous sounds as well as searching for discarded clothing or pieces of it that matched the description of what Tracy was wearing. "Don't touch anything. Take photos of anything significant. Keep hydrated and watch for poison oak. And you. Rookie," he snapped, and Matt realized the coordinator was talking to him. "You are to stay on the trails. No wandering. No deviation. Is that clear?"

"Yes, sir."

He was clear. And he was ready. There was a monster out there, trying to steal the life force of a child. And he wasn't going to allow it.

He did as the team leader had instructed: taking off at a run, following the packed, sandy trail through oak woodland at the base of the hike. Dodging sharp rocks, jumping the gnarled roots of twisted old oak trees. Slowing on the massive boulders and rock falls.

He jogged past a cattle gate, and the trail opened up into meadows with views of Los Osos Valley and the greater San Luis Obispo area. Ahead was Bishop Peak itself: a summit of rugged rock, the tallest in SLO, one of the "Nine Sisters," a chain of volcanic peaks stretching to Morro Bay.

Matt was so tense his whole body was shaking. His emotions boiled inside him. It was a state he hated, because all he could do was get in his own way. Sometimes he was so furious at things he couldn't speak.

He breathed in deep and focused on his running, and in his mind, he catalogued what he knew. First, the profile. Ninety-eight-point-five percent of non-family abductors were male. Average age twenty-seven. Unmarried, living alone or with parents. Unemployed or engaged in unskilled or semi-skilled labor. Tracy would likely have been chosen just out of opportunity. The primary objective would be sexual assault. In seventy-six percent of cases, the abducted child would be murdered within three hours; in eighty-eight percent of cases, murdered within twenty-four hours.

"Not this time," he panted, and ran harder.

It's not like he thought he was going to rescue Tracy himself. He wasn't some delusional kid.

But he was here for her.

You need to scream, he told her in his mind. *You need to scream and keep screaming. Make noise so we can hear you. I swear to you I'll come.*

The vegetation changed from shady trees to scrub and chaparral, aromatic coyote bush and monkey flower. Sweat poured down his back and matted his hair. He swigged water from a bottle on his belt and cut through hills of golden, scorched grass and sage-green scrub, heading up the granite mountain topped by the triangular crag that gave it its name. Different trails snaked off for different approaches to the peak and he veered off on the trail toward his assigned search area.

The gently rolling, sandy golden hills falling away from the path disguised the trail's real height. It was a steep and strenuous rise. Hawks soared above and Matt found himself wishing for that bird's eye view. There were far too many wooded areas in the reserve where Tracy's captor could be holding her.

On the switchbacks the trail got so rocky and uneven Matt had to slow to a panting walk.

He stopped when he reached the last ascent of the trail: enormous boulders of the peak forming natural caves and crannies. He gulped more water and walked in a circle to keep from cramping.

It was highly unlikely that Tracy's captor would have taken her this far up, so Matt turned to work his way back, searching the rock piles along the trail, alert not just to human sounds but also to the telltale rattle of sunning snakes.

And he spoke aloud, again.

"I'm here, Tracy. I'm here."

He listened with everything in him.

And heard the wind.

For the next four hours he scoured the trails in his section of the grid. The sky changed from blazing blue to afternoon haze to smoky twilight. And the darker the sky, the bleaker Matt's thoughts.

He could feel the fatigue of the intense concentration. His neck ached from looking down, searching the ground for anything: pieces of clothing, some disturbance in the sand, broken branches next to the trail, hair….

And he'd found—a big fat nothing.

It wasn't just him, either. He'd gotten a rare patch of cell phone reception fifteen minutes ago and phoned in to the trail coordinator. No one had reported anything useful.

But he was ready to go all night. He was outside. He was free. He was fine. That little girl was alone with a monster.

And there was a feeling nagging at him, growing steadily stronger.

This is a popular trail.

Tracy's abductor must know it well, and he must have headed for some spot significantly off-trail, someplace he would feel hidden.

He's not going to risk running into people—

A shrill beeping startled Matt out of his concentration. It was his phone, the timer he'd set for himself so he would make the end-of-day check in on time. There were no volunteers allowed on the mountain after dark.

He stopped in his tracks on the ridge, looking over a steep incline, the creases and folds of a valley.

Come on, Tracy, he begged her in his head. *I'm here. Give me something.*

The acres of sage brush below him moved like the sea, as wind rushed through the hollows of the valley. An eagle glided on the wind above him.

But nothing human.

He did one last scan of the valley below.

And turned to head back down the trail, his heart sinking with every step.

He checked in with the team leader at the trail head where they'd started. He looked as grim as Matt felt, but he thanked Matt for his work and gave him a firm handshake. "Search resumes here at five-thirty am."

"I'll be here, sir," Matt promised.

He had every intention of hiking back down to his car. Logically he knew: the last thing a search ever needed was some overzealous volunteer going rogue and needing to be rescued himself.

But his boots on the path were slower and slower.

How can I go home when she's up here, somewhere? How can any of us? How can we leave her to whatever is happening to her?

His thoughts became angrier.

What were they there for if not to search every square inch of this mountain until they found her? How the hell were they supposed to go home when this creep was holding Tracy somewhere, doing things he didn't even want to think about?

Six hours. He's had her six hours, by now.

Some of the searchers, a lot of them, were fathers themselves. And there were mothers, too. Would they go home if it were their son or daughter?

"No fucking way," he said aloud.

No fucking way I'm waiting until dawn.

He'd clocked out. No one was to say he couldn't camp. He had his pack. He'd done it a million times before in this park.

Okay, maybe four.

If he could do that on a normal day, why couldn't he do it tonight, when Tracy's life might depend on it?

He hustled the rest of the way to his car and grabbed his camping gear from the trunk. There were still quite a few cars parked in the dirt lot: law enforcement, the pro volunteers. But he knew a short cut up through the oak woods that would bypass the official trail head and evade the search coordinator.

What he was doing was against the rules, but it didn't feel wrong. It actually felt the opposite of wrong. And if he ran into someone who wanted to know what he was still doing there, he'd say...

Well, he'd figure that out if he had to.

He slipped into the shadows outside the perimeter of the parking lot, and disappeared into the woods.

Walking in the almost-dark was difficult enough to keep him focused. He couldn't use his Maglite or his headlamp, for fear of being discovered. Instead he moved slowly and strained his eyes through the swiftly descending shadows.

He'd decided to go back to the ridge he'd stopped on just before he'd headed back down the mountain. It was random, but he had to start somewhere.

Once the moon rose, there would be a view of the valley and he'd be able to search again. It would be full tonight. He'd pick a spot to rest and wait for the moonlight.

Twenty minutes later he'd made his way back to the ridge and a smooth, sandy spot to camp out. It was full dark now, too dark to have done anything for the last ten minutes but feel his way carefully upward, one foot in front of the other.

But now that he was on the ridge, he could see the lights in the valley, and make out the vague shapes of hills below and the tower of tumbled boulders above.

He unrolled his sleeping bag and sat on it with his back against a rock to wait for moonrise.

He groped in a pocket for his phone, checked it—but the Nokia wasn't showing any bars at all.

He suddenly remembered that he was supposed to be going to a concert with Caitlin tonight. He hadn't thought about her all day, hadn't texted to let her know what he was doing. He knew that even in these extreme circumstances, it was probably not a good sign for the relationship. But he pushed those thoughts away.

Instead he took his area map from his pack and studied it under the light of the Maglite, finding his place on it and situating himself visually, fixing the four directions and layout of the trail and hills in his head.

Then he leaned back against the boulder to look out over the valley.

He was aware of how tired he was. There was fatigue in every muscle of his body, not even really from physical exertion, but from the stress of the responsibility, the anxiety about Tracy.

But it was a whole world better than sitting at home, doing nothing.

It took him a while to calm down. His muscles, his nerves, his mind, were all jittery, scattered.

Relax, he ordered himself. And then said it more softly. *Relax.*

The night went from dark to ebony, and suddenly there were stars, as if someone had just flipped a switch. It wasn't like the jewel-crusted dome you got out in the desert. There was light pollution as well as the light of the rising moon below the horizon line that was already fading out some of the starry brilliance. But still.

There was a quick dim motion in the blackest corner of the sky. So faint he wasn't sure if he saw it or just willed it.

He decided to believe he saw it. And that he'd see more. He breathed in, breathed out,

His scrambled thoughts slipped away from him. The dome of sky above him grew darker black, expanding and deepening. At first he'd seen a patina of stars, painted as if on a ceiling. Now there were layers. He could see farther, deeper. His body seemed to sink into the earth….

A star flashed by, startling him. Not faint this time. An electric blaze. "Whoa," he said aloud.

There was another. Bigger. Almost in slow motion. Like the sky was showing off for him now.

And then they were falling like gentle rain.

Chapter 10

All of the world is moving around her.

Millions of flying stars, like a snowstorm. Every pore of her is open to the cosmos. Her stomach doing rollercoasters.

Stars flying past like snow flurries, and the—

Matt blinked awake.

For a moment he had no idea where he was.

He'd been looking up at the shooting stars and had drifted off, dozed. And it felt like he had been… somewhere else. Somewhere warmer, and deeper, and far, far away. Perhaps had *been* someone else….

He had a vague recollection of a feminine presence. But when he grasped for it, it was gone.

He was still in a soporific half-sleep state—not sleep, more a kind of hyper-clarity. He could hear the wind, infinite variations of it. Low, like breath, a whining whistle, an ebbing and murmuring. The scrambling rustle of a squirrel, the leaf-crackling, the flutter of bird wings….

When he heard the cry, it was so faint, like that first shooting star, he thought he dreamed it.

A voice, hoarse and tiny and desperate.

"Anyone? Anyone? Can you hear me?"

"Please. Please help me.

Matt sat for a moment, frozen, stunned. Then he scrambled up to his feet, straining toward the sound.

The voice had come from below him, far below in the valley.

He didn't want to use his Maglite for fear of alerting the abductor.

So he started down the sandy hill, feeling his way by moonlight, steering around pale boulders, his eyes and ears straining to hear, to see.

Sage scrub scraped at his legs and caught in the canvas of his cargo pants. He kept going, heading down, down…

The wind ebbed and flowed, and the night seemed to breathe around him. He was suddenly back in the feeling of his nightmare.

Something out there. Something so huge…

A rustle and crashing in the bushes sent his heart into his throat, his pulse skyrocketing.

The darkness seemed to part… and she was there. So unexpected it felt like a dream.

She was just as in the photo—and not. Her wide eyes were dark and glazed. Her hands and her small bare feet were bloodied from the rocks she had been scrambling over, her bare legs were scratched from thorn bushes. Her skin seemed to hang off her. In some part of his mind Matt recognized dehydration, but for a moment, in the moonlight, she appeared as a living skeleton

"Tracy," he gasped.

She wore only a ripped T-shirt, and he tried not to think about what that meant. But there was a fierce, tensile strength in her young limbs as she stumbled toward him, shaking.

"Coming," she croaked out, in a voice raw from screaming. "He's coming. We have to *go*."

He didn't think. He didn't hesitate. He scooped her up. "Hold on," he said. But he didn't have to tell her. Her wiry arms locked around his neck.

He turned and barreled through the dark, upward, uphill, through spiny brush, over jagged granite. He tried to hold Tracy high enough that the branches didn't claw at her. He could feel her ragged panting, her heart beating like a rabbit's as he ran.

And as he stumbled upward, his pulse leaped at the sound of someone crashing through the brush below them.

Pursuing.

And gaining on them.

Tracy whimpered in his arms. She too had heard.

"Hold on," he whispered. "Hold on."

His chest was on fire as he ran straight up through the brush, not bothering to look for a trail. Pumping his legs hard, harder. Tracy trembling in his arms.

He was gasping. And shaking.

The terror

It felt as if some preternatural thing was after them. He could visualize it, slobbering and gibbering behind them.

He could feel its breath—

Then his heart shot through his chest as the sound came from *both* sides. A deliberate crashing in the brush, coming straight toward them, encircling them....

A shadow loomed up in the path—

"FREEZE!" a male voice shouted. Matt stopped in his tracks, clutching Tracy to him, his heart racing like a mad animal. But the intonation of the voice was familiar. It was salvation. It was a police command.

His eyes focused in the darkness. They were surrounded by a circle of deputies with weapons drawn, all trained directly on him.

In a flash, Matt realized what the men might think. He found his voice, shouted out, "SLO police! I have Tracy Collier."

The officers surrounding them were frozen in shooting stance, deliberating.

He shouted again. "I'm putting her down."

He lowered Tracy gently to the ground, keeping his hands on her shoulders until he was sure she could stand. She threw her arms around his legs and held on.

Two deputies converged on Matt and wrested him away from the girl. Matt felt the hard impact of the ground as they threw him down.

He tasted dust, but all he could think as they cuffed him was—*It's over. She's safe.*

She's safe.

Chapter 11

Portland – present
Singh

Agent Snyder falls silent. The story is done.

Singh sits across from him in the study. Her heart is racing as if it has been she herself scrambling up the mountain through jagged brush in the dark, carrying the little girl with her.

It takes her some moments to come back to herself, to Agent Snyder's study, to the present.

Around her, the boxes have been restored to order. She and Agent Snyder have worked through the files in several of them, and those she has moved to a storage space. Other files have been sorted into their proper boxes by year, awaiting entry into the database. Agent Snyder's tale has unfolded over several days this week, on breaks, in between the dozens of ViCAP entries they have already completed.

Now that she has heard it all, her first reflection is that it is all so very Roarke. The dogged refusal to give up. The willingness to bend a rule so far that it begins to take on a different form, a new meaning.

Snyder gives her the ghost of a smile. "Now you know what happens when you let me talk. Three days later, and I haven't even begun to answer your question."

Singh has to think to recall that she had begun, all those days ago, by asking how Agent Snyder and Roarke had met.

"But I see, now," she responds. "It became a mission for him, that night. With Tracy."

Agent Snyder shakes his head. "Oh, no. It had been a mission long before then. The first time Matthew applied to the Academy was when he was nine years old."

She stares at him. "But—how?"

"He wrote a letter to the Director. Of course, they didn't take him up on it. But he's been prepping for the job ever since."

Singh has not heard this before. "At nine," she repeats, sensing some significance. "Was there something in particular..." And then she knows what Agent Snyder will say as he says it.

"It was the Reaper."

And now she feels a wave of unreality.

Agent Snyder continues. "The family massacre case gripped the West Coast, particularly California. It would've been impossible to avoid the coverage, the state of fear and anxiety that citizens were in. But as a nine-year old boy from a family quite similar to the ones that Nathaniel Hughes chose to slaughter: educated and affluent parents, children the same age as Matthew and his brother... one can only imagine how personal it must have seemed to him."

Singh knows Roarke enough to imagine very well. "And he became attached to Cara Lindstrom—at least, the *idea* of Cara Lindstrom—"

"At nine."

Singh feels a chill as it sinks in. "He decided to become an agent..."

"Because of Cara Lindstrom."

Driving on the road back to her hotel, she cannot get the story out of her mind.

And the implications.

It is a huge revelation: that Roarke's history with Cara goes back much further than Singh has ever thought. That their connection is more profound than she ever guessed.

It is an incredible secret for Roarke to have been keeping, these many months that the team has been in Cara's pursuit. Then she wonders if Damien knows. Roarke would not have any reason to tell her, but he may have told Epps. Or not. It is a mystery.

It changes everything.

She walks into her hotel room and closes the door behind her.

Then turns and stands facing the map.

She put it up days ago: a map of the continental United States depicting the interstate system, covering nearly an entire wall of her suite.

Her secret work has progressed. It no longer just a journal. She has marked Cara's known murders on the map and dated them, using a different color push pin for each year in which a murder has occurred. She has marked off Interstate 40, which she believes to have been Cara's first route. And she has begun searching databases for murders and suspicious deaths that occurred along that route in the summer of 2005.

But now there is a new factor.

She reaches into a pocket for her phone and Googles *Tracy Collier abduction.* She stares down, frozen, at the date.

June 10.

It is a sudden, shocking insight.

She knows where Cara was that day.

That very day.

Chapter 12

Grand Canyon, Arizona - June 2005
Cara

She stands looking out over the stupendous gorge. Layered bands of red and pink and black and white, rock formations as big as cathedrals. Thousands of feet deep. Millions of years of geologic history. An entire world below ground level.

The Grand Canyon.

It takes her breath away.

That first night of freedom, she'd made it across California. Fort Mojave Indian Reservation at the border. Lake Havasu at the crossing of the Colorado River. Then Kingman, at the east end of the Mojave Desert, and the strange little town of Seligman, its main street a living museum of Route 66 memorabilia and bizarre art installations.

Driving has already become a way of life.

She starts every day by looking at her map: the U.S. with the interstates in red and blue, like arteries and veins. Every night she sleeps under the stars. Even if she did know how to register in a motel, which she doesn't, after all those years of confinement the thought of being boxed inside four walls is unbearable. Instead, she lives outside, immersing herself in the totality. The smell of rain. The feel of the air when the heat breaks at dusk. The live, pulsing silence in the smoky blue twilight.

And views like these. She leans into the metal rail of the overlook, still hot from the day's sun, and looks out on this panorama of infinity, colored by streaks of sunset.

Her brain can barely process the immensity. It seems more like a vast, two-dimensional canvas than a real place.

To gaze out into this enormity compared with her two years in a cell…

It is living, breathing *Beauty.*

She found the words in a roadside gift shop as she crossed through Fort Mojave. Painted on a sandstone souvenir plaque, a Navajo prayer:

As I walk, I walk in Beauty.
Beauty above me.
Beauty below me.
Beauty to my left.
Beauty to my right.
Beauty before me.
Beauty behind me.
Beauty around me.
As I walk, I walk in Beauty.

A prayer, a gift, a way forward.

The words have kept her safe. She has not had a single intimation of *It* since the beginning of her journey. It is her secret hope that the prayer will be her salvation.

She lifts her face to the gold-red rays of the sun, breathes in the sunset.

Driving into the park, she'd taken the first stop she could, scenic Mather Point on the Rim Trail. But there are far, far too many people on this sightseeing path. She knows she must go further, deeper, out of range of humanity. To descend into the earth, into that vast beauty.

She turns from the railing and heads back toward the visitor center. On the short walk she hears five different languages, which interests her. It occurs to her that she can use her high school languages as a disguise. As a foreign tourist, she will be more anonymous. The accent, the foreignness, will be what people remember.

Back at the Visitor Center she stands in front of a huge map, framed in a glass display case, and studies it, frowning. There are so many trails: South Kaibab, Bright Angel, North Rim—

A voice speaks behind her: "Rim to Rim."

Adrenaline shoots through her. She has been so engrossed in the map that she has forgotten to be vigilant, to keep aware of her surroundings.

She twists around—

But the person standing in front of her is no threat: a girl about her own age, a year or two older at most, with sun-bronzed skin and freckles. She's dressed for hiking in khaki shorts, boots and thick socks, a faded tank top in psychedelic tie-dye. A bandana pulls her sun-bleached hair into a bouncy ponytail.

She gives Cara a radiant smile. "You're trying to decide on a trail, right? First time? Rim to Rim is the only way to fly. Are you on your own?"

There is no guile in the last question, but Cara answers, "No," quickly, automatically. She wants no invitation, no questions, no probing, no danger of letting something slip that will trip her up later.

The girl seems unbothered. "Well, either way. Totally doable. I'm Sierra," she adds, extending a brown hand.

Cara forces herself to take it for a quick shake. "Lesley," she lies. And realizes she has forgotten to try an accent.

"No trail name, yet, huh?" Sierra flashes a grin. "That'll come." And she continues her cheerful advice. "Rim to Rim is twenty-three miles, total. Start off at North Rim—less tourists! You can leave your bike or car there at the trailhead and there's a shuttle that'll take you back when you come out on South Rim. Or vice-versa. It's seven miles down to Cottonwood, where you can camp the first night, then another seven to Bright Angel Campground at the bottom. There are plenty of people there so it's no big if you do it on your own. I have a couple of times."

She is so friendly and unafraid. So *Normal.* But Cara is always wary of strangers, and loathe to get into any conversation that requires her to reveal any detail about herself. Too risky.

"Do you have a backcountry permit?" Sierra asks. Cara hasn't even heard of one. "You'll need one," the girl says. She takes off the small pack she's wearing, roots through it and comes up with a folded sheet of paper. "Take mine." She winks. "I always make a copy." She extends the paper. "Put it on your tent when you camp and the rangers won't bother you."

Cara takes the permit. "Thanks," she remembers to say.

"No worries!" Sierra says. "I'll see you at the river. *Namaste*!" she adds with a wave, as she starts off down the trail into the twilight, gone as quickly as she appeared.

Cara stands for a moment, dazed by the encounter. As she turns slowly. She has a fluttery, excited feeling.

All her life she has been told what to do. By random people, by road signs, by clouds, by songs, by the moon. There are always signs.

She looks at the pass, like a Golden Ticket in her hand.

Of course she will go.

That night she purchases supplies and fills a small backpack with provisions. Trail mix, dried fruit, chocolate bars. She adds the portable water filter system and compass she keeps in the car. And as always, the hunting knife.

She will not be taking the longer trail that Sierra suggested. She cannot run the risk of being so predictable, nor of running into her on the trail and the girl wanting to hike together, to strike up a friendship.

Instead she camps in her car on a highway pull off concealed from the road, then leaves her car on the South Rim and picks up the trailhead there at first light.

Her first view of the vast mouth of Bright Angel Canyon comes through fir trees and aspen, quaking aspen with its round, fluttering leaves, ferns and wildflowers. Beyond the trees are miles and miles of mesa-like sculptured cliffs.

The sight is a jittery thrill.

The brush in front of her moves, and she catches her breath. A white-tailed deer lifts its head and holds her gaze for a few seconds before it goes delicately back to grazing.

Cara turns and steps forward, to begin the descent through two billion years of the earth's history.

The first length of the trail is surprisingly developed, the path wide, smooth and defined by carefully built sandstone walls, and low boulders lining both sides of the trail. The path soon narrows and plunges. She adjusts her pace to brace against the jarring decline and hard ridges of earth. It is so steep that even going downhill, in the cool of the morning, her muscles are working hard enough for her to break a sweat.

Just beside her, the cliff drops hundreds of feet, with no railing between a careless hiker and certain death. The danger is nauseating and exhilarating. She veers a little closer to the cliff wall, breathes in crisp, clean air, and continues into the rainbow vista of rock.

There are other hikers on the trail. She passes a few, every five minutes or so, couples and trios, some loners, laden with bulging backpacks and walking poles. They nod and step courteously against the rock wall to let her pass. Either her quick pace or the set of her face keeps the others from conversation beyond an occasional "Hey" or "Good morning." But the smiles seem genuine and she finds herself becoming less tense with every encounter. People are so focused on their own descents, on the overwhelming views, that they pay her little attention.

We're all here for the same reason, she realizes, startled.

Beauty.

The endorphins come in a rush, and now she is floating on the sensation and colors.

The sun shimmering in liquid waves on the rock. Massive formations towering around her on all sides. The stunning reds of the Canyon, always contrasting with the green. The heat on her face, the smells of the rock and the scrub. The near-weightlessness of her own body.

Her thoughts go to the girl, Sierra. She wonders if she can ever be as happy as that, as easy and free. So at peace with herself in the world.

Sierra has obviously done this hike, doubtless many others, on her own, many times. So it is possible to live like this: bold, unencumbered.

Maybe it means… maybe it's a sign… that she can escape the darkness that has shadowed her for all of her life since *The Night.*

She feels lighter than she can ever remember feeling.

Maybe. Maybe.

Maybe this is the road.

She is so overcome with the ecstasy of beauty she wants to run, to burst free of her skin and become one with all her surroundings. She is careful, though, always careful, knowing that a twisted ankle can cripple her, leave her to the mercy of anyone who comes by. Hospitalization is out of the question, a guarantee of discovery.

She hikes over rock, over sand, past huge tumbled boulders, so many of them oddly square. There are wooden bridges across parts of the trail and over chasms. Sometimes the path narrows to just two or three feet to round a cliff wall, the trail dizzyingly close to the sheer cliff edge. She is aware of her legs shaking from exertion and hyper-attention.

The sun climbs in the sky and heat radiates from the walls. She has lived much of her life in the desert and the intensity of temperature is a pleasure. In the mid-day hours, when the sun is highest and hottest, she finds off-trail places that conceal her. The heat has the added advantage of deterring hikers from the full hike, meaning she sees people only infrequently now. She passes a few guided groups, one mule train carrying tourists and supplies, and takes note of how fast they are traveling, so she can always know how far or close she is to them.

Lower, parts of the trail tunnel directly into the rock of the cliff face, descending through redwall limestone.

It is like burrowing into the beating red heart of the earth.

The brush along the trail becomes more intensely green, shaded with white-barked birch, and she encounters more and more streams, running water by the trails, then glimpses below of the wide Colorado River.

She stoops to fill her empty water bottles, to process with her filter overnight.

Now the trail is sandier, softer, slowing her pace. Her back and legs are feeling the strain of the day. Her footsteps seem drunk, swaying. Her shadow is long in front of her as she makes her way through a copse of towering pines.

A short walk through a dark tunnel through rock, and she emerges into the sunlight.

And stops in her tracks.

In her exhaustion, and the contrast from dark tunnel to brilliant sun, she sees a shadow. A skeleton in the shape of a girl.

Ivy.

Then her eyes adjust to the sun and the vision is gone.

She catches her breath, and moves on, crossing the sturdy, fenced bridge over the mud-brown Colorado River. The surrounding cliffs are towering, mythic, jagged edifices striped with bands of red and pink and white.

And then she is at the bottom. Phantom Ranch.

In the daze of the day's hike, through the endorphins and lingering effect of the constant mind-altering vistas, the ranch seems exactly that. A phantom, a mirage of civilization at the bottom of the canyon.

She walks on meandering paths through long green grasses, under gentle birches curving overhead in a canopy.

Ahead is a small common dining hall of river stone and rough-hewn wood, with a chalkboard menu of food for purchase.

She moves tentatively to the doorway and gets a glimpse of a crowded room. Her ears are assaulted by sound: loud conversation and raucous laughter. Many of the groups at the long tables are drinking.

She backs away from the doorway, hoping no one has seen her, and hurries on, past aspen trees, feathery white tassels of pampas grass and more of the prickly pear cactus, crossing another sturdy wooden bridge above a red rushing creek into shady, grassy Bright Angel campground. She catches glimpses of one- and two-person tents in between the short twisting oak trees and scrub. The sites are well-used, some of them with battered picnic tables and tent areas defined by sandstone slabs.

She moves past these, drawn to the sites along the river itself. She finds an empty one with its own picnic table, an unexpected luxury.

She sets up her tent on the pinkish sand in a circle of scrub, far from any campers, but in proximity to a group with several women hikers. She finds a thick stick to use as a pole to hang her pack out of reach of animals.

Then she sits, or rather collapses, on the ground.

She lies back flat and stares up sheer cliffs to a pointed peak, like a bishop's hat. Her exhaustion is like a heavy blanket, settling over her.

She stays without moving for hours, listening to the rush of the stream, the aspen leaves rustling in the wind, watching the sunset, hours of psychedelic light washing over the sky and rocks.

The night grows darker, and the sky erupts in stars.

All of the world seems to move around her.

She is seeing millions of shooting stars. Lights flying past like snow flurries. Every pore of her is open to the cosmos. Her stomach doing rollercoasters.

And there is something more. A presence.

She is not alone. She is not alone, and she is loved.

When she wakes, the moonlight is nearly blinding. She can feel it, white hot and burning on her skin.

Ivy stands in the stark canyon shadows, watching her.

The skeleton girl she met at fourteen. Abducted, raped, doused in gasoline and set on fire, left in the desert to die.

Cara avenged her, killed her rapist, and helped Ivy leave her world of pain.

She lies back in the sand and closes her eyes. And she feels Ivy kneel beside her, and curl up to sleep beside her in the sand.

In the morning, she opens her eyes to blue cliffs under hazy blue sky. As the sun rises, the pinks and oranges are mirrored in the river.

Ivy is gone.

But Cara's stomach is heavy with dread.

She is washing up when she sees her again. She straightens, looking out across the river.

Ivy stands on the sandy bank on the opposite side of the water, half-hidden in the fronds of tamarisk and mesquite. She is not alone. There is a crumpled bundle at her feet.

And Cara knows she has not escaped. There is no escape from *It*.

She makes her way across the bridge to the other side, down onto the rocks beside the river.

Ivy has vanished. But the bundle is there. A huddled girl under the small, shrub-like trees, sitting half in and half out of the water, hugging her knees and rocking herself.

A wraith in torn hiking shorts and camisole.

So changed, it is a few stunned moments before Cara fully recognizes her.

There is nothing about her of the glowing hiker she encountered at the top of the Canyon. There is deadness in Sierra now, a deadness Cara knows too well.

She does not have to ask *what*. She knows what people look like when *It* has finished with them. Years ago, *It* held her in its scaly hands. She has been as close to *It* as anyone has been and survived.

She has seen *It* all her life since that night. She knows *Its* touch. *Its* foul breath, *Its* glittering eyes.

The monster has infiltrated this sacred canyon. *It* has found this girl and her life force is all but drained from her.

Cara crouches beside Sierra at the water's edge. Her voice is hollow. "Who did this?"

The girl turns her head clumsily, but doesn't speak. Her body seems disconnected from her brain.

"*What happened?*" Cara cries.

"Nothing happened," Sierra says flatly.

Cara has seen this before, too. People who have encountered *It* often say it, denying any attack, any trauma. Their minds drop a protective shield on memories.

At any rate, she doesn't need to be told. She can see the blood drops forming like sweat on the girl's brow, rivulets of red streaming slowly down her arms, dripping onto the rock.

She has seen the blood, time and time again in her life. Oozing from girls coming into foster care. Dripping from girls—and boys—in *The Cage.* The girls in the group homes who go out one day and come back with the dull look in their eyes and the scratches on their souls. Girls like Laura Huell. Like Ivy Barnes.

She pulls herself together, asks slowly and clearly, "Is *It* here?"

Sierra doesn't ask what she means. She shakes her head quickly, looks up toward the pale trail cut into the rock wall above them. The fear on her face is sickening.

"Stay here," Sierra whispers. "You stay until…" She shudders through her whole body.

"Until what?" Cara asks, but she is almost certain what Sierra is going to say.

"Until they're gone."

They. The girl didn't have to explain it. Cara feels a wave of fury. "How many of them?" she says flatly.

"Two," the girl whispers.

"Where?"

The girl's voice is dead. "Ribbon Falls," she says.

Cara takes Sierra's arm, and points across the river, making her look. "Cross the bridge. Go to Shadow Ranch." Then she turns the girl to face her and stares into Sierra's eyes until she can see the girl look back.

"I was never here. Do you understand?"

After a moment, Sierra nods.

Back at her campsite, Cara walks in an aimless circle, then falls to her knees on the sand and tears down her tent, blindly shoves her equipment into her pack.

She burns with the white-hot rage of the violation. Of the girl, of the canyon, of the safety of any woman or girl in it now. She knows the attack was a deliberate crushing of that bright, strong spirit, the light in the other girl. Her bravery, her freedom, her daring to take the canyon and the trails and the world on her own terms.

Sierra will never feel safe in nature again. The beauty of the canyon has been forever destroyed for her.

And Cara is wild with fury at the obscenity of it.

Ribbon Falls are a side trip, on the ascent to North Rim. So Sierra's attackers are on the trail Cara intended to climb today.

She yanks the zips of her pack closed and stands, following the trail signs to the South Rim.

And Ribbon Falls.

The moon is still in the sky, a full white disk against the blue, and the clash between faint sunlight and strong moonlight makes weird, elongated shadows on the trail and the canyon walls.

The Canyon is not so warm, now. It is still, its breath suspended in anticipation. The crunch of her boots on the sand is at times nearly deafening.

Her breath is hot in her lungs from the climb, but the steady upward rhythm is easier than going downward.

The sun climbs, too. And with it her rage grows.

She knows now there will be no escape. She cannot drive away from *It*. *It* will always find her. And if there is no escaping *It*, then she will fight. To the death. She would rather face *It* once and for all than spend her life running.

She comes to a fork where a wooden trail sign indicates *Ribbon Falls, 2 miles.*

She stops on the path, staring at the sign. A choice. Her last chance. She could continue, go up to the Rim and out.

She takes the turn.

In the slot canyon, the air is cooled by the water and greenery, twenty degrees less than on the sunny upward trail.

But there is a deeper chill in this crevice. Her body temperature has dropped, her breath is short from adrenaline. She is so tense she is shivering.

She slows on the rock path, to keep her footsteps quiet.

Her pulse escalates at a faint rustling ahead. She stops still, her back against the rock wall...

Water rushing. The sound of the falls.

Which means the end of the trail is coming. Sierra's attackers will be close, now.

She moves forward, every cell in her alert.

Around another curve, the falls come into view, white water cascading down a sprawling rock face and tumbling into a spreading pool forty feet below the trail she is on.

She looks out over a pile of gigantic boulders, and a thicket of green in a semicircle around the base of the falls.

She eases forward to scour the territory below for a glimpse of a camp.

There is no sign of the men she is looking for. Her heart starts to race. They could be anywhere. Behind her on the trail, concealed between the enormous rocks, watching her from somewhere on the cliff above....

She catches a flash of orange in the greenery below.

Then it is easy to spot them, camped in a sandy circle in the sage. Two one-man tents, set some distance from each other. It's an illegal set up; the only park-allowed camping is in spots with fire circles. There is no fire circle here.

Good. That much less chance of a ranger coming this way.

She stays where she is for long minutes, scanning the boulders below her, finding a ledge above the thicket where she will be able to watch without being seen, then mapping out the path over the rocks that she will take on her way down.

When she has her route fixed in her head, she begins the descent. The boulders are rough and easy to climb. She takes her time, but the small sounds she makes are drowned out by the constant churning of the falls.

She gets to her chosen ledge without incident, and it is high enough above them to keep a lookout. She makes a bowl in the sand to sit in comfortably, with her back against the warm granite of a boulder… and the hunting knife in her lap.

She holds it, turning it in her hand, learning its weight, its heft, its curves.

Beyond the thicket, the falls cascade in a soporific rush. She tunes out the falls and focuses below.

Are they sleeping? Are they there at all?

She remains like this for some time before she hears the unmistakable zip sound of a tent being opened.

Someone is moving below her.

She freezes where she is, sinks back against the rock wall.

Below her, a man in a T-shirt and jockey shorts comes out into her sightline. He stands sleepily beside a bush with his hands at his crotch, and waters the sage with his morning piss.

Her hands tighten on the knife. *Now?* Can she get to him in time, down over the rocks, while he is occupied and vulnerable, before he is fully awake?

He shakes himself off and turns away, then stops still, staring up into the rocks, like an animal sensing a predator.

She freezes, suspends her breathing, stays as motionless as she can make herself.

The camper slowly turns, walks back toward his campsite, out of sight.

In a moment she hears his voice, taunting. "Rise and shine, asshole. Time to hit the trail."

After a beat, another voice answers, muffled by a tent and slurred with sleep or a hangover. "Go fuck yourself."

The one outside the tent taunts back, "Aww, whassamatter, *Lover Boy?* That little girl wear you out? I'm all ready to go again."

Above them, Cara digs her nails into her palms and wills herself to stay still through her rage.

She hears the scrape of metal against rock. A whiff of sulfur.

After a long moment, the strong green burning smell of marijuana wafts from below.

She relaxes.

Good. Stoned is passive. Stoned is languid and stupid. She couldn't ask for a better sign that this is *meant.*

The other voice comes from inside the tent. "Hey. Pass that bad boy in here."

She hears the sound of a zipper on canvas.

She sits back to wait. She smells pot smoke, gets glimpses of the first camper taking down his tent, loading up his pack. There is no sign or sound of the other. The one is leaving his trail buddy and moving on.

She must choose. Follow the hiker, or confront the other?

Whatever she chooses, one will get away. But perhaps not. The one who has left has also left his DNA all over the camp. He will be the logical suspect for what she is about to do.

And the other is drowsy, stoned, unsuspecting, perhaps even asleep.

She will stay.

She sits back, gritting her teeth as the first camper walks out of the brush and starts down the sandy trail, the way she came. She soothes herself by imagining him stumbling on the trail, falling over the side, his bones breaking on the rocks below.

A few minutes later she hears the snoring, the sound rumbling against the rocks, audible even over the gurgling of the water.

She stands from her ledge, slowly. Unfolding herself, testing cramped muscles, flexing, letting the blood back into fingers and toes.

She slides the knife into the deep, wide lower pocket of her cargo pants. Then feels her way down through the rocks, already warm under her touch.

She slips over the last boulder and eases herself down to the sand. Light as the wind, she moves toward the tent. Its flap hangs open, unzipped.

She listens with her whole body, aware of his every breath, every rattle of his snores.

Several yards from the tent she lowers herself to the sand and crawls forward. She stops just outside the tent, poised on her hands and knees, staring in through the open flap…

Inside is the sleeping lump of his form, half-in, half out of his sleeping bag.

He is twice her size. He could crush her with upper body strength alone.

But she knows what to do. The exact point of utmost vulnerability. She knows the spot because she has felt the cold steel of a blade in her own throat.

Her hand tightens on the grip of the knife and she inches slowly forward, over the door flap, until she is half inside…

His snore is cut short and his eyes pop open… he sees her for one swift second….

She lunges forward and plunges the knife into his neck.

The man jackknifes up to sitting, with a howl of shock and rage. The adrenaline rush allows him that much. But his legs are encased in the sleeping bag, binding him.

She scrambles backward as his neck sprays blood like a rainbird.

His hands scrabble at his throat, and his fingers find the knife, still protruding from the side of his neck. It would be comic if it weren't so very deadly.

She knows there is nothing he can do. The blood loss from a severed carotid artery is one hundred milliliters per heartbeat.

Thirty seconds of blood spurt.

Unconsciousness in under a minute.

Death within three minutes.

When it is done, she stands up under the daylight moon with blood on her hands, on her clothes. Her heart is pounding. But what she feels is peace.

This filth has no place in the Canyon. No place on the earth.

She turns and walks through the scrub to the pool under the falls. She wades in, fully clothed, feeling the shock of the cold water sizzling through her like electricity. She moves her legs against the water, pushing forward until she is under the falls themselves, feeling water pounding on her head, rushing over her body.

Washing the blood of the monster away.

Chapter 13

Portland – present
Singh

Singh stands in front of her interstates map, staring at Arizona. At the yellow push pin in the heart of Grand Canyon.

The sound of the falls is still faint in her ears.

It had not been a difficult murder to find. There have only been twenty-three homicides recorded in the park since the 1800's.

On June 10, 2005, one week after Cara disappeared from her foster home in Oceanside, a hiker named Daniel Modine was murdered on a backcountry trail in the canyon on the South Rim trail. Stabbed in the throat with a hunting knife, apparently as he slept. He bled out without making it out of his sleeping bag.

He had been robbed of any wallet, ID or valuables he may have been carrying. There was evidence he had camped with a male companion, whose name appeared on their wilderness camping permit. The companion was questioned extensively, but no charges were ever filed.

If Singh is correct that Cara took I-40 across the country, the Grand Canyon would have been a natural side trip, just an hour's drive from Williams, Arizona.

The Grand Canyon. One of the seven natural wonders of the world! How could she have resisted?

If Cara had taken I-40 that summer. If she had taken the side trip to Grand Canyon. If she had decided to hike the Rim trail. If she had come across one of those men whom she seemed so eerily able to identify as predators...

If. If. If.

It is Singh's theory, nothing more.

But slashed-throat homicides are not common. And Singh has seen Cara at work, that night out in the desert of the Salton Sea. Perhaps because of Cara's own childhood attack, and the wound that left her throat and mind forever scarred, she often, and unerringly, strikes at her victim's throats.

But of course the tipping factor is that Modine had a record, for exactly the kind of predatory activity that draws Cara to her victims. A domestic abuse charge: stalking and assault of an ex-girlfriend. A dismissed sexual battery charge. All signs of a predator.

Singh looks at her map, at the dots she has affixed there. The cluster of murders in San Francisco and Oakland. The murders in Lake Arrowhead and San Luis Obispo. The murders in the Salton Sea.

These are all in red. The present. At least, the recent present.

She steps forward and writes June 10, 2005 in tiny, precise numbers on the dot she has placed on the Grand Canyon.

The murder of Daniel Modine took place on the exact same night that Roarke rescued Tracy Collier. And against all rationality, that fact makes Singh sure Cara was responsible.

In this case, this endless case, a confluence like that cannot be ignored.

Chapter 14

Portland/San Francisco - present
Singh

She wakes to the pounding of rain.

She has been dreaming of red lines. Red arteries… blue veins… glowing lifelines constantly crossing each other over the country…

Then the image is lost, submerged by the shrill beeping of the alarm on her phone.

She must get to the airport for her flight.

San Francisco is cold, crisp, beautiful as ever.

Her loft apartment in the South of Market district is like a museum gallery, with expansive spaces, dramatic lighting, art hung on tall white walls, her collection of goddess sculptures on display columns and inset altars. They are all her choices—but her own walls feel unfamiliar around her. Perhaps it is she who does not belong.

But Damien is the same. Always startling, always exciting, always new—and yet deeply familiar. Her body responds to him as it has from the first moment she saw him in the office, the first day he appeared on the team and in her life. Since that day it has been a never-ending exercise in discipline, in compartmentalization, to keep their work interaction completely, coolly professional. There are no daring secret glances, no covert rendezvous in stairwells, no skating on the edge of discovery. Damien worked years undercover, and the challenge now is the same: when they are in the office they are not the same people as the ones who meet so explosively in bed. She knows that something in both of them finds pleasure in the challenge and the secrecy, and that is part of their relationship, too.

After, he brings her a tray of scones from the bakery on the next block, with her favorite raspberry jam and clotted cream, a taste she acquired at Cambridge.

They sit up on piles of pillows and spread thick preserves on scones and catch each other up on their respective weeks. Part of their intimacy is the enjoyment they take in discussing their work.

Damien has been active on Roarke's task force, with a focus on building federal cases against domestic traffickers of minors for sex. With his gang background on both sides of the fence, criminal and law enforcement, Damien is in his element. She can see he is relieved to be working Organized Crime again, using his expertise, instead of struggling with the ineffable, endless mystery of the Lindstrom case. It had taken over all of their lives for half a year. Now, in terms of the team's stated mission, it is as if Cara never existed.

Except that Cara has changed them all. Would there be such an intense focus on trafficked children and teens—would there be a task force at all?—if not for their recent exposure to Cara's bloodthirsty solution?

Singh is sure it would not be the case.

But she does not speak aloud about her journaling or her thoughts on Cara. It is too fraught a subject with Damien. While Singh has come to think of Cara as an avatar, more a life force than a human being, Damien views Lindstrom concretely, as a dangerous fugitive, albeit one whom he no longer has a professional responsibility for.

Singh also does not mention the mystery of twice finding the case file boxes in disarray, or her unease about Agent Snyder's explanation.

Her reasons for this omission are unclear to her.

Without mentioning the monumental nature of the task, she tells him of Snyder's plan to exponentially add to the ViCAP database.

Of course Damien understands instantly, all of it. The tedium of it and the horror, and the anger that this grand, phenomenally important tool is so unacceptably unused. He understands, most of all, the importance of keeping the database alive by any means necessary.

But his face is troubled. "Still. You two, doing all of that by hand? By yourselves? Sounds like Don Quixote and Sancho Panza."

Singh leaps instantly to Snyder's defense. "Agent Snyder has consulted on an extraordinary percentage of the most heinous crimes in recent US history. Prolific offenders who may have killed scores of other victims. Killers who are still killing. Victims whose families are still living every day of their lives in doubt. There is no one in the country more able than Agent Snyder to move the needle on the issue."

Damien raises up on an elbow to look at her with feigned jealousy. "Is this hero worship I'm hearin'? Or am I going to have to go up there and sort the man out?"

Her response is perhaps ambiguous.

Predictably, this leads to another entirely satisfying encounter.

Chapter 15

San Francisco - present
Roarke

Roarke sat behind his desk, swiveled toward the window, staring out over the Bay.

On his way in to the office he'd seen Singh and Epps arriving together, meeting Lam in front of the building, chatting together, before Epps turned away from Singh with just a look and a brush of his hand against hers. Their public discretion didn't mask their passion for each other. Not to Roarke. Not even from a distance.

Before that moment, all three agents had been laughing, clearly enjoying each other's company. The kind of camaraderie Roarke valued in his team.

His team. Fractured now, held together by a thread.

For the thousandth time he wondered if he'd been too hasty in sending Singh away.

He'd been so close to the same kind of madness himself. Did he have any right to judge her?

He tried to concentrate on his work, the calls he had to make that day, the warrants he needed to get for an upcoming bust.

But his thoughts kept drifting back to Singh.

And Cara.

Only three months previously, he'd left the Bureau and was holed up on the beach at Pismo, leveled by his own protocol-shattering encounter with Cara. Feeling he'd crossed so far over a line of professionalism, propriety, morality, he'd been unsure he could ever legitimately return to the job.

He'd thought he'd come through that. Only to confront her again, her presence, in the Salton Sea…

He'd stood on the sandy concrete floor of the derelict hotel, in the midst of carnage. Ortiz's body, bloody and gutted on a makeshift wooden platform. An obese young man slumped behind a table full of video equipment, his throat slit ear to ear. Several other men lying dead in the sand outside the building. Singh bound and drugged, but alive and uninjured…

And a sudden realization.

Cara wouldn't have left her. Not like that.

His heart leaped with the adrenaline jolt.

She's here. She's still here.

He wheeled around on the cement floor and strode out the door, into the dark. Jogging out into the desert night, past the unlit MOTEL sign, where he stopped on the sand between palm trees, looking around him. The wind ruffled his hair, warm and dry and teasing.

Tumbleweeds shivered. Five billion stars shimmered in the sky. The moon was so bright it was like heat on the sand…

And he spoke to the night.

"Cara. I know you're here."

He turned, under the swaying shadows of palm trees and full moon and the hundred million stars.

"I can feel you." He paused… and then said it. "I always feel you."

The wind swirled around him, and took his words out to the night. He waited, listened, heard the keening of the wind. And that word.

Real? Imagined? Dreamed?

"Come."

Chapter 16

San Francisco - present
Singh and Lam

They take a BART train to Embarcadero, and walk across to the Ferry Building, enjoying the sun.

As they stroll the pier in search of sea lions, Lam teases her. "You look relaxed. Glowing, even."

"Shut up," she tells him in Hindi.

"*Make me*," he replies, also in Hindi. Languages are part of their relationship. They can converse at least marginally in more than a dozen. He switches back to English. "So when's the wedding? I have plans for your hen party."

The thought should be amusing. But Singh's mood darkens. She has been carefully evading talk of a wedding with Damien. She must know—must discern if she is mentally stable enough to go forward with such a commitment.

She evades the question by turning it back on him. "When is yours?

Lam blushes. "Well… funny you should mention that…"

She pauses at the railing, startled. "Are you?"

Lam nods. "We figure… while we still can. Once you've exercised a right it's harder to take it away, and all that."

The joy she feels for her friends is tainted with the remembrance of their circumstances. The very real possibility that their right to marriage will be rescinded because of a minority imposing their ignorance on the rest of the country.

"That will not happen," she assures him. "Not in California."

Lam doesn't answer. They both know there are no longer any guarantees of justice prevailing. Not as the current situation stands.

"Anyway, you're next," he says cheerily. "I can see that red thread around your ankle."

She squints through the sun at him, not understanding.

"The red string of Fate?" He explains patiently, as if this is something every schoolchild should know. "The Gods tie a red string around the ankles of people who are destined for each other, or fated to help each other in a certain way."

She stares out at the Bay, suddenly still. It feels as if lightning has just cracked over their heads.

The red string of Fate.

She is accustomed to Lam speaking of mythology as a demonstrated fact. And it is part of their bond: they were both raised in cultures far more ancient than that of the United States.

But her reaction to this particular pronouncement is fierce and unexpected. Her senses are tingling. And for a moment she is overcome with the remembrance of the image from her dream:

Red and blue lines, criss crossing the country…

Cara's murder in the Grand Canyon. Roarke's rescue of Tracy Collier on the mountaintop.

On the same day.

She had almost convinced herself it was all in her imagination, this confluence of dates. But now—

"People who are destined for each other or destined to help each other in some way…"

"The red string of Fate," she repeats faintly, when she has recovered her voice. "Is that Vietnamese?"

He corrects her cheerfully. "Chinese, but hey—we can't separate our myths from theirs any more. That's what a thousand years of political and cultural domination will do. Anyway, we keep the good ones. And this is a good one." He leans back against the railing, looking out at people drifting on the pier. Singles, couples, families. "Two people connected by the red thread are destined lovers, regardless of time, place or circumstances. The cord can stretch, it can tangle, but it will never break. You're always in that person's orbit."

He shrugs, philosophically. "How do you think I ended up with the Bear?" He means Stotlemyre. "Red string. Had to be."

Singh ponders, while Lam adds, "Supposedly with each passing year the threads grow tighter, bringing us closer to those people whose lives are destined to intertwine with ours in some way."

It is an extravagantly romantic notion. With all the charm of most extravagantly romantic notions. She feels it in her own life, with Epps. They have often marveled together at how unlikely it is that they would find each other. Born oceans and continents apart, in communities and to parents who could not have been more different. Hers, upper-class Indian engineers and entrepreneurs. His, a drug-addicted teenage mother and struggling teenage father.

And yet here they are.

But what if...

It is so intimate she does not dare say it aloud. But what if Lam is right?

She has no doubt that love binds Roarke and Lindstrom. A tragic, impossible love—yet love it is.

Even more, are they not working together, in some cosmic sense?

And if such a string connects Roarke and Cara, how many other times might their paths have crossed?

How many other cases?

And suddenly she sees it. As if the whole country is spread out before her like the map in her Portland hotel.

Criss-crossed with hundreds of red threads.

PART TWO

Chapter 17

Portland - present
Singh and Snyder

Singh arrives at Agent Snyder's house in a morning shrouded with fog. She has been up most of the night combing law enforcement databases, and is anxious to question him.

To that end, she carries a box full of pastries she has bought from a bakery across the street from her hotel. It is a ruse on her part. She wants a coffee break this morning, as soon as she can engineer it.

She balances the box as she punches in the security code for the door.

The house is quiet as she enters the hall. She steps to the archway of the living room…

And freezes, looking out at chaos.

Someone has torn through the boxes. Files are spread everywhere. Some are dumped out entirely.

She bites back the impulse to call out to Agent Snyder. Her sense is too strong that there is something else, someone else, at work here.

She sets the bakery box noiselessly down on an end table.

She has no weapon. She scans the room, and her eyes light on the fireplace, the rack of implements there: coal shovel, hearth broom, and poker. She moves on the balls of her feet to the fireplace to slip the poker from the stand.

A step comes from the inner hallway....

Her hand tightens around the poker handle...

Snyder appears in the archway of the hall, leveling his service weapon at her. Singh's heart nearly leaps out of her chest. "Agent Snyder!"

A stricken look crosses Snyder's face. Instantly he lowers the Glock. "Forgive me. Forgive me."

She is so agitated she has to stop herself from crying out. "Agent Snyder, what is happening? What are you not telling me?"

He looks devastated. He steps back to a side table, slides open a drawer to put the Glock away, and closes it with finality. He stands facing away from her, then turns to her in chagrin.

"I should have told you before." He looks around at the scattered files. "Someone's been in the house."

As disturbing as the truth is, she is relieved to hear him speak it aloud.

He turns helplessly in the room. "No valuables have been taken. I've found no sign of anyone. Just the files ransacked and left... like this. As if whoever it is wants me to see."

Singh is chilled. "But this has happened twice since I have been here. Have you called the police?"

He looks mortified. "I haven't. It was foolish of me. Pride. I was hoping to make sense of it by determining which files the intruder is after..."

Despite her distress, Singh feels a prickling of empathy. Of course his own reputation as an investigator has factored into his decision-making. He will have been feeling, and fighting, the inevitable loss of power that aging is.

"And have you?" she asks.

He gestures to the disorder. "Because of the extent and seeming randomness of the ransacking, it took me some time to determine what had gone missing. Which almost certainly was the intruder's intent. But there has been a file stolen. The file on a case I consulted on in January. Just my handwritten notes."

Singh feels an electric thrill of danger.

"I'd been troubled about this particular case before the intrusions. A few months ago, before you and I began this work together, I was called up to consult on a murder in Idaho." His face shadows. "A child killing. A five-year old boy, abducted and savaged by a predator, left in the woods."

Singh sits abruptly on a sofa. She is gripped by the familiar numb anger. *Monsters. There are monsters.*

"Local law enforcement was getting nowhere and they asked for an evaluation. I took Matthew up with me in January."

Singh looks up, startled. She has heard nothing of this. "I did not know he had done that."

An ambiguous look crosses Agent Snyder's face. "I understand he wasn't in very close touch with the office that month. The Lindstrom case was—conflicting."

As Singh knows, "conflicting" is a mild word for what the Lindstrom case has been for Roarke.

And not just for Roarke...

"Matthew had just taken his leave of absence after... well, let's call it what it was. He suffered a breakdown after Cara Lindstrom's release from prison and disappearance. He'd left San Francisco and was staying in Pismo Beach. I called him there and applied some emotional blackmail to get him to come up to Idaho to assist me on the consult."

Singh is unnerved. It is true that Roarke had been off the grid for the entire month of January. But he had filled the team in on his investigation in the Coachella Valley, following fourteen-year old Cara's trail from sixteen years ago, to find a vicious serial rapist still operating in the present. Roarke had never once mentioned a side trip to Idaho.

Snyder continues. "There was an aspect of the case that bore some similarity to a case that Matthew and I worked years ago. An older case. In Seattle… and here in Portland."

The file. The file he had tried to hide from her.

"The Street Hunter killings," she says, with absolute certainty.

He looks at her. "Of course you would be familiar with those murders."

Singh is instantly on edge. "The case in Idaho reminds you of the Street Hunter?"

"There are significant differences." He pauses, then admits, "And very troubling similarities."

"And those notes are in the file that is missing?" she asks tensely.

"I'm afraid so."

Singh's senses are buzzing. This is the undercurrent of urgency she has been sensing all along. "Agent Snyder, we must get to the bottom of whatever has been happening here."

"Yes. It's time for me to tell you everything." He stares out through the glass doors to the deck, where the fog swirls through the trees, a cold and murky presence. Suddenly he looks haggard. "But there is so much. I don't know where to start."

"Start with whatever you are thinking," she urges.

"Yes," he says. "You're right." She can see him relax, regain focus. He moves away from the doors, into the room. "You asked me, last week, how I met Matthew. I'm afraid I went off on a tangent. But I'm convinced now, it started there. It was a militia case." Agent Snyder pauses, and is quiet for a long time. Singh does not know what to think. And then he turns back to her. "Sorry. I was thinking—that all the signs were there, all along. The rise of this violent subculture of conspiracy and apocalypse. Paranoid men arming themselves, collecting into groups that feed on each other's obsession and racism and misogyny. Spreading their toxicity through the internet… and amassing more armaments." Singh can feel the force of his regret. "If we had been paying more attention to the militias. What we might have prevented…"

He passes a hand over his forehead. "Yes. The case. It was 2005, and we were investigating a militia group in Richmond. One member, specifically."

Singh's entire body is electrified by one word.

Richmond.

Chapter 18

Quantico, Virginia - June 2005
Matt

It was like driving into the landscape of a dream.

Matt sat on the edge of his seat, staring out the window of the taxi at the wooded obstacle course made famous in the eerie opening of *The Silence of the Lambs*. The FBI Academy, five hundred forty-seven acres within the Marine Corps base, about forty miles out of D.C. The campus he'd read so many descriptions of, that he'd studied so intently on obscure videos he'd searched out on a new internet site called YouTube.

The last two weeks had been a whirlwind.

That night at Bishop Peak, Sheriff's deputies had taken Matt into custody and removed Tracy Collier from the park to a hospital.

And Marcus Bannon, a drifter with a history of sexual assault, was arrested as he tried to flee the area.

Bannon had been holding Tracy in an old power facility hut outside the nature reserve, where he'd been squatting for several weeks. He'd left her in the hut while he went out for some still unknown reason, and that remarkable little girl had bitten through the duct tape Bannon had bound her with, punched out the glass of the one window, and crawled out.

In her disorientation and panic she'd stumbled into the reserve, and it was on her frantic climb up the hill that Matt had found her—at the same time that Bannon returned to the shed to find the window broken and blood on the glass where she'd crawled out.

Bannon pursued her and Matt on the hill, but was spooked by the timely arrival of the deputies. He'd panicked and made a run for it. A patrol car noticed his erratic driving, clocked the description of the vehicle given by witnesses to Tracy's abduction, and gave pursuit. So not long after Matt was lying face down and cuffed in the dirt, Bannon was arrested and booked.

And Tracy was returned to the arms of her overjoyed and grateful grandmother.

Alive. But not unharmed.

And Matt? He was a local hero. For a week, he was interviewed on the radio, in state news.

And Quantico called, offering him the internship.

Matt had no idea if they'd booted someone else off it, or created another spot for him, or if he'd always been in the running. He knew he should be excited regardless of the hows and whys. But there was a nagging doubt consuming him. He felt like an impostor.

And he couldn't push through the fog of depression that had surrounded him since Tracy's rescue.

He took his finals at Cal Poly, packed his bags, and arrived at the FBI complex in Virginia on that sweltering June day.

The taxi dropped him off at the dorm that would be home to the interns for the eight weeks of the program. At the registration desk in the lobby Matt was allotted a room and a roommate, Ed Chen, a Korean-American engineering major from MIT who'd already been assigned to the forensics lab.

In their room, Matt dressed in a new suit, impeccable shirt and tie and dress shoes—graduation presents from his parents. Then he and Ed joined the other dressed-to-the-nines interns for orientation, walking through the doors of the lecture hall under the engraved words:

FIDELITY BRAVERY INTEGRITY

The words felt like fire in Matt's chest.

After a welcome speech by the Deputy Director, during which he referred to the Bureau as a "family" no less than four times, the interns were escorted on a tour of the facilities, ending at Hogan's Alley—the ten-acre urban landscape built specifically for simulations like hostage scenarios, bomb threats and criminal investigations.

But in the midst of his fellow interns' excitement, Matt was gripped by a growing unease. Every other intern he met already seemed to have a specific unit assignment. But no one had told him exactly what he was supposed to be doing here.

That first night in his dorm room he lay awake for most of the night, unaccustomed to having a roommate again and anxious about his seeming lack of place in the structure. The angst he'd been feeling for weeks deepened into fear. Fear that he wasn't worthy. Fear that he hadn't merely failed, but had fucked up beyond redemption.

On day two he was assigned to the Visual Investigative Analysis Unit. It was another stab in the heart. He'd hoped for a place on the Tactical Squad. Again he had the nagging feeling that the powers that be were just trying to create a place for him at the last minute. Not because he'd done anything real to deserve it, but just for show.

He dutifully attended the orientation on matrix analysis, link analysis, and visual investigative analysis. He was tasked with reading and reviewing huge stacks of case reports filed by operatives in the field, along with open source news reports gathered from the internet. The job: to search for linkages.

A small, mean voice in his head whispered that it was grunt work. He ignored it. If this was what he was going to do all summer, he would make it count. He threw himself into the process, trying to shake off his funk. It was all about looking for the larger plot or narrative. Finding the connections between seemingly random facts. Finding individuals connected to a case who repeatedly crossed paths. Catching the overlaps in time or location.

Then on the third day, his life changed forever.

He emerged from his six am shower and found a scribbled note from Ed informing him he'd had a call from administration.

Report to Conference Room D - Snyder wants to see you.

For a moment Matt's heart skipped a beat.

Snyder?

Chuck Snyder was one of the original Behavioral Science Unit at the FBI, the living definition of "profiler." At least, he was what anyone who knew anything thought about when they heard the word.

Matt forced himself to check his excitement.

He knew Snyder didn't work at Quantico anymore. His beat was the Pacific Northwest, in the field office in Portland. Surely it wasn't *that* Snyder.

But when Matt walked into the conference room, the man himself was seated at the table, a file spread out in front of him.

Matt knew him from photos. He was younger than Matt had imagined. No, that wasn't true. He was stronger. Matt could see he was tall even though the agent was seated, and there was a rough male energy there that Matt had already come to expect in the law enforcement professionals around him. But with Snyder, there was something more ancient and mythic, something like a Viking about him.

"Matthew Roarke," Snyder said. And there was a long and excruciating moment of silence while the veteran agent looked him over. It was a feeling like being in a doctor's office.

Matt felt a thrill of anticipation… and immediately an attack of nerves.

What the hell is this?

Snyder reached for the file in front of him. "This is a remarkable story." On top of the file was a newspaper article that Matt recognized instantly. It was one of the recounts of his "rescue" of Tracy Collier.

Matt had to struggle not to look pained. Apparently he didn't succeed. The older man picked up immediately on his discomfort.

"You don't agree?" Snyder asked.

Matt knew he was supposed to say something like, *I was just doing the job,* or *It's an honor to serve.*

Instead he burst out angrily, "I didn't do anything. *She* did it. She bit through the tape on her hands and punched out the glass of the window and hauled herself up out of that hut. But she broke her ankle dropping out of the window and she got stuck in the valley there. I heard her calling and I went down and I brought her out." His mouth was dry and he had to swallow to finish. "That's it."

Snyder chuckled, tossed the article back on the table. "You're right. You didn't do much at all. Dumb luck."

Matt bristled, but answered tightly, "Yeah."

The agent sat back in his chair, studying him. It went on beyond anything comfortable, but Matt was damned if he was going to show it. He stood without moving, without blinking. Finally Snyder spoke.

"But you were there."

"Not fast enough," Matt said, before he could stop himself.

The agent gave him a level look. "Because Bannon raped her, you mean?"

Matt didn't want to talk about this. He'd never wanted to talk about it. But the words came anyway, low, angry, resentful. "If I'd just kept looking. If I hadn't gone back down the trail to check in. I would've gotten there sooner..."

"And you feel guilty because you think she's damaged." Agent Snyder's voice was suddenly sharp. "That's your privilege speaking. Nothing really bad has ever happened to you."

Matt felt his face flush with anger.

"You're going to learn that many, many women and girls have had the same experience, and worse. Boys and men, too." Snyder fixed a level gaze on Matt's face. "Rape doesn't make anyone 'less than.' Except the rapist."

Matt felt as if he'd been struck upside the head. "I wasn't thinking of it—like that," he admitted.

"I know you weren't. No one wants to talk about rape." Snyder indicated the file. "Tracy's case was barely covered in national news. If she'd been killed, or gotten away completely unscathed, every news source would still be talking about it."

That was true. There hadn't been much publicity about it at all. Something occurred to Matt. "How did you know about it, then?"

"It's my business to know."

But how did you know that nothing bad ever happened to me? Matt thought, but didn't say. To his surprise, Snyder answered him anyway.

"Getting through life unscathed is a kind of privilege, just like being born wealthy, or white, or male. You won the jackpot on all of those."

"Yes, sir," Matt said.

"Now you've committed yourself to giving back by helping people who haven't been so fortunate. That's good. It's the definition of what 'good' is." Snyder's voice softened. "Tracy Collier is alive—because you found her. If Bannon had caught up with her, he most certainly would have killed her."

Matt felt something like a concrete band around his chest suddenly dissolving to liquid and pouring away from him. A concrete band he hadn't even known was there.

Snyder nodded, and paged through the file, absently. "When you went back, that night. What made you go *there*? To that exact place?"

Matt tightened up again. He'd told the story a hundred times by now. He'd thought he was done with this part. "I must've seen something down there in the valley, when I was on the trail that day. A flash of—movement, or light. Or maybe I heard her calling, back when I was searching earlier in the day and it registered on some level. So I went back."

"Probably," Snyder said. But he didn't sound like he believed it.

"She started screaming for help when he left her. Maybe she was easier to hear at night."

This time Snyder said nothing. He just sat, waiting.

For what?

Matt had told the story, and he was sticking to it. Just like he had the first time he'd told it and the hundred times since. He definitely wasn't going to say anything stupid like, *"I just wanted to find her so bad that I did."*

But he had the weirdest feeling Snyder was trying to *get* him to say that.

After a time, the older man said, "You don't like the word 'intuition'?"

"I wouldn't say it aloud," Matt answered before he could stop himself.

Snyder laughed again. "Fair enough. But you can say it to me. In fact, if you're going to work with me, I might even require it."

Blood was suddenly pounding in Matt's head. *Work with him? Is that what this is?* He had to focus hard to bring himself back to Snyder's words.

"I'm teaching a seminar here this summer. But an urgent case has come up in the Richmond area and I've been asked to provide investigative support. I'll need an assistant, as it were. Interested?"

Interested? Matt could barely breathe.

"Yes, sir!"

"Then get some sleep tonight. We've got work to do tomorrow."

And so Matt's real training began.

Chapter 19

Portland – present
Singh and Snyder

Agent Snyder pauses. He stands at the window, looking out on the fountain in his garden. He seems quite as if he is immersed in another time.

Singh herself is gripped with internal turmoil.

On the surface, Agent Snyder's narrative so far seems to have nothing whatsoever to do with the Street Hunter, or Idaho, or anything in the immediate present.

But if Singh's research is correct, it has everything to do with everything.

Agent Snyder turns away from the window. "I apologize, Agent Singh. I didn't sleep last night and I seem to have lost my train of thought."

She prompts him quickly. "You took ASAC Roarke out on this domestic violence case in Richmond…"

Agent Snyder looks at her, a sharp, strange look. He speaks softly. "That's interesting. I didn't say it was a domestic violence case. How would you know that?"

Singh doesn't know how to answer. She doesn't know anything. And yet, she has the strongest feeling that she does.

Because there are two halves to the story he is telling.

Chapter 20

Wilmington, North Carolina - June 2005
Cara

She stands on the beach in Wilmington, looking out at the Atlantic.

She's done it. Ocean to ocean. A complete trip across the entire country.

A miracle, really.

It is a startling ocean, with none of the stark rumbling violence of the Pacific. Calm, with barely any surf at all, and warm as bathwater.

Everything is warmer. And the air is beyond moist. She is used to desert heat, as dry as bone. Here the humidity is so dense she can lean into the air and feel it push back.

She wades into the surf, losing herself in the softness, the soothing blues and beiges, washing the trip away.

The Grand Canyon could have been the end of everything. It almost was.

Somehow, after the *Encounter* at the falls, she'd made it up to the Rim, to the car she left at the parking lot. She has a vague sense memory of the baking heat of the sun drying the water of the falls from her skin and clothes...

But truthfully, she does not remember anything else of the upward hike. She only remembers finding herself behind the wheel, on the road again. Her survival instinct, which she thinks of vaguely like the locomotive of the freight trains she keeps passing, had kicked into high gear and kept her moving.

She drives all night in a stupor, knowing she needs to cross another border before she can rest. Back to Interstate 40, through the rest of Arizona and across the state line to New Mexico.

The obvious suspect for the hiker's murder will be the hiker's companion. His name will be on the backcountry pass of his murdered friend. He will have to account for his whereabouts, while there is no record of her anywhere. No name on the shuttle bus. No backcountry pass in her name. She is an eighteen-year old girl. There is no reason for anyone to suspect her.

Other fragments of the *Encounter* come back as she speeds on the highway. She remembers the vile power of *It* under her body as she scrambled to cut *Its* throat. She remembers blood on her face, the shock of stepping into rushing cold water....

And she remembers a moment of thinking of using the knife on herself.

In her first days of driving, of wide open road, she had been lulled into a sense of freedom and calm.

The truth is, there is no such thing as safety. *It* can follow even into a haven like the Canyon. Indeed, *It* seems to be mocking her, playing a cruel game with her—allowing her to feel safe and then striking so closely, attacking Sierra right under her nose...

She is first empty, then dazed, and then so angry she can barely drive for the shaking.

It is only the landscape that keeps her going. I-40 in New Mexico traces the southern edge of a huge Navajo reservation, at times crossing through it. She knows the wild beauty of the California desert. The New Mexico desert is something even more stunning. The colors are psychedelic. Every possible variation of red. It is staggering beauty, of an entirely different kind from the Grand Canyon, even.

And the state is so sparely populated that she seems alone on the road. Perhaps she has driven off the edge of the world. There is only one station she can find on the radio, a soundtrack of haunting native music, chanting and flute. She turns the radio off and can hear the sound even more clearly in the desert wind.

When she pulls off the road to camp, the sand is blood-red. As the sun sets she seems to be in the midst of a shimmering sphere of molten lava.

In this vast emptiness, she begins to come back to herself.

In the morning, she drives on. And the next day. And the next. She no longer thinks so often about the knife in the glove compartment, and how easy it would be to end this fight.

But now she has her guard up, always. The *Encounter* in the Grand Canyon has reminded her what she has known since she was five years old. *It* lurks everywhere. On the road, in the bodies of men who leer at her as she passes, who try to chase her car on the freeway, making obscene gestures.

She begins to dress as a boy, to conceal her hair in a cap and her eyes behind sunglasses, to wear loose jeans and bulky flannel shirts as she speeds through the long monotonous stretch of Texas. Again, it is a radical change in landscape, beginning right at the New Mexico border. There is Amarillo, with its garish billboards, the rainbow-painted upended cars of Cadillac Ranch. And then long stretches of flat nothingness. She feels exposed on the wide-open highway and drives without stopping even to sleep, to get through as quickly as possible.

The border of Oklahoma brings on another change in geography and landscape, and she begins to realize that state boundaries are not random imaginary lines, but demarcations of different physical worlds. Oklahoma is as flat as Texas, but its starkness is softened by gentle hills and the half-tree, half-bush greenery lining the road. Parts of the state have a haunting wildness that she has difficulty finding words for. She trades her car for another, leaving the Honda on a downtown street to be stolen, and jacking an old warhorse of a truck, something to fit in on these Southern roads.

She drives Arkansas, the bridge city of Memphis, Tennessee roads meandering through woods and carved granite cliffs. In North Carolina, she traverses mountains shrouded by the hazy mist that gives the Blue Ridge its name. Then on through Asheville, the farmland surrounding Charlotte, Raleigh… and now here.

Wilmington. This beach, the pinks and beiges and powder blues, the warm waves licking at her shins.

For the first time, post-canyon, she feels peace.

But she feels no pull to stay. The long stretch of driving has only made her hungry for more.

Now that she's made it all the way across, her plan is to cross the country vertically. She will take 95 North to get a taste of the South-North route and the major Eastern cities along it, all the way up to I-90, the northernmost East-West interstate.

She wants the country and its veins and arteries fixed in her mind. She intends to know every mile of the interstate system. Every road leads to every other road, eventually. A whole network of freedom. She wants the grid in her head so she always knows where she is, and where she can escape.

She turns back to the ocean and looks out at the boats on the glistening water. The moon is up in daylight, a pale, almost-full disk in the blue sky.

She'll start for Virginia tomorrow.

Chapter 21

Portland - present
Singh and Snyder

Agent Snyder sits back in his armchair. Singh can hear her own heart beating in the silence.

Finally he speaks. "Cara Lindstrom was in Virginia when Matthew and I were investigating this militia case." It is not a question.

"She was in Richmond," Singh answers.

Snyder glances at her sharply. "How do you know?"

She doesn't tell him. Instead, she drives him to her hotel.

As he walks into the living room of the suite, she can see the stunned disbelief on his face.

Her wall-sized map of the interstates system has evolved. She has the various routes traced in different colors, with corresponding dates written in the margins of the map. Now the whole country is dotted with push pins of different colors. And beside the map Singh has mounted two rectangular white boards.

At the top of one board she has written simply, ROARKE.

And on the second she has written CARA.

On each board is a timeline, starting in 2001, listing successive years to the present.

At the top of Cara's timeline Singh has filled in the early murders she knows of from the year Cara was fourteen years old, along with locations and dates. In Palm Desert, California, the group home counselor, Clive Pierson. In the desert outside Las Piedras, California, the serial rapist David Huell.

At the bottom of Cara's board is a flurry of names, dates and cities, where Singh has listed Cara's most recent whereabouts and known and suspected murders.

In October of last year, Agent Greer in San Francisco; the trucker, Brent Hartley, at the rest stop in Atascadero; the five traffickers near Blythe, California.

In November, Danny Ramirez in San Francisco. Nathaniel Martin Hughes, aka "The Reaper," in Lake Arrowhead, California.

In December, a prison guard in Burlingame, and the Tenderloin and International Boulevard pimp murders in San Francisco and Oakland.

In January, the six hunters who went missing in the Chinle area of New Mexico, hunters Singh suspects set out to rape teenage Navajo girls in Canyon de Chelly—and instead came face to face with Cara's relentless fury.

In February, three men who brought loaded rifles to a women's rally in Arizona and ended up corpses stacked in a pile in a side alley. The murder Singh herself was present for in the deserted motel in Salton Sea: Detective Gilbert Ortiz. And the four men who were participants and collateral damage that night.

Between most of those dates on Cara's board Singh has connected the same dates on Roarke's board with lengths of red string. Multiple dates, multiple fatal incidents: Greer's death, the Tenderloin murders, the desert murders, the murder of the Reaper. Every instance in which Roarke's and Cara's paths crossed. Over a dozen deaths, all within the last five months.

The middle of Cara's board also contains names and dates written in yellow, with question marks beside them. Names from Singh's list of possible Cara victims, yet to be proven.

Except that parallel to Cara's murder of Daniel Modine in the Grand Canyon, Singh has noted on Roarke's board:

June 10, 2005 *San Luis Obispo, CA* *Rescue of Tracy Collier*

And she has used a piece of red string to connect Modine's murder and the rescue of Tracy Collier.

Looking at the map, the boards, the totality of it, Singh has a moment of thinking she must look entirely mad.

Then Snyder turns to her. "Well, Agent Singh, I think you'd better explain yourself."

She takes a breath. And she becomes an FBI agent again as she talks Snyder through her interstates theory, her conviction that Cara would have traversed the country in this way.

She references the key of dates she has started in the margin of the map: a separate color for each year when she has a guess or a strong indication of the year, each route labeled where possible with the years Singh believes Cara took that route. She points out the pins marking the murders she strongly believes are Cara's.

It is as if she is back in her office, with her team, in the role that she is meant for.

Agent Snyder walks the length of the map, marveling. "We've always thought she's been killing for years. But this... this is astonishing."

She feels a quiet thrill of validation at his approval.

He stops to study the two side-by-side timelines, Roarke's and Cara's.

"There's something else here you haven't explained." He indicates the red strings she has fastened between points on Roarke's timeline and Cara's. The Grand Canyon murder and Roarke's rescue of Tracy Collier. The massacre of the Lindstrom family and nine-year old Matt Roarke's letter to the FBI director announcing his intention to become an agent. The connections between timelines with the Tenderloin murders, the murder of the Reaper, and the uncanny death of Agent Greer.

"The correlation of dates I understand," Agent Snyder says. "But is there a significance to the string?"

This is the part she feels shakiest about. "There is," she says. "But before I explain, would you finish your story about your work with ASAC Roarke on the Richmond case?"

He frowns, and she adds quickly, "It is crucial to the whole. There is something I must confirm."

"Very well," he answers. "Richmond, 2005."

Chapter 22

Quantico, Virginia - June 2005
Matt

Matt's alarm rang at five am. It was two full hours before he was to meet Snyder, but he wanted to be completely alert for whatever was in store.

He showered and dressed quickly in casual clothes, as instructed. Snyder had advised jeans and "*Some kind of concert T-shirt, if you have one here. Preferably black. Preferably heavy metal. And a duckbill cap.*"

Matt had left his concert T's at home. He'd never owned a duckbill cap. So he'd gone room to room until he found an intern who had a Metallica shirt and hat he could borrow.

Dawn was just breaking as he headed for the parking lot.

He was by nature a night owl, but he didn't mind the early hour. He'd quickly realized early morning was the only bearable time of day, here. As a native Californian, he was accustomed to heat, but he'd never experienced the paralyzing humidity of the South. The air dripped with moisture, and so did he. He'd taken to having multiple showers per day, changing his clothes constantly to keep up with the sweating.

But after his talk—or talking-to—with Snyder, he felt as if a two-ton weight had been lifted from him. And he felt excitement again, the certainty that he was pursuing something greater than himself.

A mission.

This summer it would all—or at least, more of it—be revealed.

Snyder was waiting for him in the parking lot, holding a paper tray with two large cups of coffee in one hand and a plastic bag in the other. He looked over Matt's clothes. "Not bad," he said. "Keep the hat. But try this shirt instead." He tossed Matt the plastic bag and Matt removed a T-shirt with a dragon logo and a band name: *Goatwhore.*

"More Southern," Snyder said, straight-faced.

Right, Matt thought, bemused.

"Today we're going fishing," Snyder told him, as he started into the parking lot.

Matt pulled the new shirt on as he followed the agent to his vehicle, one of the oversized four-wheel drive SUVs that Matt had noticed were standard on Virginia roads. He didn't see any fishing gear in the back—the expedition was metaphorical.

Snyder stood in back of the car and asked, "How's your driving?"

"I like to drive," Matt said. He'd read somewhere that the vast majority of people considered themselves excellent drivers. He'd worked in a police department long enough to know the actual statistics.

"Then the wheel is yours." Snyder tossed him the keys.

Inside the SUV, Snyder arranged the coffees in the cup holders while Matt motored out of the Quantico campus. Snyder directed him onto Interstate 95, south, toward Richmond.

"I've been asked to do a threat assessment." He took a surveillance shot out of a file and placed it on the dashboard between them.

Matt glanced down at a photo that seemed to have been pulled from a DMV record: a man with a round, ruddy face, a receding hairline, wire frame glasses, a stare halfway between blank and hostile.

"Wayne Gilman," Snyder explained. "He's come to our attention because of an anonymous tip that Gilman has been making threats against the Bureau and the ATF."

Matt felt his pulse jump.

"He's a resident of Richmond and he's our surveillance target today. But for now, drink your coffee and keep your eyes on the road."

Matt was buzzing with curiosity and anticipation, but did as he was told.

The freeway was lined with dense trees on both sides, a relentless corridor of green. He was used to the breathtaking coastal views of Highway 1, and the ever-changing pastoral meandering of 101. It was a disconcerting thing to drive a freeway of such sameness: no vistas whatsoever, just that impenetrable wall of trees.

Snyder spoke from the passenger seat. "I-95 is the main North-South interstate on the Eastern Seaboard. Or South-North, as it's wise to say here," he added wryly.

Matt had already picked up on the antebellum obsession. In fifteen minutes of driving, he'd passed five or six trucks with Confederate flag bumper stickers. The one directly in front of them had a second flag sticker, a coiled rattlesnake with the words DON'T TREAD ON ME. He had to call up his high school history for the name of it: the Gadsden flag. Something to do with the American Revolution. He was wondering idly what the bumper sticker's owner was trying to say when Snyder spoke.

"Do you know anything about the Dwight D. Eisenhower Interstate Highway System?"

"Not really, sir," Matt replied, and felt a stab of anxiety. *Am I supposed to?*

Snyder smiled faintly, as if reading his thoughts. "You're not going to find it on any written test. But this job is going to take you all over the country. You'll be dropped at a second's notice into a completely unfamiliar state, and you'll need to make your way."

Matt felt a quiet thrill that Snyder was talking as if he was already an agent. He had to force himself to concentrate on the veteran's next words.

"There's a precision to the numerology of the interstate system. If you know the numbers, you can always get a quick sense of where you are and how to get to the next place you need to be. We're on I-95, the major interstate of the Eastern Seaboard, traversing from Miami to New York City, parallel to the Atlantic Coast, and serving most of the major Eastern cities in between: Jacksonville, Savannah, Richmond, DC, Baltimore, Philadelphia, Boston. Odd interstate numbers mean a North-South route across the length of the country; the even-numbered highways are West-East across the width, starting with I-5, which you will be familiar with..."

"Oh, wow," Matt said. He felt like he'd just been given the keys to the country... and simultaneously like an idiot for never having seen it. Highway 1 was the California coast road, Pacific Coast Highway. I-5 was the main interstate through the middle of California. And if I-95 was parallel to the Atlantic coast....

"So the interstates go up by multiples of five across the whole country? 5 to 95?"

Snyder nodded, looking pleased. "There isn't one for every multiple of five. But the ones that are there, yes, they're divisible by five, in ascending order."

Matt had never stopped to think that there was an actual plan. He drove in silence through the green corridor, marveling at how useful that information was going to be, as Snyder continued.

"The interstate system may actually have contributed to the rise of the modern serial killer. It certainly made hunting easier for serial rapists. These men could suddenly move freely around the country. The anonymity of travel and the constant crossing of jurisdictions makes it far harder to catch them."

Roarke stared out the windshield at the dense trees. He could imagine another Green River Killer operating here. Stopping to pick up a truck stop prostitute or a lone female traveler…

The thought was a stab of unease.

Who would ever find a body in these woods?

Chapter 23

I-95, Virginia - June 2005
Cara

On the beach she had decided she would take I-95 all the way up the East Coast to the Canadian border.

But driving it is another story entirely. The freeway is densely traveled and monotonous, mile upon mile of wooded corridor. The trees are ominous; there is no way to see if anyone is coming. It is a cold and anxious feeling. In just a few hours of travel, she is longing for the breathtaking vistas of the West. Worse, she sees few women travelers in cars on their own, and she feels constantly under a spotlight. The pickup trucks with their Confederate flags and NRA bumper stickers make her queasy. She is afraid to stop even for gas, where she is watched by unsmiling men as she fuels up.

She considers abandoning the South-North route and turning back at 64 to head for the wide-open spaces of the West. But that non-major highway will take her through even more back woods.

Best to stick to major corridors. Surely she will be more anonymous in the cities.

She resolves she will make it as far as New York, then head west on I-80, ending in San Francisco.

But later that day the plan changes.

It begins when she must make another pit stop for gas, which entails driving off the highway into that endless maze of trees. Southern gas stations seem to be further off the main highways than in other parts of the country.

She fills her tank without incident and is just driving back to the interstate when a monstrous truck, an old Ford, pulls up beside her.

The humidity outside is so oppressive she has removed her cap, and her hair gives her away.

The truck slows to keep pace with her, and several men inside the truck stare into her truck at her, a lone girl-woman, driving.

She accelerates.

The truck pulls up alongside her again.

This time, one of the men inside, a sweaty round-faced man with wire frame glasses, lifts a shotgun so that she can see it, and caresses it lewdly, licking his lips at her. The other men laugh.

It is not the only firearm they have in the truck, she is sure.

And there is no one on the road to prevent anything they intend to do.

Chapter 24

I-95, Virginia - June 2005
Matt

As Matt stared into the wall of trees, enmeshed in thoughts of serial killers, Snyder spoke abruptly. "I know that you've come here hoping to work Behavioral Sciences."

Matt glanced away from the road, startled. Again, Snyder seemed to have read his thoughts.

"It's clear in your choice of major, your course selection, your psychiatric internship. I also read your thesis on Ridgeway."

Now Matt felt almost spied on, stripped bare. The same year Matt had begun college, Gary Ridgeway, aka the Green River Killer, was finally arrested and charged for more than four dozen homicides of prostitutes in the Seattle-Tacoma area of Washington State. Matt had done his senior thesis on the use of new advances in DNA technology in Ridgeway's apprehension.

"2001," Snyder said. "A banner year in the advance in use of DNA technology. And of course, the year of the 9/11 attacks." He turned in the passenger seat and looked at Matt directly. "That year the Bureau radically changed direction and focus. You need to know this, Matthew. Behavioral Science, the division you've obviously grown up learning a great deal about, and pinning your hopes on joining, is being cut to the bone. Since 9/11 the Bureau's focus has been on counter-terrorism. Budgets have been slashed. Agents have been reassigned. Prospective agents will be selected according to the new criteria."

Matt felt a sinking sensation. *What's he trying to tell me? That I'm not going to make it into the Bureau?*

"It's a rising tide and virtually unstoppable in this political climate," Snyder continued.

Matt hazarded a guess. "But… you don't agree?"

Snyder looked bleak. "It's the way of the world, to focus on outside threats, to cast the *Other* as the enemy, rather than to look for the monster within. Shadow projection, Jung would call it. Not to mention that the politics of it have very little to do with social good."

Matt was fielding a barrage of feelings. Disappointment, anger, confusion. "But—what are *you* going to do?"

Snyder half-smiled. "We keep doing the same work and call it by different names."

A thrill rippled through Matt at the "*We*."

"Violent crimes against persons won't stop because we've chosen to look outside ourselves for our enemies. Crimes within the family unit, for example. One in ten children will be sexually abused by the age of eighteen. Twenty percent of those will be abused before the age of eight. Twenty-three percent are abused by family members. These are only the *identified* cases. The estimate is that sixty percent of victims will never report."

Matt was vaguely aware of the math. It was sickening.

"I believe that in a truly moral nation, the eradication of these atrocities should be a top priority."

Matt had never heard that idea spoken so plainly. "I agree," he said. What he'd seen in his brief stint with the SLO police department was an ongoing, depressing game of whack-a-mole. "But how do you even…" He didn't know how to end the sentence, and felt the familiar, sickening surge of frustration. *How do you start? How do you make people care?*

Snyder answered his question without being asked. "I'm working on a correlation between these domestic abuses—child sexual abuse and domestic battery—and violence that's perpetrated outside the home. It's part of what we'll be looking at today."

Matt was dying to ask what he meant, but Snyder was on a roll.

"Domestic violence and child abuse are excellent predictors of other violent, aberrant behavior. If we can establish familial abuse as a marker for other, more visible crimes, I believe law enforcement and the world at large will pay more attention to those intimate abuses."

Matt gripped the wheel. "But—that's so easy."

"And yet there's a deeply ingrained national reluctance to prosecute rape and child abuse. Partly patriarchal. Partly religious. But there's a larger problem with ViCAP. At present only one and a half percent of violent crimes are making it into the database."

For a moment Matt was certain he'd heard wrong. He'd been reading about the ViCAP system for years.

Snyder glanced at Matt's face, and read his mind. "You thought that ViCAP was the cutting edge of nationwide law enforcement? It's sold that way. Excellent public relations job. The truth is, the database is almost entirely unused."

Matt stared out at the road, stunned. Snyder's voice was grim. "And because of that, almost ninety-nine percent of identified violent predators aren't being tracked at all."

Chapter 25

I-95, Virginia - June 2005
Cara

She grips the steering wheel of her truck as the driver of the red truck steers his vehicle right beside hers. The sides of the trucks scrape in a scream of metal.

She slams the gas pedal to the floor and manages to pull ahead, breathing shallowly through fear and rage.

She takes a quick glance in the rear-view mirror. Behind her, the truck is accelerating, gaining. The driver and the man in the passenger seat are laughing, leaning forward...

Her heart hammers in her chest.

No. Never.

She breathes in, scans the road in front of her, and sets her intention. It is a terrible risk, not one for anyone to take who is not willing to die.

She is willing to die.

Then she lets them draw up beside her once more… her eyes flicking from the rear-view mirror to the side mirror… watching… waiting…

The truck is side by side with her now…

She grips the steering wheel and swerves. Hard.

There is a thud and another shriek of metal as her truck plows against the side of theirs. She holds tight to the steering wheel, her arms locked, keeping her vehicle hard against the side of the other truck. And then quickly twists the wheel the other way at the sudden release of friction… as their truck runs itself into a ditch.

She straightens her truck on the road, pushing the gas pedal to the floor. Her truck shoots away, leaving her pursuers in the dust.

Her heart is beating, off the charts. The exhilaration is immense.

She bears down harder on the accelerator, burning up the road.

Chapter 26

Richmond, Virginia - June 2005
Matt

Matt had to force himself to concentrate on driving. He was feeling a sick, falling sensation, as if the ground had opened up under his feet.

Snyder's voice turned apologetic. "I'm throwing a lot at you for a first day, I know. But this is the most important thing I can tell you about the Bureau. You can create your own cases. We have great latitude in that area. You'll have no power at first, but that will come."

Through his daze, Matt understood that he was getting an offer of mentorship from the exact person he would most want to be mentored by.

"Why me?" he blurted.

Snyder took a long, level look at him. "Because you're not afraid to look evil in the face."

Matt was so startled he couldn't speak.

"It's partly your Catholic upbringing. But there's something else, something that started this. It's got its hooks in you. Maybe someday you'll tell me about it. But not today," he finished. "We're getting off here."

He directed Matt off the highway and down an industrial street into the parking lot of a fairgrounds, with aircraft hangar-style exhibition buildings.

Huge yellow and orange banners advertised:

GUN SHOW TODAY!

Matt paid the parking fee at the gate and drove the SUV into the lines of cars in the lot.

"We want to park with a view of the entrance gate," Snyder said beside him.

Matt found a space at the end of one line and parked. He and Snyder stared out the windshield toward the gated entrance.

A line of armed men snaked up to the gun-check table outside the gate, waiting to demonstrate to security guards that their weapons were unloaded. An NRA recruitment table under a tent advertised *Free Entry*—with an NRA membership signup.

Snyder put the surveillance shot of their target on the console between them. Wayne Gilman stared up out of the photo.

"The party who called in the tip said Gilman was enraged by a crackdown on illegal activity at Richmond gun shows by the ATF last year and is vowing revenge."

Matt nodded, intent.

"Gilman is a Patriot. In the militia sense of the word. He attends these gun shows regularly and always purchases multiple weapons. We believe he's stockpiling for his militia organization, the Richmond League."

"But Gilman has no criminal record. And I want to be clear about this." Snyder's tone had become severe, and Roarke unconsciously straightened in his seat to listen carefully. "I'm inclined to be highly skeptical of helpful tips to the FBI. Always remember that it was a tip from a feuding neighbor that sent the Bureau too aggressively into the standoff at Ruby Ridge. A tip that started with the truth—and then exaggerated the truth into a situation that agents could and should have vetted more carefully to avoid disaster."

Matt's stomach twisted. He'd studied Ruby Ridge, the 1992 fatal standoff between U.S. Marshals and the Bureau, and a family of heavily armed white separatists in Idaho. It had resulted in a backlash of right-wing fury that the Bureau was still reeling from today. *Would the FBI ever recover from that tragedy?*

"Nonetheless, it is a fact that our subject has been buying alarmingly large numbers of automatic weapons and ammunition at gun shows. The assault weapons ban that took the AR-15 and similar semiautomatic rifles off the market ended last year. Gilman has been especially busy acquiring these. It's legal. But sudden acquisition of numbers of weapons is never a good sign. Timothy McVeigh went on a gun-buying binge before he killed 168 people in the Oklahoma City bombing. Eric Harris and Dylan Klebold used a friend to purchase multiple weapons at a gun show before they massacred thirteen people at Columbine. I can name a dozen others and not scratch the surface."

He paused, and Matt sensed all the rest had been background to what he was about to say. "But I believe the most immediate danger is to Gilman's wife and their three young children."

Matt sat up, startled.

"The police have been called to Gilman's house on three occasions to investigate reports of suspected domestic violence. The latest was just a few days ago. Jenny Gilman went to the hospital and was treated for concussion, multiple contusions and a broken collarbone—but declined to press charges. Gilman's violence against her appears to be escalating."

Matt felt familiar anger rising. Snyder took a second photo from the file. A pretty young woman looked out of the shot, with a smile on her face that didn't reach her eyes.

Matt looked down at her, jolted. "She's so young."

"Twenty-two," Snyder said.

Matt's age.

"She has three kids already?" he asked, in disbelief, and realized immediately how naïve he sounded.

"Gilman married her when she was sixteen."

Now Matt lifted his eyes from the photo and stared at Snyder. "Is that even legal?"

The sound the agent made was not quite a sigh. "In forty-eight states of the U.S. The general age of marriage is eighteen, but there are exceptions in all forty-eight of those states that mean a minor can be married with the consent of parents or legal guardians, consent of a court clerk or judge, or if that minor is pregnant or has given birth to a child. In eighteen states, there is virtually no minimum age of marriage."

"That's disgusting," Matt said numbly.

"Oh, it's worse than that. In some states minors cannot legally divorce, leave their spouse, or enter a shelter to escape abuse."

Outside the SUV, the line of armed men grew. And Snyder continued, "The Bible says man shall have dominion over the Earth and all the animals. Dominionists like Gilman take that to mean they have God-given dominion over their wives and children, too. *But.* The anonymous caller was female. So it's possible that it was Gilman's wife who made the call about Gilman's threats."

"Looking for help?" Matt asked. He felt a prickling of hope.

"In perhaps the only way she could. Abusers are very, very good at isolating their families from any support system. We've been watching the house, hoping to get a chance to talk to her. But for the last week, she hasn't left." Snyder looked out the windshield. "For these many reasons, we're here to surveil Gilman's activity at this show."

"Let's go," Matt said. It was all he could do not to grab the door handle that very second.

"Not together," Snyder warned him. "We'll look too much like law enforcement. Go on ahead. Keep your phone on. Just look for him. Don't approach, don't interact. Walk the exhibition hall and act like a customer. I'll be nearby."

The fairgrounds were already crowded and the asphalt radiated the heat of the day. Matt could feel it through the soles of his shoes as he walked toward the gate.

He scanned the crowd, estimated he was seeing ninety-five percent men, ninety-nine percent white.

He also realized exactly why Snyder had asked him to wear jeans and the concert T and hat. It was practically the uniform of the under-thirty crowd. And many of the older crowd, too. He saw tattooed bikers, jeans and black death metal concert T-shirts, camouflage wear, cowboy hats and boots.

He joined the entry line behind a guy in an electric wheelchair with a six-weapon gun rack on the back of the chair, and studied the array in disbelief while he worked out his cover story in his head. *I'm a transfer student starting at Virginia Tech in the fall. I'm shopping for a Glock.* It was a weapon he knew well from his law enforcement volunteer work, although he wasn't about to say that part. *Sure, I'll take a look at something else if you've got it. Talk me into it.*

At the ticket booth he declined NRA membership and paid the entrance fee, then wound his way through several food trucks serving burgers and pulled pork, heading toward the exhibition hall.

He stepped through the double doors—and braced himself against a glacial blast of air conditioning. He had to pause to let his eyes adjust to the dark, such a contrast from the blazing sun outside.

He was in a long tubular hall with rows and rectangles of folding tables set up for dealers, much like any county fair. But these tables were literally bowing under the weight of thousands of firearms. Boxes of ammunition stacked on plywood and sawhorse tables. Gunpowder sold in gallon jugs.

He'd had firearms training since age fourteen. But he had never seen so many weapons assembled in one place. There were more than enough to arm a small country.

He found his mind and his body rebelling against the sight, against the sheer scope of it. It was impossible to take in, rationally. The hall was filled with death.

He forced himself to move forward, to join the hundreds of people wandering in the aisles, looking over tables displaying rifles, shotguns, handguns, gun parts, scopes, knives, machetes, nunchucks, swords.

At one booth were stacks of survival kits with weeks' worth of freeze-dried food, elaborate backpacks, camouflage suits and other wilderness survival equipment, all under a misspelled banner: *Can you're family survive the Apocalipse?*

An elderly man walked by with a rifle slung across his back, a sign with the lettering "*Ask me about my gun*" on a sign sticking out of the barrel. As Matt turned his head to look at the man, he saw another man a few feet away carrying a similar long gun with a similar sign.

Matt's internal danger alert shot up to "high." In his criminal justice classes, he'd studied the "weapons effect": the increased levels of aggression shown by people in the presence of weapons. The statistics were startling.

If the presence of weapons was a predictor of heightened aggression, he was in the psychological equivalent of a radiation hot zone.

A loud dinging went off, and everyone in the aisle turned toward a small stage at one side of the hall. A man in a ten-gallon hat stepped up to the microphone. "Hope y'all saved your entry tickets. There's a number on that ticket, and in a few minutes we're gonna be drawing the lucky winner of this brand new AR-15. Get 'em out, folks, and get ready…"

As others around him dug in their pockets, Matt moved on, scanning the faces for Gilman.

At a table displaying AK-47s, a breakdown tutorial played on a video screen above the booth, which proclaimed itself YOUR ONE-STOP ASSAULT SHOP. Two hulking, obese young men, both younger than Matt, bellied up to hold the guns.

Matt turned away and almost collided with a young couple pushing a three- or four-year old boy in a stroller. The boy brandished a toy machine gun almost as big as he was. He pointed and "shot" at Matt. The clear plastic of the gun lit up with colorful flashing lights and the sound of gunfire.

Focus, Matt told himself. *Find Gilman.*

Chapter 27

I-95, Virginia - June 2005
Cara

She drives steadily and tries to calm her buzz.

It is quickly replaced by anger.

She knows that her senses are heightened by the moon. It has always been so, and the moon will be full tonight. She also knows it is the collective effect of the freeway harassment she has been experiencing throughout the country that has led to this final straw.

Why should men like this be allowed to terrorize the highways?

Not today, she decides. *Today they lose.*

She pulls off the highway at a wooded turnoff to wait for the truck. She does not think she damaged it enough to slow them down much.

She spots it again within ten minutes, a red blur, flying by the turnoff. It is definitely *the* truck. The same group of men. The same Stetsoned driver, the same sweaty round-faced man with his wire frame glasses, the one who'd caressed the shotgun.

She lets the truck pass. And she follows.

The truck leaves the interstate at a Richmond exit with signs pointing toward a fairground. As the truck approaches the complex, she sees banners and bus stop billboards announcing a gun show.

Of course the red truck slows to join the line of vehicles turning into the parking lot. Of course.

Guns.

A parking space opens right in front of the gated entrance, and she pulls into it to think. She turns off the engine and watches the red truck drive through the gate into the parking lot.

A dilemma.

Her loathing for firearms is huge and visceral. And the vast majority of the vehicles entering the fairground are men. She cannot follow her attackers into this place. She has no desire to sit waiting for them to reemerge.

And yet she is feeling no urgency to leave.

So she puts on her cap and a hoodie, grabs her backpack, and gets out of her truck. She joins the foot traffic to walk through the gate onto the fairgrounds, into an enormous parking lot.

There are hundreds of vehicles parked: cars, motorcycles, SUVs, and trucks. Truck after truck, not a few with Confederate flag bumper stickers. Dozens of them are as big and red as the one that tried to run her off the road.

But she finds *the* truck easily, the red monstrosity, parked and empty. She can see the scrape she herself put into it, cut into the driver's side. She slips between it and the truck parked beside it, two massive walls of metal, neatly concealing her from the eyes of anyone passing by.

The red truck is an older Ford, like many she has driven in her desert joyriding. Easy to jack.

Which makes her decision that much easier.

She never travels without her kit: pliers, knife, screwdriver, coat hanger. She removes what she needs from her backpack and when there is no one walking past, she gets to work with the wire.

Chapter 28

Richmond, Virginia - June 2005
Matt

He'd found him.

Gilman stood right across from him at a large island of display tables, four tables long by three wide.

In the photo Gilman had looked grim and menacing. In three-dimensional reality he was rotund, apple-cheeked, wet-lipped, wearing a prissy pair of wire-framed glasses. He was in his forties, but Matt could still see the bullied Mama's boy he must have been as a child, and felt a surge of contempt. This would-be hero with a gun fetish. An accountant with fantasies of shooting his way through a millennial apocalypse.

And if he couldn't have his fantasy, he'd take down as many people as he could fire at. Starting with his child wife and kids.

Matt no longer felt sick. It was something else entirely.

Fury.

He stepped up to the nearest corner of the booth, pretending to browse so he could watch Gilman.

Glancing down at the display, he was taken aback to see the tables were crammed with hundreds of items of Nazi memorabilia, from cheap modern swastika flags to Nazi-era toilet tissue in a yellowed brown paper wrapper with the word *Edelweiss* printed in German lettering.

Behind the tables, an enormous man overflowing his wheelchair and a younger, more conventionally burly man were doing a brisk business.

The younger vendor shot a look at Matt. Matt forced himself to stay still and play customer. He perused a layout of antique Third Reich daggers and watched out of the corner of his eye as Gilman began a furtive conversation with another of the dealers, a large tattooed man in motorcycle leathers, wearing a bandanna.

Matt positioned himself so that he could see more clearly, and picked up a dagger, hefting the weapon, all the time keeping one eye on Gilman.

The bandannaed dealer nodded to a door with a clearly posted sign: NO ENTRY. He moved toward it. Gilman followed, and as the bandannaed vendor slipped through the door, Gilman was right behind him.

Matt circled the table, keeping up his pretense of browsing. He couldn't very well walk through the door after them—

Then the dinging bell went off again, and everyone turned as they had before, focused toward the small stage.

Without stopping to think, Matt used the cover of the momentary distraction to slip through the door.

He found himself in a long maintenance corridor, with work lights giving off a sickly glow. The door shut behind him, closing off the exhibition hall.

The tunnel was dim and vile, smelling of sour milk and trash and rubber, a whiff of rotting hot dogs and old popcorn. Matt was alone. No sign of Gilman or the bandannaed vendor—

Even as he thought it, there was a sudden, live rustling beside him. He twisted around...

A grotesquely large rat waddled out from between piled black trash bags.

Matt moved quickly away from it, revolted.

There was only one way to go: a ramp sloping down to an underground level.

He started quietly downward, sticking close to the wall to create less of a target, as he'd learned in tactical classes.

The slope evened out into a narrower tunnel which branched in three directions: left, right, and straight ahead. There seemed to be a whole warren of concrete tunnels running underneath the exhibition halls.

He stood still at the crossroads and listened hard. Down the tunnel to the left he could hear the faint sound of male voices.

Matt felt for his phone and dialed Snyder. Instead of connecting, the phone simply cut off. He checked the screen, and saw no bars.

No reception underground.

He glanced back behind him at the ramp. He knew he should go back, find Snyder...

But by then it might be too late, he argued with himself. *Gilman could be gone.*

If he'd obeyed orders at Bishop Peak he never would have found Tracy. In fact, if he'd just stayed on the mountain instead of going back to check in like a good little soldier...

Not this time, he resolved.

He moved into the left-hand tunnel.... and froze at the sound of a sharp male voice.

"You're late enough."

Matt pressed back against the concrete wall. The voice had come from another corridor.

Another answered the first. "Little accident on the road." *Gilman.*

Their voices echoed off the walls, an eerie disembodied effect. The first man said something indecipherable, and Gilman responded with something that sounded like,

"Some bitch driver..."

Matt moved silently forward toward the corner and peered into the connecting corridor.

Gilman and the dealer were walking toward the end of it. Matt dodged behind another black pyramid of trash bundled in plastic contractor bags. His shoe scuffed an aluminum can that had escaped from a trash bag. It clattered across the concrete floor.

Ahead of him one of the men growled, "The hell was that?"

Matt pressed his back against the cool hard wall, holding his breath against the stink. His heart thumped in his chest as he imagined the two of them staring back into the darkness.

"Rat, probably. There's a shitload of them down here."

"Hell, what're we waiting for? Exterminate the bitches."

Matt flinched as the voice exploded in the echoey halls: "BLAM-BLAM-BLAM-BLAM-BLAM-BLAM..."

That was Gilman, wasn't it? Not good. The guy sounds like a psycho.

So don't lose him.

Matt forced himself to move, to edge his head around the side of the trash bag pyramid.

The two men were far, far down the concrete corridor, now, headed for a set of double doors with a glowing red EXIT sign above.

Matt hovered beside the mountain of trash bags until he heard the slam of heavy doors.

They're out.

He sprinted to the end of the corridor, came to a halt in front of the filthy industrial double doors with the glowing red EXIT sign above.

He paused, his hand on the release bar, his heart racing, his neck sweating.

And then pushed the door open.

The sudden sunlight was blinding. He caught a glimpse of a concrete ramp, leading down to a back lot...

Instinctively he dropped into a crouch, below the level of a slanted concrete wall lining the ramp. He had no idea if he'd been seen.

He heard the bleat of a car alarm, the cut-off sound of a door opening mechanically.

They must be parked right next to the ramp.

He pressed his palms against the concrete of the wall and eased his way up to look over.

Gilman and the bandannaed dealer stood beside a white van. The dealer pulled open the back doors of the van. Matt could see straight down into the vehicle.

Not just a few weapons. The whole van was crammed with gun racks and ammunition. Rifles, submachine guns, bulky cases that suggested far more ominous weapons.

Matt pulled out his phone and started surreptitiously clicking off photos.

The dealer slammed the doors of the van and handed Gilman the keys. Matt continued to photograph the exchange as Gilman got into the front seat of the van. The engine flared up, and Matt fumbled with the phone to dial Snyder's number—

The door opened behind him.

Matt twisted around to find the bulky younger vendor from the Nazi memorabilia booth, and another man in plaid shirt and duckbill hat. They stepped in to surround him. Armed and definitely not friendly.

"Whatchu doing back here, boy?" the man in the duckbill hat challenged him. "This here's restricted access."

The bandannaed vendor moved up the ramp from the parking lot.

Three of them.

Matt looked straight at the bandannaed vendor. "I was following you."

He could see the vendor was startled, but the man blustered, "You queer for me?"

People really talk like this? Matt wondered. They sounded like good ol' boys from some seventies movie. But he wasn't laughing. He was the only one there who wasn't armed.

He was also pretty positive that his California accent wasn't going to win him points with this crowd. He tried to channel his upstate New York cousins as he answered.

"I'm looking for something for my father," he said. "Figured you wouldn't be showing the best stuff out there on the floor."

The vendor looked truculent and skeptical. "Best stuff? What 'best stuff' would that be, boy?"

Matt's mind scrambled back to his high school history. "Dad's nuts for anything *Reichsparteitag*," he said, using the German word for the Nuremberg rallies. "Postcards, banners."

"You want the good stuff, huh?" The bandannaed dealer's eyes were a chilling blank. "Why don't you take a ride with us, then? See if we can't find the good stuff for your Daddy."

Matt was pretty damn sure that a ride-along with the militia boys was not what Snyder had had in mind. But he'd approached them. He couldn't very well back away now.

"What kind of stuff're you—"

But before he finished the sentence, he felt a massive blow connect with his head.

And everything exploded in blackness.

Chapter 29

Richmond, Virginia – June 2005
Cara

She drives the hotwired truck out of the parking lot and double parks it beside her own truck, leaving the engine running.

Quickly, efficiently, she removes the rest of her few belongings from the back of her old truck and throws them into the back seat of the red truck. She leaves the keys in the ignition of the old truck and the doors unlocked to make it easier to steal. She doesn't expect it will last overnight in this neighborhood.

Then she gets back into the men's truck and drives off, putting distance between herself and the vehicle she has just abandoned.

A few blocks away from the fairgrounds, she pulls over to the curb to get her bearings.

Now that she is in her tormentors' truck, she is not sure what she will do with it. Stealing it may have to be enough. She cannot keep it for more than an hour or two. But she has noticed many lakes off the interstate. It would be a pleasure to sink the truck in one of them.

Not the level of damage the driver and his friends deserve, but it would be something.

She reaches into her bag and pulls out gloves to wear, then begins a search through the console and glove compartment.

The truck has a Garmin navigation system. She has seen them before in her teenage joyriding. Since the device's introduction several years before, she has made a point of discarding them in any car she drives, in case her route might be tracked. Here it could be to her advantage to have the location of these men.

She's contemplating the device, when something makes her look up. And she spots a white van driving straight for her.

In the driver's seat is the round-faced man with wire-framed glasses. The one who threatened her, caressing the gun.

His eyes are focused on the road. He doesn't see her as he drives past.

She is sure he is the same man. Right here in front of her. And that is never for no reason.

Something hardens in her.

In a pack, he's very brave. With a gun, he's very brave. Men in packs with guns are always very brave.

Hunting an eighteen-year old girl.

Very, very brave.

Rage boils up inside her.

She makes a U-turn, and follows.

Chapter 30

Richmond, Virginia - June 2005
Matt

Buzzing. Dark. Hurts.

Hurts. Head hurts—

Wake up. Now. Now.

The voice in his head was so strong Matt jolted back to a hazy half-consciousness. He forced open his eyes, only to see—

Nothing. Pitch black.

Terror swept through him. He was wide awake now. Lying on a cold concrete floor.

Can't move.

Try. Move your hands. Move your feet.

His arms moved. His legs moved. But just that slight stirring brought a stabbing pain in the side of his head.

He'd been hit hard, with some blunt object. He could feel the wound throbbing. He groped at the back of his skull… found sticky blood under his fingers and a lump through his hair. Touching it brought a wave of nausea.

But that wasn't the worst.

The blackness wasn't going away.

I'm blind.

He forced himself to breathe in, forced himself calm. *You can move. You're not bound. Use your other senses. What do you hear? What do you feel?*

There was a soft whirring from a… *Fan? Ventilation system?*

Possibly. Probably.

The air was very cool, and there was a musty, slightly damp smell. He turned his head, around, up…

And far above his head, about a story high, he saw it. A thin horizontal line of light. Massive relief washed over him.

Not blind. It's just pitch black down here. No windows. But that line is light underneath a door. This must be a basement, and there must be stairs up to that door.

He felt his pockets, searching for his phone… but of course it was gone. They'd have taken it for the photos.

And everything else…

He hoped none of his captors were tech savvy enough to open it.

He felt his way slowly to his feet, swallowing back another wave of nausea from the throbbing in his head.

He set his jaw and straightened to standing, then made his way up the narrow stairs, feeling along the rough wall. At the door, he ran his hand over the wall beside it until he found a light switch. He flipped it.

A powerful fluorescent light went on, illuminating the basement in a brightness that seemed to scorch his eyes.

He was in a deep, windowless space. The floor below was crowded with neat rows of metal shelving, stocked with an eye-popping assembly of dried foods, plastic bins of beans, rice. There were water tanks, a large generator….

It was straight out of the survivalist books he'd seen at the gun show. Preppers stockpiling for the apocalypse.

That's the kind of people you're dealing with, he told himself grimly.

He turned back to the door and examined it. It was reinforced steel, deadbolted. No possible way of kicking through.

It's someone's house, though, he thought. And the men from the gun show had brought him here… why?

On the plus side, they hadn't killed him.

Not yet, anyway.

Another huge plus was that they hadn't handcuffed or tied him. Which seemed like an enormous mistake on their part. Although they were probably thinking of him as just some stupid kid. They'd taken his wallet of course, and all they'd have found was a California driver's license, his Cal Poly student ID, some cash and a credit card. Nothing at all connecting him with the FBI. So he could rack that and his obvious youth up as one hell of a huge advantage.

Okay. Okay. Let's have a look around. Assess.

Moving as quietly as he could manage, he eased back down the stairs to the basement floor. At the bottom he glanced at the shelves around him and spotted a shelf that held camping equipment. He stepped up to it, grabbed a sleeping bag to examine it. It was sewn with a canvas label reading GILMAN, as if for some Boy Scout camping trip.

He quickly checked the other bags. All labeled GILMAN.

This was his house, then.

Okay, so again—why had the vendors brought Matt here?

The basement was an effective prison, that was a fact. And/or Gilman was the leader and would have the ultimate say as to Matt's fate.

There was nothing good about that.

He'd noticed several boxes of Artic-rated tents on the camping shelf. Now he grabbed one, tore it open, and removed the aluminum spikes. He put a spike into every pocket he had, stuck another in his belt, kept one in his hand. Immediately he felt better.

He turned from the shelf and continued his examination of the basement, walking slowly down one aisle at a time, looking for other weapons and a way out.

The next aisle was cartons, tubs and boxes of food.

At least I'm not gonna starve, he thought with grim humor. And helped himself to some protein bars from a 100-count box.

Thanks for nothing, assholes.

He bit into a chocolate-covered bar and walked on.

In one wall there was another reinforced and padlocked door to an inner room which he highly suspected was the munitions room.

What's the point of an apocalypse if you're not stocked up with your favorite weapons?

The wall beside the door was lined with propane tanks. Matt had a brief thought that he could start a fire with the fuel, burn the door down. Just as quickly he nixed the idea. He'd probably only succeed in burning himself alive, and he hated fire more than anything.

He looked upward, toward the stairs and the door.

He doubted Gilman was home yet. He'd driven off with that van, obviously with someplace to take those weapons. And if he was at the house, Matt had a feeling he would be being dealt with already.

Suddenly he recalled Snyder's briefing. *"She hasn't left for a week."*

He felt a rush of clarity—and hope.

He wasn't the only prisoner in the house. If he had any possible ally in the situation, it was Gilman's wife.

I'm going to have to get her to open that door.

Could he do that?

If she's the one who called the Bureau on her husband...

He struggled through the splitting ache in his head to remember her name.

Jenny.

Okay, Jenny. We're going to bust loose today. Let's do it.

He went back to the staircase, climbed the stairs again as noiselessly as he could. He stopped on the top platform beside the door... and hesitated. If he called out, and the men who attacked him were still there, this might be the worst idea in the world.

He focused on Jenny.

He'd seen her photo, the hospital record of her injuries.

You need this even more than I do.

He took a breath, and spoke. "Ms. Gilman, are you there?"

He listened hard, and thought he heard a faint, hurried scuffle outside the door. Then a sound like someone shushing someone else. He remembered there were children, a five-year old, a toddler, a baby in a jumper…

Was he just imagining it? Hoping for such benign sounds?

Snyder's words came back to him.

"The Bible says man shall have dominion over the Earth and all the animals. Dominionists take that to mean they also have dominion over their wives and children."

She can't believe that, can she? If she does, I'm fucked.

He squelched the thought.

Look. We're just going to talk to her.

He cleared his throat. "Ms. Gilman, my name is Matt Roarke. I'm working with the FBI and this is false imprisonment. The men who assaulted me and left me down here are going to be going to prison for a long, long time. But that doesn't mean you have to."

There was no response at all. He went on.

"I don't know if you know anything about me. But I know a little about you. Do you know…we're the same age?"

He paused. Again, heard nothing.

"That's how I know that none of this is your fault. I know you're… you're trapped."

He couldn't hear her. But he could *feel* her. More than that. He felt like he knew her.

"I think we're both trapped. I made a mistake and now your husband's buddies might kill me. Maybe it was a stupid mistake but… I don't think I should have to die for it."

His head was throbbing again and nausea rolled over him. He felt his way down the wall to sit, leaning back against the door.

"I don't know. Maybe you made a mistake, too. No one should have to get married at sixteen." He forced a laugh. "I was such a naïve kid back then. Just—unbelievably stupid. I'm not saying you were stupid," he added hastily. "But come on, what did you know compared to a thirty-five year old guy?"

He had no idea if she was listening to his rambling. But no one had burst down the door and shot him yet. That was a plus.

"There's something about that that just isn't right. It would be like… like me marrying someone my mom's age. I love my mom, but… no."

She wasn't saying a word, and maybe he just desperately wanted to believe it, but he could swear he felt her listening. So he sat against the door, and he talked.

"I'm sure you're a lot smarter than I am. I don't know anything much. But… I know I'm still too young to get married. I don't even… I don't even know who I am. I just broke up with my girlfriend last week because I knew we were too young to be serious—"

He stopped. *Whoa, where did that come from?*

Somewhere along the line he'd started to be honest.

But it's not like I have anything to lose.

"You know what? It was more than that. I think… I think there's someone out there for me. And she's going to want the same things that I want… but not the way I want them. Does that make sense? She'll have her own way of—everything. And I'll learn from her. I don't want to tell her who she is. I want her to be who she is and show me who I am."

He stopped again. Was that a sob he'd heard? Or was there anyone out there at all? He didn't have a clue. He took a breath.

"I'll tell you something else. I would never hit her. Never. Or our kids. That's not a husband. That's a monster."

He touched the door, tried to will her to—not just listen, but to hear him. "I know he beats you up. If you let me out, you can walk out, too. You and your kids."

And then, a miracle. A shaky voice from behind the door.

"He'll kill me."

Matt was electrified. And terrified. He knew he had to play it just right. "You called, didn't you? You called the FBI about your husband."

Only silence from behind the door.

"We'll get you out, I swear. You don't have to live like this."

"You don't understand." Her voice was low, strained. She could barely get the words out. "He has police friends. Army friends. They're always watching us. You don't know what they'll do."

She believed it utterly. And maybe it was true. He knelt close to the door and spoke firmly.

"My boss… he's a legend in the Bureau. I promise you, we'll get you witness protection. You and your kids can start all over."

"I can't…"

Her voice stopped and there was a silence behind the door. A living silence. A thinking silence. Matt could barely breathe.

"You can. I can tell you can. You can do this for your kids. You can do it for you."

More silence, possibly the longest silence of his life. And then the sound of a metal bolt sliding in the doorframe.

He scrambled to his feet… and stepped through the doorway, out into daylight that seemed a whole world brighter than the fluorescent tubes of the basement.

She stood in the front hallway of the house, a too-slender woman in a flowered dress. Looking ten years younger than he was, and fifty years older.

"Thank you," he said.

She was shaking, backing away from him even as he stepped forward…

Then they both twisted around at the sound of pounding on the front door.

Chapter 31

I-95, Virginia - June 2005
Cara

She stays well behind the van as it heads for the interstate and takes the onramp, going north, through more green corridors. The freeway is well-traveled today, but it's easy to keep sight of the shiny white vehicle in the stream of cars—and trucks just like the one she is driving. The ubiquity of them is effective camouflage.

After forty minutes, the van turns off the interstate onto a state highway. Densely packed trees that can conceal any number of activities. She falls further back, now, slowing to stay out of sight as the van winds through the woods.

In a few more minutes the van makes another turnoff to a smaller road, into thicker woods, past signs to a recreational area. She gets just a glimpse of a large body of water between the trees when they go over a rise.

She drives even more slowly. When she rounds the next curve, she sees the white van stopped ahead with the driver's door standing open and the man in glasses standing outside it, fiddling with a steel gate fixed between two posts marking a dirt road.

She brakes softly. While he is occupied with the gate, she puts the truck in reverse to back up, driving backward around the curve.

She stops on the road and sits behind the wheel with her pulse racing. She forces herself to be still for a good five minutes, waiting and thinking. She is fairly certain the chain demarcates a private drive. She will not be able to pass the gate. But wherever the round-faced man is taking the van is probably not that far from the road.

She makes the decision to proceed on foot.

She kills the engine, checks her knife, and reaches for a liter bottle of water. Then she gets out of the truck, stepping down into a wall of heat and humidity.

She shuts the door behind her and walks the road toward the gate. A hundred feet from it she walks into the woods, moving parallel to the gateway, staying in the trees beside the dirt drive.

Cicadas seethe in the trees around her, an alien and almost deafening sound which masks her footsteps through the underbrush. She swigs water and presses on.

Within a quarter mile she comes upon a small clearing.

The white van is parked outside a double-wide trailer set on blocks in the trees. The door of the trailer stands open, and a slanted ramp leads up to the doorway. There is a flat rolling cart at the top of the ramp.

The van's back doors are wide open, enabling her to see inside.

The whole back of the van is crammed with guns. Long guns, automatics, boxes of ammunition.

She backs behind a tree and has to swallow against the rising of her gorge. She stays put there, her heart rate elevated. After a moment, the round-faced man steps out of the trailer. She stiffens, and watches.

He steers the cart down the ramp, returns to the van and hauls a crate out of the back. He loads the crate onto the cart and wheels it up to the trailer, up the ramp.

When he disappears into the trailer, she moves further into the woods, back toward the road. If he's unloading that whole van by himself, that means she has some time.

Back at the truck, she gets in and reconnects the ignition and battery wires to start it up again. She drives to the gate at the beginning of the dirt road, and then a bit past it to a gap in the trees she spotted on her walk back to the truck. It's big enough for her to drive the truck through. From there she drives slowly through underbrush to get onto the private dirt road.

She knows that in this wilderness, the man will be able to hear the engine, the approach of the truck. So she stops the truck before the trailer comes into view, and waits there on the dirt road, idling, with her foot on the brake.

Letting him come to her.

Two minutes later he comes into view, armed with a shotgun. The same shotgun he had mimed stroking off.

He sees the truck and stops in his tracks, then loosens his grip on the gun and starts forward toward the truck he has now recognized as his friend's. "Hey. That wasn't the plan."

She is silent, still, her hands gripping the steering wheel.

Another step closer to the truck, and he sees her.

"Who the hell—?" And then it dawns on his face. "Wait. Wait justafuckingminute. You're the one. You ran us off the road—"

He is so shocked to see her, trying to wrap his mind around what it means, that it gives her that few second's advantage. He is just that one second too late to raise his gun.

It's a big, scary weapon

But hers is bigger.

She stamps on the accelerator and drives straight for him.

Chapter 32

Portland - present
Singh and Snyder

Singh sits back on the sofa. While Agent Snyder has been telling his story, she has been supplying her suppositions about Cara's place in the narrative. Now he stands from the armchair where he has been sitting, and looks out the glass doors of her suite, contemplating the river view in silence.

She has no idea what he is thinking.

After a moment she adds anxiously, "I have no evidence Cara Lindstrom was there. I only know from the coroner's report that on that day in 2005, Wayne Gilman was crushed by a pickup truck on a property he owned in the woods outside Richmond. The truck was left abandoned on the property and found to belong to an associate of Gilman's. The associate claimed the vehicle was stolen from the parking lot of a gun show he had been attending. He had many alibi witnesses and was not charged with Gilman's murder."

She pauses, remembering another point. "I am guessing that it was the police arriving at Gilman's house at ASAC Roarke's moment of peril."

Finally Snyder turns to her. "No. That was me. The T-shirt I gave Matthew to put on had a concealed tracker. When he disappeared from the gun show, I was able to trace him to Gilman's house."

"And Ms. Gilman?"

He gives her a look of quiet triumph. "We got her and her children out that day. She didn't know Gilman wouldn't be coming home, so she went with us on the spur of the moment. Fortunately, Matthew had managed to establish that much trust. Of course, as things unfolded, she didn't need witness protection after all."

Singh feels a rush of lightness that she recognizes as joy.

He nods in acknowledgment, and continues, "Gilman's body wasn't found until some days later, on that property in the woods. And we—that is, the Bureau, recovered hundreds of weapons from a mobile home that had been being used exclusively as a weapons stash."

He has not mentioned a point that Singh has been wondering about. She raises it now. "In your account, you said that ASAC Roarke saw Gilman drive away from the gun show back lot in a white van. But the van was not listed as seized property in the police report."

Snyder nods to her. "Correct. We never recovered the van full of weapons. It could've been stolen, or the items relocated. But that would leave a mystery. Why didn't the thief or thieves take any of the weapons or munitions inside the trailer? The door of the trailer was left wide open, but the armaments inside didn't seem to have been touched. Maybe there just wasn't time. We simply don't know."

Singh is thinking of the lake near Gilman's forest property. A large lake in a recreational area. If the authorities dredged it, would they find the van and the weapons, sunk without a trace, all those years ago?

Or is that more of her own fancy?

Snyder finishes, "No one was ever apprehended, for the theft or for the murder. It could have been one of his militia associates betraying him. It could have been one of the weapons dealers—"

"But nothing was ever proven."

"No," Agent Snyder answers absently. "Nothing was ever proven."

He looks toward the map and the dual timelines.

"Now. The red string?"

Singh takes a breath and relates what Lam told her of the red string of Fate.

When she has finished, he is frowning deeply. "If I am understanding you correctly, you are postulating that Matthew's and Cara's paths have crossed, not just in the Gilman case, but many dozens of times over the last sixteen years. And that their connection is the key to solving potentially dozens of murders."

He has articulated it better than she has been able to, herself. At the same time, hearing him speak the words, she thinks she has possibly never heard something so insane. She fully expects Agent Snyder to order her back to San Francisco on the spot.

"I know it sounds mad..." she begins faintly.

Snyder gives her a wry smile. "'We're all mad, here.'"

Singh recognizes the quote from *Alice in Wonderland.* It perfectly encapsulates the down-the-rabbit-hole feeling of the case.

He turns and looks at the chart again. "There's no question there is some uncanny bond between Matthew and Cara. It's so evident we may as well call it fact. Your 'red string' theory is as good an explanation as any. Better than anything I've come up with."

She bites her lip. "I have not spoken with ASAC Roarke about this theory."

Agent Snyder laughs shortly, startled. "No. No, that's probably wise."

He moves to the white board with the list of Cara's murders, then walks to the end of the map, and stands looking up at the state of Oregon.

"This may explain... *can* it explain...?" He trails off, and is so silent for so long she becomes uneasy.

Suddenly he turns to her, and his face is grave. "If your theory is even remotely true, Agent Singh, we have urgent work to do. Data entry can wait. We must fill in this timeline, these charts of yours, leaving nothing out."

He glances back at the map. "I believe we'll be needing more string."

PART THREE

Chapter 33

Phoenix, Arizona - September 27, 2008
Cara

It is her country, now.

She has been across it five times, and has traveled all of the major North-South, South-North interstates as well.

There is a unique pleasure in knowing every mile, the veins and arteries of the land, the quirks and rhythms of each region.

And there has been a vast relief in the discovery of just how much of the country is free of people. At how many places there are to escape, to hide. In wilderness, in deserts, in mountains, valleys... particularly in the national parks, with their infinitely varied, otherworldly *Beauty*—but in populated areas as well. In unincorporated desert communities where no one questions anyone else's past. In anonymous beach towns where the second and third houses of obscenely wealthy owners are left empty for predictable spans of time, providing luxurious accommodation during what the unadventurous call the off-season.

Everywhere she goes she is cataloguing, making notes. Learning distances to major highways, learning the peculiarities of state highway laws.

And planting stashes of money and other essential items.

She began the practice some time into her second cross-country drive. Now in every state she crosses, she opens a mailbox drop or small storage unit and automates the payments to one of her false identity credit cards. In these boxes she stashes emergency cash and IDs. She puts combination locks on all of them, all with the same numerical code except for the prefix, which varies with each state. Each storage unit is at a town on a one hundred-mile marker within the state, so she can never lose count and so she will always know how close she is to an emergency stash.

She takes these elaborate precautions because she knows, beyond doubt, there will be a time when she will need to use them.

The whispering of the moon has not ceased since she has been on the road. In fact, it has become more focused, its directions more clear and implacable. The closer the moon is to full, the more likely there will be an *Encounter*: a moment, an incident, that will force her to do battle. When *It* will reveal *Itself* and cannot be ignored. When the instructions—from the moon, the earth, the wind, the stars, the murmur of the planet itself—cannot be denied.

There is no questioning why. Abomination must be eliminated. Atrocity must be halted.

She knows no other sane way to live in the world.

There is still the essential question: *Why her?* Why has she been chosen for this bleak mission?

She only knows that she *sees.* She cannot in her heart believe that others don't see, as well. How can it be possible not to see: the glinting looks, the leers, the predatory intent. Predators wear masks, but there is something always that slips, that reveal *It.* Sometimes her own revulsion is so palpable that she is hard-pressed not to cry out at the sight of the monster, in random encounters at a gas station, in a hotel lobby, on a city street.

But somehow others are unwilling to fight. To stand in the street and name *It* for what *It* is.

She does not often stop to wonder why. The loneliness would be crushing. But if *The Mission* is hers alone, it is no less urgent. In fact, it is more so.

So she prepares her stashes. For the inevitable time when she will need them.

Other aspects of her road habits have evolved as well.

For the first several months of her freedom, she slept only outside. As the weather grew colder, she ventured into anonymous motels along the interstates. The novelty of having a soft bed, of not having to seek out a shower in a campsite or a gym, or bathe herself in a lake or stream, proved alluring. She was surprised and relieved to find the motel clerks pay little attention to travelers. They see so very many.

She has found it is good practice for her to speak a few words with them, to practice different accents, different languages. To blend chameleon-like into any environment.

She understands that these forays into civilization are important, even critical. If she stayed only in the wilderness she would become altogether feral, too noticeably *Other* to survive the inevitable encounters with other human beings. She must practice the mask of civilization regularly.

She doesn't stay in cities often, but she discovers the hotels near airports are also anonymous enough that she is able to add them to her routine. She finds she enjoys a gym to work out in, to keep her body toned and strong, ready to fight. Foraging in a hotel mini-bar is one more way to avoid people.

One evening in Denver, when she is taking in the historic sights downtown, she wanders into a restored mining hotel. It is old and strange and she likes it. She impulsively books a room for the night. It is by far the most expensive place she has ever stayed in.

But that night, it finally sinks in, that she has the cash to stay in any hotel she wants to if she chooses.

So sometimes she allows herself these luxuries. And sometimes she is simply drawn to the beauty of a place.

Such as the hotel where she has stopped now, outside Phoenix. A central hotel of almost extra-terrestrial aesthetic, and vast grounds with many satellite compounds of villas and suites.

She does not enter the long, low main building at first, but parks in the parking lot and does as she has learned to do before she enters any hotel: she watches the guests coming and going. What she sees will determine how she will dress, what persona she will adopt.

Far more men travel, alone and in groups, than women do. Being female, she is always aware of being in the minority and therefore dangerously noticeable. She has become practiced at blending in to whatever large group might be staying at a hotel: tourists, a sales force, a church group.

At this Arizona resort, there is a large group of some kind of business conference attending, so she drives a short distance away from the parking lot to prepare her costume.

She generally keeps several changes of clothes in the trunk of her car, clothes she uses as camouflage. A business suit, a cocktail dress, a battered hoodie, a track suit. Printed tank tops, camping clothes, eyeglasses, lanyards, baseball caps, knit caps. All bought from thrift stores so that the fabric will contain other people's DNA.

She discards her clothes regularly, and buys replacements in the secondhand shops. Even better are the ones she can find in the bins left out on the streets in many cities, as donations meant for the homeless to pick up. Because those items are usually unwashed, and several times more likely than thrift store clothes to have other people's hair and fluids and fibers on them. Elements that can naturally contaminate the scene of an *Encounter*, and add another layer of obfuscation. She has also made a habit of picking up bits of hair from gyms, and used tissues with other people's saliva and mucus, which she stores in the trunk of whatever car she is driving, and leaves in the room of any hotel or motel she stays in. Anything, really, that will make any potential investigation void.

Also in her travel accessories are makeup and sunglasses to alter her facial features. She will often wear a sweater under a shirt or jersey, or a second pair of pants under her jeans, to pad her figure.

More rarely she may wear a wig, but she is wary of keeping them in the car.

She carries props, as well. A computer bag, a phone with no battery or SIM card, that she has additionally soaked in water to be absolutely certain it is dead and untraceable. She has no use for a phone, no one to call, no desire to risk using the internet except rarely, and then only at large public libraries. But a phone is useful for avoiding conversation, for blending in.

She returns to the hotel dressed in a tailored, conservative suit and expensive shoes, and checks in without incident.

The resort is the largest she has ever stayed in. But apart from a few golf carts, the vast, open grounds seem deserted. In September, the desert heat of the day is enough that people keep to themselves in their clusters of villas.

Her room is in one of these satellite villas, a luxurious space with a marble-walled bathroom, a bed with fluffy clouds of pillows, an elegant conversation area. She is grateful for all of it, the privacy, the comfort. Especially now. She needs much more sleep when the moon is so close to full.

She showers and slides between sheets as soft as whipped cream.

To prepare herself for what she can feel coming.

Chapter 34

Portland - present
Singh and Snyder

Singh stops her narrative to catch her breath, to sip from a glass of water.

Her interstates map and charts are now set up in Agent Snyder's study, on polished wooden frames he has used as case boards in the past, in front of a backdrop of his library of criminal psychology.

It makes all her research feel active and real.

Agent Snyder has not yet explained what he meant about the urgency of her theory, and how it connects to the Street Hunter case. He has only assured her he will tell her in time. For the present, he has pressed her to tell him about other murders she has attributed to Cara.

Speaking these things aloud has made her aware that she has been indulging a fantasy about how to be a fugitive in this country, in a time when she herself often wants to disappear. Now she is relating all of this to Agent Snyder as if everything she has fantasized in her private journaling is fact. But he has listened attentively, asking questions only to clarify.

She has told him how she has put together the map by searching for murders which fit a certain set of criteria: crimes which feature grievous injury to the throat, in which the victim has some history or indication of sexual predation, and which occurred on or near a full moon. Today she has been outlining another murder from the past she has long suspected is Cara's work.

She feels the need to say again, "This is all speculation. What I know is that on the thirtieth of September, 2008, a male guest was found murdered on the grounds of the Arizona Biltmore Hotel. His windpipe had been crushed by someone stomping his throat to pieces."

Chapter 35

Phoenix, Arizona - September 29, 2008
Cara

As always when the moon is so close to full, she sleeps for the night, a day, and the next night, stirring only for water and the toilet.

On the third day, she wakes well before dawn, already restless.

Until she checked into the hotel, she had been driving for days in a row. Her body is a mass of kinks and tightness. So she eats fruit and cheese and nuts from the mini bar, dresses for a workout, and goes out into the dark to find the gym.

She has found that if she goes to a hotel gym early enough, she is often the only person there. She enjoys using the machines, the treadmill, the rowers, the weights. Testing the strength of her own body in the hush of an empty workout room. Strength is survival.

But today, despite the early hour, someone is already there working out. A man running on a treadmill, dressed in a T-shirt and shorts—and top of the line athletic shoes. A corporate type in his late twenties. Not gym-buffed, as so many of them are, but bulky and bearlike, the way men from the Northeast tend to be, with an extra layer of flesh against the cold. *Boston, maybe,* she thinks. There is an arresting intensity, there. A hungry impatience.

Normally she is wary of working out with anyone else present in the gym. But the man on the machine doesn't give her a glance. He is fixated on the TV screen above him, tuned to a financial channel.

And she needs this workout, to calm the restless, prickling agitation she always experiences with the fullness of the moon.

She picks a weight machine well away from him, where she can keep an eye on him, and begins her presses.

After a few moments of news, the man has stopped the machine. He holds onto the side bars, staring up at the TV with such intensity that she is compelled to look up at the screen.

She has seen any number of financial programs. The gym televisions in large hotels are always tuned to such channels in the morning, especially since the housing market began to collapse. She pays scant attention to politics. But she is always interested in money.

The chart she is seeing now is disastrous. The lines look like free fall. When the program cuts to live coverage of the Stock Exchange, the trading floor is in chaos.

She moves closer, mesmerized by the faces of the traders, the primal panic radiating from the screen.

"What happened?" she asks aloud.

The man turns and looks at her, as if he has just realized she's there. "Congress voted no on the bank bailout."

She takes this news without emotion. A stock market crash will have no effect on her own accounts. She holds cash, period. But she understands that what is happening is momentous.

She is surprised to find herself speaking aloud. "People knew it was coming. They must have."

He glances at her. "Yeah. People knew. That never seems to stop anyone from ignoring what's right in front of them."

She has had vast experience with that.

The man dismounts the treadmill, looks distractedly around for his water bottle, his towel. "Got to get to work. It's going to be a long day. And a long year. Or ten." He hesitates, then reaches into the pocket of his gym shorts, takes out a card case and extends a business card. "If you ever need an advisor."

She takes the card. His name is Paul Hawthorne. He's an investment banker.

She does not check out of the hotel that day. She packs her few things and stows them in her car, but adds another night to her stay and remains in the room with the television on, something she is rarely moved to do, and watches the ominous news reports.

That night, she goes out to the main building, to the hotel bar.

She enters warily. She is one of only three women in the lounge and attracts instant attention. She ignores the appraising look of a burly businessman sitting with colleagues at one of the dark booths, and scans the room.

The banker named Paul sits alone at the bar with a drink, watching the television above the bar. More financial news.

When she steps up beside him, he startles, and stands. "Hello." She nods to him. He remains standing. "I was rude, this morning. I'm sorry."

She doesn't know what he means. There is an empty stool beside him. She sits, and he sits back down. "What would you like?" he asks.

There is something she wants, but what he means is a drink. "Vodka tonic," she says. "And water."

She will drink the water and not the vodka. It's an easy enough illusion. People are always on their guard when you don't drink. It is always more useful to let them think you are.

He orders, and then turns and looks at her without smiling. "I have a rule not to chat up women in a gym."

"Good rule," she says. It is. Obvious, but rare. She glances around her at the bar. "But here?"

"Different rules."

She has not done this often. There have been a few boys her own age or about, whom she was able to talk to. Eric, the boy at one of her multitudes of foster homes who taught her to drive and to jack cars.

Chris Devlin, an older boy at one of the high schools she'd briefly attended, who had flirted with her as if she were *Normal* and had been of use when she was tracking down a predator and in dire need of local information.

Now once again, to get the thing she wants, she must play a game that makes it look like she is being friendly. Open. Even possibly willing. She has seen it. What women say. What men say.

As their drinks arrive, she glances up at the bar TV, which is all news of the crash, the same panicked footage they watched together in the gym that morning. And she pretends the next question comes from what she is seeing on the television.

"Things didn't get better."

He, too, looks at the screen. "They're going to get a lot worse before they get better."

"For how long?"

He shakes his head. "Years. Forever, unless someone who *gets* it does something drastic about it."

"But... it's like a sale, isn't it?" she asks. In all that morning financial TV, in all those hotel gyms, she has seen one consistent rule of the stock market: *Buy low, sell high.*

He laughs, startled. "Sure, if you have balls of steel." Then he backtracks. "Sorry. I meant—"

She waits.

"Yeah. Theoretically. If you don't mind a huge gamble. And you have time to wait it out."

Time is, of course, the wild card. She never assumes she will live through the next day.

But her freedom depends entirely on the money she has, in her bank accounts and physically stashed away. It is a very concrete power. As with any power, it is both useful and imperative to understand everything she can about it. And she senses an opportunity.

It's the easiest thing in the world to get men talking. She simply makes it about him. "What are *you* going to do?"

His laugh is short and wry. "How much time do you have?

She meets his gaze. "I have time."

Chapter 36

Portland - present
Singh and Snyder

Singh breaks off her narrative again.

Agent Snyder has been listening intently, without comment, and Singh knows she has been embellishing the narrative as if she is alone with her journal, writing her speculations without filter. Now she feels she has been too unprofessionally intimate with her details.

She feels heat in her cheeks, and clarifies aloud, "Perhaps I have... that is to say, all I really know is that a murder of a banker occurred at the resort on the night of the financial crash..."

Snyder nods. "So you've constructed a plausible scenario for the murder through speculation on Cara's inner life, and on how she arrived at that place and moment in time. And very credibly."

Singh feels the rush of pride even before he adds, "You're a born profiler. I always suspected so. Please, go on."

Chapter 37

Phoenix, Arizona - September 29, 2008
Cara

Hawthorne seems to know his job very well. And he's not a hustler. Without any self-aggrandizement, he gives her a concise, precise history of the housing bubble, sub-prime mortgages and the bank bailout bill, the failure of which has precipitated the current market crash.

Greed, of course. And the men who have ruined countless lives with their speculation will almost certainly never suffer any punishment for the damage they've done.

In between financial talk, he asks her personal questions. What she does. Where she's from. Often in these situations she says, "Canada, originally." When you keep the answers vague, if the other person has any working knowledge of certain areas, they will almost always volunteer it: *"I've spent some time in Toronto."* Then she can use a completely different region if more questions come up. She is very good at deflecting questions.

But this time she says, "New Orleans." She has been there recently and the place is still under her skin.

It's a city of survivors, of wraiths, of the walking dead. She feels at home in that great trauma. She has gone back there every year since the hurricane, luxuriating in the soft humidity, the great rolling river, the ghostly Spanish moss, the smell of sugar candles, the lacy black iron balconies hung with glittering beads, the defiant costumes and frillery of the people who would not give up on their city even when the rest of the country did. And the music. On every street corner, on every passing boat, in the air itself.

Paul lights up at its mention, and now she does not have to fill in her experience, because he is immediately talking about his own. She can nod and agree, and show enthusiasm for places he speaks of that she knows.

While he talks, she finds herself glancing at his forearms, the way his shoulders move under the dress shirt he wears. He has a comfort in his own body, a masculine power that cannot be ignored. She remembers his arms and chest in his workout T-shirt from the morning, his bare thighs in running shorts.

He drinks more, and she pretends to.

It is the longest conversation she has had with anyone for years. Already she regrets that. Even though she has been vague in detail, he knows too much about her. He has been too interested. And people have seen them talking.

So when it is late, too late, she goes with him to his villa, out onto the vast grounds.

They walk over the perfect lawns, weaving through arcs of water from the sprinklers. The rising full moon on the horizon stains the clouds like a spreading pool of blood.

When they step inside his villa, the lights don't even come on before they are on each other, devouring each other, pulling at each other's clothes, finding flesh.

He is startled and excited by her violence. She doesn't know any other way to be.

For her sex has been mostly a threat, that men around her have wielded like a cudgel. Something to avoid, to escape, to be constantly wary of.

But tonight, there is something about this collision of bodies, the fusing of flesh, that excites her, too. A satisfaction of hunger that creates new hunger. Her body is alive, and wired, and new to her.

A way, for a moment, of not being alone.

She does not want talk, after, but she forces herself to remain beside him in his bed, to let him hold her, and trace soft patterns on her bare skin.

Despite his best efforts to remain awake, his breathing becomes deeper. Soon he is asleep.

She removes herself from the circle of his arms, slips out of the bed. She stands in the dark beside it, watching him sleep…

Then she walks out of the room.

She dresses in the living room of his suite, and steps out into the moonlight.

The air has cooled. The wind is light and teasing.

Her body feels different to her, as if her nerves have come alive. She is aware of how she moves—her limbs, her hips, her thighs—in a way that is more heightened than it ever has been. It is an odd feeling, unfamiliar but not uncomfortable.

So this is sex.

She has wondered. It has taken her some time to get over the jittery feeling of danger whenever a man looks at her. To realize that there are ordinary men, there are good men—and there are predators.

These groups do not intersect. Now that she is older, now that she is not a prisoner to any system, it has become easy for her to distinguish the predators. She has had a lifetime of experience.

And for the first time, she wonders, *Is it possible?*

Companionship... some respite from the constant aloneness…

She is so intent on the thought, on what is newly vibrating within her, that she does not see *It* coming. The sudden lunge out of the darkness. The hands clamped around her waist and mouth, strangling her cry.

Through her terror, she knows instantly who. The businessman from the bar. Stinking of Scotch and malevolence.

He lifts her off her feet, wrests her behind a hedge border. Twigs claw at her skin as he crushes her to the ground.

Falling on top of her, knocking her breath from her…

So much heavier than she is.

Before she can recover her breath, he clamps a hand down on her mouth to silence her, and shoves the other between her legs. It is the exact opportunity she needs. She bites down hard on his fingers, jaws clamping and grinding. She tastes blood and he tries to pull back. She bites harder and twists her head viciously, ripping his flesh.

He draws the other hand back to hit her—and her own hand is free. She slams the heel of her palm savagely up into his chin, hears his teeth crunch.

"Bitch!" he mumbles. Or tries to, through broken teeth.

She doesn't give him a moment, but scrambles to standing, powered by the electric spike of adrenaline, and kicks him in the side of the head.

Then she stomps her foot hard down on his throat.

And raises her boot, and stomps again and again and again.

There is barely anything left of his throat when she stops herself. She stands gasping. The moon above her is swollen and angry, blurry with rage.

She turns and stumbles away across the lawn.

After a few steps she catches herself. She forces herself to stand upright, to walk slowly, in some semblance of *Normal.*

She does not return to her villa, but veers for the side lot where she self-parked with her suitcase and toiletries already stashed in the trunk. She must leave this place as quickly as possible, put as much distance between herself and this hotel, this city as she can before dawn.

As the terror subsides, something else builds. Fury.

Fury at the pathetic excuse for a human being who lies behind the hedge, stiffening on the resort lawn. Fury at herself, for letting her guard down and allowing *It* to so easily strike. Fury for ever thinking that *It* would not be lurking, waiting for a time that she is unsuspecting, actually feeling alive, feeling *Normal.*

Normal is not possible.

She will not forget again.

Chapter 38

Portland – present
Singh and Snyder

Agent Snyder looks out through the tall windows at the darkening sky. "No perpetrator was ever identified," he says. Not a question.

"There was never even a suspect," Singh replies.

She is experiencing a profound relief in being able to talk about it all. She has been too long alone inside her own head with these theories. "This murder stood out not just because of the injury to the throat, but also because it seems very likely to have been self-defense, given the damage done to his fingers, the angle of the injuries to his jaw. And even though he was fully dressed, the coroner found pre-ejaculate in his clothes."

Snyder nods. "Very similar to the murder of that trucker in Atascadero."

A few months ago Cara had killed a trucker with a criminal history who had followed her into the women's restroom of a highway rest stop. It was one of the first murders Roarke's team had been able to attribute to her.

"Just so," Singh says. "Also, the victim, Kendall Parsons, had several harassment complaints at various workplaces."

Agent Snyder says softly, "Making him Cara's exact sort of target." He regards her thoughtfully. "But this banker you spoke of. Paul Hawthorne."

"Hawthorne was a colleague of Parsons who attended the same conference that weekend. Hawthorne gave a statement to the police that I found..." Singh pauses, not entirely sure how to phrase it. "Incomplete. He spoke of suspecting Parsons of predatory activity in the past. He did not mention seeing Parsons with a woman on the night in question. And yet there seemed to be a gap in his statement."

"Ah," Agent Snyder says. "I see. A Lindstrom-sized gap."

A question has been looming in Singh's mind ever since she discovered the murder on the Biltmore grounds.

"Agent Snyder, I must ask you. Was ASAC Roarke in Phoenix on September 29, 2008?" Singh is aware that she is holding her breath, waiting for his answer.

Snyder turns thoughtful eyes to her. "Not that I'm aware of. But I can tell you exactly where he was two days later. Because that was the day he met Monica."

Chapter 39

San Francisco - October 2008
Matt

The moon was full in the sky, the autumnal glow adding a layer to the illumination of the streetlamps.

Matt walked the footpaths of Golden Gate Park. Above him, a warm breeze stirred the dry leaves of eucalyptus trees.

He paused at a scenic overlook to look out over the glimmering lights of San Francisco.

It was his city, now.

The week he finished his summer internship at Quantico, Snyder had asked him, "Where do you want to end up working, ultimately? Geographically speaking?"

He didn't have to think twice. He'd fallen in love with "The City," as Bay Area locals called it, when he was just a boy. San Francisco was small enough to be able to know it intimately, and had all the right proportions of city sophistication, staggering natural beauty, fascinating Gold Rush history, culture and entertainment, and endlessly diverse eccentricity.

Snyder chuckled. "Can't argue with that. Well, you have three years to fill before the Bureau will take you as an agent-in-training. If you want to really know a city, you need to work it as a cop. The Bureau won't put you straight back in San Francisco at first, but you'll have done the groundwork for a transfer later."

If Snyder had told him to pack his bags and head for the Arctic, Matt would have done it.

Now, as a uniformed officer of the San Francisco PD, Golden Gate Park was his favorite beat. It wasn't just a literal walk in the park, although that was definitely a perk. A large number of homeless made the thousand-acre urban refuge their home and there were the usual factors of mental illness and gang activity. Matt had already had to contend with six drug overdoses, two of which were DOA at the hospitals he'd rushed them to. The exposure to such human desperation took a psychic toll.

He was learning things. He wasn't changing the world on any major scale, but he was doing something to make one little part of it better. He was keeping the peace. He was being of service.

But he was impatient to move on.

Working with Snyder, that taste he'd gotten of the Gilman case with its disappeared target, the ominous background of domestic arms trafficking, the whole unsolved mystery of it, had started a hunger in him for autonomy before he'd even started as an agent. He was itching to finish his last year of required employment and get on to the Bureau where he could begin, as Snyder had promised, to build his own cases his own way.

He circled back toward the plaza of the Palace of the Legion of Honor, a three-quarter scale model of the original *Palais* in Paris, home to world-class collections of European art. It stood in the black and white of moonlight like a stage set.

Tonight the three-tiered fountain in front of the Palace was lit up in changing colors. There was some big corporate affair going on after hours and Matt had volunteered for foot patrol.

He'd been going to the museum since he was just a kid, had had some of his very first makeout sessions here, on middle and high school field trips. He wasn't sure what it was—the romantic elegance of the columns, the spectacular lighting, the pleasantly erotic relaxation of drifting through galleries, maybe just all that marble—but the Palace was still a can't-lose first date.

He'd had no shortage of those in his time in San Francisco. Dates, hookups, explorations, experiments... he didn't even know what to call them. Nothing at all lasting. He wanted the companionship, and he definitely wanted the sex, but no one seemed to stick.

In the courtyard, the statue of Rodin's *The Thinker* loomed, silent and alone on its pedestal. He paused, looking up. "What do you say, pal? Is it me?" he asked the statue wryly.

The problem was, and it wasn't anything he could ever tell anyone, but—he had yet to find anyone who was remotely as interesting to him as his work. He didn't have time, real time, for anything else.

The Thinker had nothing to say on the issue.

Matt turned away, and was doubling back past the huge circle of fountain when something slowed his steps.

A sound? A feeling?

He looked toward the marble Arc de Triomphe entrance and the columned courtyard beyond. The only sound was the splashing of water in the huge circular fountain behind him. He could feel the mist on his face...

And then he heard it. An echo of uneasy laughter. Low voices, a scuffling... then a woman's voice, frantic and rising. "No. I'm not... *Stop. Don't—*"

Her voice cut off abruptly.

Matt bolted forward in the direction of the sounds, through the parallel-set columns. The wide courtyard inside seemed deserted. He turned in a circle...

And then he saw them.

In the shadows between columns, a woman in a cocktail dress wrestled with a man in a suit. His arm was around her waist, his hand clamped over her mouth—

Matt's pulse shot up. He barreled forward, raising his voice. "Step away from the lady. Now."

The suit jerked around in rage… and then his eyes focused on Matt's uniform. In the dim light, his face went through a convulsion of readjustment, the predator receding from his features to leave a disgruntled, arrogantly good-looking corporate type of perhaps fifty.

Matt repeated, "Step away." He rested his right hand near his holster, making sure the suit saw him do it.

"It's fine," the woman said quickly. "We're fine, officer."

"You heard the lady," the suit said. "This is a private party."

Matt kept his eyes on the man's face. "Party's over, pal. Find yourself somewhere else to be."

The suit mumbled something Matt couldn't hear, which was undoubtedly for the best, and strode off into the dark, moving with stiff-legged rage.

The woman turned to him, flustered. She had dark hair and eyes and brows, an elegant profile, a slender, tensile body sheathed in a glittering cocktail dress. A guest from the corporate party Matt was here patrolling. And ringless, he noted. The asshole wasn't her husband, at least.

"I appreciate your help," she said coolly. She sounded not a bit appreciative, just a little breathless and a lot annoyed. Probably too young to be a senior partner, but she already had the command of one. "But I'm fine. He was drunk," she said. Matt could hear the tremor under the flippant tone.

"Look, miss. What I just saw was assault. If you want to file a report—"

She interrupted, horrified. "No! God, no. I have to work with him."

"So do other people."

She bristled. "So?"

Matt felt a spike of irritation, and also confusion. "So if you don't do anything, he's free to do it with the next woman, and the next—"

Now she flared up, startling him. "Fuck you. You don't have to put up with this shit, you have no clue. Don't tell me how to handle it. I've dealt with it all my life and I'm doing just fine."

It was anger he felt first, and then a twisting helplessness. She was wrong, but she was right.

After a moment he said quietly, "I'm sorry." He turned to leave.

She called after him, "Wait." He turned back. She frowned at him in the dark. "A man who actually apologizes?" She stood looking at him, then reached into the small silver bag at her side and took out a business card. She extended it. "Let me buy you a drink sometime."

He looked at the card, then back up at her. "That's probably not a good idea."

Their eyes caught, and heat sizzled through him.

"You're probably right," she said.

Chapter 40

Portland - present
Singh and Snyder

Agent Snyder pauses and looks toward the windows at the darkening sky.

Singh sits, unsure of what to make of the story. It tells her something about Roarke, certainly. She is not at all sure what it has to do with the case. She prompts Agent Snyder gently. "And this woman was Monica. Who became ASAC Roarke's wife. Now ex-wife."

Snyder nods. "Yes. I've heard the story from both Roarke and Monica. And you're wondering why I would tell it, in this context." He turns back toward her. "Because that night, not long after this encounter, the banker who was harassing Monica was found murdered in the park."

He meets Singh's startled gaze. "Stabbed in the throat."

Singh feels a wave of unreality.

"I doubt Matthew would talk to you about this, but it was clear to me from a conversation we had once that he felt the killing pushed the two of them, him and Monica, together. Monica contacted him, understandably distressed to learn of the murder of her colleague. On one level she was—"

"Wondering if ASAC Roarke had killed her harasser," Singh finishes, in a murmur.

"Exactly. Of course he didn't. But it's not hard to see how the experience created a strong bond between them. Add to that that Matthew has always been a knight/rescuer..." He stops, amends quickly. "I don't mean to diminish Monica in any way. I got to know her during Matthew's posting here in Portland. She's a dynamic, intelligent, passionate woman. Every bit Matthew's equal. But she was not..." he pauses, searching for the word. "His partner."

Singh nods, and cannot help thinking of Cara. Who is not in a million lifetimes the partner she can morally wish for Roarke.

And yet...

She has no time to take the idea further, because Agent Snyder's next words are electrifying. "As for the murder, no killer was ever found."

The agents' eyes meet with the same thought. Snyder says slowly. "I don't know if there is any way of verifying Cara's whereabouts that night. I brought the murder up, the confluence, mainly to affirm that I strongly believe you're on to something with this map of yours."

Singh is lightheaded.

Was it Cara? Was she there?

And Roarke. Knowing that Cara kills so often by attacking her victims' throats, how could he not have told the team of the murder that brought him together with his own wife?

But she knows why. It is her own theory, and even she can hardly believe it could be true.

Agent Snyder steps forward to the map. He touches a finger to Phoenix, speaks aloud. "Phoenix to Los Angeles on I-10. Los Angeles to San Francisco on I-5..."

Singh has been thinking exactly the same thing. "Twelve hours drive. A day, two at most."

"If Cara continued on Interstate 10 from Phoenix, she could easily have been in San Francisco by that date."

"Daniel Modine. Wayne Gilman. Kendall Parsons. Monica's colleague, Roy Mazzaro."

Snyder reaches to the well of the white board for a marker and uses it to write that name and date on Cara's timeline.

Then he turns to Singh. "We have more than enough correlation to convince me of your theory. It's time for me to tell you about Portland."

Singh feels a shiver of anticipation. "The Street Hunter."

"The Street Hunter," he agrees. "And the Wolf."

PART FOUR

Chapter 41

Portland - 2009
Matt

Matt's heart was beating so loudly he was afraid it would be heard through the forest sounds around him. He took a slow breath in and tried to move more silently through the underbrush.

It was a dismally overcast day, with mist drifting through the trees. Several yards ahead of him, Snyder led the way, moving as expertly as an ancient Indian guide. The rushing of a nearby river grew as the two agents crossed by stealth through streams and blackberry vines toward the kill site of the eighth known victim of the serial killer the media was calling the Street Hunter.

The killing ground was miles out of town, on the bank of the Columbia River. It felt a million miles from anywhere. But instead of tranquility there was a creepiness here. The trees dripped with the rain that had just fallen, the skies were black and swollen with rain yet to come.

The heaviness was more than humidity. A teenage boy's last sights, last sounds, last breaths were breathed here.

And the agents' intense caution, their frequent pauses, were because they knew that in Seattle, the Street Hunter had returned to his wilderness dump sites to have sex with the corpses of his victims. Necrophilia was a common pattern with serial killers. People were objects to them. Dead or alive, it made no difference to the killers' sexual satisfaction.

The two known Portland victims were the most recently found—and they had been found within less than a mile of each other, which increased the chances the killer would return to this very spot.

The agents were coming up on a field. Roarke could see the river beyond the grasses. But Snyder stopped at the last uneven row of trees and held up a hand, halting Matt behind him. The older agent lifted the binoculars hanging from his neck. Matt did the same. Both men scanned the field leading to the riverbank, looking for any human movement.

Portland PD had of course removed the victim's remains. But the crime site on its own would carry a sexual charge for the killer. There was always the possibility that they would find him there.

After several minutes visual search, Snyder lowered the glasses. "We may as well move."

The men stepped out of the trees and began the slog through the marshy grasses toward the river.

It was wet. It was cold. A killer could be watching.

But Matt was lucky. And he knew he was lucky. Other new graduates from his class at the FBI Academy were scattered to the four winds, many at grim outposts in the likes of Minot, North Dakota and Brownsville, Texas. Matt had been assigned right away to a dream placement: Portland, on the West Coast BAU team, by special request of Special Agent Chuck Snyder.

As Snyder had warned him, the BAU had greatly diminished in size from its heyday but maintained small advisory teams for every region of the U.S. The Pacific Northwest was currently up to its ears in bodies due to the Street Hunter murders. Even before his assignment to the Portland field office, Matt had read everything he could read about it, obsessively following the Street Hunter killings in Seattle.

The first victim found was a homeless seventeen-year old girl, engaged in survival prostitution, her body dumped on the bank of the Duwamish River. As the Seattle police looked into missing persons reports and started searching the riverbank, more victims were found. Three female, one male, all homeless teenagers engaged in street prostitution. And there were other missing persons of the target age who hadn't yet been found or accounted for.

The last Seattle disappearance had been five months ago. But now in the last week, just days before Matt had arrived on his new assignment, the bodies of a teenage girl and a teenage boy had been found in this wilderness area outside Portland.

Snyder hadn't even briefed Matt in the office. They'd driven straight out to the dump site.

And the question was paramount in Matt's mind: Had the Street Hunter moved on? Found a new hunting ground?

He paused and looked back to scan the woods, but saw nothing human.

If you can call the Street Hunter human.

He turned and joined Snyder at the riverbank.

The water beside the bank was murky and there was scattered, drenched trash on the bank, as if people had fished or camped without cleaning up after themselves.

Snyder had shown him crime scene photos of the two teenagers found in the vicinity. Everything in Matt was in revolt against the violation of these young lives.

"The girl, Denise Vickery, was found last week, half a mile up river. The boy was found here two days ago. His fingerprints don't match any in the IAFIS system. Portland PD has been contacted by dozens of parents and relatives trying to find out if this boy is theirs, but no hits so far. We have no idea who he was."

"There have been two male victims out of eight, one in Seattle and this young John Doe, and both were attacked differently than the female victims, by which I mean more viciously. We're waiting on autopsy results on John Doe, but he was severely battered, with multiple broken bones, and sodomized, with severe anal tearing." Snyder turned to him. "Do you have any preliminary questions?"

Matt felt a jolt of anxiety at the sudden pressure. He'd forgotten how bluntly inclusive Snyder could be. He began carefully.

"As the media here has picked up on, the case is notable for the mix of male and female victims."

"Very true. What are your thoughts on that?"

And suddenly the situation hit home. This wasn't class. It wasn't theoretical. It wasn't about grades or graduation. It was real life. Real people's lives depended on the answers.

Matt pulled his thoughts together. "You're more likely to see a mix of male and female victims with pedophiles. The younger the victim, the more likely it is that the perpetrator has abused children of both sexes. And if you see male and female victims, then it's highly likely the perpetrator has abused children younger than six. It would also be likely that the perpetrator was abused himself. Also, the presence of a mental illness in a perpetrator triples the odds of gender crossover."

"Good. Go on."

"He's likely to be between the ages of twenty and thirty-five: three-quarters of sexual predators are younger than thirty-five. Eighty percent are of normal intelligence. He is almost undoubtedly male. We see females involved in molestation of young victims, either with or without a male partner, but ninety-seven percent of violent sexual offenses against children are committed by men. Also, seventy percent of perpetrators are white. And the behavior is highly repetitive, to the point of compulsion."

Snyder nodded approval. "Very good. You've just sketched out a solid base for what we're looking for. However..." He paused.

Matt became instantly alert.

Snyder continued, "I believe someone is deliberately confusing the issue."

"How?"

"First of all, the media is reporting that the Street Hunter has moved his hunting down to Portland. It's less than three hours' drive—no great distance for a serial killer. But Denise Vickery, Portland victim number one, was killed at least three years ago."

Matt stared at him. "*Before* any of the Seattle victims."

"That's right. The article from the Portland newspaper reporting that the Street Hunter had moved his action from Seattle to Portland came out before we'd released the information that Vickery had been killed years earlier. And that article got picked up by national news, so it was out all over the country that the Street Hunter was now hunting in Portland as well as Seattle." Snyder paused, and Matt sensed something important coming. "And then suddenly the body of this unidentified boy is found here, in the same vicinity as Vickery's body. With an important difference. Young John Doe was not killed years ago, but days."

Three years between killings. Matt tried to quiet his racing mind to consider the implications. "So it was *just* this article that presented the narrative that the Street Hunter indiscriminately killed both male and female victims and that he was hunting in both Portland and Seattle?"

"Correct."

Matt thought on it. "Did the initial article mention the location where Denise Vickery's body was found?"

"It was specific, yes."

Matt looked around them at the desolate site. "Was Young John Doe actually killed here? Or was there any evidence that his body had been moved?"

"Ah," Snyder said. "You've caught it."

Matt felt a rush. "You're thinking that someone read this article and dumped Young John Doe's body here to make him look like a victim of the Street Hunter. You think there's another killer attempting to cover his own kill by staging the boy as a victim of the Street Hunter."

"Bravo," Snyder said softly.

Matt felt exhilarated and sick, all at the same time.

Snyder looked out over the river. "The truth is, I've thought through many of those same conclusions. I'm encouraged that you would come to the same theory. But it's still just a theory."

Matt was intent. "But... if someone dumped him to make it look like he was the Street Hunter's... that's a big risk."

"Yes, it would be. Why?"

"We stake out dump sites."

"When and if we have the resources, yes. Which is a big if."

"It would mean that— *if* there is a second killer—either he doesn't know that, or he's desperate enough to take that risk, to throw an investigation in his own location off track."

"Exactly. So what is that location and what is going on there that someone would risk everything to protect?"

Matt was silent. It was a rhetorical question.

"That's what I'm currently trying to determine," Snyder continued. "We're waiting on the autopsy and a forensic evaluation of trace evidence from Young John Doe's body from our national lab. I'm hoping they'll find something that will give us a lead on where the boy was moved from."

There was something else, though, nagging at Matt. He spoke aloud. "If Denise Vickery was killed over three years ago, that means she was the Street Hunter's first. At least, his first known. So the Street Hunter did move his hunting ground, but it was from Portland to Seattle..." and then it hit him, and he finished, electrified. "Out of his own back yard." Without turning or moving, he let himself take in the field, the woods, the river. "That's why we're here. You think he lives here."

"I've been considering the possibility."

So it was more than possible the killer was watching them right now. An unnerving feeling, but also an exciting one. A real enemy that it was Matt's sworn duty to bring down.

He glanced at the clearing, just with his eyes, making no body movements that would betray what he was doing. Snyder noticed, of course, and nodded.

"Yes," he said casually. Matt had to admire his cool. They could be talking about anything. "He very well could be."

Matt stood in the desolate area and something in him shivered. A horrible place to die. A horrific way to die. The fog seemed to be a manifestation of the psychic pall over it all.

Two killers, intersecting…

His eyes rested on the riverbank, the discarded trash, and something jogged his memory.

Snyder spoke beside him. "What are you thinking?"

"Given all the publicity the Green River killings got up here, in Ridgeway's own hunting ground, it's reasonable to think that the Street Hunter picked up some methods from him."

It may have been Matt's imagination, but it seemed to him that Snyder became more still. "Like what, for example?" the older agent asked neutrally.

"If this killer went so far as to move the body, maybe he's taking more than location from Ridgeway's playbook. Ridgeway contaminated his dump scenes with trash from other scenes: used condoms, hair, cigarettes. Effectively planting 'evidence' that contained other people's DNA samples and would point away from him."

Snyder nodded. "Yes. It's easy enough to do, for someone who follows documentaries on forensics and crime scene methodology. Lucky for us most rapists and killers aren't rocket scientists. Most don't have the attention span. The ones who do, they present their own problems. But sometimes planted evidence itself reveals a truth."

Matt felt a prickle of anticipation. "What do you think the Street Hunter planted?"

"I don't know if it was planted. But every other Street Hunter victim was stripped of identifying items: IDs, handbags, jewelry. By contrast, Young John Doe was wearing a plastic wristband, like the ones you get proving you paid admission to a concert or club. A wristband with the emblem of the club imprinted on it. And I wonder why a killer who was so careful to remove other identifiers would have left that wristband…"

Matt finished, "Unless he planted it himself."

Chapter 42

Portland - 2009
Matt and Snyder

The agents had stopped for dinner on the way back in to the city and so were returning some time after dark, late enough in the evening to visit the club called Church. The name on the wristband Young John Doe had been wearing.

As Snyder drove, Matt looked out through the passenger window at a dismal procession of cheap motels, fast food joints, strip clubs with names like Sugar Dance, Peekaboo Models.

And kids. Dozens and dozens of kids on the sidewalk, in micro minis and high heels, some in regular street clothes, but with no other reason to be out on this street.

Snyder spoke from behind the wheel. "This is 82nd Avenue. There are plenty of other pickup spots, but this is the track. The biggest prostitution stroll in the Portland area."

The street walkers were painfully young. Matt felt his face tightening with outrage as Snyder continued. "Portland has been a sex trafficking hub for a long time. It's part of the Pacific circuit. Pimps move the kids from Seattle, through Portland, San Francisco, Los Angeles, San Diego, Vegas—and back up through the stops to Seattle. Every few weeks a different city. That way they can't form any bonds with anyone who could help them escape the life."

Three years as a cop in San Francisco had opened Matt's eyes to the real dynamics of the street life. Hollywood and the media were glib and reactionary about prostitution, often portraying it as a choice by lazy women who wanted an easy living, or a glamorous way for pretty girls to put themselves through college. Nothing could be further from the truth. In most cases it was systematic enslavement of children and young teens that had started with sexual abuse in the home or foster home. By the average age of thirteen, vulnerable girls from wretched domestic situations were targeted by sex traffickers, and groomed into addiction and submission, in some cases virtually kidnapped into the life.

Matt felt a burning in his gut. This is what it was all for. All the training, all the courses, all the police work. To get him ready to fight exactly this.

Snyder stared out the windshield. "The financial crisis has turned a lot more kids out on the street. Domestic abuse rises during economic downturns and the runway population has skyrocketed in the last two years, not just here, but nationwide. The youth and homeless services in Seattle and Portland and the very active music culture here draws a lot of young people. That draws the pimps, the rapists—and the serial rapists who graduate to serial murder. And this is part of the difficulty of the Street Hunter case. The fact that the circuit keeps these kids moving makes it very difficult to determine who is actually missing."

Snyder slowed the SUV and pulled into a parking space in front of a large gothic structure. Not a cathedral, but an impressive sanctuary nonetheless. It hadn't occurred to Matt that the club would be in an actual church.

Snyder turned off the engine and turned to Matt. "We have two jobs here. First, if possible, to pinpoint the date Young John Doe was in the club and if anyone can identify him. And second, to make contacts in the street scene who will talk to us about 'sick tricks.' If the Street Hunter is a Portland resident, or former resident, he may be known on the street."

The agents entered at the side of the building, through a street level door, and went down a short set of stairs, which opened into a dark space with a ticket booth that Matt recognized from his altar boy days as a confessional. He stood by as Snyder showed the ticket vendor his Bureau credentials. The vendor made a call, then directed the agents up a spiral set of stone stairs. They followed pulsing music to the top, and stepped through a heavy curtain.

Matt looked around him, taking it in.

The venue had once been an actual functioning chapel. The original layout had been preserved, although the pews were long gone except for a few lining the walls for atmosphere. The dais had been converted to a stage, the choir loft was a balcony of tables, the stained-glass windows were expertly lit and glowing psychedelically.

The place was packed, and overwhelmingly young. Matt was twenty-five, but he felt ages older than these kids. He couldn't remember the last time he'd been to a club like this, even though there were plenty of them in San Francisco, even in his own neighborhood.

Onstage, a band of young musicians played what Matt figured was the next iteration of the grunge that had gotten him through some angst-ridden nights in high school. The music was dark and brooding, rough, cynical vocals with driving melodic instrumentation.

A manager a few years older than Matt met the agents and took them into an upstairs office, where Snyder showed him a photo of the wristband that Young John Doe had been wearing.

"Yeah, looks like one of ours," the manager said. He showed the agents several rolls of similar ribbon-like bands.

Matt noted the different colors and styles. "You cycle through different styles of wristbands to denote different nights, correct?" he asked.

"Right."

"Is there any way of telling from the color or graphics what dates these wristbands were being used?"

"Nah, man—there's no dates. We got ten different styles and the only rule is you don't use the same color two nights in a row."

It was as Matt had suspected would be the case. So there was no way to pinpoint the date that Young John Doe—or the killer—had gotten that particular wristband from the club.

But if—*if*—the killer had placed the band on the boy's wrist to confuse the crime scene, he would have to have taken an intact wristband out of the club, which meant in all likelihood he'd actually been inside.

As the manager took a phone call, Snyder pulled Matt aside. "I'll stay here and talk to staff. I'm likely to put a damper on any conversation downstairs, so best I stay out of sight. You go back down and circulate. Try not to look too much like a Fed."

Matt walked back down the spiral staircase, wondering just how much he already did look like a Fed. Probably too much, he concluded. He made a mental note to add a couple of battered concert T-shirts to his trunk wardrobe. He glanced around the club to get a sense of the fashion.

And maybe a flannel shirt.

And a filthy knit cap.

And I guess I'd better get started on a beard.

He went to the bar for a prop drink.

As he waited for the bartender, he felt someone watching him, and turned… to catch the gaze of a slim, dreadlocked musician type at the other end of the bar. Matt recognized him as the singer of the band that had been playing onstage when he and Snyder had first come into the club. The singer didn't drop his eyes. At first Matt assumed sexual interest, but when he looked harder the vibe he got was straight.

The singer set his drink down without finishing and wove through the crowd straight to Matt. He stopped in front of him, and leaned in to shout over the frenetic music of the band that had taken over the stage.

"Are you here working the Street Hunter case?"

Matt tried not to react. *I guess that settles the "looking like a Fed" question.*

The young man gave him a brief, ironic smile, and leaned in to shout again. "Took about two minutes for everyone in the club to hear there was FBI here."

"I'm Special Agent Roarke." Matt felt self-conscious using his title. He was used to identifying himself as "Officer." *Special Agent* felt like a whole different level.

"Jamie Kennedy," the young man returned, and then got right to the point. "This is the same guy as in Seattle, right?"

Matt shouted back at him. "Where can we talk?"

Kennedy nodded, and then gestured toward a door.

Matt picked up his Coke and Kennedy led the way outside to a far quieter patio and garden area with tables, booths, nooks, a fountain. Above them, colored lights from electric strings woven through trees and awnings glowed, hazy in the mist.

Kennedy chose a deserted corner table, and they sat. The noise of the club was still ringing in Matt's ears as he asked, "So you've been following this case?"

"It's all over the papers. It's all anyone can talk about," Kennedy said. "A lot of the street kids hang here. As soon as that girl's body was found, we started asking people to check in." He added flatly, "People are scared."

"Who's 'we'?"

Kennedy looked thrown.

"You said, 'We' started asking people to check in."

"Oh. Well… my band. Other bands. On our website, on flyers. Asking club kids to just—let other people know they were okay. Trying to get people living on the street to crash together with people they knew." His eyes darkened. "But when you guys found that second kid… well, now the whole street is freaked."

While Matt didn't want to divulge details, he knew he had an opportunity, here, a direct line to helpful witnesses. At the same time, he was wary, remembering the wrist band may have been deliberately left to obfuscate the case. Kennedy seemed sincere but Matt wasn't about to trust a gift horse.

"Do you know anyone who's felt specifically threatened, or stalked, or afraid?"

There was a flash of anger on Kennedy's face. "That's street life, man. It happens every day. Beatings, rapes, abductions, hostage situations—you name it."

Matt knew that was precisely true.

Kennedy visibly controlled himself. "So you think the killer's a trick?" he asked.

Matt kept his tone neutral. "It's possible. We're looking for someone who may have been around the scene a lot. Someone who probably has a history of assault on sex workers. If you know people who'd be willing to help us identify some of these guys, it would be a huge help."

He waited while Kennedy seemed to wrestle with himself. "I can try to set that up. I can't promise anything."

Matt reached for his credentials wallet, fished out one of his brand-new Bureau cards. "Anything you could do to point us in a possible direction..." He wrote his own cell phone number beneath the office number, extended it to Kennedy and looked at him straight on. "This is going to happen again, unless we move fast."

Kennedy didn't look away. "I get it. Nobody wants that."

"Then I hope I hear from you soon."

Kennedy nodded, and took the card.

Chapter 43

Portland - present
Singh and Snyder

A log in the fireplace snaps with a small explosion of sparks, startling Snyder into silence.

The fire is the only light left in the study; the sky outside has gone completely black.

It takes Singh a moment to fully return to the present, to take in her surroundings, so caught up has she been in his story. And the implication of it.

The Wolf. A second killer, with some tie to an active present-day case.

She speaks aloud. "Agent Snyder, the other killer, the one you called the Wolf? I have never heard of any murders from the time by a killer with that name."

"No. No, the Wolf was just a theory..." he trails off, looking into the fire.

"But you are thinking that the Idaho murder you were consulting on in January may be tied to the Street Hunter case?"

He looks at her, his face gaunt in the firelight. There is irritation in his voice. "No, Matthew. You're not listening to me."

Singh is confused. "I'm sorry, Agent Snyder?"

"Matthew," he says again, and she experiences a moment of alarm before he finishes, "I was trying to tell him in January, but he wouldn't listen."

He looks pale, fragile. Concern for him brings her fully to consciousness. Singh stands. "I can barely keep my eyes open. I am afraid I need sleep. Would you mind very much if we were to continue tomorrow?"

He nods, vaguely. "Of course. Of course."

"Rest well, Agent Snyder."

She has the impulse to hug him, which surprises her, and which she of course resists.

Outside, a thick mist drifts in the trees.

As she drives back toward the highway and her hotel, she has to use her high beams to see the curves of the road. Her thoughts swirl like the fog.

She has not yet heard the whole story. But one thing is very clear already. Snyder and Roarke were pursuing a theory that there was a second killer, apart from the Street Hunter. That that killer may have brought a victim of his own to the Street Hunter's Portland dumping ground to conceal his tracks.

And she strongly suspects Snyder may believe that second killer, the one he had briefly referred to as "The Wolf," is still at large. Not only at large, but…

Is it possible?

…. has broken in to Agent Snyder's home to obtain case files.

She shivers at the thought.

Inside the house.

She will hear more from Agent Snyder tomorrow. But she is in no mood to rest.

She uses her GPS to find 82nd Avenue, and drives the strip, staring out the windshield at young people dressed in bedraggled provocation, huddled in doorways to keep warm.

Nothing changes.

The wave of fury she feels is not unlike what Lindstrom must feel.

She has not had much time to explore Portland. But she knows that the nearby Alberta Arts District is a big hangout for musicians, with many of what Portland calls DIY clubs in the area.

She uses her GPS to navigate to the district, and cruises until she finds a well-lit strip where numerous young partiers are clustered outside bars and clubs. It seems walkable, and she has had no dinner, so she finds a parking space and leaves her vehicle to walk in the misty night.

She cannot get her mind off Snyder's story: the Street Hunter, the Wolf amongst these lambs. Roarke working this case that was the very embodiment of evil: abused and forgotten children slaughtered by a monster…

A perfect storm of what would draw Cara.

Could Cara and Roarke's paths have crossed in Portland?

She is so immersed in her thoughts that she is only now aware that a car has slowed on the street beside her, following her.

A male driver leans toward the open passenger window making slurping noises. "Hey mama. How much for a suck and fuck? C'mere, mama."

She reaches in her coat pocket for her credentials and walks straight for the car, arm extended, holding the wallet out and shouting, "FBI. You are under arrest."

The car takes off in a squeal of tires.

She steps back on the sidewalk, shaking with disgust and anger.

Then she turns and keeps walking.

A neon sign appears in the mist beside a looming building with arched buttresses. When she sees the name, she realizes why she is here.

She approaches, marveling that it still exists. She can feel the pulse of music under the soles of her feet.

She stops under the neon sign that reads CHURCH, and walks down a set of dark stairs. But she hesitates in the dark entrance.

Her aim is to find Jamie Kennedy, Roarke's young musician contact. She feels Agent Snyder would not have mentioned him so prominently if he were not going to play a pivotal role in the tale.

She knows this is hardly the way to go about finding a witness. It would take her no time to go through the usual channels to find Kennedy. Simply Googling him might well be more productive than anything she can do in this club. But she has the strong urge to see the place, to feel it. To immerse herself in the story Snyder has been telling.

She pays the cover charge at a booth which surely once was a confessional, and receives a wristband with perhaps the same emblem that was on the wristband Young John Doe wore. Then she shows her credentials to the pierced and tattooed young man in the booth. "I am looking for a musician who used to play here. His name is Jamie Kennedy. Does he ever come in?"

The guy looks at her as if she is some kind of lunatic. "Only every day. He owns the place."

After a brief phone call, the booth attendant directs her to a spiral staircase. As Singh winds upward through a turret-like cone of stone work, she has the thought, *I am entering the story, now.*

She steps out of the stairwell into the nave of a former church, elaborately re-visioned into a music club. What used to be the dais is now a stage, where a band of young musicians is playing something darkly rhythmic.

At the top of the stairs, a man who must be Jamie Kennedy moves forward to meet her. He looks much as she pictured him as Snyder was telling his story. Clear-eyed, clear-skinned, with a tranquil aura of authority about him.

Her words come before she thinks. "You bought the club. I am so very glad to know it." She is charmed by the idea.

He seems startled by her impulsive intimacy. "I'm sorry—do I know you?"

"You knew some colleagues of mine. They have told me something about you." She looks around at the obviously thriving club. "How did this come about?"

He looks away, modestly embarrassed. "My band did really well on a record and the place was up for sale—and I just went for it. It seemed like it was what I was supposed to do. I hated the idea of it being turned into something else. So..."

For the first time in a long time Singh feels a warm glow for humanity in general. She has almost forgotten what it is like to hope.

"I am pleased it is doing well for you."

"Beats working," he says, and flashes an electric smile. It gives her a sense of what his stage persona must have been. "But you're not here to talk about music or Church," he says.

Singh remembers herself. "I apologize. I am FBI Special Agent Singh, of the San Francisco Bureau. And I am following up on a case that you assisted members of my team with, in 2009."

Kennedy's face shadows. "Wow. Okay. I thought that was done a long time ago."

"Yes. And possibly no."

She has no intention of questioning him about the Street Hunter case. She does not have sufficient information, herself, and any talk of those events should take place only with Agent Snyder present.

But there is a separate aspect of Roarke's part in this investigation that she has been wondering about all evening.

She takes out her phone, where she keeps a photo of the police sketch of Cara. There is a mug shot, of course, from Cara's brief incarceration, but Singh has spent time with Lindstrom. She knows the sketch does her much better justice.

She hands her phone to Kennedy now.

And she sees it in his face. He looks down on the sketch and Singh is sure. He knows her.

Because meeting Cara—you never forget.

She was here.

Chapter 44

Portland - 2009
Cara

She stands on the Morrison Bridge, one of eleven spanning the Willamette River, and looks out over the wide band of water.

She has been across the country nearly a hundred times now. West-East, East-West, North-South, South-North. On the interstates and on meandering side roads. On scenic highways and circuitous road trips with no particular destination in mind. She has explored every state, with the exceptions of Alaska and Hawaii—because she will not get on a plane, and she will not go anywhere that requires a passport, and while there are ferries that go to Alaska without stopping in Canada, she will not risk that journey.

She has long ago stopped haunting the interstates with the single-minded purpose to drive a road from beginning to end. She knows now she should never have done it to begin with. It was a pattern that would be too easy to guess, if someone were inclined to trace her movements.

But she cannot regret the risk. Because now the country is in her very marrow. She has come to know its geography so well, she feels sometimes that all she need do is think of a place and she will be there. She can call up the map of it in her mind, could sit down with pen and paper and draw every major road in every state. She would never have learned it so thoroughly without her methodical driving.

Also because of that systematic driving, she is never far from cash, from fake IDs, from master car keys, from disguises, from a weapon. She has seeded her emergency stashes everywhere.

And she has done *The Work* across so vast a territory that it would be nearly impossible to guess the pattern. *It* has been met and defeated in hundreds of different guises. And against all odds, something has protected her. From her first encounter with the monster on *The Night*, which she knows logically she should never have survived—and in every *Encounter* since. It is proof that what she is doing is *meant.*

The effect cannot help but ripple outward. With each *Encounter* she knows dozens of people will no longer have to fear that particular predator.

But she will never again be so predictable.

Now, in 2009, she is back on the West Coast. She is still most comfortable in the West and Southwest: the Pacific Coast, the deserts of California, Arizona and New Mexico. She spends large swaths of time in the national parks. But she has become more familiar with the cities as well. Los Angeles, and San Francisco, of course—still her favorite—Seattle, and San Diego.

Now she is exploring Portland. Tucked in between the Columbia and Willamette Rivers, in the shadow of volcanic Mount Hood. So walkable, with Pioneer Courthouse Square, the waterfront, the Grotto's botanical gardens, the hippie stalls of the Saturday Market, all within easy strolls of each other. The city has a young energy and she finds it easy to blend in on the street, with its microbreweries and coffeehouses and electric music scene, venues with names like Backspace, Laughing Horse, and Slabtown.

The city's two halves straddle the Willamette River and she takes unique pleasure walking back and forth over the city's eleven bridges. It is what she is doing today, in the light drizzle or heavy mist. Walking the paved path of Waterfront Park beside the river, crossing a bridge, walking to the next bridge on the opposite side. Hawthorne, Morrison, Burnside.

She is kitted out in the uniform of the Portland underground: grunge fashion. It suits her, the knitted caps and flannel shirts and torn tights she finds in thrift shops. It is defiant and anonymous and warm enough for the damp and always chilly weather. And it is an easy disguise: in these clothes she looks years younger, a teenager, just another street waif, indistinguishable from the others on the riverfront walkway.

There are frightening numbers of them, young people living on the riverbank in rows and rows of tents under the bridge. Camping in pods in the parks. Squatting in downtown doorways. Every larger city has them, and the West Coast more than elsewhere because of the temperate weather, youth services, and youth culture. Since the financial meltdown there are even more. And the predators flock to snatch them up.

She had not meant to stay long in Portland, but the signs are telling her that this is where she needs to be. The moon is growing and there are shadows in the street—the shadows of predators, trolling for teenagers, children, young people of fluid gender who draw the concentrated malevolence of *It*.

She fingers the razor she always carries in her pocket, now. She will need to use it soon.

When she descends the bridge for the riverfront walkway, there is a young man busking under a tree, playing guitar. She slows to listen, intending to toss coins into his instrument case. But on second glance he is older than she thought, about her age. He doesn't look homeless, either. He smiles at her beatifically, and extends a flyer.

"We've got a show tonight. Come to Church."

She stoops and takes a flyer, and their eyes meet for a moment with a heat that catches her by surprise, before she turns and walks away.

The flyer is in her pocket when she leaves her Pearl District hotel that night. She has a car stashed on a side street, but public transportation is part of Portland's appeal. She jumps on the easy access MAX train to the Aurora District.

She can sense it before she feels it, a rhythm through the sidewalk, a faint, but insistent pulse. Music coming up from the sidewalk. She stops at a door at the foot of a set of stairs leading down from the sidewalk.

The neon sign over the door says simply, *Church.*

She goes down a darkly blue lit set of stairs, and pays the cover at a booth, where she gets a glowing plastic wristband. She follows the music up another set of stairs and emerges through an arched doorway… into a cathedral.

No. Not quite. But the soaring ceilings of the church give it the spaciousness of a much larger venue. It is a complete and enchanting revelation, totally unexpected from the innocuous, anonymous entrance. A blue-lit two-story space, with the stage on the former dais, walls with curtains hung between original stained glass rose windows. The middle floor is a huge dance area; she gets a glimpse of tables in the choir loft above. In one wall, double doors lead outside to a large outdoor patio and garden lit with fairy lights.

Onstage a band plays, the music dark and haunting, rhythmic and fluid. She recognizes the lead singer's dreads and beatific face. The young man who gave her the flyer. A shiver of anticipation ripples up her spine.

More will be revealed.

She pays cash for a prop drink, finds a high stool in a corner to sit. People look her over, but she doesn't interact and no one bothers her.

The band finishes its set to enthusiastic cheers, and a recorded soundtrack takes over.

She gazes up and around her. The arched ceiling is painted midnight blue, and the constellations glimmer in gold, painted astrological signs in human form, made up of stars. And around the ring of ceiling in silver are painted the phases of the moon.

She stares directly above her at a full silver disk...

When she looks down from it, the dreadlocked singer is standing beside her, smiling. "You came."

She nods to him warily. He is glowing from the show, a fine sheen of sweat and adrenaline. "I hope you liked the music. Not that I'm fishing or anything." He smiles at her.

She did. She says so.

"Well, you just made my night." he says. He is charming and somehow luminous. There is a light there that that seems a bit more than just post-performance high. "You're new. To Church, anyway. Just visiting?"

Since that night in Arizona with Paul Hawthorne, she has become better at talking to people when she needs to. It is good practice. She finds it easy to make up histories for herself. She can briefly imagine other lives that she might have lived, if not for *The Night.* If she had never been *Scratched.*

If her eyes had never been opened.

She tells the musician she's from San Francisco, because she knows it well enough to provide a detailed story.

He nods knowingly. "Great city. Portland's the same, but—smaller. Flatter. Younger. Maybe not quite so crazy." He smiles. "But what do I know?" He looks back over his shoulder toward the choir loft. "The band's going up to the green room. Want to come and hang?"

She tenses, looks him over quickly. There is no sense of anything ominous. Rather, she feels a pull of import. As if this is what she is here for.

Still she can't help but ask. "Why?"

He pushes his hair out of his face. "I like the way you watched the show. And okay, yeah, you're really freaking beautiful. I hope that's not so shallow it drives you off."

She thinks of the Beauty Prayer. Beauty isn't shallow. But the beauty of the oceans and deserts is a different thing than the "beauty" portrayed in advertisements, on billboards and magazines. She doesn't know which beauty he means, here. But these things are always revealed.

She says nothing.

But she goes with him.

His name is Jamie Kennedy.

At the top of a spiral set of stairs he holds the green door for her and she steps through warily, her body as always braced to flee or fight. She is looking into the balcony she glimpsed from the floor below. Young people are sunk into huge sofas and chairs. A makeshift but well-stocked bar and bowls of snack food are set up on a table lit with electric candles.

The constellations on the arched ceiling above are much closer now, and she can see the phases of the moon in detail. The black walls are layered in wild scribblings and sketches in colored chalk, and the air is smoky with the green smell of pot.

This is *Normal.* Not everyone's idea of *Normal.* But for the creative kind of person, definitely. An experience as alien to her as other kinds of *Normal.*

She recognizes the musicians from Jamie's band among the others. There are non-musicians as well. Street kids. Waifs. Their body language, their *scratches*, make it clear they are tricking to survive.

Jamie brings her the tea she asks for in place of anything stronger, and introduces her around as Mia, the name she has given him. She tolerates the niceties, because it gets her closer to these young people. The wounds she senses in them are not just from the past. The cloud of fear over the huddled groups is tangible, stomach-turning.

Jamie is a light in this anxious darkness, obviously beloved, a leader in the crowd. She half-listens to conversations he has with various starry-eyed kids gushing about the show, about his performance. And she waits for the reason she is here to be revealed.

It isn't long.

She spots her almost immediately. It's hard to miss the slim, flamboyant young—girl or boy, Cara isn't sure. Which is clearly the point.

Her clothes are flashy but Cara's quick eyes catch the missing sequins on the worn velvet.

Seeing Jamie, s/he stops in her tracks, with a dramatic feigned swoon. "Be still my heart."

Jamie gives her a smile. "How's it going, Brandi?"

Brandi strikes a pose, inviting scrutiny. "How does it look?"

Jamie laughs. "You're a vision, as usual." He turns to Cara. "This is my friend, Mia."

Brandi looks Cara over, and Cara gets a flash of the keen, cold perception under the camp act. A survivor assessing a survivor, without filters, without mercy. But when Brandi speaks, it's with elaborate nonchalance.

"Where you from, sweetness?"

"Here and there," Cara responds.

"Citizen of the world," Brandi supplies, challenging.

Cara gives a nod and says nothing.

"Here, there, and everywhere," Brandi drawls.

"Like that," Cara says quietly.

Brandi gives her another X-ray look, and her eyes widen slightly. "Oh my."

Cara is suddenly sure Brandi has seen everything there is to see. Then Brandi pivots to Jamie. "This is my competition, hmm? It's a tragedy, I tell you."

Jamie smiles. "You'll always be the one for me."

Cara had not been sure about Jamie until that moment. But his easy, egoless flirting with this damaged soul stirs something in her. Jamie is a genuinely kind person. More clearly so than most she has ever met.

Brandi gives her wig a preening pat. "I hate to seethe and run. But—places to go, people to blow..."

Jamie's concern is instant. "You're not going out tonight, are you?"

"Girl's gotta eat."

Jamie reaches a hand into his pocket for his wallet. Brandi stops him. "You put that right back. You wouldn't want to make me feel cheap." She smooths her hands down her waist. "Day comes I can't make my own living, just take me then and there."

Jamie put his wallet away with obvious reluctance. "Just be sure to check in."

Brandi waves a jaunty hand back over her shoulder without turning around, a diva gesture that is likely out of some film Cara has never seen.

Jamie watches her go, concern in his gaze.

When he turns back, he sees Cara watching him. "We're trying to pair people up on a buddy system," he explains. "So that anyone out working checks in at the end of the night."

And then he tells her why.

A sixteen-year old girl and a younger boy, found in the woods outside the city within the space of two weeks. Raped, slaughtered, and dumped near the river within a mile of each other. Apparently the crime scenes have been revisited. A monster taking his pleasure from the dead.

As Jamie speaks, she must use all her strength to hide what is going on inside her.

"It started in Seattle. All kinds of street kids were disappearing and they turned up dead. Now it looks like the guy's decided to move down here. So. The buddy system."

Cara says nothing, not even to point out the obvious flaw in the system. It is reactive, not proactive. Merely an alarm bell sounded after the wolf has done its bloody work.

It is the thing that makes her most angry, and despairing—and implacably dangerous. It is what most wrenches her soul, if there is such a thing as a soul, and if she has one. How people can use children, those luminous beings who are all the future of the world, like blow up fuck dolls.

And that all the power of the law is somehow not focused on obliterating these monsters.

If she had her way every single one of them would die instantly.

The world being what it is, she must content herself with one at a time.

Chapter 45

Portland – present
Singh and Snyder

Singh pauses for breath.

"Cara Lindstrom *was* here when we were investigating the Street Hunter," Agent Snyder says, with a kind of reverent awe.

She answers him. "Jamie Kennedy identified her from the police sketch. His own description of her is unmistakable. She was here."

"I remember Kennedy well," Agent Snyder says. "Thoroughly credible."

Today he shows no signs of the fatigue of the last night. His eyes are more than simply alert as he stares across the study at her, with an expression she has never seen in him before. He is focused, still, formidable. He is a hunter.

"There were always holes in my understanding of the Street Hunter case. And Matthew knew it, too. From the moment you spoke of your red string theory I suspected Cara was a missing piece. And that changes everything."

Chapter 46

Portland - 2009
Matt

Matt sat in the study of Snyder's house, surrounded by its magnificent library of all the textbooks and reference manuals he hoped eventually to own for himself. A long wood-framed case board stood in the center of the room, jigsawed with crime scene photos of the Seattle and Portland murders, newspaper articles, victim photos, a timeline of the known murders.

Snyder had tasked Matt with combing through the online "Street Action" forums, where local johns posted their reviews of the women and girls they used. The men insisted on calling themselves "mongers," "hobbyists," or "trollers." In the ultimate irony, they felt the terms "trick" and "john" were dehumanizing.

There was one of these posters whom Matt had zeroed in on with equal parts disgust and professional interest. The man who called himself "Devil Dawg" was what the other johns called a "pooner."

Matt had to see the word "pooner" in context several times to deduce it meant a senior member of the online forums, a high-status hobbyist, well-versed in the online acronyms. Someone with street cred. Matt assumed the nickname was from the word "poontang."

Devil Dawg posted almost nightly, warning other johns against law enforcement officers out cruising the track, boasting about being able to spot "trannies." Other less senior posters seemed to look up to him.

At first Matt had dismissed him as just another asshole. But as he kept reading, through night after night of depressing online chat, he was starting to think Devil Dawg was a little too interested in the Street Hunter case. He brought it up at the slightest provocation, worked it in to conversations that had nothing to do with the murders.

Matt could almost hear the guy's heavy breathing as he typed out grisly details. None of which were anything beyond what had been discussed in the newspapers. But Matt thought he should be interviewed. The problem there was that these sex forums were notoriously scrupulous about guarding their users' privacy. It was going to take more authority than Matt had, to get "The Dawg"'s personal details.

For the moment Matt contented himself with making notes and swilling coffee to keep awake. He was aware of being a little too wired. When Snyder stepped through the door, he bolted from the sofa like a track runner jumping the gun.

Snyder looked at him with mild surprise. "I've just had a call from the national lab with the results on Young John Doe. There were two very interesting forensic hits on the trace materials found on the body. A mix of calcium carbonate and sulfur—a combination of minerals that one would find in geothermal areas."

"There must be plenty of those around here," Matt said cautiously. He would expect so, anyway, with the volcanos.

"Certainly there are geothermal areas in Portland. But." Snyder paused for just the briefest second, and Matt's pulse jumped in anticipation. "The lab also found another piece of trace evidence. Wolf fur. Identified as from a species that's not native to Oregon."

Holy shit, Matt thought. *He was moved from a different* state.

"Gray wolves are endangered, and found in the Western United States mostly near the Yellowstone and Glacier National Parks. The fact that we can now pinpoint those locations means we have a better chance of identifying the boy. The national lab also concurs with the Portland medical examiner that Young John Doe is younger than the other victims. He was large for his age, but probably no more than thirteen years old."

Matt flinched. And then resolved himself. *That's the last kid you get, motherfucker. You're going down.*

He forced his attention back to Snyder's summation.

"Our other Portland victim, Denise Vickery, had no such animal fur on her body. Nor did any of the previous Street Hunter victims. Another difference between the two Portland victims is that Vickery's hyoid bone was broken, as were those bones in all the Seattle victims."

Evidence of strangulation, Matt knew.

"But young John Doe's was not," Snyder finished. "Cause of death was the blow to the head. And the autopsy shows he was beaten severely before the lethal blow. "And, the rape, the internal tearing, was post-mortem."

"So... he fought," Matt said. *Fought off the rape. And the guy killed him.*

"He fought. And he showed no signs of the rectal scarring that we often see in teenagers engaged in survival prostitution—a common indication of long-term sexual abuse."

Matt sorted the implications in his head.

"So Young John Doe's body had trace elements that were not found on any of the other victims. He was several years younger than the other victims and the mode of death was different, a head wound rather than strangulation. He was wearing the club wristband, while the other victims were stripped of any identifying ornaments or documents. And his body showed no sign of prior sexual abuse."

He had been speaking aloud. Snyder nodded approval. "Go on."

"On the other hand, the female Portland victim, Denise Vickery, is looking like a victim of the Street Hunter. Which makes her chronologically the first victim we know of. And indicating the killer is possibly a Portland resident who possibly took his hunting up to Seattle as a diversionary tactic."

"Yes," Snyder concurred.

"But there are enough discrepancies with the MO and evidence on Young John Doe to indicate a possible second killer."

"Correct on all counts," Snyder said. "There's one other thing I find interesting. We have some new information on the male victim in Seattle. Terry Laithwaite." He stepped to the board with the crime scene photos to indicate the photo of Laithwaite's corpse. The harsh lighting of the morgue revealed a bedraggled, slender young man with delicately feminine features.

Snyder continued. "He had a record for solicitation." He paused, then added with irony, "Because naturally, the seventeen-year old runaway is at fault, rather than the adult man who solicits him. But look. I've just obtained some new photos."

He turned to Matt and passed over a file. Matt opened it to look down at a photo, and experienced a moment's confusion. He was certain he was looking at a girl. The next two photos showed Laithwaite in full drag. If he hadn't known, Matt could easily have been fooled at first glance.

"What do you see?" Snyder asked.

"He did a really convincing girl," Matt said.

"Yes," Snyder said. "He did. And here's another interesting fact. Laithwaite was beaten very badly before the killer strangled him. But unlike every other of the Street Hunter's victims, Laithwaite doesn't appear to have been sexually assaulted."

Matt felt another surge of the sick urgency. "If Young John Doe was killed by a different man…" he stopped.

"Go on," Snyder said.

"Then Laithwaite is the Street Hunter's only male victim. And Laithwaite in full drag..." He walked the room, working it out. "What if the killer picked him up believing he was a girl, and flipped out when he found out the truth? He's shocked, he's humiliated… so he beats and strangles him in a rage. No sexual assault because men aren't his particular turn-on."

Snyder was nodding slightly. "I agree. Very plausible."

At this point Matt could contain himself no longer. "There was a suspect on Portland PD's list, John Lombard, who had an assault complaint on a transsexual male prostitute. Three years ago. There was a strangulation attempt. But charges were dropped." Either the kid didn't press charges or as so often happened in these cases, the DA's office didn't advocate hard enough for a transsexual victim.

Snyder frowned. "As I recall, Portland PD eliminated Lombard for the Street Hunter. And the Street Hunter's clear preference is for girls. What we need to find is local mongers who fit the profile."

Matt interrupted. "I don't mean the Street Hunter. I mean, if Young John Doe was killed by another killer. If there is a second killer who attacks boys. Lombard could be our guy."

Snyder shook his head. "I do believe for the time being we need to treat these two killings as unrelated, and pursue them as if they are separate crimes. But our priority is the Street Hunter. I'll have a researcher follow up on missing teenage boys in Montana and Wyoming, and areas close to Yosemite and Glacier. But I want you to go to the rape crisis clinics and youth shelters and follow up on attacks on teenage girls, focusing in particular in the few years prior to Denise Vickery's murder."

Matt answered, "Yes, sir."

But mentally he added, *And boys who dress like girls.*

Chapter 47

Portland - present
Singh and Snyder

Now Singh understands. "You and ASAC Roarke named the shadow killer, the second killer, 'The Wolf' because of the wolf fur on Young John Doe's body."

Snyder gestures to her. "Yes. Young John Doe was an anomaly. To explain the discrepancies, we postulated a second killer who had dumped Young John Doe's body in the same vicinity of the Portland victim, staging it to make the boy appear to be another victim of the Street Hunter. We called this killer the Wolf. But as I strongly cautioned Matthew at the time, we were officially consulting on the Street Hunter case. We couldn't go off tracking a hypothetical second killer. At the same time, we couldn't let Young John Doe confuse the Street Hunter case. We had to treat the two cases as separate."

Singh shivers at the thought. *Two shadowy, malevolent presences.*

"Two vicious predators," Agent Snyder says. Singh looks at him, startled. She had not been aware she had spoken aloud.

"And now, the Huntress," he finishes.

Chapter 48

Portland - 2009
Cara

She wakes slowly, to the sound of rain on the roof, and Jamie's warmth beside her in the bed.

They are in his small apartment, in his bedroom, in his bed: a mattress and box springs on the floor. She lies still and listens to his easy breathing.

It is not like her to let someone close to her, so quickly, so easily. But for the last few days, she has done exactly that, with Jamie. She has told herself that it is in service to whatever knowledge she is supposed to get from him, part of *The Work*. But in bed beside him now, she is aware that that is a lie. There is a sweetness about him, a directness and tranquility, that has made her long for some connection. He is not forever. But he is some *Normal.*

For the last week, she has been allowed that peace.

But last night she dreamed of the skeleton girl. And she knows that her time with Jamie has come to an end.

As if in answer to her thoughts, a sharp knocking comes from the next room, the front door. Jamie sits straight up in bed.

Cara lies still, feigning sleep even as her pulse jumps and her heart begins to race.

The knocking comes again, sharper, more urgent.

Now, of course, the deeper meaning of their time together will be revealed. And she feels a pang of regret, that it will only come to whatever this is now, this pounding at the door.

She feels him reach beside the bed, pull on his jeans, and then his warmth is gone. Outside the bedroom she hears the front door open and there is a hushed, urgent conversation.

The door shuts, and Jamie comes back into the bedroom. Even with her eyes closed, she can feel the cold anxiety coming from him.

He reaches down for clothes, and Cara opens her eyes, sits up.

"I didn't mean to wake you." He sits on the bed, reaches for her hand. She forces herself not to stiffen, to let him take her icy hand in his. "Go back to sleep. I'll be back…" he trails off. "As soon as I can."

She ignores this. "What happened?"

"That was Brandi's check-in buddy. She didn't come back last night."

Of course. Of course. She is angry with herself. She should have known. All the signs were there.

Stupid. Stupid…

Jamie is on his feet, dressing, searching for discarded socks, shoes. "She would never just go off radar like that. Not with everything going on. Something happened."

Cara leans over, reaching for her own clothes.

Jamie stops and looks at her, opens his mouth to protest. She stares back at him. He nods. "Okay. Let's go."

Outside on the street, they pile into Jamie's tiny Mazda. As he drives off into a steady rain, he hands his phone to her to call Brandi again.

She has to force herself to take it. She is wary of all mobile phones, as if the mere touch of one could alert some punishing entity to her presence. She would never keep a live device herself. But she disguises her apprehension and keys in the number. There is no answer, just Brandi's sultry recorded voice on the voice message.

Jamie glances at her from behind the wheel, and she shakes her head. He sets his jaw and drives on.

Their destination is a warren of warehouses at the edge of the Arts District. Jamie pilots the car through a complicated maze of streets that becomes more ominous by the block, with furtive transactions on dim doorsteps and filthy alleyways crammed with overflowing Dumpsters. He finally parks in front of a dark warehouse.

The two of them get out of the car, looking up through the rain at the ravaged building. Some of its windows are boarded up, some newly broken.

"The cops've been running people out of here," Jamie says, staring up at the derelict building. "But there are still ways to get in."

She follows as he moves around the warehouse to a side alley littered with trash and glittering with broken glass. He stops under a boarded-up window. The bottom of one pane is a wide, thin board, not nailed down. Jamie pulls on it to reveal an opening that a small person could slip through. As he starts to work an arm under the wood, she stops him. "Let me."

He's reluctant, but obviously too big to easily fit through himself. "Be careful. Take a look first. Don't go all the way in unless you can see there's no one around."

It's touching, his concern. He has no idea how many times she's exposed herself to far, far worse. But she says nothing as he boosts her up, holding her steady. She wedges an arm, a shoulder, then her head through the gap between the board and the window frame, feels the wood crack as she forces it further open with her shoulders and chest until she is able to wriggle through.

Inside the dimness of the warehouse space she drops to the floor and turns quickly to look around her. She is in an empty corridor with vaulted ceilings. Water pools on the floor from rain leaking through boarded-up windows. She scans the darkness in both directions.

"Mia!" Jamie calls anxiously from outside the building.

She turns to the window, pulls the board out by leaning back with her full weight, so Jamie can squeeze through.

He drops to the floor and straightens. They move silently together through the corridor and stop at the double doors at the end. Jamie pushes one open, takes a quick look inside. She watches his back, sees his muscles relax. He turns and motions her to follow.

They move through the door into a central warehouse room, a former factory floor cluttered with old machinery.

And squatters.

She stiffens, glances around quickly—but sees only young people here, kids and older teens, huddled on dirty mattresses lying in in the drier corners and on top of a conveyor belt frame. Graffiti covers the walls. There are piles of trash and a damp, foul smell.

And yet there is more than that. The soaring spaciousness. The rain falling through broken skylight windows. Cascading columns of water. There is a haunting beauty in it, something that reminds her of Church. There is a reason young people camp in this place.

Jamie moves to the center of the room and calls out. "We need some help. A friend of ours is missing. We can't get hold of her. Does anyone here know Brandi Hughes?"

Cara watches as kids get off their mattresses and boxes and drift toward him, compelled by his open earnestness. Even as she has been.

She remains near the doorway for a moment, and then pushes back through the swinging double doors to explore.

In the corridor, she moves back toward the doors at the opposite end, moving quietly so she can listen. Something has drawn her, made her step outside, away from the others.

All her senses are tensely coiled, on high alert, as she moves slowly from the outer corridor to an inner one.

Without the windows and skylights, she is moving into the dark. She can feel a large space around her, and there is some open structure in the wall ahead.

She strains her eyes into the blackness until she gets a vague impression… two big concrete circles, or tunnels. Some kind of ventilation fans.

She tenses at a sound. A moaning. Terribly faint, like a wounded animal.

She moves forward in the dark.

Inside the ventilation tunnels, gray light comes from grilles leading to the outside of the building, enough light for her to see.

In one of the circles is a heap of discarded trash. Only it's not. Cara makes out a bedroll, a blanket. And curled on top of the bedroll is a broken, bloodied person. Split lip and blackened eyes. A face scarcely recognizable as human.

Brandi.

Cara moves closer to the concrete circle, feeling the waves of pain rolling from the heap.

From behind her comes a burst of motion as the door flies open, the thud of feet on concrete.

Jamie.

He stops beside Cara as he sees the crumpled bundle. "Oh God. Oh no."

Brandi mumbles, a slurring of words that means broken teeth, possibly a broken jaw. Cara can barely make it out. "Not… one… of my better days."

Jamie crawls into the concrete hole, reaching out. On his knees beside Brandi, he carefully feels down her arms, her legs. She winces, sucks air through her breath… but there is no screaming, which Cara takes as a positive.

Jamie gently puts his arms around her, and Brandi leans against him, sobbing into his chest.

Brandi insists on no ambulance, then passes out as soon as Jamie picks her up. He carries her through the tomblike warehouse, out a side door to his car, where he lays her on the back seat and puts the front seats back as far as they will go to hold her in place.

He drives through the pouring rain, with Cara turned backward in the passenger seat to hold Brandi's hand. Blood bubbles at the corner of her mouth, the only sign of life.

She and Jamie sit for hours in the waiting room of the ER until they're finally allowed in to see Brandi.

She shares a room with two other patients. All are drugged and sleeping. Cara and Jamie sit by her bed, on either side of her.

Cara watches Brandi intently, focusing on her eyelids. When she can see the movement that means she is close to waking, Cara suggests Jamie go down to the hospital gift shop for flowers. Of course Jamie sees it is the right thing. And Cara offers to stay by Brandi's side, to watch her.

So she is alone with her when Brandi stirs to consciousness.

"You," she says faintly, squinting up at Cara through swollen, bruised eyes.

"Jamie's here. He'll be back in a few minutes," Cara says.

"That boy," Brandi says. "That boy."

The drugs she has been given are strong and lulling. They could make a person talkative even if that person wasn't as naturally forthcoming as Brandi. Cara is counting on that.

Brandi is still talking about Jamie. "So fine… so *nice.* No one nicer." She looks up at Cara. "But you. You're not nice."

Cara holds her gaze. "No."

"He deserves better."

"I know."

Brandi sighs, a long, full-bodied shudder. "I don't want him to know what that…" her voice breaks, then hardens. "What that monster did."

"I won't tell him," Cara says.

And then Brandi tells her everything.

Chapter 49

Portland - 2009
Cara

She leaves Brandi's room and the hospital before Jamie returns.

She has not gone back to her car in the past few days. Jamie has never seen her in it. She does not want the people she interacts with in this city to be able to associate her with the vehicle. And if it has been stolen, there is nothing identifying in it.

But it is still there on the side street where she left it, waiting for her, and so are the keys she has hidden in a tree down the block. She retrieves the keys, gets into the driver's seat, starts the engine, and heads over the Interstate Bridge, across the Columbia River and out of Oregon, to the adjoining state of Washington.

Brandi has been very specific about her attacker. The kind of car he drives. Where he cruises for sex workers. The name he uses: "John." Quite possibly not his own, being so obvious.

But Cara knows more than enough to find him.

So now she must do some shopping. And she must do it elsewhere.

Given the option, she will always choose to do her preparatory work in a different state. Crossing state lines is an immediate and effective contaminant to any law enforcement investigation.

She does not have to go far. Every city has a Goodwill and similar charity stores. It only needs to be somewhere fairly large, where she will not be noticed. The first town she comes to has a downtown with several such stores. Even better: outside one is a line of free boxes, in the driveway at the side of the store. She roots through the unwashed clothes to find the items she needs.

She returns to Portland from her brief road trip with the costume and all the supplies she requires for the evening. But there is one last task ahead, one she does not relish.

She must tell Jamie she is leaving.

If she simply disappears, he will be beside himself. She cannot have him looking for her. She must make a clean break.

She goes to see him at Church, after the night's lineup of bands has started. Better to have people around them, and noise. She cannot bear a lingering, emotional scene.

She meets him on the main floor under the starry painted dome. As always, he lights up when he sees her. She draws him outside to the garden, where they sit at the secluded table they have been using to meet between shows.

First she asks him about Brandi, though she already knows better than Jamie how Brandi is. It had been clear Brandi has no appetite to talk to Jamie in her condition. She'd told Cara what needed to be told, and feigned sleep when Cara left, so as not to have to speak with him.

Being Jamie, he'd been calling the clinic to check up on her. "They say she's stable." He smiles a bit. "She likes you, you know."

Cara knows that "like" is not the word. But she and Brandi understand each other, which is more useful for her purposes.

He draws a deep, pained breath. "So what is it?" he asks directly. "You might as well just say."

He knows, already.

She will regret leaving him. Perhaps there is more than regret. She has no name for what she feels. Perhaps this is what caring for someone is like. But there is nothing to be done. She cannot afford the luxury of emotion. She cannot let whatever might have been get in the way of the *Work.*

She spins out her story. She's going back to San Francisco. A job is waiting for her. Portland isn't for her.

And she says that she's leaving tonight.

If she's lucky, it will be true, about leaving tonight. If not, Jamie will have much more than abandonment to mourn.

"I'm crushed." He seeks her eyes, holds them. "I thought maybe we had something."

She ignores the painful twist in her stomach. "I'm not the right person for you."

He tries to smile. "Now how would you even know that?"

Because I'm not the right person for anyone, she thinks.

He doesn't fight her, probably because he knows she's right. And that, too, is sad.

When he reaches for her she doesn't pull away, so he takes her face in his hands and kisses her softly. "Be happy, Mia. Be good."

Her throat aches as she walks out of the garden into the club. As she weaves through the crush of dancers on the crowded floor, the haunting, pulsing music of a dark ballad surrounds her.

Be good.

It is like him to say. It is who he is. Which is confirmation that she has done the only thing she can do, by leaving him. But as she moves out through the cathedral she feels a piercing, visceral longing.

Alone.

The pain is so sharp she almost cries out.

The music closes in on her, tearing at her heart.

Chapter 50

Portland - 2009
Matt

Matt moved through the cathedral entrance of Church, into the pulse of the club. The floor was packed with a crush of young people swaying to some dark and brooding song.

As he passed through the arch of the entrance, he was hit by a strong feeling of…

Desire? Longing? Belonging?

The emotion was so overpowering he stopped and looked around him at the club. Sensation flooded through him. The lights, the crowd, the stained glass glowing from backlights, the haunting quality of the music…

Something here. Someone? If I could just be still for a moment…

Chapter 51

Cara

She stands still, forcing herself to breathe. She clenches her fists, her jaw, and forces herself to push forward against what she is feeling.

It is like breaking through glass, a visceral tearing. But she can move again.

She threads through the crowd and out.

Chapter 52

Matt

And then he felt… whatever he was feeling… withdraw, recede…

And then it was gone, leaving him breathless—and bereft.

He stood for a moment, wondering.

How strange.

He forced himself to move forward through the crowd, to shake off the feeling and concentrate on his business here.

He'd spent the day talking to rape crisis counselors and youth shelter workers looking for information about attacks, rapes that kids had escaped with their lives. At one of the shelters, a counselor had told him that there had been chatter about an assault on a young victim just the night before, but had no details to give him.

He'd checked in with Portland PD and gone through the last night's incident reports. A handful of assaults, but all by adults on adults. None on teen sex workers that would fit his criteria.

He'd been about to start on the hospitals, when it occurred to him that Jamie Kennedy might be a much faster source of the information he needed. So he texted Snyder with an update and headed back to Church.

He found Kennedy in the back garden, seated alone at a back table lit only by strings of electric lights in the trees. His back was stiff as he faced away from the center of the garden.

Matt sat across from him. Kennedy started back to himself, turned, and stared blankly across the table at Matt. Matt spoke without greeting. "I need to talk to you."

The musician answered with visible effort. "Can it wait? It's… not a great time."

Something was going on with him, that much was clear. Something had shaken him badly.

"It can't." Matt said evenly. He looked straight into Kennedy's face to get him to focus. "There's word on the street that someone was attacked last night. We need to talk to this person."

Despite Kennedy's distraction, a look flashed across his face, giving him away.

Matt jumped on it. "You do know."

Kennedy looked genuinely conflicted. He shook his head. "I can't."

"Is this person safe? Have they sought medical attention?"

Kennedy hedged. "She's… being taken care of."

Matt wasn't about to back off. "I appreciate that, and I'm sure your friend does, too. But it's misplaced. You could be putting other people in jeopardy by keeping silent."

Kennedy visibly struggled with himself. Matt tried to keep his voice neutral. "No promises you've made make any difference right now. You haven't seen what this guy does to these kids. Nothing is more important than stopping him."

He was aware that he was being harsher than he needed to be. There was something about Kennedy that was pushing his buttons. The musician's gentleness, maybe. There was something unscathed about him that was making Matt bristle with…

Jealousy? That's weird.

The musician finally relented. "All right. I'll take you to her. Just—you have to let me go in first."

Inside, Matt exulted. On the surface, he nodded. "However you want to play it."

In the car, Kennedy sat slumped in the passenger seat, staring out the window. *Pain,* Matt thought. *The guy is in pain. About this? Or something else?*

As he followed Kennedy's directions to the hospital, he pressed for more. "Anything you can tell us. Anything at all."

"I haven't been able to talk to her about it. But...I have to think the guy who did it was a regular trick. This—friend, she's not stupid. She knows all about the murders. So she must know him. She'd never go with him otherwise."

At the hospital, Matt kept his promise and waited in the hall for Kennedy to go in first. Of course, what that really meant was he stayed just out of sight in the corridor outside, well within earshot, as Kennedy moved through the door.

"Shit," he heard Kennedy mumble from inside the room.

Matt shot through the door.

The room had three beds, two filled with sleeping patients. Kennedy stood staring at the third, empty one. He turned to Matt, helpless. For a moment Matt had the sinking thought that Kennedy's friend had died. But the bed was unmade, sheets thrown back as if someone had just gotten out of it. A glass of juice sat half-drunk still on the bed stand. It looked more like the friend had taken a runner.

"Go get a nurse," Matt ordered. "Anyone you can find."

Kennedy bolted out. Matt took the few moments alone to get a look at the medical chart. The first thing he read on the chart was the thing he had suspected from the nuanced way Kennedy had used the pronoun "she" about his friend. Brandon Hughes was a biological male: aka Brandi.

He skimmed through the rest of the chart. The injuries were horrific. Concussion, broken jaw, broken ribs, anal tears. The assailant had beaten, kicked, punched, raped, and nearly strangled Hughes to death.

Strangled. Like the Street Hunter's victims.

But unlike five, or six, other victims—she was left alive. And that was its own mystery.

Matt dropped the medical chart back into place as Kennedy barreled back into the room with a nurse behind him.

The staff hadn't even noticed Hughes had gone. It hadn't been long, apparently. The nurse had last made rounds only an hour before.

Kennedy was obviously panicked about his missing friend. In this heightened state of alarm, he gave up more details. Brandi was a trans kid, age seventeen or eighteen, flamboyant and feminine, who had continued to work the street despite warnings about the Street Hunter from Kennedy and other acquaintances.

It all struck an ominous chord.

"Where would she go?" Matt demanded.

Kennedy shook his head, gave Matt a haunted look. "Any number of places."

"Call. Text. Keep trying to get in touch with her. Let me know whatever you find out," he told Kennedy.

Then Matt went outside to his Land Rover and broke the speed limit back to Snyder's house.

He stood on the porch, pressing the doorbell, but there was no answer. Snyder had given him the security code and had encouraged him to use the study as an office. Roarke didn't hesitate.

He punched in the code, and strode through the house into the office, where he opened a file box and flipped through Portland PD files on the men they'd interviewed as suspects, searching for an address on John Lombard.

Lightning flashed outside the tall windows. Matt glanced up at the flicker—and saw himself reflected in the glass. Standing in the middle of the study, his hands buried in a file box, surrounded by a library of depravity.

It was an odd feeling of déjà vu. As if he were seeing his own future. Work-obsessed, surrounded by darkness…

And alone.

He felt a chill.

Snyder shouldn't be keeping all of this stuff in his house. You can't live with it. It's too much.

And it was no wonder Snyder wasn't married. What normal person would want to have all of this with her all the time?

It doesn't matter where you work. You bring it with you. You can't ask another person to live with this.

What did that mean for him and Monica? His chances of marriage, a family?

It was a fleeting thought, instantly shut down. Too much to bear, along with all the rest of it.

He seized on the file he was looking for. "Got you," he said, too loudly, to dispel the other thoughts.

A sound behind him made him twist around to face the doorway. He'd been so fixated on his inner turmoil he hadn't noticed Snyder step into the room.

"Didn't mean to startle you," the older agent said mildly. But Roarke felt it as a rebuke. In the middle of an active case, there was no excuse for letting down his guard.

He leapt into action to compensate. "I got a lead on the victim I texted you about. Brandi Hughes, seventeen, aka Brandon. Apparently Kennedy and a friend found Hughes half-dead in a warehouse where a lot of the street kids flop."

He quickly filled Snyder in on Hughes' injuries, saw Snyder's eyes contract in empathy. But otherwise the older agent was quiet while Matt was speaking. *Too quiet,* Matt thought at one point, but forced himself to concentrate on relating the details of the attack on Hughes.

When he'd finished, Snyder walked the room absently. His gaze went to the file in Matt's hand. "And that?

"It's Lombard's. The monger with the assault on the trans kid. Another trans kid, similar assault…" He was feeling an urgency he couldn't define, a need to be out there on the street looking for *this* guy. The one who so brutally attacked Kennedy's friend. "I think this is the guy."

He had no way of knowing that. It was just overwhelmingly how he felt.

He didn't add, *And I think he's out there now. Tonight.*

Chapter 53

Portland – 2009
Cara

She stands on a dark street, the one that Brandi had named and described as "hers." The surrounding buildings loom around her, their windows blank and dark. The one corner streetlamp is out.

The only glimmer of light comes from the moon. Clouds obscure it, then pass, but every few minutes it shines through again with implacable brightness, a white heat that ripples on her skin.

She'd rented a motel room nearby, the kind of place where the clerks don't ask for ID or engage in anything by way of conversation. In the dismal little cube, she'd dressed in her new acquisitions. Looking into the mirror of the bathroom, she found herself unrecognizable.

It is part of her survival strategy to mimic, to constantly become other people. But of all the many personas she has taken on, this may be the most extreme. Even just standing on the street, she feels like a different person entirely.

She suspects that Brandi is an example of her attacker's specific trigger. A boy who is not a boy. A girl who is not quite a girl. It is almost surely that Otherness that attracts and enrages.

So she has taken Brandi as a model, has incorporated that sense into her costume. The bedraggled pop-icon-ness. The sad flamboyance. Boots that make her gait a bit clunky. And hidden in the right boot there is one more item she has obtained. The key to everything.

She stands on Brandi's usual corner, betting that "John" will stop if he sees a carbon copy of Brandi on the street. He won't be able to help himself.

A rain starts, a light mist, and she walks the block to keep warm.

Against her will, she thinks of Jamie, and the hurt in his eyes when she told him she was leaving. She knows she has been cold. Colder than he deserved.

Brandi's voice whispers in her head. *"But you. You're not good."*

How can she possibly tell someone like Jamie the truth? The things she's done… he would recoil from her in horror if he knew.

No one will ever know her. Not if she can help it.

No one should have to share this darkness.

Chapter 54

Portland - 2009
Matt and Snyder

Snyder walked the study. He took his time before he finally answered Matt.

"It does look like you're on to a serial offender. But we're talking about a substantially different pattern of assault from the one on Young John Doe. That boy was savaged in a particular way. The killer's intent was prolonged torture—it was only the boy's death that circumvented that. The beating you're describing is savage—

"And Lombard was arrested for a savage beating. On a trans kid." Matt could hear his own voice rising.

Snyder turned to face him. "All right, what's bothering you?"

Matt tried to moderate the intense emotion going on inside him. "There's something here. I can feel it."

He would never have said those words to anyone besides Snyder. But from the first day of their acquaintance, Snyder had encouraged him to trust his intuition. And Snyder didn't criticize him for it now. Instead he answered with calm reason.

"You know that chances are, whoever attacked Brandi, this person is not going to be out there tonight doing the same thing again so soon."

"Unless the killer is decompensating," Matt argued.

In the syndrome known as decompensation, the cooling-off period disappeared, and killers were known to go on sprees, with little or no time between attacks.

"True," Snyder acknowledged. "But the fact remains, Brandi Hughes was not killed. Viciously attacked, yes. But not murdered. Rape and beatings like this are terribly common in the street life."

Matt understood. And it was Snyder's case, Snyder's call. Yet the feeling remained. Something was happening, something he needed to prevent.

Something *now.*

He stood suspended for what seemed like a lifetime.... then Snyder half-laughed. "All right. Obviously your gut's talking to you. What do you want to do?"

Matt felt a tidal wave of relief. "I think we should interview Lombard."

"You have the address?"

"Yes." Matt had to fight not to shout. "Yes. Thank you."

He was already moving for the door.

Chapter 55

Portland - 2009
Cara

She spots the car cruising about eleven-thirty pm. Exactly as Brandi has described it: a dark blue Honda Civic. About as non-descript as a car could be.

The car slows as it passes her. The driver is hunched on the far side of the car and obscured in shadow. Her heart beats faster, and she shifts languorously on her feet, as she has seen so many street children do, inviting scrutiny. The car doesn't stop, rather makes a left at the corner and disappears into the dark.

She stays as she is, waiting, keeping up her pose....

As she anticipated, the Honda returns from the same direction, obviously having circled the block. This time it slows to a stop at the curb in front of her.

She thinks of Brandi's strutting swagger, and mimics it as she teeters over to the car. The driver lowers the passenger side window.

She places her arms, encased in elbow-length evening gloves, on the roof of the car, leans down to look inside….

And sees the gleaming eyes of *It.* The jagged teeth, the salivating mouth.

She hides her recoil, makes her voice low and husky, like Brandi's sultry contralto. "Want a date?

He reaches across the front seat and pushes open the door. She lowers herself into the seat, pulls the door closed.

He drives.

Chapter 56

Portland - 2009
Matt and Snyder

Matt sped Snyder's Jeep on the downtown street. On the seat between him and Snyder was a search warrant for Lombard's house, newly signed by a judge. Since the discovery of the bodies of Denise Vickery and Young John Doe, the Portland PD and DA's office had kept a judge on twenty-four hour call in order to get emergency warrants signed as quickly as possible.

Matt was sweating from tension—and an inexplicable, unshakeable certainty of mortal danger.

For Brandi Hughes? For any one of the hundreds of teenagers sleeping on the streets tonight?

But the feeling was so overwhelmingly intimate.

"Turn here," Snyder ordered.

The houses on this residential block were fairly large, though most had seen better days. Lombard's address was down a long driveway, behind one of the bigger homes. Not exactly a cottage—it looked more like a converted garage with its own fenced yard and privacy. According to the DMV, Lombard was the registered owner of a 1997 dark blue Honda Civic, but there was no car parked in the long driveway running beside the main house.

And there were no lights on in the little house.

The agents got out of the Jeep and approached.

Snyder took a position beside the doorstep with his service weapon drawn while Matt knocked, then pounded on the door. But there was no answer and no sound from within.

The warrant authorized entry, and it was no great feat for Matt to kick the door open. The impact was a welcome release of tension. The agents went in, weapons leading. The adrenaline rush of entry hit Matt like a speeding train as the agents swiveled, shouting, "FBI!" "Drop all weapons and come out with your hands up!"

Their search was short. The house was just two rooms, a cluttered living area with a kitchenette, and a stale-smelling bedroom with a small bathroom. There was clearly no one home here, just a lingering, greasy presence.

The bed was unmade. Dirty dishes were piled in the sink. Which judging by the state of the house in general, could mean Lombard was just out for an hour, or had been gone for a week. It didn't look like he'd packed anything. Matt highly suspected that what they were seeing was how the man lived.

And he was gripped by an overwhelming dread that he and Snyder were somehow too late.

Chapter 57

Portland - 2009
Cara

There is a smell to this "John," like stale grease or unwashed sheets.

Sitting in the passenger seat as he drives, Cara takes shallow breaths to conceal her terror and loathing.

He makes a right turn down an unlit street. She stares out the windshield. Dark cars at the curb. Dark buildings, closed, empty. No one walking on the sidewalk. Advantageous to him, he thinks. It will be to her as well.

In the murky dim of the car, she stares into John's lap. He is already aroused, thinking about what will come next.

Good. More blood to the area means he will die that much faster.

He slows the car, looking ahead to a space at the curb.

Now. While he is distracted.

She reaches between his thighs with her left hand, while she slips her right hand down her right leg toward the knife she stole from the thrift shop, now concealed in her right boot. The steel is cold, razor sharp. As her left fingers stroke his bulge, she closes her fist around the sheath of the knife, straightens in one smooth motion, and stabs the knife into the crease at his hip, where his leg is attached.

The femoral artery.

In the same movement as the stab, she twists the knife, opening the cut, making it deep and jagged to prevent the artery from doing its lifesaving trick of contracting to close off the cut.

She hears *Its* hiss in John's sharp intake of breath, feels the car swerve with John's shock. His first instinct is to grab the wheel to correct it. His second is to snarl a curse at her.

Both fatal mistakes. Because with every anger-elevated beat of his heart, blood spurts from the wound in his thigh as if from a cut garden hose. A severed femoral artery means unconsciousness is only thirty seconds away. Already he will be feeling drowsy.

She presses back against the passenger door, out of his reach.

The car is slowing, drifting. He no longer has the strength required to depress the gas pedal.

And only now does he grab for the wound, a late attempt to apply compression.

She reaches for the steering wheel, turning it toward her to keep the car marginally straight on the road. The bumper grazes another, parked car, which effectively stops the Honda.

"You… bitch…" he says. Barely able to keep his eyes open, now. *Systemic shock.* She leans back against the passenger door and watches the pumping blood slow. He writhes sluggishly. Slow, useless movements.

His eyes close. His bowels release.

Three minutes, total.

She stares out the windshield at the dimly lit street. There is no one moving, no sound but the wild beating of her own heart.

She uses the lever on the side of the passenger seat and lowers the seat to a nearly horizontal position. She leans toward the corpse and grabs its arms, pulls its torso across the console out from under the steering wheel and half into the passenger seat beside her. It takes some effort, but she is flying on adrenaline and the body seems much lighter than it is.

She opens the passenger door, gets out of the car and shuts the door behind her, walks around to the driver's side. She reaches inside the car to manipulate the lifeless legs over onto the passenger side, arranging the body to look as if "John" is asleep in the seat. She turns to the back seat, grabs a rain jacket she'd spotted earlier, and lays over the bloody, stinking mess on the driver's seat before sitting behind the wheel herself.

Then she restarts the car and drives.

Chapter 58

Portland - 2009
Matt

Lombard's computer was right there, as if he had just been on it.

Adrenaline was burning through Matt's veins and it was almost unbearable to have to sit, to force himself to focus and read, rather than break heads.

The first screen that came up was the Backdoor website. Lombard's bookmarks list showed other sex forums. But Matt's eyes were fixed on the log in.

Lombard was Devil Dawg.

Matt's brain was racing to reconcile the contradictions. *Lombard is online flaunting expertise with female sex workers, and warning other mongers off trans hustlers. At the same time, he's been accused of sexual assault on a male hustler...*

He turned as Snyder entered the room, and stopped, seeing Matt's face. "What is it?"

"I've been watching this guy online. He posts under the name 'Devil Dawg'. He's an active poster, what they call a pooner. Always holding forth, warning other johns against law enforcement on the street, boasting about being able to spot trannies. But we know Lombard's assaulted a transvestite sex worker before, a sexual assault. He puts on this front of being aggressively heterosexual, when his tastes are something else altogether."

Snyder finishes, "So he's been creating character witnesses—a virtual alibi for himself." The other agent raises his arm and only now does Matt notice that he is holding an oversized book. "And it gets more interesting."

Matt stands as Snyder puts the book down on the desk and they look down at a scrapbook full of newspaper clippings. News articles about the Street Hunter.

We've got him, Matt thought wildly. "He's saving his clippings."

Snyder shook his head. "I'm not so sure. He's highlighting details of the murders in the news articles. But the questions he's jotting in the margins read more like he's trying to figure out who the Street Hunter is. And there's this." He turned a page to a later article, pointed to a notation in the margin. A name, underlined several times: ***Hammerhead***.

Snyder looked up from the article. "That sounds like one of those forum handles to me."

"It is," Matt said, through a mouth gone suddenly dry. "I know that name."

Chapter 59

Portland – present
Singh and Snyder

Singh stares at Agent Snyder, realizing. "So you found the Street Hunter…"

Snyder nods. "Because of what we learned that night in John Lombard's house. We were extremely fortunate that Lombard wasn't expecting a police search. And that he was a slob. We'd specifically asked for his computer in the warrant since Brandi Hughes did some advertising online. And what we got off Lombard's computer led us to Robert Jonah Barker. The Street Hunter."

It is well after dark. Agent Snyder has been speaking for over eight straight hours, with only occasional interjections by Singh, to postulate Cara's part in the action. She can hear the raggedness in his voice. Her own body is cramped from sitting still for so long. Yet she has no desire to leave or even to get up. There is too much swirling inside her head.

She has been assuming that Lombard would be revealed to be the Wolf. And that while Cara was circling the case she somehow crossed his path.

But what Snyder is revealing now seems to contradict everything she has been thinking.

"Lombard had pinpointed Barker's online identity by following information in the news about the Street Hunter. He'd gone back into old Portland Backdoor forums and found posts that he believed were the Street Hunter's. He'd even saved printouts of conversations, which we passed on to Seattle PD."

He gives Singh a tired smile. "As so often happens in these cases, the takedown was neither action-packed nor glamorous. Barker wasn't even living in Portland any more. Seattle PD arrested him at his work. DNA tests proved he was the Street Hunter. He was arraigned in Seattle for the murders of four of the six known Seattle victims, including Charlie Laithwaite, and for the Portland murder of Denise Vickery. He pled 'not guilty' to all."

Singh's brow furrows as she tries to make sense of it. "I'm afraid I do not understand. *Was* Lombard the second killer? Did he attack Brandi Hughes, and kill Young John Doe?"

"Matthew was quite convinced of that. But when Seattle PD arrested Barker, Brandi Hughes came forward and identified him as her attacker. There was no proof that Barker was in Portland, but he had no alibi for the night. So—" Snyder lifted his hands.

"So the police were inclined to believe Brandi Hughes," Singh murmurs.

"There was no reason not to," Snyder answers. "Then as you know, Barker was killed in jail by another inmate while awaiting trial. Since Barker was dead, Brandi Hughes never had to testify under oath." He frowns. "I myself thought that Matthew was on track about Lombard being Hughes' attacker." He looks at Singh. "But now, knowing that Cara Lindstrom was here… I'm inclined to doubt everything I thought I knew."

Singh feels a buzzing in her temples. Perhaps she has not been wrong after all. "What happened to Lombard?" she asks carefully.

Snyder nods to her. "Ah. That's the question we all should have been asking. Once you told me that Lindstrom was here, I started an online search. And as far as I've been able to determine, John Lombard didn't just leave town the night we searched his house. He disappeared. There is no further public record of him whatsoever."

The two agents look at each other through the shadows of the study.

"Cara," Singh says.

"Cara," Agent Snyder repeats. "Or—we've both gone completely off the deep end."

Singh laughs shakily. They both fall into silence, contemplating. Finally Singh asks, tentatively.

"Was there any evidence at all to link Barker to Young John Doe?"

Snyder looks at her. "There was not."

"Then… did ASAC Roarke believe—do *you* believe—Lombard was the second killer, the one you called the Wolf?"

Snyder sighs. "The Wolf was a theory with numerous holes. It's true that the body of young John Doe was moved, probably from some distance, and that the pattern of attack and killing was different from the MO of the Street Hunter. But the wolf fur found on his body doesn't prove he was killed in some other state and moved here. Remember that many, if not most, of the young runaways and homeless teens here come to Portland from other cities and states all across the country. They're hoping to escape abusive or regressive situations in their home towns and states. Young John Doe could have been a recent transplant to Portland. The wolf fur and mineral deposits found on his body could have come from his own clothes, his own contact with those elements, not from the killer's. The fur was just an anomaly that we latched on to that never conclusively proved anything."

Regret creeps into his voice. "Our best chance at learning the truth about Young John Doe would have been questioning Barker himself. But dead men tell no tales. And the Seattle and Portland police departments closed the Street Hunter case."

She looks at him in the firelight. "Yet you believe that this recent child killing, the Idaho case, is somehow linked to the Wolf."

He suddenly looks haggard in the low light. "Agent Singh, I don't know what I believe. Barker is dead. Lombard appears to be dead."

She leans forward impulsively, puts both her hands on his. "We will get to the bottom of it. We will sort it. But now I must leave you and we must both rest. Tomorrow we begin."

Driving back to her hotel, Singh is in turmoil. Not one, but three mysteries remain.

What happened to John Lombard?

Who killed Young John Doe?

And who broke into Agent Snyder's house to search his case files?

And she knows she is not going to wait until morning to find out.

When she walks in through the cathedral entrance of Church, the club is in full swing. Kennedy is there behind the bar, talking to one of the bartenders.

He recognizes her instantly, and excuses himself from his conversation to step over to her.

"I had a feeling I'd be seeing you again," he says.

His upstairs office is papered in posters and flyers from two decades of shows: on the walls, on the ceiling. The artwork is arresting, and many of the names recognizable to her. She takes it all in only briefly before she turns to him with her purpose.

"I understand that you knew a victim of the Street Hunter. One who survived."

Kennedy gives her a brief, startled look. "She… yes. It really was a miracle."

The next part Singh offers casually, as if this is information he has told her himself. "And it was you and your friend Mia who found Ms. Hughes after the attack?"

"Yes, we—" He stops, realizing what he has just admitted even as Singh is reaching for the police sketch of Cara.

Finally he says, "I don't think I'm going to answer that."

His hesitation tells all. Singh knows there is no need to produce the sketch of Cara again. Both of them know of whom they are speaking. She moves on.

"Did Brandi talk to you about who attacked her?"

"She didn't want to and I didn't want to press her." His face tightens. "I know it was Barker, though. That came out later after she went to the police and identified him in a lineup."

"Did Brandi talk to your mutual friend about it?"

The question surprises him, enough so that he responds. "Not that I know of."

"But she may have."

Singh is almost certain that Roarke was correct, that it was John Lombard who attacked Brandi, not the Street Hunter. She is almost certain that Cara killed Lombard. And perhaps... Brandi never mentioned Lombard so that his murder would be less likely to be discovered.

She can tell from the distant focus in his face that Kennedy is thinking of a specific incident. "She could have," he says finally. "When we visited Brandi at the hospital..." He trails off, then says abruptly, "You know Mia, don't you? Is she all right?"

Singh hesitates. Will Kennedy's life be improved by knowing the truth about this woman who clearly meant something to him? She thinks not. So she says nothing. The pieces are there for him to put together, should he choose to do so.

"Is Brandi all right?" she asks instead.

"Brandi's fine."

More than fine, as it turns out.

Singh is able to see her first thing the next morning, because of the job that she does, as an anchor on an early morning local TV talk show. When Singh calls the station, she is told she can see Brandi after the broadcast; the show finishes its live filming at eight am.

She goes not because it will change anything, or help anyone, but because of the allure of the mystery. Perhaps because she needs some real world, tangible confirmation of the tale she is weaving in her own head. She needs to know.

A production assistant leads her to a green room, where Brandi Hughes sits on a sofa in front of a low table with a tray of coffee and pastries.

The street waif Singh has been picturing has grown into an elegant, sophisticated woman, with sharply cut hair, sharper cheekbones, and a commanding style. She indicates an armchair with a manicured hand, and looks Singh over so frankly Singh feels a frisson of sensuality.

"So that doll Jamie Kennedy sent you." Brandi's voice is a smoky purr. "That's a flash from the past. What can I do for you, my love?"

"I am Special Agent Singh of the San Francisco FBI."

Brandi arches an eyebrow, leans back and crosses exquisite legs. "I surrender."

Singh half-smiles. "I have only a few questions, if I may. They concern Robert Jonah Barker."

Brandi's face shadows. "That *is* ancient history." She is agitated, as of course one would be. She puts a hand out, reaching for the table, and stops mid-reach. Singh has seen it before: a gesture that smokers make before remembering the smoking ban.

"Damn," she murmurs.

But is that agitation also a show?

Singh leans forward. "Barker is long dead. The case is closed. There is nothing whatsoever official about my interest, only my personal need to know." Brandi sits silent, waiting, so Singh continues. "Are you quite sure that it was Barker who attacked you?"

Brandi laughs. "Sugar, I like attention as much as the next girl. Maybe a tad bit more. But that doesn't extend to breaking my own ribs to play like I'm the one surviving victim of a serial killer."

"I have no doubt the attack was real," Singh says quietly. "I am deeply sorry for the trauma you endured. It is the identification of your attacker I have questions about. Is it not possible… that you were wrong?"

To her credit, there is no flicker of recognition on Brandi's face. "Oh, I know the man who attacked me."

Singh does not relent. "I believe that man was not Barker. Could it instead have been a monger named John Lombard?"

Brandi looks at her steadily, unsmiling. "Why would I lie?"

"Perhaps... to protect a friend."

"A friend?"

"A friend who went after your real attacker." Singh places the police sketch of Cara on the coffee table in front of them. Brandi stares down at it.

"Why, isn't that the woman who's been reported to have killed so very many men across the U.S.?" Her eyes slide up to meet Singh's. "Very bad men, if I'm not mistaken. Surely you don't think I know her?"

Now it is Singh who sits, silent, waiting.

"Well, don't I wish!" Brandi laughs. "That would be a newswoman's dream, to say the least. No, alas. I've never had the pleasure." Her voice hardens. "But good on her."

She pushes the sketch back to Singh. "Are you hunting her?"

Her tone is admirably casual.

"That is not my job," Singh answers evenly.

The two women sit across from each other, silent, unmoving. After a moment Singh puts the sketch back in her bag and stands. "I thank you for your time. I am happy to see life has turned out so well for you."

Brandi stands as well, extending a hand to shake. "It's been a pleasure." She meets Singh's eyes, before looking away. "If you ever do find her, give me a call. I would kill for that interview."

Chapter 60

Portland - present
Singh

Singh drives from the studio to Agent Snyder's house under black skies and pelting rain. The radio is full of ominous warnings about flash flooding in several counties.

Snyder's study seems a complete haven by comparison. There is a fire in the fireplace and Singh sinks gratefully into one of the tall armchairs, feeling her lack of sleep like an undertow as she fills Agent Snyder in on her talk with Brandi Hughes.

Agent Snyder's eyes are clear this morning, and he is sharply attentive. "You believe Brandi told Cara about her attacker, and Cara killed him. Meaning Lombard."

"And Brandi identified Barker, the Street Hunter, as her attacker in order to protect Cara. Brandi would never say it aloud, but..." she remembers the look in Brandi's eyes. Satisfaction. Amusement. "It is my strong guess," she finishes. "I needed to confirm because there is still the question of the intruder who has been after your files."

"It seems we can eliminate Lombard," Snyder says wryly.

"Agreed," Singh says. "So now we must consider the Wolf." Before he can interrupt, she continues. "Yes, it is only a theory, but the theory seems more than plausible to me. We need to examine the case of the murdered boy in Idaho."

"Montana," he murmurs.

She is certain he had said Idaho, but for the moment she does not press him. She leans forward intently. "You and ASAC Roarke went up in January to investigate reports of a murder of a young boy. And your notes on that case are now missing."

Agent Snyder pauses at some length before he speaks. He seems to be consolidating his thoughts. "I was advising local law enforcement on the investigation. But yes. On the surface, it appeared a completely different case. The victim was a much younger boy who had been held for several days and horrifically abused before he was killed. We know that statistically killers of teens are not likely to suddenly start hunting much younger children. But—the boy had been abducted during a family trip to Glacier National Park in the fall."

The mention of the national park gives Singh a start. She has been acutely interested in national parks during her chronicling of Cara's story. But more than that...

"Glacier is a geothermal region," she says. "You were thinking of the mineral deposits found on Young John Doe's body. And the gray wolf fur."

He nods to her gravely. "Yes. Exactly. Gray wolves are indigenous to the region. And the nature of the violence done to this boy... the MO was similar to the attack on Young John Doe. There was no way not to think of the Wolf. So I asked Matthew to come up to the crime scene with me." He stops, shakes his head. "'Ask' is perhaps not the correct word. To say he was reluctant would be putting it mildly. I called in some chips."

Chapter 61

Spokane, Washington - three months ago
Roarke and Snyder

Roarke felt the mistake of it as soon as his plane began the descent. What he saw beneath him was a city spread over a high plain, ringed by mountains. And snow. Snowy trees, snowy streets, snowy buildings, an ice-white river.

Spokane. The eastern edge of Washington, where the desert meets the Rockies.

Snyder's crime scene was near Kellogg, in the Idaho panhandle, alongside the Coeur d'Alene National Forest. Kellogg would be a seventy-mile drive, over the border into Idaho, but Spokane was the closest major airport.

Roarke's first stop was to pick up a rental vehicle.

"Make it an SUV," Snyder had warned him. "Get chains."

That should have been Roarke's clue. That and the fact that the panhandle was practically Canada. But as a native Californian, Roarke thought of snow only in the abstract, and as a necessary evil to be endured during ski season. Luckily there was no actual snow falling during his drive, though the white stuff was banked along the highway and frosting the trees. It looked damned cold out there.

But the drive on I-90 was spectacular, there was no denying that. He passed through the town of Coeur d'Alene, which according to billboards had a staggering fifty-five lakes, and into the Silver Valley of Shoshone County. Which was almost solid ice.

What the hell am I doing here?

But he knew.

He'd been hiding out in Pismo Beach, with no intention of doing law enforcement work for the foreseeable future, if ever again. But Snyder wasn't a psychological profiler for nothing. He knew exactly where Roarke's pressure points were, and he'd hit every one of them in his phone call.

"Based on missing persons reports we may be able to attribute at least one other child to this killer. The first disappearance was in Yellowstone, the second in Glacier National Park. Aaron Light's body was found only three weeks ago, and the level of damage done to the boy was extreme. It's almost certain that the killer has killed before."

Roarke's body and his mind flinched at once. *I can't do this,* he thought. His decision-making, his sense of judgment, his professionalism, had been completely shattered by the Lindstrom case, and his unforgiveable lapse with Cara herself.

Snyder had continued, quietly relentless. "There are no FBI field offices in Idaho or Montana. I can't help thinking that our unsub knows that. That fact, and the sheer acreage of those national forests makes these two states a perfect dumping ground. Add to that this region's isolationist tendencies… it's good hunting ground for a predator."

"And why do you think you need me?" Roarke asked.

"Fresh eyes," Snyder said instantly. "I'm not sure I'm thinking entirely clearly anymore."

I know the feeling, Roarke thought at him.

Snyder waited through the silence, finally spoke. "I understand your duties have become conflicting, of late."

He meant Cara. Snyder knew, or guessed, Roarke's ambivalence about chasing her, about jailing her. Snyder in fact had refused to help Roarke on the last bit of his search because he considered Cara's victims a far lower priority than the victims in his own case.

"But there's a difference between duties and the job, the work that you're meant to do. You can leave the duties for now and do your job. I need you on this, Matthew."

Before Roarke could demur, Snyder continued seamlessly. "Of course I won't mention all the time I've put into your Huntress investigation."

Roarke felt a wave of anger, and then amusement. Not only was Snyder right, he wasn't above some emotional extortion. "Of course you won't," he said dryly.

In the end, Roarke had promised him three days.

So here he was, winding the rental vehicle through the snowy wilderness. And despite his reluctance, despite his distaste for winter weather, he felt the familiar surge: the excitement of the hunt. And a strange relief. Whatever else was in store for him here, he knew that Cara Lindstrom would be nowhere near where he was going. That alone might save him—

He applied the brake at a sudden, startling vision.

A thirteen-foot tall coal miner with glowing headlamp loomed up through the snowy trees, defiantly brandishing his rock drill skyward. A turnoff indicated the *Sunshine Mine Memorial,* a tribute to the victims of one of the worst mining disasters in US history.

Right, Roarke thought. *Welcome to Idaho.*

Snyder's hotel was a lodge on one of the myriad lakes, and the view from the front deck, looking out over the water, was impressive, if icy. Snyder had booked Roarke into a room. After a quick shower and a change to extra layers of clothes, he met his former mentor in the lobby, where antique mining equipment and hunting traps and animal head trophies made up the décor.

Snyder was easy to spot, encased in a high-tech parka, the kind of coat Roarke should have brought. The men shook hands and clasped shoulders warmly. As Snyder pulled back, though he said nothing, he gave Roarke a probing look that Roarke didn't like at all. He wondered if what was going on inside him was showing on his face, in his body.

Snyder himself showed a certain haggardness, a worrisome fragility. A long case, unsolved, took an exponential toll as the days went on: the frustration of dealing with local law enforcement, the psychological murkiness, and above all, the fear for the next victim. But Snyder wasted no time. "I want to take you out to the kill site, before we lose the light."

Roarke felt a bolt of adrenaline, simultaneous anticipation and unease. He followed Snyder out the door.

Outside the hotel, the cold hit them and Roarke shivered. Snyder gave him a withering look. "You and your California blood."

He zapped open the trunk of his SUV and pulled out an extra Arctic-rated parka, handed it over silently.

Roarke took it, muttered, "I'm getting too old for this." He halfway meant it.

Inside the vehicle was warmer. While Roarke drove, Snyder filled in the details of the case. The kill site was a hunting camp in a forest outside the border of the Coeur d'Alene National Forest.

"The boy was abducted from Montana. His body was found in the woods near a hunting cabin here," he said. "His blood was found in the cabin. The savagery of the killing bumped the case up to priority child sexual homicide right away."

Roarke felt a drop in his stomach. The violation of children was the worst of the worst. "But this hasn't been publicized?"

Snyder shook his head. "At first because Aaron Light wasn't seen being abducted. And he's from a complex family situation."

"Complex" never meant anything good.

"Turn here," Snyder said.

Snyder directed him off the main road to a trail head, where they parked the SUV. Outside the vehicle, Snyder went around to the back and pulled snowshoes out of the trunk. Roarke stared at him. "You're kidding."

"Unfortunately not. It's a miracle the boy's body was found before the spring thaw. Of course the killer was counting on that."

There was no more talking. The agents strapped the shoes on and set out through the forest. The snow was deep and showshoeing was a grueling slog. Roarke was sweating and both hot and freezing by the time they hiked between the last trees into the clearing of the camp. At which point he was seriously worried about Snyder. The older man was in good shape, but Roarke's own legs were shaking from exertion.

Any thought of his own discomfort dissipated as he surveyed the clearing.

It may have been only a mile from the road, but it felt like the end of the earth. Roarke swallowed against the tightening in his throat. It was a terrible, desolate place to die.

The shadows were already lengthening, the sun sinking in the sky, and now that they had stopped moving, the air had a chilling, lethal bite.

Snyder surveyed the area. "Three months ago there wouldn't have been snow, but it would have been close. That's undoubtedly why the unsub felt safe to leave the body in a relatively shallow grave. It wouldn't have been found at all, or not anywhere as soon as it was, except that animals sniffed it out, and the first big snow was late."

They removed their snowshoes by the side of the hunting cabin and entered. It was a dismal little wreck, apparently open for the use of any sportsman who wanted shelter.

Snyder looked around at the dark, dank, walls. He rummaged in his coat and pulled out the autopsy report. Roarke used his phone light to scan through. It was heartbreaking reading. Sodomy, lashing, bones broken while the victim was still alive. And the boy had been burned, with some implement.

"There was enough flesh left on the bones to get a tox reading. The free histamine levels were off the charts. He kept the boy for days."

Roarke listened to the list of injuries. It was all so sickeningly familiar. The same thing they saw over and over. Dominionism.

Men who thought they had some right to own other people. Women, children, other men. Hunters who thought they had the right to savage other living things.

A name came to him, unbidden.

The Wolf.

Snyder looked around the cabin. "Crime scene investigators found a significant quantity of the boy's blood here. And there's quite a bit of DNA evidence. Unfortunately it's from dozens of people, and animals as well. Possibly hundreds." He shook his head. "And I can't help thinking the unsub knew that was the case. He's confident. Arrogant."

The air in the cabin seemed to darken around them, and it took a moment for Roarke to realize it was not just his mood. Night was falling.

"This trail is cold," he said, and he didn't mean literally. "Why are we here?"

"I wanted you to see it," Snyder answered. "Feel it."

Roarke nodded. To get inside the mind of a killer, there was no substitute for being on site. This man was comfortable in the outdoors, in this bleak wilderness setting. He did not bring his young victim to his home, or any place in the indoors. He was a hunter, of animals and children. They would find him in a mountain setting. He would own guns. Lots of guns.

An animal howled somewhere in the distance, and Roarke felt a chill that was not from the freezing air. Suddenly he wanted very much to be gone.

"I've felt it," he said. "Now tell me what you really have in mind."

Snyder nodded. "Back at the lodge."

The night was pitch black, studded with icy stars.

Back at the hotel, the agents both changed out of sweat-soaked clothes, showered, and met downstairs in the dining room. The bar area had tables in front of a floor-to ceiling fireplace with a blazing fire, and Snyder had managed a table near the heat and away from other patrons. After they'd ordered, Roarke just said it. "Look, I know what you're thinking."

"Do you?"

"The Wolf."

Snyder raised his hands. "It's true. There was wolf fur and the same kinds of mineral deposits, sulfur and calcium, found on Aaron Light's body—"

Roarke interrupted. "If you're going just on the basis of some wolf fur and mineral deposits, you can find that in other places besides Glacier..." he trailed off, remembering the other child disappearance in Yellowstone that Snyder had mentioned. If that other boy had been murdered—*if*—then that autopsy might well turn up the same kinds of mineral deposits and animal fur.

Snyder held up a hand. "The Wolf is a side issue. Just hear me out. The joint task force of local law enforcement agencies is focusing its efforts here, in Idaho, because this is where the freshest crime scene is."

"But?" Roarke said.

"But they don't need us for that. I have something else in mind. Hours before Aaron was abducted, the family passed through a town called Snake River, Montana. There's a witness there, a female who phoned in to the tip line anonymously, saying a local man was watching Aaron. I want to go to Snake River and try to find her."

He looked across the table, and the plea was naked in his eyes. "Three days, Matthew. All I'm asking is three days—"

A harsh bleating shatters the silence.

Chapter 62

Portland - present
Singh and Snyder

Singh nearly jumps out of her skin at the sound. Snyder has risen from his armchair, equally startled.

The alarm is coming from both of their phones, and the Amazon Echo, and Snyder's laptop—all devices shrilling at the same time, sounding an alarm. A recorded voice speaks mechanically.

"This is an announcement of the Emergency Broadcasting System. This is not a test. Flash flooding has been reported in parts of Multnomah, Clackamas, Columbia and Washington counties..."

The spoken warning repeats over the klaxoning of the alarm.

Singh is on her feet, moving to the window as if mesmerized. The sky outside is blacker than she has ever seen it in daylight. The rain looks like a solid wall of water.

Snyder is behind her. "You can't go out in that. You'll stay in the guest room, of course. I can rustle up dinner."

Singh surrenders to the moment. "And you can finish your story."

Snyder is silent. She turns to find him staring into the crackling fire.

"Agent Snyder?"

He looks at her blankly, and then shakes his head. "There isn't any more to tell. We didn't go to Montana. Matthew got the call from Sheriff's Detective Ortiz. He returned to California and went out into the desert."

Singh begs off dinner, as she has had next to no sleep the night before.

When she runs out to her car to fetch her go bag from the trunk, the violence of the wind and water is unnerving. She comes back into the house completely drenched and thankful she does not have to venture further out in such chaos.

Agent Snyder shows her to the guest room, which is clean and uncluttered by files.

She changes from her wet clothes into a T-shirt and leggings, then calls Damien and leaves a voice message to report on the flash flooding and assure him she is safe at the house.

She disconnects with a relief out of proportion to the situation that he is not there to answer her call. She needs time with her own thoughts, to process Agent Snyder's story.

She has many unanswered questions.

She settles into bed with her laptop and starts her own hunt.

She is able to find numerous reports of Aaron Light, the five-year old missing from Glacier. The boy was vacationing with his mother and stepfather and the stepfather's two other, older children. All the news reports focus on a possible parental abduction by the estranged father. Singh can find no reports of a body being discovered. The National Center for Missing and Exploited Children database lists Aaron as still missing.

She frowns and checks the time. Still before 5:00 pm. Impulsively she picks up her phone and dials information, asks for the Snake River Sheriff's Department.

The male voice that answers is steely. "Sheriff Preston."

She knows rural sheriff's departments tend toward skepticism, if not outright hostility, toward the FBI. She introduces herself instead as a child advocate from an organization to which she is a regular contributor.

"I have just a few questions regarding a murder investigation you conducted in January—"

The sheriff does not let her finish. His voice is hard. "Lady, I don't know what country you're calling from, but you're confused. We got no murder up here."

She flinches at the casual xenophobia, but keeps her tone even.

"I am speaking of the five-year old missing from Glacier National Park in—"

Preston interrupts her. "The kid's father took him. I suggest you get your facts straight and stay the hell out of people's business."

Before Singh can speak again, he has hung up on her.

She sits still in the bed, unnerved by the outright denial. Outside, the wind lashes rain against the windows.

After some minutes she stands from the bed and runs through a yoga set, using the stretches and meditation to dissipate the negative energy of the encounter.

Then she settles back into the comfortable bed. But for some time, sleep eludes her. There is something about the whole story that feels strange to her, feels wrong.

When she does drift off, it is to anxious nightmares of a formless pursuer.

And sometime after two, she wakes in terror. With the absolute knowing there is someone in her room.

Chapter 63

Singh doesn't breathe. She inches a hand out toward the drawer of the bedside table, where she always keeps a weapon.

Then she remembers she is not at home. There is no weapon to reach for.

In the days after she was attacked in the garage of her loft building by the armed online trolls, she slept with the Glock under her pillow, in addition to the knife she has always kept in her bedtable drawer.

But she has surrendered her sidearm to Roarke.

"Agent Snyder?" she asks, and hears the tremor in her own throat. Her pulse shoots higher when there is no response from the shadow.

"Matthew," the intruder says hoarsely, and through her terror she recognizes his voice. Her eyes focus in the dark.

Snyder stands, swaying, dressed in pajamas and a robe. His eyes are unfocused and he is in such distress, she is sure that he is sleepwalking, not conscious of where he is or who she is.

She keeps her own calm. "Agent Snyder," she says firmly.

"Matthew," he says again. "It's the Wolf. We didn't get him. We didn't get him. *He's out there.*"

Instead of turning on the bedside lamp, she rises from the bed, slowly, cautiously. "I'm here," she says, not attempting to identify herself or correct him.

"The Wolf," he says again, urgently. "We have to get him."

"We will talk about it in the morning," Singh says. "Now you must sleep." She approaches him with soft footsteps, touches her hand to his arm. "Come."

He does not speak again, but allows her to lead him out of the room, down the L-shaped hall to his bedroom.

His room is a master suite, a bed area and a sitting area with fireplace, a bathroom off to the side, sliding glass doors to another small deck. There is a small lamp on and files are spread all over the table and love seat of the sitting area. He must have been working long into the night, and their grisly subject matter worked its way into his dreams.

She leads him to the bed. He sinks down into it like a child, and she pulls the down quilt up over him. He is instantly asleep—if he was ever awake at all.

She returns to her own room, and with reluctant practicality bars the door with a chair.

Her heart is racing as she lies down on the bed. She feels as if the solid walls around her have suddenly dissolved.

Immediately she rises again, and reaches for her phone.

Roarke answers on the first ring, his voice tense with adrenaline. She regrets the late-night call, but it is far beyond time for them to talk.

She forces herself to sit calmly at the small writing table in the guest room. Methodically, succinctly, she explains everything. The ransacked files and the file Agent Snyder claims is missing. The murdered boy from Montana. The similarity of that attack to the killing of Young John Doe, and Snyder's conviction that the murders are related, and possibly connected to the theoretical killer Roarke and Snyder called "the Wolf." And her own call to Sheriff Preston and his denial of the Aaron Light investigation.

Roarke is silent for such a long time she is not sure he is still on the line. Then he says, "Chuck is confused. The only case we were ever on in Montana was one we worked years ago."

For a moment she wonders if he has not understood. She begins, "He has been speaking of when you went to Idaho in January to follow up on the case—"

"We didn't go to Idaho to follow up on the Wolf. Ever."

The agitation in his voice is so pronounced, that Singh knows her worst fear has been confirmed.

Roarke speaks again. "I called Chuck in December when the team was investigating the pimp murders in the Tenderloin and on International Boulevard. He told me then he was in Idaho, assisting in a child killing investigation."

She is grasping for questions that will help her understand. "Did he say that investigation involved the Wolf?"

"*There is no Wolf.*" His voice is hard. "It was a theory we had a long time ago. Chuck wasn't in Idaho in January or Montana in December. He's confused."

Singh can hear Roarke's harsh and elevated breathing. She knows, beyond a doubt, that he would never lie about something like this.

"I understand," she says, barely able to force the words out.

"I didn't send you up there to—" He stops, and she senses he is unable to finish.

"I will take care of Agent Snyder," she tells him, softly.

"Thank you," he says. And for a moment she thinks he has disconnected. Then he says, "He needs to rest. That's why he's retiring. Just get the files in order."

Singh places her phone carefully on the table and sits in silence.

She is reeling. But there is so much she understands, now. Perhaps even that she is not in as much disgrace as she had thought, except possibly with herself. She has completely misinterpreted her assignment. Roarke has sent her to watch Agent Snyder, not the opposite.

This does little to alleviate the heartbreak she is feeling over this revelation. Or the profound responsibility she feels, to be worthy of the task she has been given.

Her phone pings, announcing a text. She lifts her phone and sees a message from Roarke.

It is a phone number and a name: Doctor Morales. She will call, of course she will. But she is already sure what the doctor will say.

Chapter 64

Portland - present
Singh and Snyder

She knows when she wakes that he is already up.

Fog is thick outside the windows. The rain has diminished to this lingering mist.

She has barely slept. Instead she has spent the night castigating herself.

Of course the signs have all been there, plain for anyone to see. The difficulty maintaining his train of thought. The confusion of dates. The nighttime ransacking of his own files with no memory of doing it. The paranoia.

But she has been caught up in her own mad theory, and has missed every warning. Instead of offering clarity and support, she has led Agent Snyder down her own rabbit hole of obsession.

She throws back her quilt, and forces herself to stand, to re-dress in the trousers and sweater she wore the day before.

Her heart is heavy as she walks down the hall toward the study. Agent Snyder is standing at the glass doors to the deck, and turns when he hears her step.

"I believe I owe you an apology."

His eyes are clear, his voice rueful. He is back from wherever he was. But now she knows that clarity is only temporary.

Last night she rehearsed a dozen different approaches to the subject in her head. Cautious, deferential, oblique.

But in the end, when she sits down with him on the familiar sofa and looks into his beloved face, she speaks straight out. "I have spoken with ASAC Roarke. Agent Snyder, he says there was no trip to Idaho in January."

He looks stricken, and before she can lose her nerve, she adds softly. "I believe that there is something you have not been telling me. It is time to tell me now."

And that is all that is required.

He confesses his diagnosis. Early stages of the scourge known as Alzheimer's disease.

"One morning I looked in the bathroom mirror and I didn't know if I was the person looking back at me. I knew then."

He is shaky, seeming so very much older than she has ever seen him. His body is racked with emotion.

"My mind. Feels like Swiss cheese. There are holes. The holes…" He presses his hands against his temples, as if to squeeze his brain. And then he looks up at her with stricken eyes. "Does this mean that none of it happened? None of it is true?"

She summons all her conviction. "Agent Snyder. *This* is true." She stands and turns in the room, gesturing to take in the files around them, the books, the news articles and photos on the walls. "You have done all of this. Yours has been a lifetime of fighting evil."

He is intently focused on her. She continues in a burst of enthusiasm.

"And there is more to do. We will do what we have been doing. We will enter all these files into ViCAP, just as we started. *That* is the work."

She is sure she can feel his energy lift, his spirit returning.

"Of course you're right. I forgot..." he stops, and finishes with irony. "I forgot myself."

They spend the rest of the day doing straight data entry into ViCAP. And there is something solid and right about doing this fastidious, repetitive business. It is not dramatic. It is not the stuff of movies. But it is the work that will put the predators away.

It is the path.

Chapter 65

Portland - present
Singh

For a third night in a row, she lies awake in her bed, listening to the hollow spiral of the wind.

She meant every word about the database being the *Work*. There is nothing better that she and Agent Snyder can do to bring his life to a culmination, to make a powerful stand against the dark. She cannot mourn what may come for him, because the present is all any human being ever has. She believes with everything in her that the decline of the body, and death, is a release from this world of shadow into a higher consciousness. Of all the people she has ever known, Agent Snyder deserves that transcendence.

And yet her throat aches with unshed tears. She is missing Damien desperately. But to talk to him about all of this seems a betrayal of Agent Snyder. And she does not want to cry.

She turns over in her bed for the thousandth time that night, trying to find some comfort.

Then for some reason she recalls her brief phone call with Sheriff Preston.

His drawling, dripping voice. The deliberate insult to her citizenship. So scathing. So arrogantly insistent that there was nothing at all to her query about the murder of a child.

And he had been lying. She is utterly sure of it. Going so far as to deflect her inquiry with a racist comment. And for that moment in time, it had worked.

And so? Roarke has told you that there was no investigation in Montana. Agent Snyder has confirmed that he is ill. His story about the Wolf is a hallucination, nothing more.

She has even called in to the Bureau to inquire about Snyder's January assignment. He was never assigned to a child killer case, nor any case at all in Idaho.

And yet.

Perhaps more than anything it is the mention of the national park called Glacier that she cannot dismiss. In Singh's own theory, Cara spends much of her time in national parks.

And who is to say that theory is not just as insane as Agent Snyder's story? The murder in the Grand Canyon is the only one you have so far been able to find.

But is that not the entire point? That the chances of finding a corpse in the vastness of a wilderness park are next to nil?

Singh is certain Cara seeks the wilderness. She has seen her, if only briefly, that night in the desert. She will never be able to banish the image of Cara in the palm grove, in the desert wind, under the moon.

If Cara is able to see the very worst of people, then how else can she possibly survive, other than finding places where the number of human encounters she has is reduced to the absolute minimum?

This woman, this avatar, belongs in these uninhabited spaces. Surrounded by such haunting beauty.

So once again a national park has surfaced in this convolution of a case. And though it does not mean anything coherent on the surface, Singh finally realizes what she must do.

In the morning she drives to Agent Snyder's house.

She finds him in the study, seated at his wide desk, already at work at data entry. She stands across the desk from him. "Agent Snyder, I believe you."

Agent Snyder looks up at her through dazed eyes. But it is not the haze of disease, just simple confusion. She crosses to his side of the desk, pulls up a chair across from him, very close, and takes both his hands. "The night before last, when you mistook me for ASAC Roarke, you spoke of the Wolf.'"

He looks at her sharply. "What did I say?"

She takes a breath. "You said, 'He is out there. We didn't get him.' And I believe you. Your details may not be exact, but there is something you are sure of. You have done this too long not to know when there is grave threat."

His eyes light with determination—and hope.

"We are going to work this all out together, you and I. We will go to Montana. We will proceed as if it is all true. We will separate facts from confusion. If we do not, we will never know. And if there is any chance, any at all, that the lives of children are at stake, it is the only possible thing to do."

She feels his hands tighten on hers. "Yes. Yes. Thank you, Agent Singh."

PART FIVE

Chapter 66

San Francisco – present
Roarke

Roarke and Epps hovered in the upstairs corridor, running through silent preparations for entry. The weapons check. The slow breaths in to still pounding hearts. Establishing the eye contact that will keep an invisible thread of communication between them. A mutual nod of readiness.

Then they rounded the corner, striding through the hall with grim purpose, service weapons heavy on their hips, unbuckled and at the ready.

It was the third raid Roarke had taken part in in the last few months. One at a concrete plant being used as a meth lab and prison for a shipment of trafficking victims. One at a residential brothel operating out of a storage facility. Fatalities at both, after an entire career of none.

And now this one. Going down not in a stinking back alley or a filthy prison of a brothel, but in a clean, well-lit, well-maintained office in one of San Francisco's most prominent high-rises. There was no breaking the front doors open with a battering ram. The agents walked through the doors like businessmen, into the offices of Backdoor, the website where pimps posted photos and contact information for the women and teenagers they trafficked.

Roarke and Epps approached inner offices with warrants out and handcuffs extended, and the looks on the faces of the men behind the desks were the same as on any street hustler. Rage. Indignation. And that haunted flicker that maybe, just maybe, this time they were the ones who were well and truly fucked.

While Roarke and Epps recited Miranda warnings and cuffed their quarry, a team of Bureau accountants was already pouring in behind them, seizing records, confiscating computers.

It wasn't quite the adrenaline high of a street pursuit or shootout. But it was every bit as satisfying to perp-walk the suspects past the gathered clusters of their white-collar neighbors and peers, out through the front doors onto the street, and load them into the backs of the SFPD patrol cars that would take them in for booking.

Roarke and Epps shut the squad car doors on their collars and stood on the sidewalk with other onlookers, several of whom were shooting video with their phones as the black and whites drove away.

Roarke breathed in deep as Epps said, "Damn. That felt good."

Roarke had to agree. Taking down pimps in a back alley was one kind of triumph. Taking down privileged men who thought that the color of their skin protected their atrocities was a whole other kind of rush.

The high continued back at the Bureau, as Roarke and Epps did their victory lap around the office. And then Roarke headed for home on BART.

He sat back in his seat, watching the blur of tunnel through the train window, still pleasantly buzzed from the takedown. He had to admit he missed hunting. He missed the face-to-face.

But he knew the administration was the most important. He'd been aware of the festering sewer that was Backdoor since his first case as an agent, working on the Street Hunter killings. The owners had spent years making millions of dollars on the sale of teenage girls, laundering the profits.

He knew his emphasis had to be on shutting down the source, changing the mindset in law enforcement that still led to the arrests of the women and girls instead of the men pimping them and using them. Changing the mindset of the customers who told themselves and anyone who would listen that they were doing nothing wrong.

And there was a grim pleasure in holding the line. In saying, *Not on my turf. There might be a sexual predator in the White House, two on the Supreme Court, but that shit won't fly in California. Not while I'm still breathing.*

He got off at 24th/Mission to walk the last blocks, and he was already thinking ahead. Planning.

They'd just arrested half a dozen of the founders of one of the most profitable online "escort" ad websites. Next up was a targeted series of street busts, coordinated with the San Francisco and Oakland police departments. Arresting the pimps and funneling the teenage girls into MISSSEY and the Belvedere House to get the trauma counseling and life skills training they needed and deserved.

Roarke felt a pang at the thought of Belvedere. His mind went to Rachel Elliott. Rachel, the heart and soul of the Belvedere House. Rachel, who'd committed her life to rescuing these girls. He should have been working with her on this operation.

He wouldn't be on this path if not for her.

And Cara.

His phone buzzed in his coat pocket. Adrenaline shot through his already overloaded system. There were too many things the call could be, and almost none of them good.

The number was blocked. He clicked on without speaking, waiting for the caller to speak first. After a moment, they did.

"Hello."

The voice was agonizingly familiar. A voice he thought he might never hear again. Of course. Of course she would call now, today.

"Hello," he answered, and found himself unable to speak further.

"I saw what you did this afternoon," Rachel said. "You and Epps. Thanks for taking those scum down. But that's not why I'm calling. I got a package from a mutual friend of ours."

A mutual friend.

Cara.

A package?

"An electronic package," Rachel continued. "It's millions, Matt. I mean… millions."

She went silent, letting him work out what she meant. Money. An electronic transfer. A donation to Belvedere House?

As unlikely as it seemed, he could see it. Cara must have learned something about investing, to grow her inheritance into the kind of money it sounded like Rachel was talking about.

"It's not hard to guess what she wants done with it—" Rachel started.

"Don't—"

"I won't tell you," she finished for him. "But I thought you should know because…" her voice became careful. "Giving away your money, your possessions… it's something people do—"

When they're planning to end it all, a voice in his own head finished with her. His throat was suddenly dry.

"Yes. I see."

"So. That's about it." Her voice was a sigh.

"Rachel," he said.

She waited.

He wanted to say that she could come home. That whatever she was complicit to, she would almost certainly never be prosecuted for it. That he wanted her here, in the way that she wanted him to say that.

But none of that would be true. They were tied together. He could never deny that. But not in the way she wanted.

"Take care of yourself," he said. And heard the silence as she disconnected.

And immediately his mind was full of Cara.

She's alive.

He is flooded with exhilaration. And fear. Not for what she will do, but for what he might do.

He can hear her voice in the desert wind.

"Come."

Chapter 67

Death Valley, California – two days ago
Cara

She lies on her back in the sand, looking up into infinity. The vast blue-black bowl of sky blazes with a trillion stars. The desert wind is dry and gentle, matching her breath. Fine particles of sand brush her bare skin.

She should have left the state after that bloody night, a month ago in the Salton Sea. But the closest route, and the only realistic road, would have been I-10. Closest, and most obvious to anyone tracking her.

Instead she fell back, instinctively, on her lesson from the *Encounter* in the Grand Canyon, a dozen years ago. The only thing she knows to do in these moments is to seek *Beauty.* She followed the signs out of the Salton Sea and onto a complicated series of roads headed north through the center of the state. Then veered toward one of the wilderness places she is most comfortable with.

Death Valley National Park. Hundreds of microcosmic wildernesses all in one vast desert preserve: volcanic craters and blazing white salt flats and rainbow-colored canyons and sand dunes worthy of the Sahara.

She has stayed several weeks in this endless, alien landscape. After the refuge of Canyon de Chelly, returning to the world as it has become, and doing battle so soon after that, had been a profound shock.

But her old enemy is dead.

Overpowering Ortiz had been easy, thanks to the unexpected assistance of Roarke's teammate, Agent Singh. Faced with the two of them, the detective had had no chance.

She does not believe his online followers will come after her. Not now that they have seen the live online stream of Ortiz lying on the platform in the derelict hotel that he intended to use to broadcast his homemade torture porn.

Lying on the platform, fileted like a fish. His own equipment used against him.

She shuts the door on that horror, and turns her mind to other thoughts.

She does not want to leave this beauty and venture into the winter cold of other states. But she has indulged herself for too long. She must move, she must always move. Staying still is an invitation for *It* or anyone else to find her.

So for this last night, she lies with the one memory of that night she wants to keep. The feel of the wind on her skin, the sound of it rustling through dry fronds in the palm grove. And of Roarke standing in the sand under the desert moon, calling to her.

"I feel you. I always feel you."

The next day she drives.

She crosses the state line to pick up State Route 374 in Nevada. Through the ghost town of Rhyolite, with its sand-swept ruins of buildings, barely recognizable as a school, a train station, a bank.

She stops to explore the stone foundations of the buildings, and lingers at the skeletal bank. It pulls into focus a thought that has been growing in her mind.

From Rhyolite she picks up the 95 to Las Vegas.

She takes the precaution of switching vehicles. Many of the vacation houses in this corridor keep sports vehicles on the property, languishing in garages. She finds a Jeep Wrangler with black tinted glass, rugged enough for winter travel, and with a ski rack on the roof. She lifts some plates from a different car, also tucked away in a vacation home, and installs them on the Jeep. And helps herself to two sets of skis, always useful as a cover story.

She makes several stops for supplies. Traveling in cold climates in winter requires its own emergency gear. It is why she does it so infrequently. There is too much chance of something going wrong. She purchases snowshoes, Arctic gear, a powerful portable car heater to keep in the back of the Jeep.

And she makes one more stop. To a branch of her main bank. To do something she has been contemplating in the desert.

A near-death experience focuses the mind. She has never before been so certain of what she needs to do. The money has served its purpose. It has a new purpose now, and it is in good hands. Unburdening is a relief.

And now she drives.

I-15 is one of her favorite south-north routes, cutting through Arizona, Nevada, Utah, Idaho and Montana, with easy access to some of the greatest national parks in the country. Bryce, with its otherworldly rock spires. Nearby Zion, with its majestic domes. Then up through Wyoming, into Montana and all the way up to Glacier National Park, the "Crown of the North." In the winter there are far fewer visitors to these stupendous sites. She begins to look forward to the adventure.

What she does not wonder about is what she will do next. She will be led, as she always is. The signs will be clear.

Chapter 68

Portland - present
Singh and Snyder

And so they are off.

They have traded Singh's rental SUV for one with a ski rack installed, two pairs of skis locked into it. Just tourists on their way to the magnificent Northern slopes. It will be their cover story as they retrace this "imaginary" case Snyder has talked about, to investigate if there really is a child killer hunting in the national parks of Montana.

They have packed the car with winter gear, food, a portable heater. While Singh arranges the trunk, Snyder brings other items out. Two Glocks. A shotgun.

Singh's distaste must be evident on her face, because he looks at her wryly and apologizes. "We can't forget what we're going in to. No matter where we go, we will be out-gunned by people looking for any opportunity to use their weapons. We can't minimize that threat."

She nods, resigned, and watches as he stashes the weapons securely in a lock box in the back. She has a brief, uncomfortable moment of wondering if she should be worried.

But she has resolved to trust him. And that is what she intends to do.

They settle themselves into the vehicle, Singh at the wheel, Snyder in the navigator's seat. Their first destination is seven hours away. Kellogg, Idaho, where Snyder told her that he summoned Roarke in January. Where, in his story, the agents snowshoed out to a desolate hunting cabin, and Snyder told Roarke a tale of a young boy, abducted, assaulted, tortured, murdered; his savaged body left in the woods.

It now seems likely that Agent Snyder superimposed the details of the Portland victim, Young John Doe's murder, onto his mind's imaginings of what might have happened to Aaron Light, the five-year old missing from Glacier National Park.

And yet Singh is compelled to follow Snyder's story, to see what might be true in it. *True* is not the word she means. The better word is *real*.

Because there is *truth* throughout the story. It is the *real* that must be determined.

There is a troublingly illicit taint to the journey. She cannot tell Roarke of their plans, therefore she has not told Damien. He would object, and so strenuously and rationally that she would have difficulty arguing with him. It is not lost on her that she and Agent Snyder are headed into two of the whitest states in the entire US, in the middle of a virulent white supremacist wave. Ordinary activities, ordinary travel, have become perilous for persons of her skin color. She will proceed with all wariness.

But as she drives I-84 through Mount Hood National Forest, the meditative trance of the road begins to relax and lull her. It is hard to imagine viciousness in so pristine a wilderness. She notices details in appreciative silence: the glimmer of sun through primeval trees. The glint of river beside the road. She understands the pleasure Cara must take in the driving. The empowerment, and the peace. On the road it is easier to see this troubled nation in all its natural wonder and potential.

Snyder has been silent, also contemplating the scenery outside his window. He suddenly turns to her, and his face looks twenty years younger.

"I can't tell you how good it feels to be on the road again. It reminds me of the early days with Matthew… so much of those years together was driving."

"It reminds me of—" She stops, because she is about to say something that is not strictly true.

"What?" he asks.

"Cara," she admits.

Certainly Cara will have driven this exact road they are now on. In fact she may have taken it after her short stay in Portland, in 2009. Singh is almost positive that Cara did not go "back" to San Francisco, as she had told the musician Jamie Kennedy. Whatever she told him would have been the exact opposite of what she actually did.

"Ah. Yes," Agent Snyder says. "The road is Cara's domain. Its own universe, with its own rules. Something a bit magical."

It has been in Singh's mind. It is not unthinkable that they should find her.

"We shall see," Snyder says. And Singh has the feeling that he has heard her thought exactly.

Chapter 69

Utah - present
Cara

Outside her Jeep, flat desert turns to carved sandstone formations, and the paler colors turn to vivid pinks and reds.

She has been driving six hours through Nevada, now is entering Utah. She has decided on Bryce Canyon as her first stop, and has just made the turnoff at the UT-20 exit when she sees him.

A man in the road ahead. A dark figure who casts a shadow so long it can only be a dream... or destiny.

He does not extend his hand for a lift, but there can be no other reason that he stands there in the middle of nowhere, so still and waiting.

Picking up hitchhikers is not something she does. Ever. But as she drives past, she gets a glimpse of his face.

She has seen someone like him before. Perhaps she has seen him before. His ancient, ravaged face recalls the other, the man she met the night of her first kill. The man who called her "Monster Slayer."

She brakes the Jeep, and reverses along the road, bringing the vehicle to a stop beside him.

He nods to her and reaches for the door handle.

He pulls the door shut behind him and settles himself in the passenger seat, smelling of the earth, the wind, and sky.

As she shifts back to *Drive* and accelerates, he speaks to her harshly in what she recognizes as Diné. Navajo. The words she doesn't understand. But his gestures are unmistakable. He is pointing back the way she came, in the opposite direction, back to the interstate.

She looks at him. And he looks at her full in the face.

She slows the Jeep and makes the turn.

Chapter 70

San Francisco - present
Roarke

He woke from a dream of the road.

Without even getting out of bed, he reached for his phone to call Singh. And then he called Snyder, both his cell phone and his landline.

Neither was answering on any line.

And that wasn't good.

He called again en route to the Bureau. And once again in his office. Each time with the same result. Then he buzzed Epps, and paced in front of his desk, trying to define his unease. There was some kind of a confluence of things. Chuck's obviously worsening condition. Singh, believing his dementia fantasies. Rachel calling out of the blue, even as he had been thinking of her. Cara, suddenly on the radar again....

He was jolted back to the present at Epps' voice. "Chief?" The other agent stood in the doorway, frowning in at him.

Roarke shut the door behind him and got right to it. "Have you spoken with Singh today?"

The unease on Epps' face confirmed Roarke's suspicion. "Not since yesterday morning. We've texted and left messages, but—" He took a beat. "Her messages sound different. I feel like…" He said the next with obvious reluctance. "I feel like she's somewhere else."

All of Roarke's worst fears came flooding in on him. He was a fool to have thought Singh would passively accept a rehabilitation assignment. He was a fool to think he knew anything at all about women.

"What?" Epps said. The raw worry in his voice scared Roarke.

He spoke reluctantly. "There's a case I think they may be reinvestigating. Unofficially. There's nothing active about it—"

"But," Epps said grimly.

"But I think Singh may be taking it seriously."

He filled Epps in quickly. The strange call Chuck had made a few months ago referring to a serial child killer in Montana, which turned out to be completely untrue. Roarke's discovery that Snyder was exhibiting early signs of Alzheimer's. And then just a day and a half ago, Singh calling Roarke, believing that he'd actually gone to Montana with Snyder in January to consult on the case.

"I didn't go to Montana, and neither did Chuck. There was no child killing case. He was imagining it."

Epps' face was intent. "You explained all of this to Tara."

"Of course. Because of what Chuck had told her, she was thinking that this non-existent case in Montana was connected to a real case of ours from 2009. But that was before I talked to her. I told her, and she understood."

I hope, he added in his head.

Epps stood in a live silence as he thought it over. "*Have* you ever worked with Agent Snyder in Montana?"

Roarke felt his body tightening, his defenses going up. A sure sign that he knew exactly what was going on.

Epps looked at him with a sudden, keen awareness.

"Singh texted you this morning?" Roarke asked.

Epps said tersely, "A little after nine."

Roarke picked up the desk phone, punched in an extension. "This is ASAC Roarke. I need to trace some text messages. Expedite it. Special Agent Epps will give you the details." He handed Epps the receiver.

While Epps spoke to the tech, Roarke's mind was racing. They'd just finished an operation. All that was left for the next few days was paperwork. And suddenly he knew.

When Epps put down the phone, Roarke said, "Get your go bag. We're going to Portland.'

Chapter 71

I-15, Idaho - present
Cara

She has been driving for hours now, through Utah and into Idaho, and the Diné man in her passenger seat has not spoken again. He sits like a statue, not acknowledging her.

Then as they approach a sign, he speaks harshly in his own language, indicating the turnoff to Highway 20 at Idaho Falls.

She looks at him.

It is another road she knows well. Follow it for one hundred miles and you will hit the West Gate of Yellowstone National Park. Not just the first national park in the nation, but the first in the world. A wilderness on top of a volcanic hot spot, with dramatic canyons, alpine rivers, thick forests, world-famous geysers and bubbling pools of hot springs. Still the most visited park in all the U.S.

She has done this particular journey before. Once in summer, when the wildflowers are spectacular and the air is like crystal. She found it too crowded with tourists for her to fully enjoy.

But she has also done it once in snow.

Her passenger repeats whatever he has said, insistent. It is clear he wants her to make the turn.

She makes it.

A sign is a sign.

Two hours later they have crossed the state line into Montana. Outside the car is a world of white. Drifts of snow, white-powdered evergreens, and the black ribbon of cleared road winding through the snowy silence.

The Diné man speaks again at the turn to Gardiner, the only entrance to the park open in winter.

Before them are commanding views of the rocky Gallatin Mountain Range. Shops straight out of the Wild West line a road right at the boundary line of the park.

She turns the Jeep in to the one gas station to fill the tank. As she pumps fuel, she gazes out at the Roosevelt Arch, the original park entrance from 1903, rising out of the middle of the plain.

She returns the nozzle to the gas pump, opens the driver's door....

The Jeep is empty. The Diné man is gone.

She looks out at the gas station lot. There is no sign of him. She didn't see or feel him get out of the Jeep.

Perhaps he was never there.

His reality does not concern her. He was a clear sign, and clarity is easier than ambiguity.

She looks down the long road toward the arch, standing in the middle of the snowy field like an ancient portal to another time. She starts the engine and drives for it.

Chapter 72

Kellogg, Idaho – present
Singh and Snyder

Singh leans forward in the driver's seat, peering out the windshield. The night is growing too dark to continue on these twisting, pitch-black roads.

Out of nowhere, a giant figure looms up in the trees.

Singh brakes, startled. And realizes the figure is the monument from Agent Snyder's story, the miner with the headlamp, lighting the way to the collapsed Sunshine Mine outside Kellogg.

She had thought Snyder was sleeping in the seat beside her, but now he looks at her.

By silent agreement between them, she makes the turnoff to the mine memorial, follows the miner's lamp glowing through the trees in the twilight.

The agents get out of the Jeep on their opposite sides and stand looking up at the thirteen-foot tall coal miner, defiantly brandishing his rock drill skyward. In front of the statue are ninety-one miniature tombstones. Monuments to the lost miners.

Small, like child's graves.

For Singh, it serves as a stark reminder of how many children are missing and lost each year. And why she and Agent Snyder are on this mission. If this wilderness killer exists, there could be many more child victims than anyone suspects. There almost always are.

Snyder contemplates the small gravestones without comment. Singh does not know what that might mean. But she does not press him.

The hotel in Kellogg is also as Snyder described it in his narrative, a rustic lodge on a lake with icy views of the frozen water and forest.

After a brief stop at their rooms, the agents meet in the restaurant. Antique mining equipment makes up the décor. It is an apt metaphor. She and Agent Snyder are mining.

It is only after they have ordered their meal that he addresses the issue. "I know we're waiting for a memory to shake loose. Some kind of proof."

She does not need to ask. If it had, he would have told her.

He continues, "I remember the mine memorial. And I remember this hotel, being here with Matthew. All I can say is that I was here. And I know it was a case."

He sounds haunted. According to Roarke, he was never here. Singh does not know what to believe.

"I know," he says. "One of us is wrong."

She smiles, with effort. "It has been a long day, a long drive. We will investigate the town in the morning. We are just beginning," she assures him. But inside she is not so sure.

She looks out the tall black windows and sees the moon rising over the tops of pine trees, nearing full.

What is the truth? How can we get to it?

When Agent Snyder goes upstairs for the night, she lingers in the lobby.

And then, she pushes out through the front doors, into the night.

She must brace herself against the stinging cold. But the night is clear, and still. She walks down the front steps, and onto a landscaped path winding through the hotel grounds. The silence is intoxicating. The moon casts blue shadows on the glittering snow.

Ahead of her, the brush moves, startling her.

And she sees it.

A magnificent gray-white beast, with gleaming teeth, coal black eyes.

The wolf raises its shaggy head, and for a moment, they look at each other. Then it turns on powerful haunches and trots away.

Singh exhales, one long, slow, suspended breath.

And she thinks, *There is more to this, here. Tomorrow we shall see.*

Chapter 73

Yellowstone National Park, Wyoming – present
Cara

Mammoth Hot Springs Hotel is the only winter lodging in Yellowstone accessible by the relative anonymity of automobile. She has stayed here before during the off season. It is a known quantity, which makes it far less of a risk. And the winter sights are unworldly: the contrast of the bubbling, cauldron-like hot pools and geysers against the ice and snowdrifts, the live, ethereal mist.

The small, cream-colored original hotel has expanded and now connects to a five-story modern hotel block, but the lobby and restaurant in the old building retain the rustic décor, the simple carved wood curves. She is pleased to find the Map Room is still there, a common room beside the lobby with one wall covered by an enormous map of the U.S., each state done in woods of different colors, like a massive jigsaw puzzle of the country. Several TV screens on another wall broadcast shots from various webcams throughout the park: Old Faithful geyser, the Minerva Terrace, a wolf den in the woods, a hollow tree housing a hibernating bear family.

Registering at the desk, she uses a German accent and keeps her speech minimal and halting. She has found this to be a reliable disguise for travel in the national parks, where German tourists abound in all weather and young German women often travel alone.

She asks for one of the hotel's stand-alone cabins, which come with enclosed yards for more privacy, and no need to walk in the common hallways, offering far less chance of encountering other guests.

The cabin is small and functional and has no television. Another point in the hotel's favor. She brings food supplies in from the car, but hesitates in her doorway, looking out toward the main building. Her instinct is always to remain alone in her room, far from other people. But tonight something is pulling her toward the hotel again.

She locks her door, and walks across crunching snow to the main entrance, under darkening skies. Across a field of white, plumes of steam rise from the hot springs.

Inside the restaurant she finds a quiet booth and orders soup and bread and salad.

Two older men are in the next booth, talking in gravelly voices, spinning tales. She eavesdrops as she eats, at first catching only parts of the conversation.

"… started up again."

"… here last June… Glacier, in October."

The men's voices are hushed, portentous. "Ever notice…. in clusters? ….turn up miles away from where they disappeared from."

"Dozens a year," his friend agrees.

Their intensity is arresting. She focuses her attention to hear more.

The man furthest from her is the one driving the conversation. His voice drops to a hush. "So this internet guy…. got a map…. tunnel system underground. Connects the parks. Shows how the clusters of disappeared folks are related to this underground tunnel system…"

Cara sits back in her seat. She has heard such conspiracy talk before. There is a sickness building in remote parts of the country. She can hear it in the hysteria of talk radio, in small-town conversations like these. People buying into twisted interpretations of biblical obscurities, layering in medieval superstitions.

She is no stranger to mysticism, but her peculiar belief system stops well short of supervolcanoes, contrails and Illuminati. Or people kidnapped from national parks by aliens using underground tunnel systems.

She tries to block out their talk, but something penetrates her consciousness.

"... two kids, last couple months."

The mention of missing children puts her on alert. And then one of the men pronounces the name of the town.

"Fam'ly drove through Snake River before the kid disappeared."

Suddenly she is chilled to the bone.

She knows that town.

She goes back to her cabin, and stands outside in the frozen dark, under the almost-full moon. The clouds of mist are like something out of a dream.

To hear that name, in this place. Again.

This is what the Diné man has led her to. It could not be more clear.

A low howl reverberates through the dark. Then a group howl, as the wolf pack joins in.

Just as all those years ago.

Chapter 74

Kellogg, Montana – present
Singh and Snyder

At breakfast, Singh chooses a table away from other patrons, with a view of the snowy landscape outside the wide hotel restaurant windows. Quietly she relates her plan for the morning. "Officially, Aaron Light is only missing. But you described a hunting cabin nearby in great detail, where you say Aaron was taken and killed."

The look on Agent Snyder's face is anxious, doubtful. But she holds down her own apprehension and continues. "So we are looking for anything that points us in the direction of the cabin you remember visiting."

They check out of the hotel, load their bags into the trunk and begin their drive through the town. There is not much to the town center. Aside from the central golf course and golf club, there are bars, auto body shops, several storefront ministries.

Then Singh feels Snyder sit up straighter in his seat. He stares out at a glass-fronted business called *USA Power Sports.* Large cardboard signs advertise snowmobile brands: Shoshone Honda Yamaha, Arctic Cat. Sales, Service, Parts. Ski and snowshoe rentals.

"That's the shop," he says.

"What shop?"

"I told you," he answers impatiently. "Where we rented snowshoes."

Singh holds back her dismay. He had not mentioned such a shop in his story, nor renting equipment. She prompts him gently. "You told me you and ASAC Roarke snowshoed out to the hunting cabin in the forest. You did not mention a shop."

"Hunting cabin?" he repeats, uneasily.

Singh is suddenly afraid she is losing him again. She pulls the SUV to a parking space at the curb. "We will go inside."

Bells jangle on the door as they enter.

The man behind the counter is mountain-dressed, rugged, but with a beer gut, and strangely bulbous eyes. He looks up immediately at their entrance.

"What can I do for you folks?"

His voice is pleasant enough, but his eyes crawl over Singh in a way she recognizes too well. A toxic combination of sexual interest and racist contempt.

Agent Snyder notices. She feels him stiffen beside her. He puts a protective hand to her back, but speaks to the man in an amiable tone. "Do you have ski boots back there in a size twelve, men's?"

"Rent or buy?"

"Buy."

"I'll check."

As the counter man disappears through the stockroom door, Snyder tells her, very low, "We have to go. Now. Quickly. Quickly."

He almost pulls her along in his haste to get outside, and will not speak until they are in the car and driving away from the shop. Only then does he explain.

"We weren't here to rent snowshoes. We *said* that. But we came to the shop to talk to a salesman. *That* salesman." His eyes are bright, focused. "It was a real case."

Singh's heart sinks. Her call to the Bureau had made it clear Agent Snyder was never assigned to a child killer case, or any case at all, in Kellogg.

She does her utmost to break the news gently. "Agent Snyder. I checked with the Bureau after my phone conversation with ASAC Roarke. There is no record of any assignment to Kellogg."

Agent Snyder looks at her, undaunted. "It wasn't a Bureau case. It was ATF. A favor for a friend. And the year was 2011."

Chapter 75

Portland – present
Roarke and Epps

Eighteen hours later, the agents finally arrived in Portland. A delayed flight had kept them in San Francisco overnight. No word had come from Singh or Snyder.

Driving from the airport into Portland, Roarke felt himself slipping back into the past, the white-hot urgency of his first case as an agent.

While he drove, he filled Epps in. The Street Hunter case. The anomaly of Young John Doe. Roarke's and Snyder's theory that there was another killer covering his tracks by moving the boy's body to the Street Hunter's dump site. Roarke's own nagging feeling at the time that John Lombard had something to do with the attack on Brandi Hughes, that he might have been responsible for the murder of Young John Doe.

"But this Lombard just—what? Disappeared?" Epps asked, perplexed.

That was the thing. Roarke had never found a trace of him. So had he disappeared, changed his identity, moved his killing ground elsewhere? Was Lombard the trail that Singh and Snyder were pursuing?

He shook his head, and answered Epps, "I think we're about to find out."

There were no cars in Snyder's driveway, and no one responded to the bell.

Roarke had last visited Chuck only four months ago, and Snyder had given him the door code the night he'd stayed there. He knew Snyder cycled through a set of passwords, so he hoped for good timing and punched in the one he remembered. It didn't work. But an older one did. The door clicked open.

The agents moved inside.

The entry hall was quiet and dark. Roarke called out, "Chuck?" Epps followed with "Tara!"

No response came. Of course, Snyder and Singh could just be out. But the house felt empty.

The agents stepped into the living room. They both stopped in their tracks at the same time, hit by the sight of dozens of file boxes, scattered and piled on the table, the floor, every available surface.

Epps looked around them in consternation. "What the hell have they been doing?"

Roarke had expected files and some degree of chaos, but this much was unnerving. Especially with Singh involved. It was unlike her usual meticulousness.

Epps looked equally disturbed by the sight.

The two men moved through the house, checking rooms. Epps went for the hall to the bedrooms, while Roarke walked into the kitchen.

It too was empty, with no dishes in the sink or on any countertop, no sign of recent meal preparation, no coffee in the coffeemaker. Roarke crossed to the inner door to the garage and opened it to look in. There was no vehicle parked inside.

He closed the door and stepped back into the kitchen. He checked the trash bin. It was lined with a fresh plastic bag, completely empty.

He stood in the middle of the room, running through options. There were things he still hadn't told Epps. His agent still had no idea of what Roarke suspected about that night near the Salton Sea. The night that Singh was ostensibly kidnapped and left bound, drugged and unconscious in a derelict motel, while Cara's nemesis, sheriff's detective Ortiz, was murdered.

Roarke was certain Singh knew more, had done more that night than anyone might ever know.

He had also been sure that sending her to work with Chuck was the right thing, not just for Chuck, in his declining condition, but for both of them. Snyder had a lifetime of experience understanding and predicting violence, and infinite depths of insight and compassion.

But now Roarke wondered if he might have created a perfect storm of obsession.

Epps' voice came from the living room.

"Chief."

His tone made Roarke bolt out the kitchen door and take the living room in three strides, toward the door of Snyder's study.

Epps stood in the middle of the room, surrounded by more file boxes. He was facing a long case board, with a full-sized map of the U.S., dotted with push pins and photos and Post-it notations, and two parallel timelines pinned to the side of it, with dates connected by lengths of red string.

Roarke's initial, sinking feeling was: *They* are *working on some case. An active case.* He moved closer to the board. Epps turned to him and nodded to the timelines.

Roarke focused on the two long columns of dates and notations. And he experienced a hot spike of unreality.

The name on the top of the first timeline was his own. The name on the top of the second was Cara's. And it didn't take more than one long look to grasp that the red string showed correlation between his whereabouts and Cara's on over a dozen dates.

Not just in the past year. Going back fourteen years, to the year 2005.

Chapter 76

Kalispell, Montana – present
Singh and Snyder

The truck barrels up over rocky snowy fields, through a winter landscape of mountain peaks, valleys, forests, and an enormous, encompassing cerulean sky. Singh holds tight to a bar in the passenger seat, Agent Snyder is in the middle seat. Two bouncing border collies occupy the back.

At the wheel is Agent Morris Ziskin, Federal Bureau of Alcohol, Tobacco and Firearms, retired. He has met Singh and Snyder on the road where they have left their vehicle so he can drive them up to the ranch he'd bought for himself when he left the ATF.

Perhaps it is the oxygen-rich atmosphere, perhaps the breathtaking beauty, but Singh feels practically giddy. Agent Snyder is right, and there was a case, and they are on the right track. Or *a* track, anyway.

Ziskin smiles her way. He is dressed for all the world like a rugged Montana rancher, boots and jeans and flannel shirt and parka, a Stetson over a wind-burned face. But when he opens his mouth, pure Atlantic City comes out. "They say no one who comes to Montana ever leaves on purpose."

Surrounded by the sheer drama of the mountains: the plunges of cliffs, the enormity of the landscape, Singh can understand the sentiment.

"Of course they tend to say it in the summer," Ziskin admits, and adds, "This place is off the grid. Anyone who wants to can get lost here. Problem is it's so far off the grid a lot of batshit crazy people come up here to hide out." And then he warns, "Prime example coming up. And it ain't pretty."

He stops the Jeep and points out through the window at a swath of red in the brilliant white snow. Singh's heart plummets at the sight of a woolly white carcass.

"Wolves?" she asks tentatively, already knowing it is not the case.

"The human kind." Ziskin says grimly. "Not the first time, either. They want the Jew—meaning me—out, and they want to be able to hunt the wolves. So they kill my sheep and blame the wolves. Two birds with one stone." He glances in the back of the truck, at the beautiful, joyful dogs. "These days I have to keep the girls with me wherever I go. So the 'wolves' won't get them, too."

Singh feels a flare of outrage. *It is a sickness, this compulsion to conquer. To come into beauty like this and think only to take life.*

Ziskin evidently picks up on her distress. "Sorry to put you into the middle of my domestic squabbles. But you need to know what you're dealing with. These people you're looking for—they're nothing to fuck around with."

In the living room of Ziskin's ranch house, floor-to-ceiling windows look out on pristine white fields and snowy peaks. Ziskin brings a huge pot of coffee to sofas in front of a river rock fireplace. As he sits, he says to Singh, "I'm sure Chuck has told you most of this already..."

Agent Snyder's face is neutral. "I'd like her to hear it from you."

Ziskin shrugs expansively. "2011. It was a total clusterfuck, excuse my French. We were picking up chatter—a couple of lowlifes in Montana and Idaho belonging to a militia called the Northwest Brigade, making barroom boasts about an upcoming attack on federal law enforcement. The Brigade's alleged plan was to assassinate a couple of police officers. In their larger scheme, they were thinking that when law enforcement showed up in force for the funerals, they could bomb the ceremony and take out dozens of our guys at once."

Singh stares at him, overcome at the monstrousness of the idea.

Snyder speaks quietly beside her. "And that of course would be the spark to ignite the uprising against the government."

Singh glances at him. His eyes are focused and clear.

Ziskin nods. "It's the pattern we see over and over again. Militia amasses a stockpile of ammunition, weapons and survival gear. Plans a bloody attack or series of attacks on state and local officials, with the goal of forcing the state to call out the National Guard. Militias are always on the lookout for an opportunity for a small, 'heroic' private band of warriors to engage the big bad government."

Snyder adds, "And to be blunt about it, to suffer some fatalities. They want the fatalities because in their minds, it creates martyrs. Which is exactly what happened in Waco and Ruby Ridge. We're still paying the price."

Despite being alarmed by the subject matter, Singh is aware and pleased to see that in context, Agent Snyder's memory is functioning perfectly.

Ziskin spreads his hands. "These guys are absolutely convinced that that's all it would take for a majority or a significant minority of the U.S. population to take up arms against the government and overthrow it. But try to call it terrorism, and see what happens."

Snyder is fully into the memory now. "2011 was an especially active year on the militia front. There was a two hundred forty-four percent increase in militias, minutemen, and other anti-government patriot groups. Three hundred sixty-three new groups in a single year."

"Because of the election of an African American president," Singh guesses.

Snyder nods to her. "Exactly. The combination of economic distress and racial animosity sent militia membership skyrocketing."

Ziskin returns to his story. "We had a multi-state investigation into the group. There was a ticking clock on it, too. Word was they were planning the attack on April nineteen."

"The anniversary of the Oklahoma City bombing," Singh realizes.

"You got it. Like other terrorists, militias are big on anniversaries. We'd been watching known Northwest Brigade members in Kellogg and in this little town called Snake River, near Glacier National Park. We were focused on a few key players. The owner of the snowmobile shop you just ran into, name of James Furman. Abraham Strauss, a hardware store owner in Snake River. And Jeremiah Hardee, aka "the Colonel"—the owner of the sports vehicle chain. We believed Furman was moving arms for the Colonel through his snowmobile sales route. And that the militia was getting significant funding for arms from the Colonel as well. The destination of all this arms movement was Snake River."

He glances at Singh to be sure she is following. She nods, riveted. "So we're putting this whole case together. Then an eleven-year old kid, Timothy Whitcomb, disappears during a family vacation at Flathead Lake, in Montana."

Singh sits up straighter, electrified. Ziskin continues grimly.

"Hundreds of officers, volunteers and cadaver dogs combed through several square miles of wilderness area. Various organizations offered tens of thousands of dollars in reward money. Tragic, but nothing to do with us, right? A month goes by, no sign of the kid. We're putting together our case, watching our players. And then the tip line for the missing kid triggers a name on an ATF list. We had a flag on all the main Northwest Brigade players so that anything related to any of these guys gets passed on to us before someone else takes action. They trace the call to Snake River. A woman, calling anonymously, with a tip on one of the militia members we'd been watching: Strauss, the owner of that Snake River hardware store. The caller says the Whitcomb family passed through Snake River the day

Timothy disappeared, and that Strauss had been watching him. And that," Ziskin made air quotes. "'It wasn't the first time.'"

Singh feels a chill that has nothing to do with the snow outside. It is Agent Snyder's story, exactly as he told it to her. The locations nearly all the same. Only the date and the missing boy's name and age are different. She looks toward Snyder. He is nodding, intently processing.

Ziskin stands, too caught up in his story now to stay still. "I made the request to state police to let me handle it. We didn't want another investigation compromising our surveillance on this domestic terrorism threat. That bought us some time, but it was tricky. 'Specially because the sheriff in Snake River was tied up with the militia. We didn't know if he was a card-carrying member, but it sure as hell looked like he was doing some covering for them."

"Was that Sheriff Preston?" Singh asks.

"Preston, right."

Singh can still feel the unpleasantness of his voice on the phone. "He is still the Sheriff, there. I have spoken with him."

Ziskin's face darkens. "Not a good guy."

"That is my impression," Singh agrees fervently.

"Preston is, or was, an Oathkeeper. It's a far-right organization that encourages law enforcement and military veterans not to obey orders that they believe would violate the Constitution. Basically meaning anything to do with suppression of gun rights."

Singh understands instantly. "So if there had been some criminal activity by a militia member, Sheriff Preston may have chosen not to look too closely at it."

"Bingo. Anyhow, we're running out of time on that April nineteen anniversary of the Oklahoma City bombing. We can't *not* follow up on a potential child abduction. And I'm undercover, can't move on it." Ziskin nods to Agent Snyder. "Chuck has a shitload of experience on both militia activity and child abuse/abduction. So I ask him to come up and take a look at the situation as a favor."

Snyder's next words are a quiet triumph. "And I brought Matthew up with me to investigate."

Chapter 77

Portland - present
Roarke and Epps

Roarke stood in front of the case board, paralyzed, mesmerized.

Singh's work, as always, was precise, clear, meticulous. She had tied unsolved murders in Cara Lindstrom's style to locations, dates and cases that Roarke himself had worked on since 2005.

All he could think was, *It can't be...*

Beside him, Epps seemed equally unnerved. "I know what this is. She has this crazy..." He stopped himself. "No. Crazy isn't the word. There's a *myth* that Lam told her that she's—taken with, I guess you could say. About a red string that signifies Fate."

As Roarke listened to Epps' explanation, he could feel his heart rate elevate. *A red string that binds people who are meant to work or be together. An unbreakable, uncanny connection.*

It was eerily how he felt—*what* he felt with Cara. It seemed as if Epps was laying Roarke's own soul bare. He was bristling at the violation, so agitated that he almost missed what Epps was saying.

"She brought it up in the context of her and me. But she was really talking about herself and Lindstrom."

Roarke was startled out of his absorption. He looked at Epps.

"She feels that connection, somehow," Epps finished. "I know she does. There's something between them."

Something between *them.* Roarke wanted to laugh. He stared at the board, trying to process it.

The year of his college graduation. His first case as an FBI intern, in Richmond. Here in Portland, on the Street Hunter case…

In every instance, if Singh was right, there was some connection to Cara.

His past rose up around him, threatening to overwhelm him.

Epps was still talking, but Roarke could no longer hear him. He turned without a word and walked out.

PART SIX

Chapter 78

Portland - present
Roarke

The air was heavy with the promise of rain.

Roarke walked in the woods in a daze.

It was a trail he'd hiked many times during his years working with Snyder, a path he could pick up from the back end of Snyder's property and trek all the way into Portland proper on days when he had the time and the mindset.

He'd left Epps at the house, without excuse or explanation. He'd had to get out. To get away from that map, those charts, the double white boards, the implications.

Those lists. Dates, names, places. *Richmond. Portland. Snake River. San Francisco.*

He couldn't begin to wrap his mind around the idea.

Six months ago his life had changed forever, the day he saw Cara Lindstrom standing on the sidewalk across the street from him, just before Agent Greer had been crushed by a delivery truck.

He'd reeled to find that she was the girl whose survival of the Reaper massacres had been the beginning of his life path. The synchronicities of their lives had sometimes felt overwhelming.

But it was now clear that Singh honestly believed, and Chuck, too—Chuck, the rationalist, the statistician—they both believed that his path and Cara's had crossed over and over.

He had to stop on the trail, overcome with a breathlessness that had nothing to do with the pace of his walking.

Wherever I've gone, she's been there.

His rational mind was fighting it.

But the cop part of him, his blue sense, knew. And he was already back in the past, feeling her presence.

Chapter 79

Montana - 2011
Roarke and Snyder

Roarke stood beside the Tundra in the parking lot of the gas station. Chuck was inside the small station store, buying what was probably his seventh coffee of the day. It had been a long drive from Portland.

It was freezing outside. Roarke had to keep stamping his feet to keep warm. But he didn't mind waiting. He'd never been at a gas station with quite such a breathtaking view.

It was his first time to Montana and "Big Sky" didn't begin to cover it. It was mythic. The layers on layers of peaks and valleys. The contrast of blinding white snow and black volcanic fields. The fog, carved out into mountains and valleys of its own. The hush of it all, that made it feel like he could hear for miles and miles... the snap of an icicle, the hoof step of a deer.

He hadn't wanted to come. It was the wrong time to take off and leave Monica, effectively in the middle of a fight—*discussion*—about their future. Which by all the signs was looking rocky, not even two years into marriage. She'd moved up to Portland reluctantly as it was, and every road assignment opened up another fissure between them.

This trip wasn't even a regular Bureau assignment, rather an off-the-grid favor for one of Snyder's friends. Chasing a hotline tip, of all things—something Chuck had always warned him to be skeptical of.

But it was all true in Richmond, he reminded himself.

No doubt there were similarities to that case, here. The small-town, squirreled-away militia. The insane stockpiling of arms. And the possibility of abuse.

More than domestic abuse, this time. A missing boy, a potential murder.

And that was what decided it, even over Monica's objections. Anywhere a child might be in jeopardy was where he had to be.

All of that anxiety had melted away in the face of the sheer staggering beauty of the place. He felt an excitement about it that was more than just the thrill of the hunt. There was something for him here. Something of import.

He turned as Chuck returned with coffee, holding out two trucker-sized cups. Probably the last thing Roarke needed at this point, but he took one anyway.

Chuck looked out at the valley, the ring of mountains, and drew in a long, satisfied breath.

"Not bad," he said, with straight-faced understatement.

"No," Roarke agreed.

Then they got into the Tundra and drove on. *Toward something*, Roarke thought. He didn't know what. But something.

Chapter 80

Yellowstone National Park, Wyoming – 2011
Cara

She wakes to the strange half-light of snow clouds outside the cabin window.

The moon last night had been bright and insistent. Something is coming. It has drawn her here already, brought her into this unfamiliar landscape. Today, more will be revealed.

The snow report posted at the front desk last night said that snow is not expected until late day. She dresses in layers: GORE-TEX and wool, an Arctic-rated parka. She drapes binoculars around her neck, pulls a pack onto her back, and steps outside into a sea of white, under a sky layered with thick, moody clouds.

She is not at home in the winter world. It is too unfamiliar, too risky. It requires too much preparation, too much caution, too much equipment, too much clothing just for basic survival. And yet, she cannot deny this aspect of life, of nature, of *Beauty*. It has taken some time on the road, but she has realized it would be against the laws of Nature not to spend some time in the frozen depths of this season.

The parking lot of Mammoth Hot Springs Hotel is surprisingly bustling, with several sets of visitors busy loading gear into two SUVs. It is not tourist types who brave the winter cold. These are wolf watchers. After centuries of unchecked hunting, the animals were re-introduced into the park in 1995 and since then have been protected, studied, chronicled, storied by scientists and environmentalists. The region has become the world's wolf-watching capital. She hopes to encounter them herself today.

She removes her snowshoes from the SUV she has been driving and kneels to strap them to her feet. She is close enough to the wolf-watchers to hear their destination. She manages to catch more interesting information as well, before the group splits up to pile into their cars and depart, vehicles spewing white clouds of exhaust in the frigid air.

After six years on the road she has become attuned to the threads that draw her, the signs that lead her inevitably to the next *Encounter.* Sometimes the signs are subtle, a feeling, a quick change of mind or direction. Sometimes they are blatant.

The wolf-watchers have given her a hint.

She had intended to hike to the Minerva Terrace today. But now she has a new, further goal. She turns toward the trail head of the nature path and sets out.

The path takes her along the edge of a frozen lake, pure aquamarine against the white of snow. The cold is crisp and clean, slightly metallic in her lungs, with hints of pine and sulfur. Above her, bare branches are coated in ice. The approach to the falls soon becomes stunningly alien, with mammoth volcanic formations in weird shapes sprouting from the ground, golden against the white. Weirder still are the boiling pools, in shades of aquamarine and turquoise, set in the midst of all that ice.

Her breath comes heavy now and she is sweating in the cold, feeling the flood of endorphins from the work her body is doing.

The nature trail opens up to a view of the Terrace. A succession of enormous, shallow pools descends in a series of chalky white limestone formations, like a staircase in some fairy tale palace of the Ice Queen. Round hot pools bubble, witch's cauldrons in the icy ground.

Her head is buzzing with the exhilaration of the sight. It is an ecstasy of feeling, sensing, seeing. Worth the trip for this alone. And yet she is certain there is more to come, today.

She removes the snowshoes to walk the boardwalk pathways over the boiling pools, through a steam bath of great billowing plumes of white. At the end of the boardwalk she puts the snowshoes on again, following a path that will circle through the Lamar Valley before returning to the hotel. This she has learned from listening to the wolf-watchers: in winter, elk, bison and moose move down into the valley to graze, and the wolves follow them.

She descends through trees, and comes out into a meadow, a pristine snow field, a perfect viewing spot. It waits, like a blank canvas. The vast stillness of it is pure pleasure and calm.

She stands between the trees, lifts the binoculars from around her neck and uses them to survey the meadow.

After what seems like seconds, as if summoned, a wolf pack emerges from the trees. A huge alpha, six others of various sizes.

They are breathtaking, magnificent creatures. Powerful. Dangerous. Purely, entirely alive.

For a moment all time stops.

And then something begins to gnaw at her consciousness. A heightened awareness, a ripple of fear. *Danger.*

She shudders, a primal spasm of anxiety.

It's not the wolves she fears. They are much too far away to be any threat to her.

And yet the stillness is ominous, loaded.

Loaded.

She keeps back inside the copse, and scans the edges of the forest at the periphery of the meadow.

And spots him, a dark stain against the winter landscape.

He has concealed himself in the trees. But the long barrel of the rifle gives him away. A hunter.

Her heart hammers crazily in her chest.

This, too, she has heard from the wolf-watchers. Hunting is illegal in the park. But since the gray wolves were removed from the endangered species list in 2009, some of the trophy hunters wait outside the borders of the park to take down the creatures as they roam across the border.

Because they can. And to defy the government, which they perceive as their enemy.

She has no weapon to stop the hunter's intention. She cannot even run forward to attract attention, not in these oversized tennis rackets attached to her feet. There is no way to reach him. His bead on the pack is a perfect shot.

So she screams.

In all her years, with all her *Encounters,* she has never screamed. Not once, since she was a child. There has been no point. She has never expected help to come, so there is no reason to try to summon it. Screaming would be a waste of several precious seconds which could and must be devoted to killing.

She does not even know if her damaged throat has the capacity to make such a sound.

But what comes out of her body is fearsome, reverberating. The surrounding rocks and mountains amplify the sound to a preternatural cry. A shower of snow falls from nearby branches of trees.

The wolves bolt in one synchronous leap, and run for the woods they've emerged from, bounds of pure muscle.

The echo of the scream lingers in the shattered air, while the hunter staggers and twists around him in shock and confusion.

She is breathless, her whole body aching with the effort. But it is done. The wolves are safe, disappeared into the forest.

Far across the meadow, the hunter stomps about in a circle, enraged. She has spoiled his vicious pleasure for the day.

And rage begins to boil up inside her, as well.

She understands hunting for food. If she had to she would kill to eat.

But someone who would deliberately break the law to slaughter these majestic animals... someone who derives pleasure from the risk of lawbreaking, who clearly thrills to killing....

There is no end to the mischief he might be doing. He has come across her path, and this is never for no reason.

It begins to snow, huge, thick, silent flakes. Visibility drops.

She gathers herself, and keeping inside the trees, she plows through the snow after him.

Chapter 81

Snake River, Montana – 2011
Roarke and Snyder

Roarke cruised the Tundra down the small main street, while Snyder looked out through the passenger window.

Like so many towns in Montana, Snake River had a Wild West feel. Storefronts that looked like a film set, wood benches on plank walkways, old-fashioned shop signs hanging by chains. It was picturesque, and close enough to Glacier National Park that it could have been a natural tourist draw—had it not had the bad luck to be eclipsed by several towns that provided better gateways to the park. In Snake River there were no ski resorts or nearby archeological finds to coax vacationers those extra few miles off the highway.

The agents did an initial drive through the town, past a post office, pawn shop, general store, the hardware store, called Snake River Mercantile—and the Huckleberry Diner, advertising "World-Famous Pie."

They were armed with Ziskin's information. They'd listened to the tape of the anonymous tip: a tentative, youngish female voice, obviously conflicted. *"That family passed through town and the boy was being watched. And then I read that he disappeared..."* And then a quick, low appeal: *"You need to check out Abraham Strauss. It's not the first time."*

Not the first time.

A pre-teen boy, missing in Montana, a habitat of gray wolves. And rife with geothermal areas.

It was impossible not to think of Young John Doe.

It was never a good feeling, an unsolved murder involving a kid. *Although maybe it* is *solved,* Roarke argued with himself, as he looked out the windshield at the main street shops. *Portland PD thinks so.*

Of course he'd double-checked the missing persons databases, the National Center for Missing and Exploited Children. He'd found no thirteen-year old boy reported missing from Snake River or the surrounding area in 2009.

Why should they make it complicated for themselves, on no real evidence?

But the agents listened to the tape once more as they cruised past Snake River Mercantile, to fix the woman's voice in their heads, and it chilled Roarke all over again to hear that final whisper:

"It's not the first time."

Whatever the anonymous tipster knew, she believed it utterly.

He parked on the street, some way down the block from Strauss's store, and the agents got out to walk the final half block to it, their feet crunching on newly salted sidewalks.

A string of bells on the door jangled as they entered and stood taking a quick look around. The mercantile seemed to have a little of everything. The front racks were ski accessories: gloves, sunglasses, hand warmers. Useful impulse purchases in the weather, and a good excuse for their drop-in to the store.

A man stood behind the counter, with broad cheeks and a jowly neck, a grizzled goatee that failed to conceal a double chin, and flat dark eyes. Strauss, looking much like his ATF surveillance photo.

The agents had decided on their cover story when they met with Agent Ziskin: father and son on a ski trip. The SUV was loaded with a ski rack and equipment, luggage in full view. They did the family act for Strauss now, Roarke calling to Snyder from another aisle to summon him. "Dad. This what you were thinking?"

He brought a pack of hand warmers over to show Snyder, nodding to Strauss as he passed. Behind the counter animal heads were on display on the wall, along with moose antlers, deer antlers. A bumper sticker was affixed to the countertop glass, aggressively yellow, with the image of a coiled snake: the Gadsden flag, with its *DON'T TREAD ON ME* warning in all-caps.

While Strauss rang up Snyder's purchases of hand warmers and sunglasses, Roarke took the moment to check out the photos framed on the wall behind the counter.

He spotted a group shot: Strauss standing beside a slaughtered elk and three other men posed with rifles beside the animal. Roarke recognized one of them: Furman, the snowmobile shop owner with the bulbous eyes. It was the same photo Furman had had up behind his own counter in the sports shop in Kellogg, when Roarke and Snyder had stopped in earlier in the day, renting snowshoes as a cover to check the militia man out.

And under that was a photo of Strauss in a coaching jacket, beside a baseball team of middle-school age boys.

Roarke's profiler mind leapt into gear. *Classic hebephile. Volunteers with middle-school age in some community service capacity—Boy Scouts, church group, sports team—to get close to potential victims. Sets himself up as an authority figure that parents and boys trust.*

Strauss had noticed his attention to the photo. Roarke gestured to it, channeled his high school jock memories, that coach-to-coach proprietary tone. "I do some middle school coaching myself."

"It's our congregation's district team," Strauss said.

Not exactly the point, Roarke thought, but gave him a smile. "It's all about the boys, though. Nothing like 'em."

Strauss's eyes went strangely blank. "You headed to Whitefish?" His voice was insincere, falsely jovial.

"Flathead Lake," Snyder said. "You know it?"

Strauss gave a terse nod.

"But we're looking for a motel here for the night," Snyder continued. "Got any recommendations?"

"You could make Whitefish by supper," Strauss said.

An obvious invitation to get the hell out of town. So blatant it would've been comic—if they hadn't been dealing with a suspected child predator.

"We're in no hurry," Snyder said pleasantly.

Strauss handed him the bag with their purchases with a stone face. "Have yourself a good one."

The agents were silent as they walked out of the store, and back in the direction of their vehicle. Once they were outside of Strauss's sight line, Roarke said softly, "Here's your hat, what's your hurry?"

"Interesting reaction to your coaching questions, too," Snyder answered.

"He's in the right position to do a lot of damage," Roarke agreed tightly.

But was he a monster? A child killer? Roarke warned himself not to make assumptions and said aloud, "So. The diner?"

According to Ziskin, the tip call had originated from there.

Snyder gave him the ghost of a smile. "I never pass up an opportunity for huckleberry pie."

Chapter 82

Yellowstone National Park – 2011
Cara

She stands between trees, watching the hunter as he throws his snowshoes into the back of a windowless van parked on the side of the road. He takes much more care with his gun.

She notes the van's license plate number, memorizing it. And there is another item of interest: a bright yellow bumper sticker.

Watching, taking visual notes, is all she can do. Obviously she cannot follow on foot.

Plumes of exhaust spew from the van's tailpipes as the hunter starts up the vehicle.

She turns in the snow and consults her compass to find the trail back to the hotel. There is nothing to do but return there.

It bothers her not at all.

If she is *meant* to find the hunter, she will find him. It is the way.

Chapter 83

Snake River, Montana - 2011
Roarke and Snyder

The diner had the warm, homey feel of a town hub, where everyone would know each other and people dropped in for the local gossip as much as for the food.

And the wide front windows had a perfect view of the mercantile.

The agents staked out a table in the front, and ordered pie and coffee from a waitress in her late twenties, dark blond, and carefully made up to conceal circles under her eyes.

The pie came immediately and was mouthwatering, a sweet and sour kick.

Snyder raised his fork in salute to the waitress, who was watching him from across the room.

"I think we've got someone's attention," he said softly, casually.

When Roarke met the waitress's gaze, she blushed and turned away quickly.

Could it be? Roarke wondered. *Not a random townsperson, but someone who actually works here?*

"Wait," Snyder said. "Let her come to us."

The rest of the meal passed without incident. The waitress, whose nametag pinned on her uniform read *Jean*, was polite, if cool, and said nothing to the agents beyond, "Anything else for you two?" and "Have a nice day."

But she left them a note with the check. The words *Alpine turnoff, Whitefish, 4:00.*

Chapter 84

Yellowstone National Park, Wyoming - 2011
Cara

The snow has stopped by the time she comes off the trail back at Mammoth Hot Springs.

And the first thing she sees is the hunter's van, parked in the restaurant parking lot.

So. A sign. It is *meant.*

She takes a moment to look over the vehicle. A van, rather than a truck, for hunting. Not especially shocking. But interesting.

Beside the license plate she can see the graphic on the toxic yellow bumper sticker: a rattlesnake coiled to strike and the capital-letter warning *DON'T TREAD ON ME.*

She contemplates it stoically. She has seen its kind before, a historical emblem given ominous new meaning by current political fury.

She has left nothing in her room, it is all in her vehicle. Beside the SUV she removes and stows her snowshoes, then moves up to the main doors of the hotel. In the lobby she checks out at the front desk, glancing into the restaurant as the clerk prints out her receipt.

The hunter is alone at a table. She takes him in quickly. He is in his thirties, dark-haired and mustached, lean and twitchy, with bad skin on his face and tattoos on his wrists. There is something snakelike about him.

Don't Tread on Me.

She steps back from the doorway and moves out of the hotel to wait in her own vehicle in the parking lot, employing the portable heater rather than running the engine.

When he leaves the restaurant and climbs into the van, she starts the SUV and follows.

Chapter 85

Snake River, Montana - 2011
Roarke and Snyder

According to Google Maps, the Whitefish turnoff was fifteen miles out of town.

A promising sign. Jean was willing to talk, although nowhere any locals could see.

While Roarke drove the winding road to the meeting spot, Snyder phoned in to the Bureau to get details from her employment records. He jotted notes, then reported aloud to Roarke.

"Jean Lange, age twenty-eight, graduate of Mountain View High, two towns over. Employment history indicates she also works in Glacier National Park during the season, which doesn't start until June. No criminal history. And she's married, with an eight-year old son."

Roarke glanced away from the twisting road, at Snyder. "Which is why she's willing to go out on a limb, here."

It was reminding him of the Richmond militia case again. A woman who might be under the thumb of her husband, the town, or both, but who'd summoned the courage to say no. Or at least to ask for help.

"Or maybe she just doesn't like Strauss," Snyder said.

Roarke's hands tightened on the wheel. *I don't either,* he thought.

Chapter 86

Idaho - 2011
Cara

She drives.

Out of the park on the Wyoming side, up toward Idaho, following the van and the hunter on the road.

Her anger is back, a slow boil under the surface of her skin, like the hot pools under the ice. She is not surprised to be back on the hunter's tail. From the moment she heard the wolf-watchers talking, she suspected that the wolves would lead her to the next step. And she is fully aware of the irony. Because what she heard the watchers talking about, what they were in the park to prevent, themselves, was exactly this. Hunters like this one, who cross into the park deliberately, illegally, to hunt the storied wolves. A wolf with a tracking device, one marked for scientific study, fetches a bigger bounty, bigger bragging rights. As if hunting endangered creatures for sport is not enough.

The predator is now the prey.

This part of Wyoming's landscape is flat, so he is easy to follow. It also makes her easy to be seen. It requires total vigilance not to let the hunter guess that he is being tracked in this way. Any time he turns off the highway, she must slow her vehicle and hang back on the road.

The fact that she is able to do it at all, that she is able to follow without ever losing him or being detected, is more proof that she is being guided. It is almost as if she is invisible.

And once the roads turn mountainous and forested, it is even easier.

He stops for the first time in a town called Kellogg, not far over the border into Idaho. He turns into the side driveway of a snowmobile shop and heads around the back of the store.

She drives past the store to park on the street and walks quickly back toward the shop, skirting the side of the shop building, staying close to the wall. At the back corner she looks around the side of the building into the lot.

The hunter's van is gone.

She scans the back of the building. There are no windows to the shop on that side, just a huge, corrugated, automated warehouse door. It is the only place the van could have gone.

She steps back, and makes her way back down the side of the building. She returns to her SUV and drives it down the block, out of sight of the shop windows. She parks, and takes a blue tarp and some boxes from the back of the SUV. She ties the tarp on to the ski rack, with the boxes underneath to create a bit of bulk. She has learned that vehicles can be as easily disguised as a person. Now when the hunter looks in his rear-view mirror, it will be the blue tarp he notices.

After nearly an hour, the van emerges from the side alley. And as the hunter drives out, the van dips, and scrapes the driveway in a screech on the way out.

It is riding lower to the ground. There has been a pickup of some kind, with weight to whatever the cargo is.

A cargo of nothing good.

The hunter drives out of Kellogg, going back the same way he came. She follows as he retraces his route back toward Montana, across the Idaho state line, and continues on 90 North to Missoula.

He makes a few more stops. In Missoula, a small city in a wide, flat valley surrounded by snowy mountains, it is at a survivalist shop. Here, while she waits, she removes the blue tarp and boxes, and locks two pairs of skis into the ski rack.

The hunter resumes driving, with Cara in careful pursuit. A few miles after Missoula he turns off 90 onto 93, heading due north, and stops off in the next town at a pawn shop. By now it is not difficult to guess what he is buying, or selling.

As the miles go by, her mind drifts to Richmond, the year of her first journey across the country. Her *Encounter* with the same kind of man, the same kind of energy. And, she strongly suspects, the same kind of cargo.

On 93 the towns are small and far apart. She follows the hunter's van for many miles along the western shore of enormous Flathead Lake. He does not stop again and she relaxes into the drive, savoring Montana's big sky magnificence.

The hunter passes through Kalispell, a small city she has been through several times before, en route to Glacier National Park. She follows the van past hotels dating back to the 1800s, bars called saloons, a drug store with an old-fashioned soda fountain.

Not long out of Kalispell, the van comes to an outpost like so many in these unpopulated states. The town of Snake River. Barely a thousand people, if that. Its wooden storefronts give it a frontier feel.

As the hunter drives the main street, a man standing outside one of the shops looks toward the van and touches a finger to his cap brim. She has seen it before. In rural counties, there is always a town signal. An acknowledgment of someone who belongs or is welcome, as opposed to a stranger.

Or perhaps this is something specific to this hunter, this shipment he carries.

So now it becomes imperative that the hunter not know he is being followed.

As the van slows mid-block, she stops at the corner, signaling a turn. Ahead of her, the van parks on the street in front of a store called Snake River Mercantile. The hunter gets out of the truck and walks toward the store.

Cara moves her SUV forward down the block and parks in another space just short of the Huckleberry Diner, advertising "*World Famous Pie.*" She has a clear view of the front of the store through the SUV's windshield. She leans over and pretends to be rummaging in her glove compartment while she watches the hunter through the plate glass window of the store.

The hunter greets the jowly, goateed man behind the counter with a nod and they exchange a few words. There is a middle-aged woman customer in the shop, and the hunter looks toward her before stepping into one of the aisles to browse.

The woman brings her purchases up to the counter and the counter man rings her up.

As soon as the woman leaves the store with her bag, the hunter steps out from the aisle, not carrying any purchases. The two men speak quickly, furtively.

She has no idea what they are saying. But she doesn't need to hear them to see the dark intent flowing around and between them.

The man behind the counter glances out toward the street… reaches under the counter and produces a handgun.

The men stand where they are, waiting, watching the window. Cara sits in her SUV watching them.

In less than a minute, a Range Rover pulls up outside the mercantile and parks at the curb. There is a Sheriff's Department logo on the side. A bulky, uniformed man sporting a handlebar mustache gets out. He is perhaps fifty. Not a deputy. Cara can see the gold badge on his chest.

He shuts the car door and walks toward the mercantile, with a revolver heavy on his hip. He opens the door to what Cara imagines as a faint jangle of bells.

She watches as inside the store, the three men exchange a few terse words. They turn to stare through the front windows of the shop toward the street. Then all of them walk through the door behind the counter, into what must be the stock room.

Cara sits, absorbing what she has seen.

The twitchy, tattooed hunter. The potbellied hardware store man with his blank stare. And this sheriff, now.

There is good law enforcement and there is bad. This one is not good.

Bad men. Bad cargo. And a bad sheriff to ensure that no one will interfere with their bad intentions.

Chapter 87

2011 – Whitefish turnoff, Montana
Roarke and Snyder

There were two parking lots at the lookout the waitress had designated, an upper and a lower. Roarke drove through the first one and down to the lower, which was not visible from the highway. Parking there wouldn't draw attention.

In the seat beside him, Chuck mused, "I know what we've found. There was no thirteen-year old boy reported missing from this area in 2009. But if Strauss is coaching regionally—"

Roarke knew where he was going. "If he's going to away games…"

In his capacity as a coach, there would really be no end of boys available to him.

Roarke turned off the engine, started to turn to Snyder to speak. Then the view caught him.

It was a misty afternoon, fog as thick as snow wreathing parts of the mountain range. But there wasn't enough fog in the whole world to obscure the view. It went on and on, layer after layer of mountain range of dull purple, iron, obsidian, with ivory white caps, silver ribbons of waterfalls in the crevasses.

In all his years of hiking, wilderness training, backpacking, he had never seen anything so vast. Ancient, deep, eternal.

The agents sat in reverent silence.

What would it be like, to just disappear out there? Roarke thought.

Never to come back to this world. To stay in that timeless beauty and find... something he'd never been able to define. Himself, maybe.

It felt so close, right now...

And he was suddenly clear. It wasn't going to work with Monica. They'd tried. They would keep trying. They respected each other. There was love there. But sooner or later they were going to have to face the truth. She belonged to the city, to big business, to the challenge of corporate life. And he was most himself in these lost spaces. There was something else for both of them—

He stopped mid-thought, at a glimpse of movement in the rearview mirror. A vehicle driving down from the upper parking lot, a pickup truck with salt splashes along the sides.

"Here we go," Chuck murmured beside him.

And Roarke added silently, *Talk to us, Jean.*

Chapter 88

Snake River, Montana - 2011
Cara

She is back on the road again, following some distance behind the van on a winding road. Now without the skis on top of the SUV. She'd taken a short drive to remove them, and re-parked to watch the mercantile from a distance until the Sheriff reemerged from the store and left in his vehicle.

A minute later the hunter had come out of the store, carrying nothing. He got back into his van and drove on, through the town.

And Cara had followed.

Outside Snake River, the road is narrow and winding. Many unpaved roads branch off into the woods. She must brake constantly and hang back on the curves to keep far enough behind the van to avoid detection.

Inevitably she rounds a curve and finds herself too close to the van, close enough that it is likely he has seen her. She slows at one of the branching roads and turns into it as if that is her destination. She waits there, out of sight, letting the hunter continue.

After half a minute, long enough for him to get past the next curve, she backs out and continues on the road, driving past a cluster of mailboxes with a chainsaw-carved wooden grizzly bear looming behind them.

She rounds the next curve of road—

The van is gone.

She has an unimpeded view of another long stretch of road ahead of her, and it is completely empty.

She makes a U-turn, cruises back the way she came, looking out at all of the nearly invisible side roads winding away from the road. Driveways, pathways. Many of them private, gated, or posted NO TRESPASSING.

The van could have turned down any one of them.

She drives slowly, considering.

Perhaps she is not *meant* to follow him further. There is never any point in forcing the issue. She will be instructed when she needs to be instructed.

So she accelerates and drives back toward Snake River.

This time she passes through on the main street without stopping. There is no possibility of staying in the town. Small towns are a kind of trap, especially in the least populous states. Everyone knows everyone, and knows everything about everyone. Outsiders have a spotlight on them. She cannot use her German tourist persona because strangers with accents are doubly unwelcome in this region, and lone women are particular targets.

And so she takes the road heading back to Kalispell. An actual city, big enough for her not to feel on display. A gateway to Glacier, for tourists who don't want to camp in the summer or who are looking to ski in the winter. Where the ski rack and equipment in the SUV will explain her presence to anyone who looks twice.

She has not eaten for some time so she parks on the first main road she comes to, lined with restaurants, saloons, hotels, and a small museum.

She finds a café and orders hot cauliflower soup and a cheese sandwich.

And she sits looking out the large plate glass windows to see what the street will present to her.

The restaurant is warm, with a fire in a river rock fireplace. After her long day of driving she finds herself drifting into a detached haze. She is sure she has not made this day's drive for no reason. She is willing to wait for the next sign.

While she is finishing her meal, she becomes aware of teenagers walking the sidewalks, alone, in pairs, in groups. School has let out for the day.

One girl walking alone catches her eye. She is young, thirteen or fourteen, with short spiky hair and baggy trousers under a thick parka. She stands out for her nervous energy and alert wariness.

And for something else that makes Cara's heart stand still.

The girl is bleeding. Crimson trails of blood in the snow behind her.

Not real, of course. And real nonetheless.

The girl is scratched.

Chapter 89

Whitefish turnoff, Montana - 2011
Roarke and Snyder

The old truck passed by their Tundra and stopped in a parking space some distance away.

"Wait," Snyder said, from the seat beside him, and Roarke could see his hand was on his weapon.

The driver's door opened. Then the waitress from the diner climbed down from the cab and hurried toward the Tundra. She was no longer in her uniform, but dressed warmly in jeans, boots and a parka.

Roarke hit the automatic lock to open the back doors of the Tundra and Jean Lange slid into the back seat, pulling the door closed behind her. The vehicle's temperature dropped with the sudden breeze from outside. But Roarke was sure the pale of her face and the tremor in her shoulders had little to do with the weather.

Snyder looked to Roarke, with a subtle nod to take the lead.

Roarke turned in the front seat, opened his credentials wallet for Lange to see, and handed her their Bureau business cards. "I'm Special Agent Roarke. This is Special Agent Snyder. We appreciate you being willing to talk to us."

She nodded, not responding with her name.

Roarke wanted to start from as general a place as possible, to let her tell the story her own way. "In these situations, time is our enemy."

She nodded again tensely, so keyed up that Roarke wasn't sure she was hearing him. But then she spoke, so low he had to lean in to hear her.

"When I read that he went missing in the park... it's got to be connected, doesn't it?"

Roarke and Snyder exchanged a glance. *Connected to what?*

"It's not the first time," she'd said on the phone.

Snyder's face was open, encouraging. "That's why we're here," he said. An invitation for her to keep going.

"I saw the family. They came in to eat at the diner." Lange's voice dropped to barely a whisper. "And he was watching. Not them—him. The boy."

She hadn't said the name yet, and Roarke didn't want to say it for her.

"After lunch, they—the family—went in across the street to shop before they went on out of town."

Roarke prompted her, quietly, easily. "You're talking about the mercantile across the street from the diner?"

She nodded, barely, keeping her head down. "And next thing, I was reading about the boy going missing."

"Who was watching him, Ms. Lange?"

"Strauss," she whispered.

"Abraham Strauss, from the Northwest Brigade?"

She was instantly wary. More than wary. Frightened. "The… who?" Then more firmly. "No. I don't know anything about that."

Lie, Roarke thought.

Lange shifted in the back seat. "I'm here because of the boys. There's nothing I can tell you about any Brigade. Do you understand that?" Her voice was so vehement that the agents were stunned into silence.

But Roarke was almost positive she'd said "*boys*." Plural.

"We understand," he said, reassuringly, he hoped. "But you just said, 'It has to be connected.' What did you mean by that?"

She looked from one to the other of the agents.

"Oh God. You don't…" There was a sudden, stricken look on her face. "I can't be here. I have to go." She fumbled for the door and fled the car, walking fast to her own vehicle.

Chapter 90

Kalispell, Montana - 2011
Cara

She puts cash on the table and leaves the restaurant, moving outside to follow the girl. As she crosses the street, a wildly oversized truck zooms around a corner, sitting high on bloated tires, its engine husky and growling, far too loud and intrusive for the snow-blanketed streets. It swerves to the curb and stops.

The group of teenage boys that spills out of the tricked-out truck is pure trouble. She would know that even without the dark girl's reaction, a stiffening, a bracing for what is to come.

The boys have spotted the girl, too. She walks faster. Other kids on the sidewalk suddenly become very interested in the shop windows, or reverse course to avoid the pack of troublemakers.

The boys ignore the others and follow behind the dark girl, four of them, then surge forward, surrounding her in a horseshoe shape, a deliberate intimidation.

"Where you off to, Mays?" "Can't hide those tits under your Pop's coat."

They have not noticed Cara gaining on them. They are teenagers, oblivious to anything not in their direct line of vision. She must skirt around the side flank of two burly, parkaed boys and stop right in front of them to halt them on the sidewalk.

They are slow to take her in. Two of them are obviously slow in general, the leader marginally less so. He is bigger, bulkier. Handsomer in a brutish way.

"Who the hell are you?" he demands. Cara says nothing, just stares back at him without moving.

"I'm talkin' to you, bitch," he snarls.

The girl takes advantage of the distraction and slips silently away, with a quick, dark look at Cara: alarmed, suspicious, grudgingly grateful.

Cara keeps her eyes on the pack leader and remains silent.

"Are you dumb, or just dumb?" he quips. The other boys laugh dutifully.

She stands on the sidewalk without moving, with no response. Already her silence and stillness is making him twitchy. He is not used to being challenged by a woman.

The other boys shift beside him, shuffling uncomfortably. And she sees a flicker in his eyes. A deep-down fear that this is something he has never seen before, and might be more than he can manage with young, brute force.

She steps up close to him, puts her hand on his arm, and whispers. The look on his face turns from unease to sheer amazement at his luck.

"Aw, hell, yeah." He grins at his pack. "Catch you guys later."

The others respond predictably, leering and catcalls.

Cara backs away from them, deliberately. The leader turns and follows her, swaggering, as she moves into an alley between two buildings.

Here, out of sight of the street, she ducks behind a Dumpster and stops, waiting for him.

He is not long behind. Immediately he traps her against the icy wall, palms flat against the bricks, arms barricading her. Which suits her well, because it gives her room to bring the knife right up between his legs, jabbing its point into the base of his balls.

His eyes go wide as he yelps.

"I wouldn't move," she says flatly. He has enough consciousness to heed the warning and freeze.

She puts more pressure on the blade so he can feel the sharp metal slicing through his jeans, grazing his skin. But stopping short of cutting. "You bother that girl again and you'll lose it all. Don't think I won't find you." She recites his truck's license plate number.

He nods frantically.

Another jab to be sure he understands. "Step back. Slowly," she says.

He complies, edging backward.

"Now go."

And he is off, stumbling in the snow.

When she exits the alley, the boy is far down the street, not looking behind him.

She glances around and sees the girl across the street, between two buildings. Waiting. Watching.

Cara stops on the sidewalk, looking across the road at her. The girl flinches and moves quickly along the sidewalk.

Cara is no longer interested in the hunter. The boys she has forgotten already. She will follow the girl.

Chapter 91

Whitefish turnoff, Montana - 2011
Roarke and Snyder

Jean Lange's truck sped out of the parking lot, disappearing around the upward curve of road. The agents sat in the Tundra, and Roarke gripped the steering wheel in frustration. "I spooked her. I went too fast."

Snyder's response was calm, reassuring. "No. She was surprised that we knew about the Northwest Brigade. She's obviously terrified of doing anything to cross it."

Across the chasm in front of them, gray mist rolled off the sides of the mountains. Roarke stared at the mist, replaying the conversation in his head. He spoke, repeating Lange's words, "'It has to be connected.' What has to be connected to what?"

Snyder nodded, considering. "She has reason to think Strauss would abduct a child."

"And not just one," Roarke suggested, wondering if Chuck had heard what he had.

"No," Snyder agreed. "Not just one."

So Roarke hadn't imagined it, the plural. *Boys.*

"She's looking out that window at Strauss's store every day she's working. No telling what she's seen. Do we go after her?"

Chuck reached for his phone. "Too many variables. We'll need to check in with Ziskin. We can't dig into this until we find out what he wants us to do next."

Chapter 92

Kalispell, Montana - 2011
Cara

She stands against the outer wall of a liquor store, watching the girl walk across the parking lot of a motel. A not very nice motel, in a not very nice part of the city. Cara has seen many of them. Not a good place for this girl to be. She waits, tensely.

The girl walks along a row of rooms toward a cleaning cart standing unattended in front of a room with an open door. A slim and harried woman in her late thirties steps out of the room. And Cara relaxes. She can see the family resemblance even before the girl approaches and gives the woman a dutiful kiss. They have a brief exchange of words, then the girl walks back to the office and goes inside.

Cara waits for a minute or two, then moves close enough to catch a glimpse of the girl through the not very clean front window. She sits on a sagging sofa, earbuds in her ears, scribbling homework.

She looks fairly settled, no doubt waiting for her mother to get off her shift.

So Cara walks back to the street she started on to get her SUV. She drives back to the motel and parks it at the edge of the lot, with a view of the office, where the girl is still seated on the couch.

It is in moments like these that Cara is glad to have the portable heater. She turns the engine off and the heater on and waits, warming herself in the SUV in the parking lot for another half hour, before the girl's mother emerges from a hall without the cleaning cart, and gestures to the girl inside the office.

The girl emerges through the door, zipping up her backpack, and mother and daughter climb into an ancient truck.

As the two drive out of the motel parking lot, Cara follows.

She is not in the least surprised when they make the turn toward Snake River.

The old truck drives through the main street of town without stopping and on to a more rural road. After about ten minutes the truck turns again at a cluster of mailboxes with a familiar chainsaw-carved grizzly bear looming beside them.

Cara is right back where she lost the hunter and the van.

The path is always revealed.

She stops the SUV beside the mailboxes as the old truck proceeds down an unpaved road. She can see a barn through the trees.

She drives on a few hundred yards, parks the truck and gets out into the icy cold. She circles back on foot through the wooded property, crunching through snow in a copse of trees, and stops inside the tree line to look out at a rundown farm. A rail fence. The small barn she spotted from the road. And a clapboard farmhouse, with the old truck parked under a sagging carport.

There is a dog inside the house that stirs up a fuss when she skirts the side of the barn, but a woman's voice speaks faintly and the dog is silent again. Cara slips through the barn doors. The musty space has several stalls, inhabited by a cow and a horse, some chickens, and a large, furry, sleepy cat.

She finds an unoccupied stall with a crack in the plank wall that allows her a view of the house. The horse in the stall next to hers nickers softly at her but doesn't seem bothered.

Within minutes the girl leaves the house, heading straight for the barn. Cara steps further behind the stall door. But the girl walks past the barn, out into the woods.

Cara watches which way she goes, then leaves the barn and follows at a distance.

The girl drifts through the mostly bare trees of the woods. It is not quite the aimless wandering of a teenager. Cara senses some more focused purpose.

It is like following the hunter in the van, staying back far enough that the girl cannot see her. But there is no need to keep close. It is easy to spot her boot prints in the undisturbed snow.

About a half mile into the woods, in the midst of the towering, sticklike bare trunks, she comes across a single, small perfect tree covered in flaming red leaves.

Cara stops in the snow, arrested by the sight: the tiny, vibrant tree surrounded by the much taller bare ones.

She moves on, thoughtfully.

The trees open up into a clearing. And in this snowy circle is a small, old plank church, obviously no longer used. The windows have been shattered by rock throwers and gunshots. There are bullet holes in the walls.

No sign of the girl. But the boot prints lead up to the warped front steps.

Cara approaches the church, mounts the steps, pushes open the door and slips inside.

Inside it is dim and wrecked. Light filters through the bullet holes in the walls. Some of the pews are broken up.

There is a crunch of snow on wood flooring behind her.

Cara turns to see the girl, standing ten feet away. Aiming a shotgun.

The girl knows how to hold the gun. They face each other in silence for a long moment, then the girl speaks.

"I can shoot."

"I know you can," Cara answers.

"Did you follow me here?" the girl demands.

"Yes."

This obvious truth seems unexpected. The girl's grip tightens on the shotgun. "Why?"

Cara takes her time answering. "I think you have something to show me."

"I don't know you," the girl says belligerently.

"That's true. But we crossed paths." She lets the girl think about that for a moment, lets her remember the incident on the sidewalk with the pack of boys.

The girl is silent. But she is listening.

"You knew I was following. You led me here. I don't think it was to kill me. You know things, don't you? Things that are eating you up inside."

For a fleeting second, the look on the girl's face is total trauma. "How do you know?" she cries.

Cara thinks of the hunter, the shopkeeper, the sheriff, the strange, furtive exchange in the hardware store. "There are men in your town who think they can hide what they are. But you can see it, can't you?"

The girl looks nervously around her. "They'll kill you if they find you here."

Now they are getting somewhere. Cara nods. "Not just kill me. Killing would come later."

The girl gives a shudder of revulsion. Involuntary, Cara thinks. The girl doesn't know what she knows, but she senses it deeply.

"Because men like that, they only do one thing with girls."

The girl mumbles something incomprehensible. Cara doesn't hear. But she knows that whatever it is, it is the crux of everything.

"I'm going to sit down," she says.

The girl doesn't respond, so Cara lowers herself slowly to a seat in the nearest intact pew. She waits a moment, and when there is no response, she speaks again. "There's something wrong in this town."

And she waits. The girl fidgets, conflicted. She's also tired of holding the gun. Cara can see the barrel starting to droop.

"It's hurt you."

The girl doesn't answer, but there's no telltale flinch. Not her, then.

"Or it's hurt someone you know."

Now there is not a mere flinch, but a full-body shudder. "Why should I trust you?" the girl demands.

"Maybe I can help."

This gets the girl's attention. Her eyes become very focused and still. Cara presses the point.

"I did before, didn't I?"

"*Those* guys," the girl says, with a contempt that shows surprising strength. "They're just assholes." The boys on the sidewalk were bigger, older than she is, but she's not afraid of them. It's the men she fears.

Cara says it aloud. "There's a bigger problem, though."

The girl's face ripples with anguish. "You don't get it. They will fucking kill you."'

"If they would kill me, they would kill you, too."

The girl is trembling now. The gun is shaking with her.

"But you know that. That's what men like that do." And now, carefully. "You said something, before. What was it?"

She whispers it. But this time Cara hears.

"Not just girls."

Chapter 93

Portland - present
Roarke

Roarke sat on a boulder in the woods. He had not moved for some time, as he forced himself to review the timeline Singh had built of his life.

For a moment, he'd put aside unthinkable questions of Cara.

Because in a sea of bewildering unknowns, there was one solid revelation. He would bet any amount of money that Singh and Snyder were off in Montana, retracing that 2011 militia case. Following the loosest of threads, in search of a theoretical killer he and Chuck had called "The Wolf." Investigating the million-to-one chance that somehow Young John Doe had disappeared from Montana without anyone ever coming forth to claim him.

With no apparent evidence, his colleagues—and friends—were off in pursuit of a child killer.

But there was much, much more to it.

According to the case board in Snyder's study, Chuck and Singh had eliminated Roarke's own main suspect for the Wolf, John Lombard, because they thought Lombard was dead.

Because they thought Cara had killed him.

The thought made him shaky.

Here. She was here. In Portland, on that night we were after the Street Hunter. I was in that study feeling mortal danger because it was her *out there, going after Lombard herself.*

It was the most mad of thoughts. Far beyond what he'd ever let himself think before. Uncanny. Almost supernatural. But every moment of their…

Relationship

Connection

Connectedness

It had all been that, and more.

The red string.

His rational mind was still saying, *"It can't be."*

But the larger part of him, the knowing part, was focusing. If Cara had been here in Portland, there was someone who could actually tell him so.

He stood abruptly and started down the path again, headed for the nearest MAX train stop.

Chapter 94

Snake River, Montana - 2011
Cara

Outside the sky has gone to blue twilight. Cara can see the moon rising through one of the broken windows.

The church is freezing inside. The girl is shivering, unconscious of the fact. Now that she has opened up, she can't seem to stop talking.

Her name is Maise. She had a brother, Danny. Two years ago she was eleven and Danny was thirteen.

"But everyone always thought he was older. He was just bigger. All the coaches wanted him for football, baseball."

The man Cara saw in the hardware store, behind the counter, is the store's owner. Strauss. He is one of the baseball coaches for a church team, which Danny started playing on a little while after their dad took off and left the family.

Danny was only on the team for a few months before he quit. He didn't tell their mother, but he confided to Maise that Strauss was making up excuses to touch him. An arm around the shoulder. A playful spank. Progressing to more blatant touching.

Cara can only feel a dull rage. The whole town, most of the town, probably knows all of this. Certainly if Maise does, there are adults who know.

"And then one day Danny... he was just gone. Everyone says he ran away." Maise is shaking so hard her teeth are chattering. "That kids his age do. That he went to find our dad, or he just wanted to be someplace more cool. But he would've told me." Her voice rises. "He would have *told* me. He would've texted. Called. Something. He'd never let it go so long without... without telling us."

Cara speaks carefully, neutrally. "What does your mother think?

"Sheriff said he was seen in the bus station in Kalispell, so Mom believes him."

But you know better.

The girl swallows. "Last month this family came through the town on the way to Flathead. A bunch of people saw them. And now their boy is disappeared, like Danny. I saw his picture in the paper." Her eyes are dark in her pinched face. "He looked like Danny."

"You think Strauss killed your brother."

It's more a shudder than a nod. But the answer is clear. "They think they own everything."

"Who are *they?*"

"The Brigade. That's what they call themselves. The Northwest Brigade. They go out on the weekends, into the woods, and do drills. Like how to survive. Only it's more like how to take over than surviving. They go out in the woods in camo and do training for the War."

"The War," Cara repeats without inflection.

"Like they say is in the Bible."

Cara feels her gorge rise. It is a weird madness some people have. Affecting more people in the country than anyone civilized would want to admit. Belief in imminent apocalypse.

She suspects many of the "believers" don't really believe. It's an excuse to play with guns, to live out videogame fantasies of warfare and alpha male heroism. And exact bloody revenge on anyone who doesn't swallow their end-time scenarios.

"So they have guns," she says aloud.

The girl laughs shortly. "They have guns."

"That's very dangerous," Cara says. "Stupid men with guns... that's a bad combination. They can come to bad ends."

Maise shakes her head rapidly. Her breath is elevated. "You don't... you have no idea how many. More guns than you've ever seen before."

An arsenal. Even better. This may be easier than she could even dare to hope. They may have set their own trap. And again, she thinks briefly of Richmond. She's seen this kind of thing too many times since then. These pockets of madness. Of *It.*

"They'll kill you," Maise says again.

Cara looks at her. "Maybe I'll kill them."

The thought electrifies the girl. Cara can see it galvanize her body. "How?" she asks.

"How would *you* do it?"

And there on the girl's face she sees the thought, *the* thought, the idea that will make this work. To defeat whatever vile thing is in this town.

Chapter 95

Portland - present
Roarke

The young woman who opened the door to him in the TV station green room was elegant, urbane, knowing.

Roarke stood still at the sight of her. For a moment he could only look at her, remembering the medical chart detailing her injuries. It was a miracle Brandi Hughes was alive, much less thriving.

A cynical smile crossed her face. "Didn't you say the San Francisco Bureau? Surely I'm not that exotic to you."

She'd misinterpreted his surprise as transgender judgment.

He apologized quickly. "I'm sorry, no. It's just—I remember the attack on you. It's good to see you well."

An inscrutable look crossed her face. "That's kind of you. Please. Sit."

He did, and she lowered herself gracefully to the sofa across from him. He leaned forward, his arms on his knees, palms up, the body language of appeal. "I understand that this subject is difficult. But I'm here about Robert Jonah Barker."

The name did not produce the reaction he'd anticipated. Brandi merely arched her salon-tended eyebrows. "My goodness. The FBI certainly is suddenly very hot on a very cold case."

Roarke sat back, frowning.

Brandi explained, "I spoke with a lovely Agent Singh about the same thing just a few days ago."

It was exactly what Roarke had suspected. Singh *was* thinking Cara was here in Portland in 2009, during the Street Hunter investigation.

He leaned forward again. "Ms. Hughes, I believe we have a mutual friend."

"And who would that be?"

Roarke paused. "I don't know what she would have been calling herself at the time. But I think you knew her."

He reached for his phone, and put it down on the table between them. The police sketch of Cara looked up from the screen. Brandi did no more than glance at it. And Roarke knew.

He spoke slowly. "I think you told the police that Barker attacked you—to protect her."

Brandi's eyes widened in a surprise Roarke was sure was feigned. "That's quite a story."

Roarke surrendered to what he knew he had to do, and spoke the truth. "I'm not going to arrest you for protecting her, Ms. Hughes. I'd have to arrest myself."

Brandi's eyes widened. "Oh my," she said softly. And there was something else in her face, now: pity. "She does have her fans, doesn't she? But I'm afraid I have nothing to tell you. What does it matter now? A bad man got himself killed, ages ago. That was then. This is now." She lifted a hand, languidly encompassing the elegant office, the framed posters of her shows on the walls.

"Barker is dead," Roarke agreed. "And quite possibly John Lombard is as well." Brandi remained carefully neutral, not reacting to the name. "I'm not shedding any tears for either of them. No one is." He leaned forward, made eye contact. "But the boy who the police thought was the Street Hunter's last victim was never identified. Somewhere out there is a family that has no idea what happened to their son."

He watched Brandi's face, saw the empathy there. He added softly, "And I think his killer is still out there, too."

Brandi's eyes contracted, in fear, or anger, Roarke wasn't sure. When she spoke, her voice was toneless. "All I can tell you is—that 'mutual friend' you spoke of—she wouldn't let that go. Until it was done."

It crystalized what Roarke hadn't known he knew.

If Snyder and Singh were in Montana pursuing the Wolf, then Cara would be, too.

Chapter 96

Snake River, Montana - 2011
Cara

The sun sparkles like diamonds on a crust of snow outside her SUV, as she sits watching the street.

She has passed the night in a motel out of town.

Now she is parked again outside the mercantile store. Maise has pointed her here, but the hunter had already led her straight to him. The hunter and the hardware man are brothers in criminality and fanaticism. Arms traffickers. End-time dominionists. And if Maise is right, this one, this Strauss, is much more.

She is sure that Maise is right. The girl *knows* what happened to her brother, knows he is dead. She knows it in her soul. She has lived in this town her whole life. Like everyone alive, she is innately attuned to the essential nature of the people around her. Maise is simply more willing than most to accept the clues she is given.

And yet with these stakes, Cara needs to see for herself, to be sure.

She gets out of her vehicle and heads for the mercantile. She will buy a few innocuous items on pretense, so that she can see Strauss face to face.

There is no recreational store in a town this size, so the mercantile stocks items for the slopes, and advertises those items in its window. *Get your ski gear here*! No doubt in the hope of catching trade from tourists passing through. That is the part she plays.

Strauss watches her from the first moment she walks in through the door to the jangling of a bell. She does not have the luxury of lingering. She gives the store a glance, zeroes in on the front racks of ski accessories, and crosses directly to them.

She chooses a few ten-packs of hand warmers and foot warmers, several cans of oxygen, a knitted face mask, and a dark hat with earmuffs. All things a skier en route to the slopes would buy, and perfectly useful for tonight's *Work*.

She takes them up to the counter and drops them on the counter beside the register. Under the glass of the counter is the same violent yellow bumper sticker with its coiled rattlesnake that she had followed all the way up from Wyoming.

She feels Strauss studying her, but she doesn't look at him yet. She focuses on a front rack stocked with gloves and glances over the selection without acknowledging him.

"Headed to Whitefish?"

She turns to look at him for the first time.

She is wearing polarized glasses—a pair that looks like prescription lenses, with a tint that slowly fades indoors. The tint shields her eyes but doesn't draw the attention that sunglasses would.

In the few seconds she is staring at him, she sees hunting photos framed on the walls behind him, smug men showing their dominion over slaughtered animals. And a photo of Strauss beside a baseball team of boys just Maise's brother's age.

She puts the gloves down on the counter with her other accessories. "How much?" she says. Her voice is flat and cold, intended to provoke.

She sees just a flash of him, just for a moment. But it is more than enough. The seething hostility. The burning eyes. The simultaneous fear of her—of all women—and a desire to crush out all life. The blind hatred she knows as *It.*

Then he turns away to ring her up.

She takes her purchases and returns to her SUV. Although no one is following her, she locks the doors and drives immediately out of town, putting distance between herself and the man she has just seen.

She takes the turn back toward Kalispell.

There is a Walmart and a Home Depot there, where she will be able to buy several innocuous items in bulk. Flares. Fertilizer. Lighting fluid.

As venal men have proven over and over, it doesn't take a rocket scientist to build a bomb.

She even knows where to find a very large truck that might be very easy to steal. While its owner is busy at football practice, for example.

Poetic justice. Using Maise's teenage tormentor's truck will put him in dire straits with the men Maise calls the Brigade.

She will have no compunction about leaving him to worm his way out of that situation.

The wild card in the mix is Maise, herself.

Cara doesn't do this. There is no "we" in her journey. But this girl has stayed strong despite ultimate powerlessness in a town which assigns women and girls not one shred of value. She has earned the right to justice for her brother. Cara will not deny her that.

She will let Maise choose for herself.

Chapter 97

Snake River, Montana - 2011
Roarke and Snyder

After a night's sleep in a hotel in Kalispell, the agents spent the first part of the day reading over every entry in the National Center for Missing and Exploited Children database for the last three years, making notations they would be able to cross-reference with Strauss's coaching activities.

In the afternoon they met with Ziskin in a motel room that was one of the ATF's centers of operation, Snake River being too small for the Bureau to have set up inside its borders. Snyder filled Ziskin in on their brief but tantalizing conversation with Jean Lange. Ziskin confirmed that he knew of no other missing children from the area.

Roarke and Snyder headed back to Snake River as the blue shadows of night crept across that enormous sky. Snyder got out of the Tundra a few blocks away from Main Street to walk the rest of the way into town, where he planned to sit at a front window table at the Huckleberry Diner and order a large, leisurely meal.

Roarke drove the Tundra the rest of the way into town to park on the street and watch the hardware store from there.

Sitting in the chill dark, he typed out a text that said simply, "*Moving.*" He didn't send it. He only wanted it on hand in case he had to go without being able to contact Snyder.

Then he sat, watching the plate glass windows of Strauss's store, while Strauss moved around in the aisles, straightening, stocking, counting money from the cash register.

This man who may have killed children, after torturing them for his pleasure.

It was the most incomprehensible thing to Roarke. Equally incomprehensible that Strauss's militia buddies probably suspected this of him, if not outright knew it, and that somehow didn't disqualify him from the inner circle.

The twisted logic of dominionism in action.

Right on the dot of seven pm, Strauss moved away from the store counter, and crossed to the front door. He turned the sign from OPEN to CLOSED and shot the deadbolt.

Almost simultaneously, a Range Rover with the Sheriff's department logo emblazoned on the side pulled up in front of the diner.

Roarke's adrenaline spiked as he watched a bulky, deliberate, uniformed man get out of the car. The handlebar mustache made him easy to recognize from the photos in Ziskin's file. Not a deputy, but the Sheriff himself. Preston. An Oathkeeper, Ziskin had said.

He walked with heavy, booted steps up the sidewalk to the front door and entered the diner.

Roarke watched through the glass as Preston went straight for Snyder's booth and stopped there, in front of the table.

Even as Roarke tensed, he was telling himself, *Chuck knows what he's doing. Keep your eyes on your target.*

A minute later he saw a heavy Toyota truck pull out of the alley beside the hardware store. He hit SEND on his pre-written text.

And he followed, as far back on the road as he could stay.

Preston took a seat in the booth across from Snyder, settled in with an easy smile and flat, assessing eyes. "Fed, right? It's customary to let local law enforcement know you're in town."

Snyder knew Preston was either a militia member or an ally of the Brigade. As far as Snyder was concerned, his main goal was to keep the man talking, so Matthew could move if he needed to move.

He pushed his plate away, leaned back with an open gesture. "Sorry if there've been some crossed wires. I doubt my business has anything to do with your town, though. I'm Special Agent Snyder, with the Behavior Analysis Unit, Portland FBI. Violence against children, specifically. We've been asked for assistance in the disappearance of Timothy Whitcomb in Flathead Park in October."

To Snyder's surprise, the Sheriff tensed slightly, his pupils dilating.

That's interesting, Snyder thought.

Outside of Snake River, Roarke followed Strauss's truck on a dark and incredibly winding road. He kept easing further back on the gas, knowing he had to stay far, far behind to keep Strauss from catching on that he was being tailed.

After fifteen minutes of following, he called Snyder and got voice mail, which gave him a spike of unease. It likely meant that Chuck was still stuck with the Sheriff.

"I'm on Lenzie Road, heading east, following Strauss in a Toyota 4Runner." He recited the license plate number. "About nine miles out of town now—"

He broke off, startled, at the sight of a looming shadow beside the road. An enormous standing bear.

His heart started a crazy hammer in his chest, until he realized the bear was a sculpture, one of those chainsaw-carved things.

Strauss's truck had disappeared.

Roarke put the Tundra in reverse and backed up toward the bear. He spotted an unpaved, unlit road to the right, curving into the woods.

He made the turn.

Chapter 98

Woods outside Snake River, Montana - 2011
Cara

Dark has fallen and stars are popping out in the frozen sky.

Cara and the girl sit in the stolen truck on a low wooded hill, Cara watching the small valley below through binoculars.

The setup she sees through the lenses is one she has seen before. A couple of doublewide trailers buried deep in the forest within the property adjacent to Maise's family's farm. It seems to be militia standard: the doublewide weapons warehouse.

Cara suspects that the stockpile's proximity had been lethal for Maise's brother. But now, it is a point in their favor. Maise knows how to navigate through those woods, how to get to the trailer by truck via a just-wide-enough path on her grandfather's property.

Everything has proceeded without a hitch. The truck acquired, fertilizer and other items bought and loaded. Every part of the operation so smooth it is clear that the way they have chosen is correct.

Even if she had not seen the man called Strauss for herself, the number of guns Maise has told her about is always the work of *It*. The damage these men can wreak is unfathomable. She has been led here, one sign after another. She does not need to know what precisely these townsmen have planned with the weapons to know that it must be stopped. It is the only reasonable thing to do.

It will not be long, now. Now that it is dark, she could let Maise out, and drive this truck with its cargo of explosives down the hill, then jam the accelerator and let it crash into the trailer. But Maise has said that Strauss visits the trailers almost every night after he closes his shop.

Strauss is worth waiting for.

The girl is talking. She started fifteen or twenty minutes ago and now she can't seem to stop. Cara understands that. She cannot imagine what would pour out of her if she ever began to speak.

"People in this town believe these crazy things. Like they say God is gonna Rapture up all the Christians any day now. But so far they're all still here. Even my Mom believes it. I don't think she all the way believes it but she's scared to not believe it. You know? I think maybe she wants to believe that Danny got Raptured because he was too good for this world. And he was."

Her eyes are wide, dilated.

"They *want* the end of the world. They *want* it. They want a war so they can fight and hurt and kill. And everyone knows it," the girl says in anguish. "Everyone knows, and they don't do anything." She is overcome, barely present in her own body.

Cara puts her hand out to halt the mad outpouring of grief. She doesn't touch her, but the girl stops anyway.

"We are doing something," Cara says. She sees the girl's rapid breathing slow, and consciousness returns to her eyes.

Now that Cara has Maise's attention, she says to the girl, "But you need to leave. Here. This place."

Maise shakes her head automatically. "I can't leave my Mom. She's lost my dad, my brother..."

"You and your mother both. You need to get out of this town."

"She'll never go."

"She'll go—for you." She has seen Maise's mother. She believes this is so. "Not right away. But soon."

The girl withdraws into herself. Thinking. And Cara does not speak again… until she sees the sudden flash of headlights in the woods.

Chapter 99

Woods outside Snake River, Montana - 2011
Roarke

Roarke had slowed way down to navigate the unpaved road. It had branched early on, one path leading off to a farmhouse with a barn. He'd hesitated over it, then caught the flash of the lights of Strauss's truck ahead, down the other fork.

He followed. The night, and the road, got darker.

Suddenly there was a pale streak of movement in his headlights. A wraith, darting across the road.

Roarke slammed on the brakes, fishtailing the Tundra. The SUV skidded to a halt at the side of the road.

He stared out the windshield into the dark. The headlights shot into the trees beside the road, two white beams. His heart thudded in his chest.

He drew his service weapon, got out of the SUV, staying behind the open driver's door. The woods felt alive: an icy wind breathing through the trees, rippling branches. The stars were brilliant, pulsing.

And there was someone out there. He could feel... *Her? Could that be?*

In his mind's eye, he called up the figure he had seen on the road. *Young. Feminine.* Not the size of a grown woman. *A teenager?*

He lowered the Glock. "Hey. Are you hurt?" He listened into the silence. It felt loaded, occupied. "Do you need help?"

The feeling of presence receded.

He twisted around to move back toward the driver's door....

And stopped in his tracks, staring toward the back tire, opposite.

He moved up to the vehicle, shined his phone light at the tire... and saw the deep cuts. Slashed.

Damn.

There was no way to follow Strauss on foot. Not without knowing where he was going, or how far he was going.

And whoever had slashed his tires was in the vicinity, watching him.

He turned and shouted into the darkness. "I'm armed and I'm pissed. You should move along."

No answer came back.

He set his jaw, checked his service weapon, then pulled the tire jack and spare out of the back of the truck and got to work.

He was angry, and he was very aware that being outside the Tundra, changing the tire out here on the road, made him vulnerable. He had no idea who might be out there in the dark.

He wasn't going to sit cowering in the car. But all his senses were on high alert as he jacked up the vehicle, unscrewed the nuts and switched out the tire. He kept stopping to look out into the woods.

It felt weird. It felt *wrong...*

A tremendous explosion rocked the night, shook the ground beneath his feet.

Instantly he could feel the heat of it, like a tidal wave in the air. Trees in the near distance went up in flame, orange fire crawling up the trunks, seeking the upper branches.

Without stopping to think, he sprinted in the direction of the fire. Then some force whooshed through the dark. Suddenly he was on his back on the ground, the wind knocked out of him.

Before he could regain his senses, another explosion rocked the night. This time the wave of heat rolled right over him. For one endless moment of terror he thought he was in the center of the fire...

But it was just air, blazingly hot air. And through the ringing in his ears, he could hear rapid popping.

Gunshots.

Chapter 100

Snake River, Montana - 2011
Snyder

Snyder felt the buzz of his phone against his hip, but kept his eyes on the sheriff, kept talking in a casually professional tone. "Apparently the Whitcomb family stopped here in town before Timothy's disappearance."

Preston wasn't giving him anything. "I'm sure they stopped a lot of places. Doesn't mean there's some pervert in my town. Everyone knows each other here. It's good people."

Snyder answered mildly, "We have no reason to suspect anyone in town. But in the last few years, have there been any other disappearances? A preteen boy, maybe thirteen or fourteen?"

The sheriff's lip curled in hostility. "You think I somehow forgot about some child abduction?"

"Not an abduction, necessarily," Snyder suggested. "Might have looked like a runaway situation."

A sound came from under the table between them: the radio on Preston's hip crackling. The sheriff ignored it, but the crackle came again, insistent. He stood and stepped away from the table to answer.

Snyder couldn't hear details, but the Sheriff's face seemed to pale under the fluorescent lights.

Without a word or a look back at Snyder, he was striding out the door.

Snyder watched him with an elevated heart rate.

Something just went down.

He put money down on the table to pay for his meal and easily, casually, walked out the door.

From the porch of the diner, he watched Preston squeeze himself behind the wheel of his official SUV. The vehicle started off with a roar of engine.

Snyder was just reaching for his phone when it buzzed again. He hadn't known how tense he'd been until he heard the sound of Matthew's voice, speaking fast, words jittery with adrenaline.

"I'm out on a private offshoot of Lenzie Road, about a mile in. There's been an explosion. A major blast—"

Snyder didn't wait for the end of the sentence. "Are you safe?"

"I'm some distance from the origin. I can see the fire, maybe half a mile away. Trees are blazing. I had a tire blowout. Best luck of my life, it turns out—" His voice stopped. "I can hear—"

His voice dropped off for an alarming moment, and Snyder felt himself age ten years in the silence. And then Matthew was back.

"Popping. Like fireworks. Ammunition, I think."

"An explosion the size you're talking about—it could be the militia stockpile." Snyder glanced back toward the diner. "I was deep into a very interesting and evasive conversation with Sheriff Preston when he got a radio call and rushed off without explanation."

He could hear the tension in Matthew's voice. "He's coming here, then. Unless there's some other back road from town, he's going to run right into me."

"Is your tire fixed?"

"Just."

"Then drive now," Snyder ordered. "When you're stopped, show your credentials. Say you're consulting on the Timothy Whitcomb case. You were on your way to West Glacier when you saw the explosion and drove toward it as a first responder. I'll be there as soon as I can—"

"Hold on. There's someone coming...."

"Matthew," Snyder said quickly.

But the phone had disconnected. Matthew's voice was gone.

Roarke turned to face the approaching headlights. All he could see against the brights was the dark shape of an SUV.

It pulled up beside him and the passenger door opened. And he stared in at a male shadow, crowned by a duckbill cap.

Chapter 101

Kalispell — present
Snyder, Singh, Ziskin

Singh leans tensely forward in her seat. "It was Sheriff Preston?"

"It was me," Ziskin says. "We got word of the explosion through the National Forest Service. I was on my way three minutes after the fire started."

And though it is years after the fact, the action long concluded, Singh lets out her breath in relief.

Ziskin continues, "We figured it was an explosion of stockpiled armaments. I say 'figured' because the sheriff didn't let us anywhere near the fire or the investigation. His deputies were in there immediately, blocking off access that night. But whatever happened with the explosion, it's a good bet Strauss had something to do with it, because he disappeared that night."

Singh looks to Snyder, startled. He is perched on the edge of his chair, elbows on his knees, intent, nodding.

He remembers, she realizes.

"The mercantile was closed the next day, mid-week, and folks at the diner and on the street were buzzing about it. An employee was there manning the cash register later that afternoon, saying Strauss had to leave town on business. We took a look around his house. His truck was gone, no answer at the door. We followed up several times. Never a sign of him." Ziskin shrugs. "He had no relatives to speak of. Within a month his store got taken over by the Colonel, the snowmobile chain owner."

Singh raises her eyebrows.

"Yeah. So. Strauss may have been killed. He may have absconded with some of the arms. He may have been responsible for the detonation, either deliberately or through negligence, and the militia eliminated him. Whatever happened, Sheriff Preston made sure it was kept under wraps. County sheriffs in isolated areas are the masters of their own little domains. But April nineteen came and went and there was no attack or attempted attack on any government officials or buildings anywhere in the Pacific Northwest. We had a strong suspicion the explosion took out whatever arms cache the Brigade had, or at least a good bit of it. When there was no April nineteenth action, and nothing for months afterward, we moved on to more active threats."

Singh finishes softly for him, "And no one ever heard from Strauss again."

It is late in the day when Ziskin returns Singh and Snyder to their vehicle, and Singh drives them back in to Kalispell to find a hotel for the night.

She concentrates on the dusky road, but she is brooding as she drives, turning over Ziskin's narrative in her mind. Suddenly she pulls off to the side of the road and turns to Agent Snyder.

"The case was about the potential militia attack. But your deep recollection from that time is of the missing boy. Timothy Whitcomb. Who is still missing, to this day."

In the seat beside her, Snyder nods, intent. "True."

"In your recollection, you superimposed the details of the attack and murder of Young John Doe. You said the missing boy was hurt in the same way. But the missing boy you described was actually Aaron Light, the five-year old boy who disappeared from Glacier National Park in October. You have been connecting not just two cases, but three. Young John Doe, Timothy Whitcomb, and Aaron Light."

It is heartbreaking to see confusion back on Agent Snyder's face after his confident certainty of the day. "I suppose... I may have been thinking that Snake River is so close to Glacier…"

She prompts him. "And you were thinking of the forensic evidence on Young John Doe. The gray wolf fur and the calcium carbonate."

"Yes," he says more firmly. "All of that felt like Glacier."

"And also that Aaron Light was a similar abduction to the Whitcomb case: a boy taken from his family in a wilderness park. Your investigative mind is connecting Aaron Light to the other two cases."

"Yes," Snyder says.

"So my question is: *Was* there a boy of Young John Doe's description missing from the Snake River area in 2009?" Before he can speak, she continues. "I realize there are none listed in the Missing Children database. And Sheriff Preston told you that there was no missing boy in town in 2009. But if Preston was the investigating authority…"

"He may never have entered Young John Doe into the database." Snyder says, and Singh hears the electric realization in his voice.

"Precisely." She looks at him, her eyes alight. "And what I am wondering is, what might Jean Lange have to say about Young John Doe?"

Chapter 102

Portland - present
Roarke and Epps

On the sidewalk outside the TV station, Roarke fished for his phone and called Epps. He was met by stony silence on the other end of the line, and he knew he owed his agent more than an apology.

"I lost it," he said into the phone. "I couldn't deal. But I need to apologize to you on the road. We need to get up to Montana. Pick me up and I'll explain on the way to the airport."

He paced the sidewalk while he waited for Epps.

Brandi Hughes had been all the confirmation he needed. He was now sure: Cara had been in Portland during the Street Hunter investigation.

Was she also in Snake River in 2011, the night of the explosion? The night of the fire that might have killed him?

The wraith he'd seen on the road that night...

Not Cara.

He didn't think so, anyway. She would have been younger, it was true, but not that much younger.

It hadn't been a vision. There had been a girl.

She was real.

The sound of a horn pulled him from his thoughts. Epps pulled up to the curb in the rental SUV.

Roarke pulled open the passenger door, climbed up into the seat and turned to face his agent. Epps didn't wait until Roarke was buckled in before he was pulling back out into traffic. His face was set and he didn't wait for an apology or explanation.

"Tech called back with the location of Tara's and Snyder's texts. They're in Kellogg, Idaho. I've booked two flights to Spokane. We've got an hour and a half to takeoff."

Epps pushed his foot down on the gas, and spoke no more.

But Roarke's mind was racing.

Kellogg was where their militia investigation had started. And Spokane was the closest airport to Kellogg.

But those texts that got traced were from two days ago.

And in our investigation in 2011, Kellogg was just a pit stop. What if they've moved on to Snake River?

His mind ranged quickly over the options. Spokane Airport was closer to Kellogg, but the airport in Kalispell would be closer to Snake River.

He spoke aloud. "Not Idaho. We need to go to Montana."

Epps glanced at him in consternation. Roarke reached for his phone to dial the airline.

He hoped to God he was right.

PART SEVEN

Chapter 103

Snake River, Montana – present
Singh and Snyder

Global warming is on full display as Singh and Snyder arrive in Snake River.

The surrounding peaks still have plenty of snow, but the towns she and Agent Snyder have driven through en route from Kalispell are showing signs of green. On the hills, at the side of the road, ice is melting everywhere. Not just rivulets of water, but whole crashing waterfalls. Another early spring. Good for them, bad for the planet.

The agents know Jean Lange still lives just outside of the town, but they do an initial drive through the town center. It is quaintly picturesque, but the first word that comes to Singh's mind is "sleepy." Post office, pawn shop, general store.

Agent Snyder stares out the window. "It's still here." He nods out to a shop. "Strauss's store. And the store name is the same: Snake River Mercantile."

Singh looks to the other side of the street, and sees the Huckleberry Diner, advertising *"World Famous Pie."* All as in Agent Snyder's story. As if time has stood still.

She parks the SUV on the street and the agents get out to walk toward the diner. They are dressed casually, she in jeans over silk leggings and a lightweight parka. More cover, like the ski racks.

But she gets sideways looks on the street, from a couple of older men sitting on one of the wooden benches outside the diner, from a truck full of teenage boys slowing at a stop sign. In this place, her skin is exotic. She has not seen any non-white persons since they drove into town.

Which is a problem right away, in terms of anonymity, Singh can see. The town being too far off the highway to be a tourist stop, every stranger appears neon-lit, and herself even more so.

She is acutely aware of the gazes as she and Agent Snyder enter the diner.

Inside it is exactly as he had described. They are able to seat themselves at a table in front of a huge plate glass window looking out on the street, with a perfect view of the mercantile just across it.

They have worked out their roles, their topics of conversation. They are headed to Whitefish, a ski town that is the most logical destination in the area at this time of year, with rustic charm, views of the Rockies, authentic dining, a historical railroad depot.

As their waitress hands them menus and pours them coffee, they use their phones to look at websites and chat about what Whitefish attractions are open, which restaurants require reservations, about the ski conditions and recommended microbreweries.

Singh glances up at the waitress, half expecting Jean Lange, but Snyder gives her a barely perceptible shake of the head and continues their tourist talk. "I've also heard the Bonsai Brewing Project is excellent, and they have live music. Let's see..." He scrolls on his phone.

The bells tied to the door jangle and someone enters behind them. Singh hears not steps, but a sound of metal thudding against glass before she turns.

And sees a man in a wheelchair, piloting himself into the diner.

She is frozen for a moment in horror and pity.

Most of the flesh on one side of the man's face has been melted away, and the burn scars continue down his neck, disappearing into the neckline of his coat. His hands on the wheelchair arms have been burned into claws.

She quickly reminds herself, *The body is a shell, a container for spirit, no more.*

But her revulsion does not diminish. Rather it grows stronger.

Help me out of my fear, she prays. *Help me to see this differently.* She is so intent on her inner struggle she nearly jumps out of her skin when Snyder's hand closes around her arm.

She looks at him. He meets her gaze, and releases her. "Nothing live at the Brewing Project tonight," he says. "Maybe at the hotel." He types a bit, and Singh's phone flashes a text.

His eyes direct her to take it.

She picks up her phone to see a two-word message that chills her to the bone.

That's Strauss.

Chapter 104

Snake River, Montana – present
Singh and Snyder

Agent Snyder pays their bill unhurriedly, thanks the waitress, and the agents leave the diner, heading for their vehicle.

As soon as Agent Snyder shuts the SUV's door behind him, Singh turns to him from the driver's seat and blurts, "Are you sure?"

The burned man had been barely recognizable as human, much less as a specific human being.

"Not a hundred percent," Snyder admits. "But he looked straight at me. It was almost…"

"What, Agent Snyder?" she asks, unable to wait.

Snyder speaks slowly. "It was as if he came in to look at us, specifically. He looked right at us. At me. I think he recognized me." He indicates the steering wheel. "We should drive."

Singh starts the engine with shaking hands, and steers away from the curb. The town is so small there are only two ways to go, and instinctively she drives out the opposite road from the way they came.

Snyder is thinking aloud. "He disappeared the night of the fire because he'd been burned. We couldn't find him because he was in intensive care somewhere, under another identity. He would have had to have some major medical work. Burn unit, rehab."

Singh watches the road and forces her jittery mind still. She continues his train of thought. "He could also have been in hiding. Thinking he had been personally targeted, that it was imperative for him to disappear. Perhaps the Colonel paid for private care in some off-the-grid setup. It would have taken years of surgeries and skin grafts for him to be functional again."

"The question is, how functional is he?" Agent Snyder asks, his voice tense.

Singh looks at him, her breath suddenly shallow.

Snyder continues. "In his condition he wouldn't be able to subdue a teenager, even a young teenager. But a five-year old…"

She shivers, but is following him. "Aaron Light. Strauss is choosing younger victims because that is all he is capable of now."

The agents look at each other in realization. And Snyder says softly,

"Child predators never stop. They do it until they die."

When Jean Lange returns to her house a few miles out of Snake River, Singh and Snyder are seated on the sagging couch on the porch, waiting for her. They stand as she exits her vehicle.

Lange recognizes Snyder instantly. It is clear from the terror on her face.

Snyder steps forward toward her. His voice conveys firm, implacable authority. "Ms. Lange, I think you know we're not going to leave. And I know you don't want to be seen talking with us on your front porch. The sooner you let us in, the safer it will be. For all of us."

It is only another moment before she unlocks the door and lets them pass, closing and bolting the door behind her.

The house is cluttered. Beer cans and liquor bottles on the coffee table, dirty glasses on the windowsill and the floor, overflowing ash trays.

Singh suspects the debris is not Lange's. The woman seems embarrassed, even mortified, reaching to picking up carelessly discarded chips packages and beer cans as she speaks nervously. "I haven't had time—"

"It's quite all right," Agent Snyder says kindly. "Please don't bother for us."

His reassurance calms her somewhat, but she continues to tidy as Snyder speaks.

"You remember me, don't you, Ms. Lange?"

She shoots a glance at him, gives a quick, distracted nod.

"Seven years ago, you knew something that you wanted to tell my partner and me, despite the potential danger to yourself. Are you aware that a five-year-old boy went missing in Glacier National Park a few months ago?"

She stops her nervous cleaning and straightens, standing with her face turned away from them.

Snyder continues, gently. "It seems whatever was going on seven years ago is still going on, or it's started up again. Maybe it's time to tell someone what you know."

She begins walking the room, seeming far too jumpy to sit down. "I knew you'd be back."

"Did you?" Snyder asks. "Why is that?"

"Cause Strauss came back."

Singh's eyes meet Agent Snyder's. He speaks casually. "We thought he'd died in that explosion in the woods, the one that happened the night after we met you."

Lange shifts, uncomfortably. "I guess you'd know about that, him getting caught in that fire."

"But he came back into town recently?" Snyder suggests.

"Four or five months ago. Hurt real bad." She shivers.

"Do you know where he'd been?

She gives a quick shake of her head. Singh thinks there is no reason not to believe her.

Snyder continues. "Seven years ago you were speaking to us of Timothy Whitcomb, who disappeared from Flathead Lake that October. But there was another, wasn't there? That's why you called us."

She drops her eyes, her head, and speaks, so low that Singh has to stop breathing to hear. "Danny Porter."

Snyder and Singh lock eyes. A new name.

"Tell us about Danny," Snyder says.

Chapter 105

Portland - present
Roarke and Epps

It took the better part of the drive to the airport to fill Epps in on the ATF case in Snake River. The other agent was scarily intent at the wheel.

"So the intel from this waitress was that the hardware store owner, Strauss, had abducted Timothy Whitcomb."

"That he might have," Roarke corrected. "Nothing was ever definitive—"

"But you met the guy," Epps said, glancing at him from the driver's seat.

Roarke was remembering the photos of the baseball team on the hardware store walls, all those boys. And the flat, unfocused look on Strauss's face when Roarke tried to talk to him about the coaching.

"Yeah. I met him. If I had a kid that age, I wouldn't want Strauss around him."

Roarke hadn't let it go. Not entirely. He'd checked the databases occasionally over the next few years. Plugging in missing boys from eight to fifteen. Putting a flag out for murders of boys of the same age range. In two or three years, he'd followed up on three potentials, but two were eventually solved and the other—just didn't fit. And he'd never been able to find the slightest trace of Strauss.

He said so to Epps, and finished, "As far as I know, no one ever heard from Strauss again. Best guess is he died in the explosion."

"But you don't know."

"I don't know." Roarke continued reluctantly. "And then in October, Aaron Light disappeared from the Glacier area. I didn't know that until Chuck called about it in December. We—the team—was so focused on the Lindstrom case... and by then we were dealing with the pimp murders..."

And Jade, and Rachel, and Bitch...

"And you didn't think Aaron Light fit because he was just five." Epps pondered it, staring out at the road in front of them.

"More to the point, Chuck was never *on* the Aaron Light case. It was his mind, playing tricks—"

Epps interrupted. "Obviously Tara thinks there's a hell of a lot more to it. Why else... why would she go off—why would they go off on their own like that...."

Roarke realized it was beyond time for him to come clean. "There's something I have to tell you. Singh isn't talking to you because... what I mean is, it's not about you. There are things you don't know—"

Epps exploded. "I don't know? No. *You* haven't said. *She* hasn't said." His agitation was clear in his voice, in his body, in the clenching of his hands on the wheel. "How much of an idiot do you think I am?"

And Roarke realized Epps was right. *He* was the one who had been an idiot, for ever thinking Epps hadn't sensed it all, all along.

Epps drove on in agitated silence. When he spoke again, his voice was toneless, but calm. "What these women have been through. We can't judge it. The violence of their everyday lives. That—predator in charge, appointing more predators every day. They are insane with rage and grief. And Cara…" He trailed off as he stopped the SUV at a light. As the engine idled, he turned in his seat to face Roarke. "Maybe Cara just knew it sooner."

The agents looked at each other, really looked at each other. And Roarke felt the wall between them crumble softly to sand.

Chapter 106

Snake River, Montana - present
Singh and Snyder

The agents have finally convinced Jean Lange to sit. Her face and voice soften as she speaks of these people she has obviously known for some years.

"The Porters are local, longtime. Grandparents, great-grands. Trish Porter married an out-of-towner, and four, five years ago he up and left her. Her and the kids moved back in with her dad." Her eyes are dark, empathetic. "So she's there raising two kids on a farm... caring for her father until he passed. She had to get some shit job in Kalispell to make ends meet." She stops for a moment, lost in thought. When she continues, it is with great reluctance. "Danny was twelve or thirteen years old, sweet kid."

Hearing this age is electrifying. It takes all of Singh's self-discipline has not to react.

"Trish's girl Maise is the smart one. A little younger than Danny. Neither of 'em really fit into this town, if you know what I mean. And

Danny… he was big for his age, really handsome boy…" She stops, looks away, jiggling her crossed leg nervously on top of the other.

"And that became a problem for him?" Agent Snyder suggests.

She nods to him. "I saw you and your partner sitting in the diner watching Strauss's store and that's when I thought you'd put it together. The Whitcomb boy, and Danny…"

"What happened to Danny?" Snyder asks evenly.

Lange looks down at her hands in her lap. "What everyone says is he run off. California or some such. Trish told me the sheriff found a lady working at the bus terminal in Kalispell who sold him a ticket for cash."

Snyder and Singh exchange a glance. *The sheriff.*

"Well, what are you going to do? Sheriff tells you something like that…" Lange trails off, looking bleak. "What are you gonna do?"

Singh has the sense she is talking about more than the situation. About her entire life.

"But Maise didn't believe it. She'd come in the diner and sit right up at that same table you guys were at. She'd do her homework there at the window and make a Coke last a long, long time."

"She was watching Strauss's store?" Singh asks softly.

Jean nods. "I mean… other people seen Strauss looking at various boys…"

"Like you saw him looking at Timothy Whitcomb."

She drops her eyes. "People knew. She was close with her brother. She would know."

"Did you ever talk to her about it?"

Again she looks away. "I told her to pray for her brother and don't give up hope, but she should help her Ma 'stead of sitting in the diner all day. I told her it was no good for her or her Ma."

She looks at them now, defensive. "No good was gonna come from her staking out Abraham Strauss."

"Of course not. You're one hundred percent right about that," Agent Snyder assures her.

"Everybody talks. And she was a kid. What could she do?"

Singh thinks of Strauss, the melted man in his wheelchair, and has an odd, electric flicker of intuition. *No, nothing a lone girl could do. But what if she had help?*

Then Jean Lange is speaking again.

"When I read about the other boy missing in Flathead it brought it all up again. And you Feds showed up and I just knew that's why you were here. I guess I figured… I owed her."

Agent Snyder says gently, "But you didn't tell us about Maise."

She stiffens. "You said you was—*were*—here about the Brigade. I'm sorry, but I can't have nothing to do with that. You don't know. You just don't know."

Snyder's voice is gentle, an absolution. "You're right, we don't. But Ms. Lange, I just need to ask you… when did Danny Porter go missing?"

Even though Singh knows what Lange is going to say, the words are like a thunderclap.

"It was 2009."

The year Young John Doe was dumped by the Columbia River.

Lange continues, "But Strauss disappeared and folks said he was dead. There were no more kids, you know, missing. So I thought, well, that's the end of that."

Not the end for Danny's sister and mother, Singh thought. *Not for Timothy Whitcomb's family.* She feels a wave of nausea, thinking of the limbo they must all still be living in. Never knowing.

Jean Lange bristles, as if hearing her thoughts. "No, I didn't call any police. What good would it've done? Sheriff has jurisdiction and they'd only pass it on to him."

Of course it must feel inescapable, Singh thinks. *Growing up in a town like this, run like an isolated kingdom by a group of fanatic, authoritarian, heavily armed men.* She must force herself back to the conversation at Agent Snyder's next words.

"We need to speak to Maise Porter. Do you know where she is?"

Lange gives him a quick, furtive look. "Left town. Pretty soon after you feds came here. Her and her Ma both."

Especially if Maise had anything to do with the armament explosion, Singh realizes.

"I got Trish a job at the park," Lange finishes.

"Glacier, you mean?"

"Yeah. I do some work there, summers. Trish asked if I could put in a word. The two of 'em moved house and didn't come back. Don't know 'bout Trish, but I'm pretty sure Maise works there, now."

"Isn't the park closed until spring?" Agent Snyder asks, surprised.

"They hire people in early to do the cleaning and prep for the season. The hotel at Many Glacier."

Singh and Snyder exchange a glance.

"Thank you, Ms. Lange," Agent Snyder says, softly. "Thank you."

Back in the SUV, Singh has barely shut the door before she is turning to Agent Snyder. "It was Strauss we saw."

Alive, horribly burned and injured.

Snyder begins, "And Danny Porter—"

"Is Young John Doe," Singh finishes.

"We need to move on," Snyder says, glancing out at the house. "And hope for Lange's sake that no one saw us here."

Singh drives to the next town, where they park outside a motel and use their tablets to connect to the database of the National Center for Missing and Exploited Children, searching for Danny Porter's name.

The search quickly confirms what they already know: Danny Porter is not listed among the missing.

"Sheriff Preston made sure he never got listed," Singh guesses.

"Or he removed him," Agent Snyder agrees.

"So Strauss, with or without the help of the other militia men, moved Danny's body and dumped him in the vicinity of the Street Hunter's newly unearthed victim."

Snyder stares out the windshield. "He may have done it himself. But the militia had a lot to protect. The snowmobile sales route and their weapons buying took any numbers of the Colonel's salesmen all over the Pacific Northwest. It wouldn't have been difficult to transport a body in a delivery van."

Singh felt a fierce hope. "If Danny is Young John Doe, Maise can identify the body. We will be able to confirm through matching their DNA. We can bring him to rest, and ease her mind."

"Yes. Maise is the key."

But Jean Lange has also informed them that Many Glacier Hotel is far enough into the park that there is no internet—nor even cell phone reception. They have no way of contacting Maise except to go to her.

The agents simultaneously reach for their phones to cue up the GPS directions. They study the maps on their phones.

It is a four and a half-hour drive to Many Glacier Hotel, on the east side of the park. There is only one direct route through the park, the legendary Going-to-the-Sun Road, and it will be impassable this time of year. They will have to drive up into Canada and circle well above the park on Canadian 3, then re-enter the US, to access Highway 2 on the east side of the park to get to the Many Glacier Entrance Station and the hotel there.

The agents look at each other.

"Let's go," Snyder says softly.

Chapter 107

Alberta, Canada - present
Singh and Snyder

Singh wakes to motion. She opens her eyes to find herself in the passenger seat of the SUV, with Agent Snyder at the wheel, driving the winding road. She had been lulled into sleep by the soporific motion of the vehicle.

Her body is cramped, both from the seat and from one of those irritatingly real-life dreams in which she had been hunched in a chair over a computer keyboard, doing endless data entry.

Her subconscious rehashing the feeling of their ViCAP work. As boring a dream as it could be.

And yet…

She frowns, trying to remember.

The dream dissipates as Snyder smiles at her, speaking from behind the wheel. "Good. I was about to wake you. The view is getting pretty unmissable."

Singh lets the dream go and turns to look through her window. The scenery outside the vehicle is indeed, breathtaking. The layered black and gray and white clouds in an endless sky above. White-barked birch trees. Wide snowy fields under sharp blue glacier-carved peaks. Sheer cliff faces. A river running alongside the sidewinder road.

A highway sign flashes by, indicating the miles to Many Glacier Entrance Station. They had been driving in Canada and are now back across the US border—

And Singh goes still, remembering.

In her dream, she had *not* been entering data into ViCAP. It had been the ViCLAS database. The Canadian version.

Her assignment here with Agent Snyder, from the start, has been the database.

Of course.

"Agent Snyder!" she says, so loudly he brakes and pulls off the road to the shoulder.

"What in the world—"

She is already unbuckling her seat belt to fumble for her phone. "In your narrative, you said the Wolf crossed borders to kill: Montana to Idaho. If we are this close to the Canadian border, would he not have done some of his hunting across the border, perhaps thinking that that would confuse jurisdictions even more? And if he crossed the border into Canada..."

Snyder finishes with her. "They have ViCLAS."

The agents look at each other, electrified. And Agent Snyder says softly, "We've been searching the wrong database."

Chapter 108

Snake River, Montana - present
Roarke and Epps

The agents stood beside the sagging couch on Jean Lange's porch, knocking on the door. And again. And again.

No answer.

They both shifted on their feet, uneasy, reluctant to leave.

Roarke reached out and tried the knob. Locked.

The men looked at each other. "We can't," Roarke said simply. "Nothing even close to probable cause."

Finally they turned to leave. But Epps stopped on the steps. "Wait."

Roarke paused to look at him.

"Something's off," Epps said, frustrated.

Roarke nodded, tense. "But what?"

Epps turned, and looked around the porch. "Tara," he said. Roarke frowned. Epps lifted his hands. "I feel like she's… here. Or she's been…"

"Okay," Roarke said carefully. "Just stand there. What is it? Something you see? Something you heard?"

Epps breathed out, composing himself. He stood for several beats, and then said, "I feel her. I..." He looked around him at the flooring, the painted planks, the battered chairs. And then he focused on the couch below the window.

Roarke watched as Epps crossed to it, bent to it. He picked up a cushion and brought it to his face.

He twisted around to Roarke. "It smells like her. It's this exotic thing she wears. Frankincense. Saffron."

Roarke turned and strode to the rental car. He opened the trunk and rooted around in his suitcase, pulled out the Maglite he always stowed with emergency supplies in his travel bag. He walked back up the porch steps and pointed the beam of the Maglite through the window.

He put his face to the glass and stared inside as he played the beam over the shadowy living room. Worn furniture, beer cans on the coffee table, a TV that undoubtedly cost more than the sum total of other objects in the room...

Normal...

And then he saw it. Something sticking out behind the couch. Just the end of a wooden leg of some small table. *But parallel to the ground.* The end table was lying on its side.

He jerked back from the window, turned, and kicked the door in.

They found Jean Lange in a crumpled heap on the floor of the hall outside one of the bedrooms.

While Roarke knelt beside her, feeling for a pulse, Epps was already on the phone to emergency services, shouting the address into the phone. "I need an ambulance *now.*"

Lange's pulse was erratic, but present. Roarke checked her over carefully. Her eyes were blacked and swollen, her mouth split and oozing blood, her scalp bleeding where lumps of hair had been ripped from her head. Her breathing was shallow, hitching around broken ribs.

He took her hand, held it in both of his. "Jean, an ambulance is coming. We're going to get you to a hospital."

She was trying to say something through a broken mouth. *"Help... me,"* Roarke heard. Only the "me" came out with a long "a."

Roarke leaned in closer. "We're Federal Agents, Jean. You're safe. We've got help coming."

"May," she said again. Her voice was a broken whisper. *"They... want... May..."*

Epps lowered the phone, and the agents exchanged a glance. "Who wants May? Who did this to you?"

"Mays. They want Mays."

Chapter 109

Many Glacier Hotel, Montana - present
Maise

The glacial lake pools at the bottom of one of a series of valleys surrounded by spiky Alpine peaks. Wind sweeps down the ski-jump shaped slopes, blowing puffs of snow from higher altitudes. Gray mist pours off one towering cliff like a waterfall.

Below a massive cliff face, on the edge of Swiftcurrent Lake, nestles a huge Swiss-style lodge: brown with white trim, slanted roofs, carved beams, gingerbread cutouts adorning the balconies. The long five-story main building is lined with wide windows. Two shorter side wings branch off from it. A marquis-shaped car port stands empty.

Inside the hotel is a soaring, empty lobby space surrounded by three upper stories of balconies supported by columns of enormous whole bare tree trunks. A bow-beamed ceiling with skylights rises in a dizzying arch like the inverted hull of a ship. A double spiral staircase leads down to a lower story.

Inside this vast silence, a lone young woman in a dark blue hotel uniform, trousers and tunic, walks past the long reception desk, the couches and chairs grouped in conversational areas, the grand piano.

She is small, but lean and strong, with striking coloring, dark hair and dark eyes against pale skin, freckles prominent by contrast. Armband tattoos show at her wrists.

She seems at home in the empty hotel. She circles around a central stone hearth with a triangular copper fireplace suspended from the ceiling by a web of cables, and pauses at a deserted row of couches and rocking chairs facing the panel of windows that overlook the wide, empty deck. The partially frozen lake is ringed by glacial mountains. An empty boat dock juts out into the ice.

She sighs out in satisfaction. She loves this view, the expansiveness of it. The pure, elemental peace. Even better, she has it to herself today. The other members of the skeleton maintenance crew are on a day ski trip and she has volunteered to stay.

During the season, the guests will come, thousands, tens of thousands of them, and that is good, too. She enjoys the variety of people from all over the country and all over the world. It is what she and Danny always dreamed of: adventure, escape. She has the money to travel herself, now. And she will—when she is done with what she is here to do. It is coming together. She can feel the signs, something just around the corner. An end to this long search.

"Soon," she says softly to her dead brother.

She turns away from the windows to continue toward the wide doors of the dining hall.

She does not see the figure watching her from behind the reception desk.

In the dining hall she walks across the gleaming bare pine floor, under a slanted pine ceiling hung with dozens of cylindrical lamps, vaguely Chinese in design. A huge river rock chimney and fireplace dominates one wall.

She unlocks a door at the side of the room to reveal a janitorial closet. She steps inside, reaching for an upright floor polisher.

She plugs in the length of cord and switches it on, feeling the vibration flow through the machine into her hands. She turns in a slow circle toward the center of the room…

And gasps… at the sight of a shadow in the doorway.

Chapter 110

Many Glacier Station, Montana - present
Singh and Snyder

Singh drives the SUV on a winding road beside a lake of powder-blue.

The agents have tried at several stop-off points to connect to the ViCLAS database, but the road is too remote for them to catch a signal.

Agent Snyder is thinking it through, aloud. "We'll need to search two distinct victim pools: preteen and young teen boys, like Danny Porter and Timothy Whitcomb, in the years before 2011. After 2011, for younger boys like Aaron Light."

Singh frowns out over the lake. She is feeling a growing anxiety. "We must find cell phone reception. Not for the database. We must alert authorities in the park that Maise Porter may be in danger. We must find someone who can get there before we may be able to."

She has no concrete reason for thinking it. And yet it is an overwhelming urgency.

Beside her, Agent Snyder shakes his head. "We can't. Absolutely not."

She glances at him, not understanding.

"There is no internal law enforcement authority that governs national parks," he explains. "Investigative power belongs entirely to the sheriffs' departments bordering the parks."

Singh's stomach sinks like a stone. "Sheriff Preston..."

"Exactly," Snyder says grimly. "We're not on his side of the park. But anyone we contact from any other bordering department is almost certain to contact him first."

Singh feels lightheaded, a sensation like falling. Agent Snyder touches her arm reassuringly. "We're not far, now."

Indeed, it is less than a quarter of an hour before Singh is slowing the SUV to drive through the unmanned park gate, the entrance to Glacier National Park.

As she follows the winding road toward Many Glacier Hotel, she notices something she has seen before when entering a national park. As stunning as the scenery has been on the drive to the park, it cannot begin to compare to the breathtaking vistas that unfold inside the park proper.

She counts ten distinct peaks lined up along the lake, massive triangular gray mountains, and conical volcanic summits, before the SUV rounds a curve and she has to start counting again.

She pulls over a few minutes later at a redwood ranger station, intending to show their credentials, explain that they are here to talk to one of the hotel employees, and perhaps enlist help. But no lights are on in the building and no one answers their knock on the door.

The agents turn to look at each other.

"Maise," Singh says. Snyder nods.

They return to their vehicle and continue into the park, past parking turnoffs at scenic points. Singh must drive more slowly because of the multitudes of potholes newly opened by the brutal winter.

And again, for no good reason, she finds herself gripped with unease. As if there is reason to rush.

She eases the speed up, mindful of potholes.

Chapter 111

Many Glacier Hotel, Montana - present
Cara and Maise

Maise fumbles for the switch of the sweeper and turns it off.

Cara steps forward into the room, and the two stand, looking at each other across time.

Cara often returns to places. She does not often return to people. Now she knows she has kept up with this girl because *The Work* is not finished. And the moment she heard the two old men talking in the restaurant in Yellowstone about children missing from national parks, it was clear to her what must be done.

Maise knows it too. It is there in the way she looks at Cara now. There is more for them to do together. It ties them like a string.

They exchange no more than a few words, and then Cara is following Maise up several flights of stairs into the employees' wing of the hotel, corridors of small rooms.

Maise walks down one of the halls to the very end, where she opens a door and steps through into a room with slanted rafters.

Cara steps inside... and turns in the room, looking at clippings of news articles taped to the wall—along with printouts of photos of children. Some as young as four and five, others ten, eleven, twelve.

"Missing," Maise says flatly. "They're all missing."

Chapter 112

Many Glacier, Montana - present
Singh and Snyder

They pass under a high trestle bridge into what the park map calls Many Glacier Village.

There the road splits in two, one leading to an empty parking lot of the hotel for guests and employees. The other fork leads up a hill toward a much larger parking lot for tourists and buses just passing through.

Singh turns toward the employee parking lot. Around the next curve they get their first glimpse of the hotel.

Singh has skied in the Alps. The chalet-style lodge would not be out of place there. The setting is equally breathtaking.

She parks their vehicle in the empty lot beside the carport and gets out of the driver's side, looking up at the hotel. When Agent Snyder does not immediately join her, she turns back to the vehicle.

Now Snyder shuts the passenger side door and circles around the SUV to her. She sees he has strapped on a sidearm. He holds the second Glock in one hand, extending it to her.

She hesitates.

"Humor me," he says.

She reaches for the weapon, checks it, and slides it into the pocket of her parka.

Then she zaps the vehicle locked, and the agents walk toward the hotel main entrance.

There are no steps up to the huge double doors, just a smooth concrete surface leading from the carport to the lodge.

There also is nothing like a doorbell at the entrance. Looking up at the massive, unlit hotel, Singh realizes it may be harder than they anticipated just to get someone to come to the door. Not to mention that Maise may be in any one of the wings, or in the building beyond the parking lot which seems to be separate housing.

Then Agent Snyder reaches out to the door and pushes on it.

It swings open under his pressure.

The agents move through the doors into a short entry that opens up at a long reception desk, empty. They walk past the desk into the vast open lobby, and stand looking up around them at the three stories of balconies, the high beamed ceiling. Singh is amazed to realize that the gleaming four-story wooden posts supporting the balconies are whole tree trunks, stripped of bark and polished to a high sheen.

The silence is live, resonant.

"Call her," Snyder says. "Better you than me."

Singh raises her voice. "Maise Porter! Are you here? We have been sent by Jean Lange."

They listen to the vast empty silence of the hotel.

"Anyone?" Singh calls.

They move further into the lobby, past a grand piano and rows of couches and rocking chairs looking out on the lake.

Agent Snyder stops, turns. Singh thinks he is about to speak. Instead, he raises a hand, motioning her silent.

Her eyes widen at the faint, ominous sound of approaching vehicles.

Agent Snyder crosses quickly toward the front-facing windows. Singh follows.

But she stops, and instinctively ducks behind of the tree trunk columns. To her right, Snyder has done the same. She eases her head around the trunk to look through the windows, and sees a massive truck and a van without side windows round the curve of road and enter the parking lot.

The vehicles stop outside the carport beside the agents' SUV, and men get out. Two from the truck, one from the driver's side of the van.

Singh feels her throat close as she sees the faces.

Sheriff Preston, with that unmistakable handlebar mustache from his photos. Furman, the snowmobile shopkeeper from Kellogg. Some tall, black-haired, tattooed man she does not recognize. All three of them are packing side arms, and as she watches, they all pull long guns from their respective vehicles. Preston walks over to their rental vehicle and tries the driver's door she has just locked. He peers in through the window.

Then all three men turn toward the van as the side panel slides open and a wheelchair rolls out onto a platform at the side of the van.

Strauss. The shine of his ruined face is unmistakable.

Singh feels for the weapon in her pocket, and silently thanks Agent Snyder's "Blue Sense," that instinct that protects cops and agents in the field.

He crosses quickly to her side. "They've come for the same reason we have," he says. "They're after Maise."

He points an index finger upward toward the overlooking balconies, then nods his head to the side stairs leading up to the balconies.

The agents hurry for the staircase and mount in silence.

Chapter 113

Many Glacier Hotel, Montana - present
Roarke and Epps

From their high position on the bridge outside the hotel, Roarke stared down at the men in the parking lot.

On approach, he and Epps had driven the loop to the upper parking lot. And as they circled back toward the hotel, they caught a glimpse of the monster truck and the van driving the loop toward the hotel.

The agents had stopped their SUV out of sight and taken positions on the trestle bridge.

They crouched, observing, evaluating, as the men in the parking lot stood beside their vehicles and checked their rifles, looking up at the hotel. The man in the sheriff's uniform, almost certainly Preston, walked over to the SUV parked in a nearby spot and tried the door.

And then the man in the wheelchair rolled off the motorized ramp of the van and joined the cluster of others.

Even from this distance, Roarke could see the horrific scars, the half-melted face. He felt as if someone had punched him in the stomach. Not just because fire was his own personal horror. Because he instantly knew what—and who—he was seeing.

"Jesus Christ," he said, low.

Epps looked to him in agitation.

"Strauss," Roarke said. "It must be. I was following him that night..."

He stopped again, his gorge rising. He'd been following Strauss's truck, right behind him. If not for that wraith of a girl... if he hadn't been stopped on the road....

He was looking at what would have happened to him that night. If he'd lived at all.

The realization was a wave of nausea.

The agents watched as the men head for the doors of the hotel.

Roarke tersely identified them. "The big one is Furman. Uniform is Sheriff Preston. Whose jurisdiction this is. The other guy I don't know."

There were no steps to climb; the militiamen walked straight in through the double front doors, Furman holding the door open for Strauss to motor past in his chair.

"We need to get in there," Epps said, his voice knotted.

Roarke scanned the front of the hotel, and focused on the broad, sturdy staircases criss-crossing the exterior on both sides of the main building and both wings. This was fire country. The stairs went all the way to ground level, providing safe, easy exit.

And entrance.

"They're at the bottom," he said aloud. "So we go up those to the top."

Chapter 114

Many Glacier Hotel, Montana - present
Singh and Snyder

On the first balcony, Singh and Snyder take positions, each hiding behind one of the huge tree trunk columns. They train their Glocks downward at the entry beside the reception desk.

Singh wraps her support hand high on the grip, softens her knees, breathes in and fixes her gaze to take in the floor space beyond the doors and reception desk.

The three militiamen walk through the door, their gaits heavy from the handguns on their hips. Each man bears a rifle.

In her mind, Singh smells gunmetal and testosterone....

From behind the men comes the motorized whir of Strauss's wheelchair as he rolls forward to join them.

The men stop in the lobby entrance, brandishing rifles, staring up and around at the balconies, the staircases, the rafters, the skylights.

Their voices echo in the empty space, disembodied, easy to hear.

"Fucking place is a mall. Where do you think we're gonna find her?"

"So we split up. It's just one little girl."

"Not just the girl," someone says. From behind her tree trunk column, Singh recognizes Furman's voice. "That's *their* SUV. Those Feds."

"Aww, whassamatter?" another of them taunts. Singh envisions the tall, twichy one. "You worried about an old man and a Muslim bitch?"

"They're Feds—"

A hard voice cuts the other off. "Exactly. *They're Feds.*" Singh recognizes Sheriff Preston, now. She can hear the ugliness of his smile. "Who do you think folks are gonna believe? This is my jurisdiction. They have no rights, here." There is the sound of a shotgun racking. "We take out the old guy and the black cunt. Then we grab the girl and go."

Singh sees a flash of movement in one of the windows across the balcony. A human form. Her pulse skyrockets. She is reeling with the impossibility of it… then logic kicks in.

There's another one. There are more, climbing up from outside…

She lifts her weapon…

And almost cries out in shock, as a face she knows as well as her own appears behind the glass.

Damien.

He spots her almost instantly. Roarke appears beside him. Damien lifts his service weapon to break the glass and Singh shakes her head frantically, puts her finger to her lips to indicate silence. Then she points down toward the lobby level and holds up four fingers.

Roarke and Epps nod tensely.

She holds up a hand, palm flat, to tell them to stay there.

Then she takes slow steps to back up from the column until she is against the inner wall, out of sight range from the lobby below.

Softly, swiftly, silently, she moves around the rectangle of balcony, hugging the inner wall, rounding one corner of the balcony, then the other, until she arrives breathless at the window.

Damien's eyes caress her through the glass as she fumbles at the window lock, twists it open. Roarke holds up both hands, his gesture cautioning—*Slow. Easy.*

The three agents grasp the bottom of the window from both sides and begin to ease the window up. A freezing wind blows through the opening and Singh flinches, wondering if the militiamen below can feel the change in the air.

A hard male voice speaks from the end of the balcony. "Gotcha."

Singh twists around… to see Furman standing in the stairway door, aiming his rifle straight at her.

Damien shouts her name from behind the glass—

A shot BOOMS, a double CRACK—

Singh feels fire in her arm… at the same instant Furman is blown backward, a crimson bloom opening in his chest.

Singh staggers on her feet, grabbing for her bleeding arm, dimly aware of Agent Snyder walking forward past her, arm straight, Glock raised. He fires again toward Furman. The wounded man twitches on the carpeted floor… then lies still.

Through the ringing in her ears, Singh hears glass shattering as Roarke and Epps break the window and scramble through the empty frame.

Damien catches Singh, holding her up.

Chapter 115

Many Glacier Hotel, Montana - present
Roarke, Epps, Snyder, Singh

Roarke strides past Epps and Singh to the balcony, taking position behind a tree trunk column. He can't see the men in the lobby, but he shouts down.

"This is ASAC Roarke of the San Francisco FBI. Drop your weapons and come out on the floor with your hands up."

There is a burst of deliberate laughter from somewhere below.

"You got zero jurisdiction here, *Fed*. This is my turf. You are in violation."

Against the wall, beside a guest room door, Epps pulls off his coat and ties the sleeves tight around Singh's bleeding arm.

"I am fine," she protests fiercely through the stab of pain. "Go. Go."

Suddenly Snyder is kneeling a bit slowly down beside them. "Go," he repeats to Epps.

Singh feels Damien's arm tighten around her in a quick embrace. Then he quick-crawls over the floor to Roarke's column.

He crouches there beside Roarke, Glock drawn, peering through the slats of the balcony wall. The militiamen have disappeared from the center floor space.

"This game is over," Roarke shouts down. "One of your guys is down already. You get anywhere near the doors and you get shot."

"We got plenty of time and plenty of ammo, A-Suck," another voice taunts from somewhere below.

"These guys are crazy," Epps mutters. "What do they think they're going to do?"

"They want casualties," Roarke answers, without taking his eyes from the main floor. "Militias want martyrs. This is the kind of standoff they're always looking for. A war against the government."

"Fuck that shit. We have to get Tara out and find the girl," Epps says.

One of the men below exclaims, "What the hell?"

The agents turn to look down… and see a slender figure in a hotel uniform walk out onto the middle of the floor.

"I'm right here, assholes."

Chapter 116

Many Glacier Hotel, Montana - present
Roarke, Epps, Snyder, Singh, Maise

Hearing the young, feminine voice, Singh feels her heart jump into her throat. A ripple of dread passes through the four agents on the upper balcony.

Epps gets a glimpse of the tall man hovering behind a chair. He shoots to his feet, aiming his Glock. Roarke leans over the balcony, training his weapon on Furman while he shouts down, “Don’t move. Anyone tries to hurt her, you’re dead.”

Maise stands on the lobby floor, against the militiamen.

On the floor, Singh feels Snyder take her hand and press something cool and rectangular into it. His phone.

“Film it,” Snyder says to Singh, low. “We need proof. They’re going to twist this story every which way. Whatever happens, we need the truth.”

He pulls her to her feet, supporting her as he walks her across to the nearest column. He leans her up against it, looks into her face. "You're good?"

Singh presses her back against the hard, solid wood. "I am good." She lifts the phone with her uninjured hand and points it below.

Snyder moves off to the next column and takes aim.

Singh eases her head around the tree trunk until she can see the lobby floor.

From her new angle she can see the militiamen beneath the balcony. Maise stands in the middle of the semicircle of them, Sheriff Preston and the tattooed one with rifles leveled at her, Strauss in his wheelchair, clutching a handgun in one of his clawed hands.

Maise is very still, her chin lifted. "What are you going to do, kill me like *he* killed my brother?"

"Shut your fucking mouth, bitch." The tall, twitchy one raises his rifle, pointing it straight into her face. She doesn't flinch.

From the balcony, Roarke shouts, "We've got every one of you covered. Anyone touches that girl, you're going to get shot. Drop your weapons *now*."

The militiamen don't move. Maise stands her ground. She is vibrating with anger. Singh can feel it in the air.

"You don't get to make this world. You all… you preach the Bible." Suddenly Maise turns—

The three militiamen lift their weapons in tandem—

On the balcony above, Roarke and Epps and Snyder raise their weapons—

Singh prays to all her goddesses at once as she holds the phone steady on Maise and the men.

The girl raises her arm and points at Strauss. "He raped and killed my brother. And that was okay with all of you."

Maise slowly lowers her arm, and looks at Sheriff Preston. "You think you can tell any story you like and stupid people will just believe you. So go ahead and kill me. But smile while you do it," she adds flatly. She turns her face up, toward the balconies. "Cause you're on the Many Glacier webcam. Broadcasting live."

Her gaze returns to Strauss. And her eyes bore into his.

"The whole world's going to know what you did. The whole world."

There was a silence that seemed to Singh to last forever.

And then chaos.

Chapter 117

Many Glacier Hotel, Montana - present
Singh

Even in retrospect, no one could be precisely clear what happened next.

It seems to Singh that Sheriff Preston jerks forward, with a curse. Instantly Roarke fires, hitting Preston's shoulder and spinning him around. The tall, twitchy man twists and stares past Preston—and Epps shoots him in the back of the thigh. The militiaman falls forward, his rifle jumping from his hands and skidding on the floor. And as Strauss howls in rage, Maise bolts out of sight behind the copper fireplace.

Roarke shouts to Agent Snyder, "Cover them!" and Snyder leans over the balcony railing, taking aim on the men on the floor below. Roarke and Epps run for the stairs.

Singh hugs the tree trunk column and holds the phone steady, filming, as her eyes search below for Maise.

Then there is another, single shot, just *before* the agents burst through the doors on the first floor.

And Singh gasps… as Strauss slumps forward in his wheelchair, his own handgun hanging from what is left of his mouth.

Chapter 118

Many Glacier Hotel, Montana - present
Roarke, Epps, Singh, Snyder, Maise

Sheriff Preston's own departmental vehicle provides convenient secure transportation for the wounded militiamen.

Roarke and Epps load the captives into the caged back seats and lock them down. Roarke takes the wheel, with Snyder riding shotgun. The plan is to rendezvous in Browning, the closest town with a law enforcement presence and a hospital.

Against Singh's protests, Epps carries her downstairs and outside to tuck her into his rental vehicle in a nest of blankets and pillows Maise pulls from a linen room, before she climbs into the back seat with Singh.

And sits there, calm, stoic, glassy-eyed.

Shock, Singh thinks dimly. She is drifting that way herself.

Epps gets into the driver's seat, and looks at Maise in the rear-view mirror. "That was pretty damn brilliant about the webcam. Was it true?"

The girl seems to rouse herself, and meets his eyes in the mirror. "Online for everyone to see."

Epps smiles grimly, starts the engine, and drives.

Maise is able to ID Young John Doe as her brother even before Singh is able to show her photos. She tonelessly describes a cluster of moles on Danny's left shoulder that Singh recalls from the autopsy report. Not that she had ever been in any doubt.

She reaches out, puts her unwounded hand gently on the back of Maise's neck. "I am so deeply sorry."

And finally, Maise leans into her and cries.

Chapter 119

Browning, Montana - present
Singh

Singh wakes in a hospital bed in the town called Browning. Much has gone on while she has been in surgery.

Sheriff Preston and the tall militiaman, Frank Saccaro, are now in the custody of the Glacier County Sheriff's Department.

Roarke has returned to Many Glacier with Agent Snyder and a team of sheriff's deputies to process the crime scene.

Epps of course has stayed in the hospital with Singh. His large frame is hunched in a hospital chair by her bed, so his face is the first thing she sees as she awakes.

She is glad to be injured, to have Damien worried and protective. It will help ease her way when she confesses to him. And she has much to confess. She must ask his forgiveness for standing apart from him and keeping secrets. She has hidden her darkness from him for too long.

It is time to let in the light.

At the moment, Damien is thinking of none of this. He is overcome with gratitude toward Snyder.

"I owe that man everything. If he hadn't...if you..." He cannot finish. She has never seen him so close to the brink.

She puts a hand to his face. "We are fine. It could never have been otherwise." She can feel some narcotic working in her bloodstream, but she needs to speak. "We were drawn, all of us, to be exactly where we needed to be. Precisely. Perfectly. We are connected. It is all connected. That is our power."

He turns his head to kiss her hand. For the first time in a long, long while, she feels her goddesses around her. And she knows the lightness of serenity.

Later, when Agent Snyder walks into Singh's hospital room, Damien stands to greet him, so effusively it is several minutes before he notices Roarke's absence.

Snyder explains, "Matthew stayed at the hotel. He said he wanted to walk through the whole episode in person and in his mind, while the memories are fresh."

He steps to Singh's bedside. She smiles up at him, and sees his eyes are focused and clear.

"Heal fast," he says. "You and I have some work to do with Maise. She's been collecting records of missing children. It'll make our ViCLAS work a walk in the park."

"How is she?" Singh asks.

"She needs this," he says simply. "I'm going to check on her now." He bends and kisses her forehead.

As Snyder disappears through the doorway, Damien's face is stormy.

"Bullshit he's 'walking through the episode,'" he says. Meaning Roarke.

She does not know how to answer. Damien lowers his voice. "I saw your map. Those timelines. The red string. He's there because he thinks *she's* there."

Singh looks at him. There is nothing she can tell him that he does not already know, in his soul.

He looks toward the door, fretting. "Should I go back?"

She reaches for his hand, raises it to her face. "That is not our story." He looks at her, and she rests her cheek against his palm.

"Our story is here."

Snyder steps out through the hospital doors into the brilliant sun, with all the glory of Montana's sky before him.

Maise sits on a high stone wall to the side of the path, looking up into that blueness.

He walks over to the wall. She looks down on him from her perch. Open. Calm. Ready.

"Young lady," he says. "You and I have work to do." He reaches up, extending his hand gallantly, as if this is some Golden Age Hollywood movie. She puts her hand in his, and lightly jumps down.

Chapter 120

Many Glacier Hotel, Montana - tomorrow
Cara

She stands in snowshoes and hiking gear, looking down from the trailhead at the shimmer of Swiftcurrent Lake, and the hotel slumbering beside it.

She tips her face to the rising sun, and feels the calm of an *Encounter* brought to a perfect conclusion.

And more. There is a new kind of peace. Perhaps, for a while, she can rest.

Because this *Encounter* has shown. There are good people. There is good law enforcement. And there is the future.

There is Maise.

She turns away from the hotel, toward the signpost: *Swiftcurrent Pass Trail.*

She knows this trail, has hiked it. There is snow now, but spring will come early under this sun. There will soon be a riot of wildflowers on the hills, explosions of color in oceans of emerald green. Glacial lakes of powder blue. A wind so pure it is like breathing liquid crystal.

And there are backcountry lodges, small chalets along the trails. Just seven miles to the first, Granite Park. Built of native stone to withstand the winters. Stocked with dried food and propane for the stoves. All she could need. And deserted now, doors and windows bolted shut, as the park is closed to all visitors for two months, still.

She will have it nearly to herself.

Nearly.

She breathes in and steps forward, into *Beauty.*

Chapter 121

Many Glacier Hotel, Montana - tomorrow
Roarke

Roarke wakes to feel the warmth and weight of the sun on the blankets covering him.

He slowly comes to full consciousness, opens his eyes to bright sunlight streaming through the slanted windows of the hotel room across from Maise's.

He lies in bed, listening to the wind against the windows.

Yesterday, after he and Epps had secured Sheriff Preston and his tattooed compadre with Preston's own cuffs, Roarke had checked them over for injuries. And had found a wound he wasn't expecting.

There was a hole in Preston's uniform, and a bleeding gash in Preston's back. A knife wound.

As if someone had thrown a blade from behind him.

Roarke had asked Maise, of course. At the hospital. In private. "Was there another person here with you? Helping you, maybe? Someone who threw the knife?"

She'd just looked at him.

As knowing and inscrutable as Brandi had been, when he'd asked about their "mutual friend."

After a shower he dresses for hiking, then takes up his emergency backpack, as always filled with basic camping supplies, dried food for several days, a water purifier.

He exits the room and descends the stairs of the staff quarters. At the floor below the lobby he pauses at the side door.

A framed map on the wall confirms what he has seen on several other maps scattered throughout the hotel. Outside, he will find a path that leads to several world-famous hikes. Highline Trail. Granite Park Trail. Swiftcurrent Pass.

He pulls open the door and steps outside into the cool, crisp wind.

The warmth of the sun beams down. The air sparkles like crystal. He can hear the gentle lapping of waves in the glistening lake. On the peaked hills, snow is melting and the grass is miraculously green under the white.

He turns and walks the path, breathing the sweetness of mountain air, feeling an energy he hadn't realized he'd lost.

At the trailhead, several paths branch out. He stands at the crossroads, surrounded by the peaks of more glacial mountains than he can count. Seeing hundreds of miles into the horizon. Smelling the trees and grass and a promise of wildflowers. Feeling the beauty.

And a sense of presence.

Feminine presence.

"You are not alone. And you are loved."

He steps onto the path and into the wilderness.

Acknowledgments

A million thanks to:

My agents, Scott Miller, Kristin Cipolla, Frank Wuliger and Lee Keele.

My producing team: Tucker Tooley, Jason Barhydt, Al Munteanu, Claudia Schorr, Ingrid Pittana, David Scharfenberg, Hannah Grossmann, Christian Parent and Gregoire Gensollen.

My fantastic editor, Pat Verducci, who miraculously made sense of it all.

Lee Lofland and his Writers Police Academy trainers/instructors: Dave Pauly, Dr. Katherine Ramsland, Corporal Dee Jackson, Andy Russell, Marco Conelli, Lieutenant Randy Shepard, and Robert Skiff, for forensics, investigative, and tactical help.

R.C. Bray for his terrific narrative interpretations of the books.

The team at Thomas & Mercer, past and present, who have continued to support and enrich this series: Alan Turkus, Jacque Ben-Zekry, Ahn Schluep, Megha Parekh, Grace Doyle, Sarah Shaw.

The WriterSpace and Spark Creative Partners teams for brilliant publicity support.

Robert Gregory Browne, for the series cover concept.

The initial inspiration for the Huntress from Val McDermid, Denise Mina, and Lee Child, at the San Francisco Bouchercon.

My writing group, the Weymouth Seven: Margaret Maron, Mary Kay Andrews, Diane Chamberlain, Sarah Shaber, Brenda Witchger and Katy Munger.

Website designer extraordinaire Madeira James, at Xuni.com.

Tracy Fenton, Helen Boyce, Teresa Nikolic, and the administrators and readers of THE Book Club, who've been so supportive on the other side of the pond.

My husband and family for putting up with all this angst.

For *Shadow Moon* I am especially grateful to:

- Mom and Dad, for dragging us to every national park in the country, every summer of our childhood.
- R.C. Bray, Rinelle Harkin, and Blue Heron Audio for this extra special audiobook.
- Cissy Hartley, for the *Shadow Moon* cover.
- Ellen Margolis, for decades of friendship, creative inspiration, and that hugely helpful Portland visit!
- Siegrid Rickenbach, the knower of roads.
- And the singing staff of Many Glacier Hotel, my musical and hiking compadres that magical summer.

* * * *

I love to hear from readers! Visit my website at http://alexandrasokoloff.com to contact me and find me on social media.

Join my mailing list to receive a free book, my quarterly newsletter, and to be automatically entered in my monthly website contests for chances to win Amazon gift cards:

Join http://bit.ly/AlexandraSokoloff_Free_book

Author's Note

Before I was a full-time screenwriter and author, I worked as a teacher in the Los Angeles County juvenile court system. I have not in any way exaggerated the plight of children and teens in the Social Services and justice systems and the prevalence of child sex trafficking. All the predators and crimes in the Huntress books are reflective of real-life predators and real-world events.

Lasting change will never happen until we all make it our responsibility to educate ourselves about what's really going on in our own communities, and to open our eyes to the presence of sexual predators in all walks of life—those hiding in the family next door and those flaunting their abuses in high office.

If you'd like to learn more about organizations in your country, state and community, and how to stand against sexual predators of every kind, I have links to places you can start on my website, http://alexandrasokoloff.com.

About the Author

Photo © Israel David Groveman

Alexandra Sokoloff has won the Thriller Award and been nominated for the Bram Stoker, Anthony, and Black Quill Awards for her supernatural thrillers *The Harrowing, The Price, The Unseen, Book of Shadows*, and *The Space Between*. She has also earned a second Thriller Award nomination for her Huntress/FBI Thrillers series (*Huntress Moon, Blood Moon, Cold Moon, Bitter Moon,* and *Hunger Moon*). The series is in development for television with Sokoloff as executive producer. The *New York Times Book Review* has called her a "daughter of Mary Shelley" and declared her books "some of the most original and freshly unnerving work in the genre."

As a screenwriter, she has written original screenplays and novel adaptations for numerous Hollywood studios, and is the author of the nonfiction *Screenwriting Tricks for Authors* writing workbooks: *Stealing Hollywood* and *Writing Love.* She also writes the acclaimed blog www.ScreenwritingTricks.com, based on her writing workshops and books, and has penned erotic paranormal fiction, including *The Shifters*, Book 2 of The Keepers trilogy, and *Keeper of the Shadows*, from The Keepers L.A. She lives in Los Angeles and in Scotland with crime author Craig Robertson.

Printed in Great Britain
by Amazon

29390197R00260